As she turned to leave, she remem

under the seats. They were designed to hol

a caravan, sitting low to the ground to keep the weight near the axle when you were towing. She lifted the first and saw it filled with plastic boxes with lids. She held the seat up with her shoulder and pulled the first box out. Inside she found five pairs of wellington boots. All different sizes. She lined them up on the table like Russian Dolls, largest to smallest. One was stripey, another spotty, one had Thomas the Tank Engine cartoons and one covered in pink butterflies. The final and smallest pair were a complete rainbow covered with a glittery sheen. She remembered each one perfectly. She had loved her boots, she would have worn them all day if allowed, even to school. He had kept them; she hadn't given them a second thought but here they were in front of her and ridiculously she realised she had missed them.

Allyson was born upstairs in a village pub, in Pease Pottage, West Sussex in 1964. Born into the licensed victualler trade, she learnt about life from the characters she served from behind the bars, before embarking on her teacher training degree in the early 1990s. Once qualified, she became a full-time primary school teacher across West Sussex, Northamptonshire and Cambridgeshire. She became a Headteacher in 2008, leading three primary schools, including special educational needs centres. After moving to the East Yorkshire coast, in 2016, she moved into Further and Higher Education, leading departments including setting up a supported internship programme. She rounded up her career as a Quality Manager in Hull College before taking early retirement where she now enjoys life on the road, touring full-time in her motorhome, along with her husband Paul and their two feisty chihuahuas. She now has the time to dedicate to her own writing after nearly thirty years of supporting others to do the same.

Seeds of Change

Allyson Croucher

COPYRIGHT

For Nevaeh, my beautiful granddaughter, born at the start of the pandemic and who has filled my heart with positivity and love. To my lovely dad, who sadly was lost at that same time.

For Sally and Wendy, for patiently sticking to my story over many months, receiving sections on random Sunday afternoons to read and comment upon. Your feedback was so kind and kept me motivated.

To Paul, my husband, for agreeing to all my madcap ideas, including living life in a seven-metre box!

And to the thousands of talented young writers, I have had the pleasure to teach and work alongside, may you continue to fill our world with your creativity, wisdom and resilience.

Contents

Madeleine Richards contemplated the jug of water, midway across the marble desk. She wondered if she could reach far enough across to pour some without a) having to splay herself face down on its vast expanse or b) interrupting the splendid pontification by John Murray, Head of Procurement and therefore spoiling what was clearly his big career moment in Claremont and Butler's launch of Our Vision for the Future.

She risk assessed the weight of her chair (which would need to be pushed ever so slightly back) the distance to stretch and the height of the top button on her crisp, white shirt. Madeline decided the risk of humiliation was just too great, and stayed rooted to her chair, dehydrating in the unbearably stuffy (in more ways than one) board room.

The room was impressive by any executive standards. Highly polished; the metaphor for all activity seen within the oval expanse of glass, gloss and gleam. Buttons inlaid into each leather armchair changed the mood lighting of each persons' seating pod. You could dim your lighting to concentrate on a presentation, create a reading spotlight to thumb through the meeting notes or change colours to suit your mood or simply transport yourself off in a kaleidoscope like an 80's disco when John Murray's voice droned and drained the life blood from your body. The thirty place settings around the desk, each demarcated by sunken planters filled with indoor palms and weeping figs, were akin to a James Bond movie. The artwork adorning the three solid walls are vast and borrowed from the Wallraf in Cologne, the Galerie Emmanuel Perrotin in France and The Tate. The fourth wall consisted of vast panes of glass, floor to ceiling, with minimal supports in between, giving the illusion that there was nothing at all between you and the City of London in all its glory. Ahead and to the left, The Shard towered, dwarfing its rivals and casting a morning shadow across the streets below. To the right, a teasing glimpse of Tower Bridge. Madeleine had once stood so close to the window, her toes touching the glass and her nose pressed against it to look downwards and experience the nauseating vertigo such a drop instilled. It had unnerved her and from that day ensured she sat the opposite side of the desk, far from the fear of falling out. Trained cameras sat discretely amongst the artefacts and ferns, yet despite the oxygen giving foliage, the lack of air in the room was unbearable as Petra, the P.A. ran around trying to find someone from estates to fix the air con system.

"And so," John was clearly building to a crescendo, arms now rotating like a windmill and his pitch verging on hysterical, "to secure our Vision for the Future, we are looking towards you all, our brightest stars, our creative and bold progressors, our dynamic and insightful influencers, to be our lions of success...."

Madeleine stifled a giggle and for the hundredth time in that lustrous and luxurious room felt a wave of imposter syndrome wash over her.

"Claremont and Butler's values place their staff at the heart of every decision in the company's development. In our strategy for the future, we want to be key players in marketing and advertising on the international stage and we want you to be central in that journey. That's why, we are opening up further opportunities for you to make a significant impact in the future of C&B. For the first time we will be rewarding a team who procures the marketing contract for the Bittern Quay's Business Development. The team will receive a promotional deal to include

.... drum roll please.... double bonus for three years, lifetime Platinum membership to the Prestige Health Club and an office suite on the twelfth floor...."

A collective intake of breath swooned around the room, nodding of heads towards each other in an unspoken sign of appreciation and excitement. The normal procedure for securing the top deals would never be entrusted to mere marketing managers, only Directors and Heads are permitted such heady heights of faith. As John Murray unpacked the terms and conditions to his audience, it became clear that a gauntlet was being laid down of never seen before proportions in the life of C&B and Madeleine realised this could be the springboard she needed to inject some renewed vigour into her work and career. She felt a small spark of interest, perhaps more of a flicker, but she definitely started to listen.

Bittern Quay was an area earmarked to be the next Canary Wharf, with the digital new age its primary sector and technology advancements being central to its design. The Quay was to be developed in phases over the next ten years, the marketing of the site was rumoured to be worth millions, if not more. It was the type of deal that would have been brought to the team on a salver, as a fete accompli, and Madeleine would have been charged with a small contribution; deciding on the radio promo sound effects or transporting the costumes for Dame Judi Dench to record a witty film segment for a corporate charity event. As a Marketing Manager she always felt her title outweighed her actual responsibilities several times over.

Not that Madeleine's mother and father would agree. To them, when she spoke of radio and filming, all they heard were the ARIAS, the Audio and Radio Industry Awards. The very fact that Madeleine commuted, not just travelled to work, no, actually commuted into London Bridge meant they elevated her above the reality and this in turn meant they were heading for disappointment, if they knew exactly how she spent her working days.

Madeleine had worked hard to be given the job at Claremont and Butler's. After school she had taken college business courses which led her to a Business and Marketing degree. To begin, she had been enthusiastic, dreaming of starting her own business, working for herself with a small team of loyal and close staff. She would be a generous boss, they would choose to spend their free time together, bowling, meals out, meals in. They would be as comfortable in their professional surroundings as they were in their personal lives together. No one would leave her employment; they would skip to work each day and leave fulfilled and happy. In her plans there was one small flaw; she didn't know what she wanted her business to do. How can she draw up a business plan if there is no product, no vision, no passion? She could advise and guide others through their ideas, she could be inventive, creative and original when presented with another person's project, but she was yet to find the theme or core to her own venture, one that she wanted to live and breathe for the rest of her working life.

Claremont and Butler had expanded several years before and had taken on a handful of new recruits, mostly apprentices. Madeleine had the advantage over the others of already holding a degree but even with this certification she never felt any more knowledgeable or capable, and in many ways, never felt that she measured up to her peer's abilities. She could hold her own; she had built a good portfolio of work but she always felt on the edge of the action, taking part but not driving. Being part of a team was all well and good but what could she genuinely put her name to, that she could claim as her own achievement?

Her mother filled in the gaps to Madeleine's vague recollections of how her day had been, with embellishments at every opportunity. She had a knack of turning the mildest activity in Madeleine's day into an international event. The Reigate and Banstead Cricket Club lunches heard tales of Madeleine's latest television advert, "Georgia May Jagger appeared as a favour to our Madeleine you know, almost begged to be in it." In fact, Madeleine had called the agent of GMJ and almost sold him her kidney to agree to her taking part. Madeline had the giddy responsibility of shopping in Waitrose for a selection of drinks and fruit for GMJ's room, calling in an electrician to sort the flickering roof light in the old warehouse they were using as a set and arguing with the makeup artist that gothic blacked out stripes across GMJ's face did not really match the floral notes of Springtime Eau de Parfum.

Madeleine was grateful to C&B. She was always aware of the privilege it was to work for a prestigious marketing company and be in a world that others could only dream of. On the days when her greatest achievement was to choose colour swatches for a mood board and empty her inbox, she never took for granted the fact she had employment, had a job title and worked alongside fairly decent people on the whole. So why did she feel so unfulfilled? She was paid well to be on the edge of a world of glamour, close enough to brush its cheeks but far enough away to have her own life and balance. Why did she swallow down a niggle that threatened to coil its way slowly up into the sunlight, that questioned what was she still doing staring at that computer screen, sitting in board meetings (or Ideas Factories as Jan, Head of Creativity would insist) or standing still, very still, at the age of twenty-seven looking in to where others flourish and shine with abundant energy?

As John Murray concluded his presentation, a junior flicked off the concealed projector with a flourish of a remote control, like Andre Rieu in a Maastricht extravaganza. The Board Room became something resembling the set of The Apprentice. John Murray set out the rules of how the game would play out. Teams of between two and five would be allowed to form, to create a marketing campaign so fantastic that it would launch Bittern Quays across the world and place Claremont and Butler firmly in the international league. The teams will pitch their ideas first to C&B's own Board of Directors and CEO, from there, just three teams will go forward to the final stage, presenting to Bittern Quay Investment Holdings, the company who owned the entire site and project. The winning teams will be up against teams from some of the largest and most successful marketing houses from across the world. There was no doubt in the room of the enormity of the task and the impact on the winning team's career and future advantages. To win the rights to the advertising campaign for Claremont and Butler would bring company rewards but the personal achievement of winning would catapult your career beyond even this gloss tower.

Normally, at the end of a meeting, a silent signal would send everyone spilling out into the corridors and scatter back to their respective offices. But this time, no one wanted to stray from the nerve centre and there they remained huddled in groups, dissecting and analysing the news that had been shared. Then, just as gazelles at a water hole scatter in unison at the scent of their predator approaching, realisation dawned. The key to success would be in the team you build or join and so a scurried selection process launched. Memories of school P.E. lessons unfolded, picking each other out in turn, cruelly whittling down the field until the last to be chosen. Veiled brutality emerged as all normal mild-mannered inclusivity and politeness stepped aside for callous declarations of each other's strengths and failings.

"You're crap at projecting to an audience," and so, Peter Sallis was ceremoniously dumped.

"Remember that tag-line for Klean's toilet paper, 'For Your Happy Place?' who was responsible for that social media shit show?

"That would be me......."

"Oh, right... I think I've got a full team now; we'll see you later."

"Xander, Xander, over here.... you can be our analyst mate, you're the strongest one here. No, no, don't go with Ana's team, they've got Klara and let's face it, she's gonna drag them right down."

Warm breath on Madeleine's neck signaled someone leaning in close to her ear.

"Madeleine, will you join me, in my team? You know, with your logic, strategy and attention to detail and my confidence in the pitch we could work really well together. I've asked Nadir for the digital stuff and Roseanne for her research and writing. What do you think? Will you join us?"

She turned to face Dominic Eaton, who stood just behind her shoulder. She smelt his shower freshness and observed a faint shaving rash on his shiny, moisturised cheek. His black hair parted far on one side leaving it cropped short and spiky above one ear, the other side a floppy long fringe combed over and held in place with a medium hold product and Madeleine suspected just a hint of hair spray.

Dominic gazed intently into Madeleine's hazel, kohl lined eyes and waited- expecting her to leap at such an opportunity. There was something self-assured about his request, he didn't plead or push any further, just gazed and waited for her to snatch his suggestion up gratefully.

It was at that point that Madeleine remembered the time. She glanced at her watch and swore. Calculating at speed the time to get to London Bridge Station and onto Reigate meant she was cutting it fine.

"Yes, okay, we'll have to talk tomorrow," as she grabbed her handbag and shot out of the door. leaving Dominic staring blankly at the fire escape instructions on the back of the door.

Mr. Kauffman sat opposite Madeleine. His desk was worn mahogany, fine scratches left by the collection of silver and pewter photo frames, turned slightly away from him to show clients Mr. Kauffman's commitment to family life. Smiling, but slightly stiff, group poses of Mrs. Kauffman and their immaculate children throughout the years reassured the many hundreds who had sat there before her, that Mr. Kauffman was honest and kind.

To her left, Madeleine's mother sat clutching her best handbag, the one Madeleine had given her two Christmases ago. A simple tan leather Michael Kors' tote that would match any outfit, but today looked slightly ridiculous against Fiona

Richards' thick, nylon navy skirt, pilled with aged bobbles and the silk lining hanging down too low, twenty denier tights and sensible, black court shoes. Fiona's cream blouse tucked firmly into her skirt's waist band and a neat string of mock pearls completed her 'best' look. With hair twisted up into a chignon, Madeleine's mother looked more like she was going for an interview than sat listening to Mr. Kauffman reading out her father's will.

Henry Richards sat beyond his wife, the desk not quite wide enough to seat everyone in a row, so his chair was turned slightly, as he sat angled at the far corner. His face was no softer now than a few minutes ago, when he growled his disappointment at Madeleine's lateness and tapped on the face of his watch just to prove the point. Henry's light grey suit was probably bought for the same occasion as her mother's, perhaps some thirty years ago for a wedding or christening in the eighties. The trousers had pleats across the top and baggy shapeless legs. His jacket crossed over very low and had a single button pulled tight now as he sat on the chair, leaving his jacket done up yet gaping open.

Fiona started to twist her tote tassels around her fingers, fidgeting slightly as Mr. Kauffman continued to open envelopes and uncurl large paper clips, laying each pile of papers neatly in a row in front of him. There was a respectful silence as each patiently waited for the solicitor to prepare himself.

To Madeleine's right sat an empty chair. Her brother James had promised to be there but in usual form had not made an appearance and had not bothered to call to explain why. Madeleine's father had clearly been irate with her own tardiness but no mention of dear James' absence, of course. Even if he walked through the door now, he would be greeted as the all-conquering hero, returning from battle, the prodigal son, unapologetically asking for his taxi fare to be refunded and being handed it without a word. Madeleine's every decision, every activity, every movement was put under the spotlight and questioned to whether it was the right thing to do. She found herself explaining herself before she was even asked; justifying why she had booked a few days off work to visit friends in Brighton, why she moved her furniture around and now had the sofa sat in front of a radiator, why she hadn't changed her credit card yet to get another year's 0% interest. But James, his whereabouts, his friends, his working life were all a mystery and he enjoyed the glorious freedom of never being asked. Most of the time Madeleine accepted the difference with a gracious 'That's families for you' attitude but there were times when a deep resentment bubbled and brewed at the injustice of it all.

'Ahem," Mr. Kauffman cleared his throat. "I think we should proceed as I don't think anyone else will be joining us today."

Mum nodded her agreement and silent permission to start.

"My name is Joel Kauffman, and I am a partner here at Kauffman & Banks. We were entrusted with Mr. Albert Williams' Last Will and Testament in 1985 after his wife sadly died. He then updated it in 1998. Mr. Williams, your father (he nodded towards Fiona in case she hadn't realised it was her father they were talking about) added provisions for his grandchildren in the update. I can confirm the 1998 Will is legally valid and has not been superseded. The beneficiaries have been invited here today but as we can see, James Richards is not here to witness the Will being read out. I am able to share the entire contents of the

Will today and you are free to relay the contents to James, however any gifts or entitlements will be awarded through our offices when he makes contact with us. The Will is straightforward as Mr. Williams had made all of the arrangements before he passed. I have been able to carry out the Estate Administration and as you know, we have not needed a Grant of Probate in this instance. I have concluded my financial review and as he had paid for all funeral arrangements and he was not bankrupt or in debt, we can now proceed."

Mr. Kauffman paused and looked at each of the waiting relatives to allow for any questions at this point. There were none.

"To my only child and daughter, Fiona, I leave my house and possessions (with the exceptions listed below) for her to do as she sees fit. I am grateful for her help and support after her mother died. She has been a good daughter and I hope this gift will make her life a little easier without her parents there for the future."

Fiona Richards hung her head down and quietly sobbed into her tissue. Madeleine squeezed her mother's arm gently but respectfully didn't glance at her distress.

"To my son-in-law Henry, I leave the contents of my garage, the tools and equipment therein, including my Triumph Toledo car and Sinclair C5. I know he will take good care of them. Also, to Henry, my gold signet ring. Henry has been a good son-in-law and father to my grandchildren, and I hope these gifts bring him pleasure.

Henry said nothing.

"To my grandson, James, I leave the trust fund set up for him to access when he is 30 years old. I hope by then James will be looking to settle down and set roots and I want this fund to provide him with a good deposit for a house. I will also give James my own father's watch. I hope that he will one day leave it to children and grandchildren of his own."

Again, a pause, and a look around for questions. There were none.

"And finally, to my granddaughter Maddie, I leave the tenancy to my allotment plot in Queens Gardens, for her to keep as long as she wishes. The council allows plots to be passed to family members and I hope she finds here what she is looking for. It was here I was at my happiest and I hope she comes to love it as much as I did. That concludes the Final Will and Testament of Albert Williams."

"What? Wait…. that can't be it…. what, really that's it? … James is left a trust fund, a house deposit in Surrey no less and I am left nothing but a plot of mud? I don't even like gardening, I've not been there for years, so why would grandad think I would be happy with that? I don't want to sound ungrateful, well yes, I guess I am ungrateful, but that's just not fair. Why should James always get the special treatment? He hardly ever visited Grandad, at least I went to see him every week. James has only ever popped round to sponge money off him, seriously… really… this can't be right!"

Madeleine could hear the rising pitch in her voice but was powerless to control it, a surge of fury propelled upwards into her head spilling out of her mouth like an exploding firework. She crackled and spat, twisting to face each person in turn, to plead her case and seek some kind of acknowledgement that yes, it was unfair and it can all be changed. No reassurance came. Just a simple, "That's enough!" from her father as he rose and left the room in disgust at his daughter's outburst.

Madeleine leant towards her mother.

"You must see what I'm saying. This is really unfair."

She could hear the small inner child creeping out but couldn't do anything to stop it. "You know how much Grandad and I got on. James hasn't worked hard for anything in his life. He just gets it all on a plate. I work really hard; you know I do. So really, all this time I should have just bummed around like James and waited to be given a house!"

The shock of her mother's response hit Madeleine like a slap across her face. Fiona simply stood and turned to leave the room. Nothing. Not a word. Then despite Madeleine's every effort she burst into tears.

Her parents' house was modest compared to many on Whitepost Hill. Sat just outside of the town, you pushed open a wooden gate and stepped through an archway cut into the immaculate hedge. It gave the impression of entering church grounds. The house was rendered white on the bottom and exposed red brick on the first floor, which jutted out a little wider than the lower half, in a type of mock-Tudor fashion. The front gardens were immaculate with deep borders of trimmed conifers of every shade from lime to dark seaweed. the lawned pathways in between were closely clipped and weedless. To the left of the house, you could see a large, wooden conservatory with an elaborate chandelier hanging in the centre. Movement behind the glass told Madeleine that was the venue for the debrief and it was underway.

As she entered the garden room, Madeleine was not surprised to see a small gathering being entertained with ready prepared trays of sandwiches, sausage rolls and small bowls of crisps. Despite the lack of originality, the food was beautifully presented on long, black pieces of slate, covered with a flourish of scattered rocket and a swirl of Modena balsamic vinegar. Her father, Henry, oversaw the corner bar, serving close friends by proudly turning to the bottle optics on the wall behind him and by delving into the ice bucket with a pair of ornate silver ice tongs.

The ladies sat on large, cream sofas in the sunshine, some with their gin and others with a cup and saucer of tea. The men mostly stood around the edge chatting in pairs and occasionally throwing back their heads in a shared joke or tale. Her brother James had made an appearance and was clutching a can of lager in one hand and the other holding onto the bar in deep conversation with father's brother Michael. Fiona flitted from one to another with her offerings, encouraging just one more egg and cress.

Madeleine looked on briefly, considering turning and leaving as unnoticed as she had arrived. The scene before her was unnervingly jolly, a far cry from the previous occasion following her grandfather's funeral. The mood then had been rightly somber. Madeleine had expected the same today. She had only lingered a short time longer in the solicitor's office, composing herself and being reassured by a nervous Mr. Kauffman that she was clearly loved, to have been left such a gift. Yet, this gathering appeared to have fast-forwarded in time. She seemed to have missed a memo that may have read 'Will Reading Party - come help us celebrate our good fortunes, eat, drink and be merry' and she felt suddenly very much out of the loop, not fitting into this scene, definitely not in the right headspace and at a loss on what to do now. She had walked in, expecting to carry on complaining and to try and persuade her family that she had a point to make. She had expected to see these visiting friends and family but had imagined there to be a quietly spoken address to explain that "Yes, father did leave us well-looked after but we don't want to dwell on that, we want to just remember him and mourn." She was side-lined with the mood before her and the celebratory back patting. It looked crass and disrespectful and she couldn't feign anything other than the miserableness that she felt.

"Madeleine, there you are!' Michael's wife, auntie Irene, beckoned from the couch and patted the empty space beside her. "How are you my lovely, you're looking very striking in your suit. Did you go to work this morning? Have you tried the sandwiches, they're very nice? Michael, Michael, would you get Madeleine a drink please? What do you want love?"

Irene was permanently cheerful and Madeleine always enjoyed her company. She could talk for England and rattled off questions without stopping to hear the answers. Although they didn't see each other very often, her aunt and uncle now lived on the south coast near Hastings, she was fond of them both. When they did get together, there was an easy repartee between them and as Madeleine felt her aunt's warmth through their touching thigh and arms, she felt her anger and frustration subside a little. She smiled and turned acceptingly to Michael, "Pinot Grigio for me please."

"So, Fiona has told us all about the Will. I gather you're not very happy with the outcome?"

"Well, no, I know how selfish and ungrateful I must sound but it does seem incredibly unfair. I really don't know why grandad thought for one minute that I would be happy, being stuck looking after his allotment….forever. I haven't been there since I was really small, I think the last time I was there I was probably about eleven or twelve. I outgrew the wellies and children-sized gardening tools. I outgrew the interest in it. I still saw grandad all the time, of course. I loved his company, but I went to his house instead. Or saw him when he came to ours. I really don't know what he was thinking when he made his decisions for the Will. And James…. I can't even bring myself to talk to him at the minute. I know he didn't ask for it, but it just sums up everything. He gets a real gift that will set him up for the future. He probably doesn't even want to get a house and settle down. I would have used the money so wisely, but I can just see James totally wasting it and not appreciate what he has been given."

Irene nodded gently, she didn't interrupt and waited a few seconds to make sure Madeleine had finished speaking.

"You know, I think you're looking at this all the wrong way. It's not a competition between you and James. The gifts aren't a measure of how much he loved you. Your grandad loved you both equally and would have put a lot of thought into his Will. Maybe he thought you are very capable in achieving the house and the investments. Maybe he just thought James needed that extra boost."

"But why the allotment for me? I don't have the time or the inclination. It's going to just sit and ruin and I'll just feel guilty for that. I can't look after it like he did. I'm just too busy at work, we have a competition for a contract and if I win, I could be travelling the world and maybe get promoted. I won't be able to go over there and just dig mud!"

"Look, who knows what lies ahead. Maybe this'll turn out to be something that you enjoy."

"I really can't see how that can happen when I have no time to go over there and no interest in getting dirty with grandad's friends."

Well, I don't suppose he meant you to do that!" Irene laughed. "That's going a bit too far."

"Ha ha, you know what I mean. Hanging out with Dougie and Doris, or whoever they are, really isn't my thing and I'm going to end up handing the plot back to the committee."

"Well, don't do anything hasty, at least visit it and see what he's left you to do."

"Well, he did say in his Will that I might find something I've been looking for. Maybe he has buried treasure there after all." Madeleine laughed at her own joke and felt the wine ease her angst. "I had better go and see James and congratulate him." Madeleine relented, rose and gave her aunt a smile as she moved towards the bar.

Dominic lent against Madeleine's glass door frame, his arms folded and one leg crossed over the other. He wore a different suit from the day before, the inside of his jacket flashed a floral silk lining, cerise and violet perennial geraniums teased a lighter side to his usual earnestness. Madeleine looked blankly at him looking back at her with a quizzical furrow on his brow. Realisation fell, she had totally forgotten about the competition teams, in fact she had totally forgotten about the competition entirely. She had managed to be at work for two hours, passing pleasantries at the barista coffee machine, asked Petra for the photocopier ink to be refilled and answered several emails without giving it a second thought. She had been so absorbed in yesterday's events that the competition had slipped to the far recesses of her mind. Shouldn't it be just a little bit more of a priority in her thoughts?

"So, have you had a chance to think about us?"

Us? She wasn't aware there was an 'us.'

"The four of us," he confirmed, as if reading her mind.

"I'm sorry, I have had a family thing," why did she feel the need to apologise?

"Oh right, it's just that most people have formed their teams and even started on ideas already. You and I will make a great team together." (There it was again, a suggestion of a different union or was she imagining it?)

"And Nadir and Roseanne?" she clarified.

"Yes, yes of course, them too. Do you want to go to San Martin's for lunch later and talk about it?" He took out his phone to write it in his online diary without waiting for a reply. "I'll send you an invite and block us out a few hours. 12.30 ok with you?"

Again, without waiting for a response, he turned and left, typing onto his phone. Her computer pinged an incoming invite moments later.

San Martin's was owned by Martin, not from the Mediterranean but from Southend-On-Sea. Living near the coast had obviously influenced him, as he served up the best seafood tapas for miles. San Martin's oozed atmosphere. The heady smell of garlic drew you in from the pavement and as you stepped into the darkened room you were transported to a lunchtime once spent in an Andalusian, white-washed bar drinking sangria. Each table owned a wine bottle, layered with multicoloured wax dripping down and spreading out carelessly onto the tabletop. One wall was covered with the bottom of wooden barrels, each stamped with the image of a bull and the names of sherry and wine producers. Every inch of space was adorned with paraphernalia, brass trays with etched scenes of Spanish towns, coloured tiles of Mediterranean flora and fauna, blackboards listing specials of the day and wine lists, trails of silk Bougainvillea, Spanish flags, piles of terracotta dishes and carafes of every size and shape, posters celebrating holy festivals, open fanned pericons and castanets. It had taken Martin years of collecting and friends and customers donating, to achieve the gaudy yet compelling interior.

Dominic was already seated, Madeleine noted instantly that it was a table for two. Suddenly the intimacy of the venue seemed inappropriate for discussing business.

"Are Nadir and Roseanne not joining us?"

"I didn't invite them this time, I thought just you and I could get the ball rolling. They are there to help with the mechanics, our wing guys. We are the creative team, the ideas guys. We can take our plans to them once we have made a start."

"Don't you think they may feel left out? I mean, this is a team competition and we need their input." Madeleine felt uncomfortable, as if she were being set up. She didn't want the other two to think she wanted it this way.

"Look we're here now," reasoned Dominic, "and I'm starving." The waiter appeared with menus right on cue. Dominic didn't take them from his hands.

"We'll take your lunchtime tapas selection please, just keep refilling the plates and the glasses, will you?" The waiter glanced at Madeleine to check that she was happy with the choice, she felt of both the menu and her lunch partner. She nodded to him that it was fine. She asked for a house white and a jug of water, she wanted to keep her senses sharp.

"So, I've been doing some research," Dominic began. "Bittern Quay Investment Holdings are made up of a Board of Directors who were each involved with the now disbanded Taiwan Financial Group and Co. When they were operating, they owned and controlled half of the container shipping that enters Hull. They moved into the property market when they saw a decline in Hull's cargo movements by selling off large areas of dockland which contained empty storage sites, mechanical workshops, that kind of thing. They sold to another holdings company who then developed the Queen Anne Village. The village is now made up of executive flats, gyms, food outlets, retail parks and it was marketed for the young, up and coming singles and couples to see Hull as a hip place to live. It was completed in time for the City of Culture thing, which was an added bonus for the developers of course. The flats all sold, the shops filled, and it breathed life into the area again."

"Ok, so what's the link with Bittern Quay, that's going to be a digital hub not a residential village?" Madeleine moved her phone and keys from the middle of the table to make way for the first few dishes to be set down.

"It seems the same people who will be making the decision for the marketing of Bittern are the same who awarded Queen Anne's. The success of Queen Anne was documented in a case study, which was used across some of the northern universities, to teach regeneration and image change."

"Okay, I think I can see where you're heading with this." The Gambas pil pil was divine, scalding hot and still bubbling in the dish, bright red from saffron soaked olive oil and spicy enough to make Madeleine flush. She dipped her bread into the grease and pulled a head off from a giant prawn.

"The winning marketing campaign for Queen Anne focused on health promoting success. If your body and mind are healthy, so you will succeed and achieve, It turns out this ethos is a major contributing factor to the values of the members. One of them, Nobuaki Ito, personally owns that health club chain with that logo.... you know the family holding hands in a swan dive...."

"Konnect?"

"Yes, that's the one. So, you see, we need to focus on health. Yes, Bittern Quays is all about technology and digital advancement but that can sound stagnant and images of being stuck glued to a screen or plugged into headphones are the first things that people think of. If we can find a way to promote health and fitness within our concept, I reckon we are onto a winner."

The meal was exquisite, padron peppers and simmered squid, sweet clams with salty Serrano ham, tiny croquettes filled with cheese, pan-fried prawns with lemon and parsley. Madeleine watched as Dominic accepted several offers to top his wine, she kept the palm of her hand over her glass. The conversation remained mostly work related and Madeleine found she was enjoying the ambiance and surprisingly the company. Ideas bounced back and forth, each received with a listening ear and professional critique. Suggestions were offered in a safe environment, no fear of ridicule or rebuff. Dominic wasn't as boastful and bombastic as she had expected. She had entered the bar with an armour, fully expecting to be railroaded by her colleague's pushiness but she was yet to need to raise her sword.

There was no doubt that Dominic Eaton oozed confidence. He knew he was going to achieve; he had no doubt that he would enjoy a successful career and absolute assurance that he would be offered any promotion that he applied for. He epitomised Claremont and Butler's values and ethos; sharp, focused and driven. Madeleine wondered several times throughout the meal why he had chosen her as his ally. The competition could be his golden ticket, the big opportunity to launch up the ladder and receive acknowledgement and reward. She felt sluggish and uninspiring by comparison. Where Dominic was vocal, she was reserved. Where he was quick and animated, she was thoughtful and serene. She admitted she had compartmentalised him, she anticipated he was an arrogant, self-appreciating egotist. However, she had the good grace to accept she was wrong and she found him to be surprisingly selfless and willing to work as a team, putting personal career risk aside. She increasingly felt she needed to match his enthusiasm and raise her game, in order to not let him down. He had put faith in her and despite her reservations of her own ability, she accepted the gauntlet and lent forward.

"Okay, let's do this!"

"You won't regret it," Dominic replied earnestly, reaching across and squeezing Madeleine's fingers.

Chapter Two - FEBRUARY

That Saturday morning was what Fiona Richards called 'A Conservatory Day.' Bright, cloudless blue sky, sunglasses to be worn against a low sun but blowing a chilly easterly wind, so sitting behind the conservatory glass was the best place to relax and appreciate the warmth and hope of spring ahead.

Madeleine lived at home with her parents and brother. She was well aware that at 27, she should be living her own life but with house prices and rentals so expensive in the south, the low rent option of staying at home worked, mostly, just fine. It allowed her to commute and save towards a deposit of her own one day. Her parents afforded her a fair level of privacy, her large bedroom had a sofa and an en-suite bathroom and a walk-in cupboard which she used to house her collection of work suits, shoes of varying heel heights and handbags. She reasoned she needed the designer labels for her job. If you are serious about your appearance, then you are serious in your work. Keeping her collections updated did mean she used more of her wages each month than she would have liked, but it was a means to an end. She can't work for C&B and not look the part. The downside to living at home was her parents' involvement in all she did. They meant well and did on the whole treat her as an adult, but they couldn't hold back from instilling their wisdom at every opportunity.

"You need to learn to drive and you should use Peter Wilcox, he taught all of the Hamilton children, they all passed first time."

"Why did you get your hair cut there, you should have gone to Tops and Tails and asked for Anna, she would have done your layers much neater."

"Have you checked your bank statements this month? You know you should always do it, you'll be surprised how many errors you can find."

Madeleine had never heard James be subjected to top tips and advice, thinly disguised criticisms. He came and went freely without being asked what time he got home last night, if he came home at all, what state his bank account was in, has he got a job yet…...?

James was older by eighteen months. This added to the irksome difference of approach. Surely, as the firstborn, James should be the one to be under scrutiny to uphold the family values and be successful in every aspect of his life, career, family, home. But somehow, he was by-passed and all hope and expectation fell upon Madeleine to achieve well and each day as she chose her outfit, boarded the train and sat in another meeting, she accepted that at least they were happy.

"Are you off out? It's freezing out there today, make sure you wrap up." Fiona glanced up from her supermarket shopping on her iPad and looked Madeleine briefly up and down. "Why are you dressed as a bag lady?"

"I'm wrapped up as it's cold, like you said. And I'm going over to grandad's allotment to take a look."

"Oh, I see, it's not grandad's anymore don't forget, it's yours now."

"Well, it is for now. I'm going to have a look and see what needs doing. If it's too much, I'm going to offer it back to the committee, there's bound to be a waiting list of people dying to take it on."

"Well, make sure you take a flask of coffee with you. It really is bitter out there today." Fiona turned back to her iPad and chose a pack of rather nice pork chops.

Madeleine had rummaged around to find suitable gardening clothes; she didn't anticipate actually doing any gardening but guessed a neat pair of slacks and a blazer wasn't going to be the sensible choice. She had pulled on her jogging bottoms, that only got worn in front of the TV of an evening and a new pair of Nike trainers that had never seen the light of day since she had bought them about six months before. She placed several T-shirts and jumpers over her top half and pulled a beanie hat over her raven hair to stop it blowing over her face. She remembered to collect the allotment keys from her dressing table drawer and went downstairs to receive her mother's advice.

The allotments were an easy walk from Madeleine's parents' house. After cutting through the park and the new housing estate she found herself on the road walking alongside the perimeter of the allotments until she reached the green metal gate, with spiked barbed wire tied across the top and a chain and padlock holding it closed tight against a post.

The last time she had approached the entrance was probably about sixteen years before. Back then, it was a wooden five-bar gate with a lighter chain, and you could climb over it, if you forgot your key. Now, tied to the gate with cable ties were laminated notices of rules and regulations, signs warning of being watched by the CCTV and a washed-out advert for a wheelbarrow which needed a new wheel. Just ask at plot number three. On the post was a reminder that dogs must be on the lead and all poop must be bagged and binned.

She took out the bunch of keys, two of them looked possible for the padlock of this size. The rest were smaller and surprisingly large in number. Madeleine was not sure what could require so many locks to be opened.

The lock took quite a lot of jiggling before it gave way. The chain had to be passed back through the railings and left to dangle whilst she pushed the ten-foot-high gate open. Madeleine bent forwards to put her weight onto the gate, she maneuvered her body round it once the gap was big enough and left it to bang shut behind her, with a loud, wobbling clatter. Pulling the chain through again, she secured the padlock and removed her keys.

Madeleine already felt the effort outweighed any possible reward but nevertheless walked into the compound which suddenly seemed very familiar.

There was a small parking area full of potholes and loose gravel. Along one side were six huge bays made from scaffold boards, filled with various stages of decomposed waste. The nearest bay held a steaming concoction of vegetables, grass cuttings, twigs and what looked like several copies of the Reigate News and corrugated cardboard packaging. As she scanned each bay to the left it became harder to distinguish the contents until the final bay, which held the completed product, dark brown, soft compost with just a few twigs to be seen. Next to this stood a large pile of wood chippings and bark. Madeleine turned left away from the car park and followed the main gravel path, past the shed with a handprinted sign, stating simply 'Shop.'

She scanned the site, dotted around stood old touring caravans, each painted a different shade of green. They were all streaky with only one coat of matt slapped onto the shiny caravan surfaces, as if hurriedly camouflaged against an air raid from above. Most still had their windows intact but many were without doors, open to the elements. Flattened tyres gave an easy entry to the vans, many had an old metal chair outside, where proud owners sat as if on a plantation porch, surveying their land.

Mowers had cleared the centre of the grassy paths that divided the patchwork of allotment squares, leaving the edges to their natural growth of grass and weeds, filling in the underside of the caravans so that they looked sprouted from the earth, caravan cabbages. Madeleine had forgotten this quirky feature of the allotments. Some were used as sheds, storage and somewhere to hang drying onions and garlic. But some had been made into cosy little rooms, with a gas burner for tea, a battery radio and somewhere to sit in the rain and contemplate. There was a variety of ways to display the plot numbers, ranging from simple white slops of paint directly onto the caravan sides, complete with streaks where the paint had run down, to hand crafted wooden signs stuck on top of posts with colourful painted flowers and bees to add a touch of artwork. One had a wrought iron number 8 hanging from a small imitation Victorian lamp post.

Madeleine continued up the central path, swinging her gaze from left to right as she passed each plot. Each were laid out in a different way, some were just one open patch of soil, with no paths, no means of walking across from one side to the other. Some had been divided up into smaller rectangles; she noted the preferences that each owner had over grassed or barked divisions. Some grew their vegetables at ground level, some had built raised beds from various wooden boards collected from reclamation yards and pallets begged from local trades and companies. You could easily identify each person's plot without the need for fences or hedging. The individual personalities of each, separated whose was whose. On all plots, the soil was now mostly bare, cleared from last year's harvest, huge cabbages remained in neat rows, sticks of Brussel sprouts left over from Christmas still intact and floppy leek tops were all that that were to be seen. Bare branch wigwams and arches of intertwined sticks stood ready for this year's action. Here and there a weathered, damp section of carpet was laid over the earth, keeping it warm and stopping the early weeds from seeing the light. She marveled at the endless combinations of how the same size and shape pieces of land could be laid out. Many had a greenhouse, all varying states of repair, some with whitewashed smears over the glass, some with ragged net curtains against the panes, others empty and clean. Sheds, ranging from huge and very new, which could easily house a small family, through to small handmade sentry guard boxes which stood gardening tools upright to attention. Madeleine began to separate mentally which plots were owned by very serious gardeners, no paraphernalia, simply a whole patch of uninterrupted earth maximising as much growing space as possible. Others she felt enjoyed the whole allotment experience, not just growing their fruit and vegetables but decorating their little place of happiness with bunting, mini cloth scarecrows on sticks, metal painted flowers and insects hanging from fruit trees and even a picnic table. She suspected some of their caravans may even hold a mini bar and gas BBQ.

Although she felt she could remember which plot was her granddad's, even after all these years, she still looked at the keys in her hand to read the paper tag that the solicitors had tied onto them for her with string. Number 15.

As a child, he would bring her to the allotment most weekends or collect her from school for an hour or two's pottering. They would come in his old van, which he used to help anyone and everyone with their errands. He would collect people's items to take to the tip, pick up bargains bought from the free-ads and deliver to their houses, drop off neighbours' garden waste to the allotment compost area and a hundred other ways he could be helpful but mostly, now as she looked back, she realised it kept him busy and more importantly, purposeful. It was rare that she saw her grandad sitting down, he would have his shirt sleeves rolled up his brown arms, busily preparing to do his next odd job. If he were at home he would be in his garden or garage, which doubled as a work shed. His 'best' car would be sat covered over with a dust sheet at one end and all around the edges would be workbenches adorned with power tools and hand tools hanging from screws on the walls. He would recycle everything he needed to house his collection of utensils and gadgets. Old chests of drawers under the work benches held every size nut, bolt, chisel and hammer ever made. Nan's old wooden jewellery boxes with pull-out drawers kept his washers and panel pins. Washed out plastic milk cartons hung from wire strips, threaded through their handles, with their ends cut off to house string, lollipop sticks for labels, eye protection goggles and everything that a good hardware store would be proud to provide. She had joined him in the allotment from an age so young that she couldn't remember her first visit there. He would let her join in with every activity, digging and weeding, setting seeds into old toilet rolls and the joy of pulling up a carrot that was so long her little arm was already stretched to its limit. She has spent many, many hours here and now, walking up the path towards his plot, she suddenly felt an overwhelming urge to cry.

The previous week had been full-on at work with a sense of pace to every phone call, email or meeting throughout the company. After the lunch at San Martin's, Madeleine had met with Dominic a few times, mostly ad hoc as each of them devised another idea or formulated a plan. By Thursday, she insisted they met with Nadir and Roseanne, as she was starting to feel they were a group of two and as enjoyable as it was turning out to be, she knew it was only fair to bring the others in.

Madeleine had worked with Nadir several times before. He was the Digital Marketing Executive and had helped her build new websites for her clients. More importantly, he single handedly drove up interest on every social platform, so that after entering just the first few characters into Google their company web page was top of the list along with reams of hits and links to Twitter, Facebook, national and international newspaper clippings, even research studies from some of the largest Universities in the U.K. It would take some companies years to build such as collection of interest, but Nadir had flooded every avenue and her client's company had surged up the internet top charts, all fair and legitimate, and her clients were delighted with her. She has received the accolade, the bonus and thanks from C&B's Board but deep down she knew once again it was not her magic that had weaved its wand, but Nadir's. Again, she felt like a disappointment despite the success.

Nadir Bowen was a technical professional through and through. He was studious, serious and private until you got to know him and thereafter you were considered a friend, on a small level, and you felt honoured to be in his circle. When he divulged a snippet of his life; what he had done at the weekend, how he and his boyfriend had had a wonderful meal in Hove, that his mother was in hospital, you felt entrusted into his inner realm. His mother was from Israel, his father Welsh. He said his mother named him the Arabic name of Nadir as it meant scarce or precious. Madeleine thought he had upheld his name admirably as he was very much admired amongst his work peers yet did absolutely nothing to promote that fact. He was true to himself and worked hard, helped others and took no glory. It was this last trait that meant Madeleine always felt a tinge of guilt over the work he had done with her, which resulted in her praise and not his. He deserved better than that.

She and Nadir now sat in one of the small meeting rooms that were available to book amongst the staff. They were early for the meeting and she was enjoying having time to catch up on the latest recipe he had picked up from Yotam Ottolenghi. He had made a vegetable winter stew but with various savoury yoghurts and toppings followed by a clementine syrup cake. He had taken it to his father's house who was home alone whilst his mother was in hospital with 'a lady's operation.' Nadir wore a tie adorned with Tom and Jerry; his novelty ties were his outlet to balance the more serious approach to his work. He would never banter or be part of a large group's exchanges, but on a one to one you could see occasional glimpses of a wicked dry humour. His ties were different each day, he must have a huge collection as Madeleine had never seen the same one twice. As they sat catching up, she realised how infrequently she had a normal conversation at work. Rarely did anyone give anything away and more importantly, no one asked questions of each other. She had realised this early on in the firm, that people, as nice as they were, generally didn't have the slightest interest in anything about you. No one asked about your health or how your evening was the day before. No one knew where she was from, her family, her recent loss. Did she have children? Husband? Wife? The normal convention of a conversation is that one person asks a question to the other, to ignite a topic. Then you exhaust that thread before the next question is asked by the other person... and off you go, a two-way conversation. "Do you have to travel into London or are you local to work?" "Have you always been into publishing/marketing/computers/lobsters/fresh air basket weaving?" So, although Nadir was known for his quietness and solitude, she had actually enjoyed a deeper connection with him in the last twenty minutes than most people in the whole time she has worked or C&B. For all other communications you stick to work related themes, that was the norm and Madeleine had become used to it. However, she was surprised at how much she was enjoying just sitting, talking, in such a gentle and genuine manner.

Roseanne Kirk was new. Madeleine was yet to meet her but knew she had come over from a rival company to head up a department for research. Her remit was to build a small team, to identify potential new marketing opportunities and also to further research the background of clients, to give any advantage to the success of pitches but also to ensure there were no hidden skeletons in cupboards of the companies that C&B represented. C&B prided themselves on their core values, integrity being a buzz word often heard in staff development and one of the six words printed on the back of everyone's staff passes, to serve as a reminder of what the company strive for. Every so often there was a warm-up activity at the start of a staff meeting with one of the core values as a focus. Madeleine secretly felt it paid lip service to someone's tick box but others in her department seemed genuinely pumped up by the team approach. She had even seen guys fist pump the air at the very mention of 'shared goal!' C&B could not afford to risk their reputation by backing a company who were not squeaky clean, therefore Roseanne, the detective, was brought in.

Next in the room was Dominic, he smiled wordlessly at them both and started to remove a few chairs from the desk and pushed them to the side of the room, setting a scene more suited for a small group. He pressed a button on the wall to lower a TV screen from the ceiling and typed in his log-in details into his iPad. Once connected to the shared drive, he connected to the screen, opened and then minimised several saved pages which he wanted to refer to during their discussion. Only once he had set everything up did he turn again and speak. "How is everyone today? We'll wait for Roseanne and then make a start on our timeline." Madeleine noted with interest that he hadn't waited for a reply to his first question and that he was assuming the lead role in the meeting, that this was his team, his leadership. She knew it would sound petty to raise the point so just smiled in reply.

The glass door flew open crashing into one of the chairs Dominic had placed behind it. It bounced off and hit the newcomer straight onto her hand, bending it back and making her shout, drop her iPad and swear.

"What the fuck is that doing there? Doesn't anyone here know about escape routes? I wish people wouldn't meddle with furniture. My iPad had better not be broken, it's new."

Dominic looked fleetingly embarrassed but recovered to straighten himself taller and welcome Roseanne into the room.

"Everyone, this is Roseanne. Are you ok, do you need your hand looking at, I can call First Aid for you?"

"I am quite capable of calling First Aid if I need it, I wish people wouldn't start putting chairs against the walls, it's not a bus stop. It looks untidy and is obviously dangerous!"

Dominic coughed and turned to the screen in an attempt to collect himself.

"Well, I am guessing you are Nadir and you are Madeleine!" Roseanne stated. Madeleine nodded affirmative then realised that it was rhetorical, as it was very clear who was who. She immediately felt foolish.

Roseanne remained standing and started passing out glossy folders. "Right, well let's start then shall we? I've put together a pack on the background to Bittern Quay Investment Holdings and each of the members of the Board. They are, more or less, the same Board from the now disbanded Taiwan Financial Group and……."

"Oh yes, we know a lot of this," Madeleine flicked through the first few pages and recognised much of the same information that Dominic had already found and shared when they dined at San Martin's.

"What do you mean 'we'? I've wasted my time preparing this. Dominic, you invited me into this group for the research."

Dominic glanced at Madeleine, "Yes, yes we do need you to…."

"I don't have time to double up on things that you've already done," Roseanne cut in. "I thought this meeting was the starting point to the project, yet it seems I am a step behind and that's not where I like to be."

"Well, we met just once to start exploring ideas …." Madeleine once more regressed into child mode and heard her own voice pitifully explaining.

"Dominic, I was actually talking to you!" Roseanne blatantly turned aside from Madeleine and ignored what she was saying.

Dominic remained unflinching this time and stepped up a gear in his measured reply.

"Madeleine and I just scrapped the surface of what's out there. We know you can bring so much more to the table. We just wanted to fast track over the other teams and get a little ahead. I'm sure you have delved far more than we possibly could, it's probably a bit further on in your report. Can you talk us through it please?"

Placated, Roseanne picked up her copy and turned a few pages more and started to brief the others on each of the Board members. She had everything there, family trees, known associates, hobbies and membership clubs, even in some cases known lovers and current mistresses. She had C. Vs for each and summarised it all in a biography pulling out known likes dislikes, successes and failures. By the time she had stopped presenting Madeleine had to admit she was good at what she did.

"Questions?" Roseanne sat with a smirk to her impeccably made-up face. Her lips were the brightest red lipstick imaginable and now pursed smugly, they seemed somewhat comical. Her dress was the tightest grey linen and as she eventually settled down into the chair, the seams strained, despite Roseanne's incredibly slim silhouette. Her pillar box red stilettos matched her lips as she laid one leg over the other in a sideways slant. Her silver-streaked hair was clearly deliberate and added to her blonde base by a top London stylist. It was pulled back in the simplest of ponytails, smooth and healthy, not one disobedient spilt hair sticking defiantly out.

"I have a few," Nadir answered, who up to now had said nothing since Roseanne had walked in. "How have you found out about the personal and private stuff? I mean, let's face it, how could you possibly know Elaine Edwards is paying her pool cleaner for more than just a chemical check and water change? If this is obtained by any illegal means then we are all finished, not just in this project but in the company"

Madeleine was impressed. Nadir wasn't not fazed by Roseanne's confident presentation and his sense of duty overrode his usual muted contributions.

"You do want to win this contract, don't you?" Roseanne slowly turned her gaze and fixed it pointedly at Nadir. "I have been brought into C&B because I am the best in the business. If I am in a team, then it will be the winning one. So far, I haven't seen much from any of you to give me that confidence. Perhaps I need to take this elsewhere"

Dominic stepped in.

"Look, let's just start again from the top. Roseanne, I know you don't yet know us very well, but I can assure you we are a strong team and I have every reason to believe we can put in a good bid for the Quays contract. Nadir is a brilliant DME and Madeleine has pulled together some of the most successful projects the company has seen over the last few years. I also have an excellent record within the firm and fully intend being on the winning team. I propose we start by establishing our specific vision, the roles we will each take, some of the initial ideas we have and then form an action plan with a timeline. How does that suit with everyone?"

Madeleine didn't recognise herself in that description. If she were to introduce herself, she would have included her ability to pulls strings, ask favours, magpie ideas from other people and places and somehow turn them into her own. She would have added that she had no single achievement that she could hold up as entirely worthy of note. She couldn't identify her specific strength as A or B. What she excelled at was 'getting by' and filling in the gaps by using other people's skills. As a school leaver, Madeleine's choice of career path was never really explored in depth. Her Career Adviser meeting at secondary school was accompanied by her parents and she couldn't remember any part of the conversation including her. They had left with the decision of sixth form and then a selection of universities. Her father, Henry, had wanted her to work towards a Law degree but looking at her predicted grades the safer option was to look at business and marketing, something she could apply to any industry or sector. Henry had retired from The Bar and had in his time been a very well-respected lawyer. His hopes of his daughter following in the family footsteps were squashed during that school meeting and Madeleine felt he never fully recovered from the disappointment. Her mother had never worked. Well, that was not quite true, she once worked part-time in a local Builder's office as an administrator, answering the phone, matching invoices with payments, filing and completing stationery orders. She took the job when Madeleine started

Reception Class in school, James already in Year Two. She stayed there for about four months but left when she felt it was too much, juggling the school run, the house, children and a job. Yet this was how she based her never ending advice and wisdom of the working world upon Madeleine, as if her four months, about twenty-five years before, somehow superseded Madeleine's own knowledge and experience. Madeleine's biggest mistake was to choose a university close to home, she didn't need to move away and cut the strings. At the time it suited her, she saved money and had no reason to escape. She didn't realise the impact of not loosening the parent / child ties in those essential years and now it seemed too late. Madeleine always felt the need to please and impress and show her parents that she was being a good daughter, working hard and achieving something they could boast about. One day she would branch out, turn her skills into her own business and enterprise. That thought often crept into her head but was quickly diminished when she realised she had absolutely no idea what her business would be. In the meantime, she went to work, went through the motions of a life and kept the even keel.

The meeting between the four settled down to be more constructive than at the start. Dominic shared his ideas about combining the digital environment with health. He and Roseanne loosened their antlers which had become firmly locked at the start and after three hours they left having formulated a plan. They would create a series of video clips and images showing what the future working environment could be for Bittern Quay staff. There would images depicting high energy activities, everyone standing up, moving, fast paced, the opposite of computer desk-based stalagmites. Actors would interact via handheld devices or earpieces whilst on the move, in the gym, at the sports club, blending work and play. International imagery would be included, meaning the actual physical working location becomes almost irrelevant. They would focus on what it would feel like to work there and have your business based at the Quays, not the physical buildings and resources. Madeleine would start to pull together contacts to create a set of backing tracks to be played on corporate videos, adverts and played out across the site during various launches. Dominic would start on recruiting actors and story boarding for a selection of videos. All would have the same theme and tone but be of varying lengths and purpose. Nadir was to start building a website and creating pre-launch taster posts for social media, to build interest and curiosity. Roseanne was to research other known projects around the world, to ensure the team's proposal was unique and original. They gave themselves one week before meeting again to see what they had all achieved.

On the way back down the corridor, Dominic pulled gently on Madeleine's elbow to slow her down and fall behind the other two. He slowed his pace and allowed some distance to grow between them and the other pair, who were already disappearing around the corner.

"What do you think?"

"What do you mean?" Madeleine wasn't sure what he was getting at.

"Roseanne" he whispered.

"Well, I think she knows her onions, as my grandfather would say."

"She certainly does. I'm not sure how she found out all of this," waving his folder "but there is a lot here we can build on and use to our advantage. Look at Elaine, Edwards, she took on the Board of Directors at Accentis Buildings Corporation when she realised she was the token female amongst eleven men. She fought until five had been replaced and there was a fifty per cent split. She unearthed reasons to oust the five men and picked them off one by one. In all of our imagery we must ensure we have a gender balance and strong women represented."

Madeleine felt a rush of indignation, "I would have thought that was a prerequisite. Why should that even need to be a consideration"

Dominic looked genuinely upset. "I'm sorry, that's not what I meant at all. Of course, that would be the case. All I meant was we ensure we draw the point out, that Bittern Quays is an equal ops environment and we make sure it's one of the values we really promote." He looked Madeleine earnestly into her face. "I wouldn't have it any other way."

Madeleine accepted she must have misunderstood and nodded to confirm all was okay between them.

"Madeleine, I don't suppose you're free tonight, are you? I have a couple of tickets for Les Mis, good seats. They were a thank you present from that company I re-launched last week. I wouldn't want them to go to waste."

Madeleine hesitated. Claremont and Butler's policies were very strict about relationships in work, they felt it could encourage biased ethics and that business deals and arrangements could get misconstrued. But this wasn't a date date. It was almost a business event, a chance to discuss work further. Madeleine hadn't been out in Town for a long time. She always left work and jumped straight onto the train, turning down offers of a drink after work. In fact, she had made so many excuses over the years not to go out with her colleagues that they didn't ask any more. It wasn't that she didn't like them; it was their insistence on talking about work all night long. She spent all day talking marketing figures, the competition and the work gossip. She didn't need to extend that into her own free time. If they were keener to let their hair down and talk as old friends do, chat about each other's lives, family, silly things that had happened to each other. But no such closeness had ever happened even though she had worked with some every day for six years. She considered a one-to-one night out may be a little more lighthearted and she really needed to break the cycle of work - home - work. She had also found she was enjoying the time she was spending with Dominic, as a friend, and found herself agreeing to meet downstairs at 6 o'clock.

Plot 15 was on the left-hand side. Madeleine spotted it immediately by its familiar bathtubs sat outside of a large, somewhat lop-sided shed. The baths were filled high with strangled nettles overspilling across piles of wooden posts and over a white plastic chair, lying on its side and half buried under a web of brambles. Madeleine sighed as she stood in front of the shed and realised how derelict it had become. Where it was once proudly painted racing green, it had peeled away in huge sections revealing crumbling wood slates, bleached white from exposure. The window frames were rotten, the putty exposed and panes filthy. The felted roof was hanging on, only just, flapping at one end to give a glimpse of soggy chipboard. The padlock on the door still held on loyally, yet the hole at the rear of the shed could be crawled through easily if anyone so desired. To the left of the shed stood a few apple trees now emptied of their fruit and leaves.

Apples lay everywhere, blackened and half eaten by grateful hedgehogs. Madeleine remembered how she would run giggling as her grandfather shook the branches with the end of his rake, darting from left to right, catching the apples in her bucket that fell off the sides of the vast sails he had tied underneath like a hammock. Afterwards, she would sit under the cooling branches against the late summer sun and sort the bounty into eating apples or cider apples. Unblemished apples were packed into wooden trays, each separated by a sheet of paper and all others went into large buckets ready for the press. Madeleine had marveled at how nothing was wasted, all blemishes were accepted into the cider pile, even those picked from the floor, a little bit nibbled. "Makes it taste extra special," granddad would say. The wasted harvest on the floor in front of her, pushed a lump into her throat. The memory of those special days, long forgotten and under-appreciated reminded her now of how happy, carefree and safe she had felt. She had loved her grandfather greatly and seeing this sad decline just proved that those days would never be experienced again. She would never spend a single moment in his company, hear him call her My Maddie, be scooped up under his arm squealing with feigned fright thrashing about her arms and legs, sitting quietly after a long day's gardening unwrapping cheese sandwiches together from greaseproof paper, popping cherry tomatoes like sweeties and sipping hot sweet tea from a flask. She had expected everything here to still look the same. To have stood still in time. To be as it was. She had not been prepared for the sorry sight before her, his heart would be equally broken if he were able to see this, of that she was sure. This patch of land had been his life, his personality, it was part of him, and he had been part of it. They were intertwined. His years of toil, his nurture, his love had been poured into the care of his plot. He was proud of it, others envied it, not in a million years would he have let it get like this willingly. She felt devastated for him and despite often hoping, that in some kind of 'after life', he was able to still view everybody, she hoped beyond everything he wasn't able to see this.

She turned to take in the rest of the allotment. It was indistinguishable. Where once there had been raised beds brimming with vegetables, there was now a sea of waving brown grasses, at least waist high. Peeking out above were old cane trellises and wigwams, broken and covered in bindweed. Huge clumps of thick, green grasses had mounded up into hillocks. Pathways were hidden and as Madeleine tried to walk through, flattening down with her feet what she couldn't push aside, she kept feeling her ankle give way as she slipped into a ditch or tripped over an old plank edging strip. As she used her arms as scythes, she found old plant pots buried into the ground, discarded metal rods which had been used to hold up weighted produce and a blackened dustbin which was once an incinerator. She wasn't sure where the funneled lid was, but she was sure it was underneath there somewhere.

The poly tunnel was now only a carbon rod frame. The plastic covering had long gone and now all that stood were rods, still intact at one end, but at the other, completely collapsed. The weeds rampaged through it as if it didn't exist, well it hardly did anymore. The poly tunnel had been erected since Madeleine was last there. She had never seen it in its prime. He had told her about it of course, asked if she wanted to come and see it. "No, sorry, I'm going out with my mates," "I'm going into town," "I'm going to the pictures." It had taken quite a few people, she understood, to erect it. Friends of granddad's had helped and there had been a ceremonial opening tea. She was invited, of course, but she had been busy. Madeline stood facing the ruin and felt, not for the first time recently, guilt. Guilt for not giving just a small amount of her teenage time, guilt of not doing more as an adult. She had felt popping round for a cup of tea had been enough, but clearly it wasn't. Had he needed help for a long time? Had he been struggling? He had been gone for a few months now but what lay before her had taken a lot longer than that to decay. When did he start not being able to keep this all up? Had he lost interest? She didn't think so as he still talked about his allotment all of the time. Was he not able to work on it any longer? Had he asked her to help him recently? She couldn't recall, but if he had, did she hear him? Now, as so many bereaved before her, she was repent at the lost opportunities to have made a small difference to his life and at the same time build even more happy memories of her own. What would an hour of taking an interest have harmed her? Would she really have lost out on friendships because of choosing him for a short while? She knew, with her adult reasoning, that youths can be selfish, they can't fast-forward and see their older selves in this moment and have foresight. She knew that if she were to live those years again nothing would change, her teenage self would still have chosen to spend time with her friends. But, oh what Madeleine would do now to change that if she could. She really hoped her grandad had understood it wasn't personal, it was just His Maddie growing up.

Madeleine made it to about halfway across the plot. It was a full-sized allotment, the size of a football pitch painted onto a school playground. She could see granddad's caravan embedded at the far end and decided that would have to wait for another day, when she could bring gloves. It was just too deep to negotiate. She would need to find or borrow some shears. The greenhouse, that preceded the poly tunnel, had at least four panes missing, the evidence lay smashed around the paved surround. She would need thick gloves! But really, if she were honest with herself, what was she truly able to achieve here? It was only right that she tidies up the dangerous things; the greenhouse glass, collect up the metal posts before someone became impaled and just tidy around the edges a little before handing back the keys. She couldn't just hand them back in this state, that wouldn't be fair. And by tidying up a little, she was somehow paying back the time she had not spent there over the years. Perhaps it would alleviate some of her guilt she reasoned, it had taken her many years to eventually come here and help but she got there in the end. Yes, too little too late, but she can only manage this small token as homage to her grandfather, she just didn't have the time in her life to commit to anything more. She would peek into the shed to see what tools were there and come back next week with anything else she needed to tidy the place up a bit. One morning should be enough to do what was needed, maybe she could persuade her father to meet her with his car, they could go to the tip with all the rubbish. She noted down the phone number of the Chair of the Committee, which was stuck to a post with a drawing pin and would ask where to send the keys. Before she left, she took a few photos and a video on her phone, to remind herself of what she needed. She wondered if her mother would like to see the allotment, but she didn't wish to upset her needlessly. No, she would just get it tidied and handed back and put it behind her. She headed back towards the shed.

Madeleine took the longer way home, wanting to walk firstly past her grandfather's house. The allotment had shaken her, but she knew his house would look the same. Her parents had been helping him to keep the gardens looking neat. They weren't gardeners but did know their way around a lawn mower and clippers. Their own clipped hedges at home were immaculate, along with nothing more challenging than a few hanging baskets, all very neat and tidy and pretty in its own way. As she turned the corner, she could see her father's car in the driveway and guessed he was there sorting things out. Her mother had not decided what to do with the house but was taking her time to slowly go through his belongings and sort into keep, sell and throw away piles. She heard rummaging in the garage.

"Oh hello," welcomed her father as she stepped out of the crisp sunshine into the darkened workshop. "Your grandfather certainly had a lot of tools; I don't even know what most of these are for. They are very rusty and to be honest the power tools all look pretty dangerous. Look at this drill, I think he had cut the lead here and added another piece here and it's all taped up, look.

I won't be plugging that in anywhere! It will have to be thrown away. Some of these things are good to keep, look, like this chisel set. It's been kept in a box so it's in nice condition. But to be honest, I can't use a lot of it, I may contact that salvage place and ask them for a price."

"I know, I've just been over to the allotment and it's in a really bad state. I had no idea he had left it to get like that. There's no way I can keep it, it's the sort of project for someone who doesn't work and spends all day, every day over there. It needs an expert."

"Really? It wasn't too bad when I last went over there, let's see, that must have been spring last year. Just before he got poorly, around March time, I guess. Well, I suppose that is almost a year. You'll be surprised how quickly a garden can get out of control, it's a constant battle to keep the weeds out. You can potter for hours and not look like you've made any difference sometimes. You're right, it's a big job and you have your own work priorities."

"Do you think mum would mind, you know, if I gave it up?"

"I think she'll understand. She used to go over there when we first were married but once you children came along, she was too busy. And then she went to work of course….."

There it was again, the reference to mother's long working career being so challenging. A familiar irksome niggle rose in Madeleine, it never gets noted how much more she does than her mother, or brother, ever did. It's somehow expected as the norm for her. Anyway, her mother would have no right to complain about her giving the allotment back. She is the one who says concentrate on your paid job above all else. If it's an issue, then she could always take it on herself, but she knew that would never happen. No, her mind was made up. She has her work commitments and no time in her life to take on the allotment. Her head must rule her heart on that score.

"Can you pick me up from the allotments next Saturday please, to go to the tip?

"No love, I'm sorry, I'm playing golf with Uncle Michael and some friends. It's all booked up. It's a whole day-er. I can do it tomorrow if you like."

Madeleine had planned to catch up on some work emails, her washing and shopping before Monday came round again. She felt a little behind her usual schedule after going to the theatre with Dominic on Thursday. Not being used to staying out late in the week, she had achieved very little all day Friday too. She couldn't afford to fall behind and wanted to be a fully contributing partner at work the following week, proving her worth and place on the team. But she also didn't want to delay giving the allotment back. The longer she waited, the more overgrown it would become. So, she agreed a time to be collected the next day and set off to get a few bits from the local hardware store and then home to pop some washing on.

Sunday morning and the wind had changed direction, the sharp chill had dropped slightly, and it was a beautifully warm day, as long as you stayed in the sunshine. Madeleine collected a few tools from her father's shed, with his permission, along with the items she had bought from the store and decided to push it all in the wheelbarrow she had found at home, leaning up against the back wall. She could put the damaged glass and metal in the wheelbarrow to load into the car. She dressed in several layers, reasoning that she may get hot, doing physical activities she wasn't used to. She could take off and put back on clothes as she needed to. She pulled on her Nike trainers, which were less white than the day before and set off. Before getting to the next street, she was already removing a jumper, a sweatshirt and the cowl from around her neck. Pushing a wheelbarrow was harder than it looked!

Madeleine removed the keys from her pocket and opened her grandfather's shed. She had found most things she thought she needed there yesterday, some shears, a few buckets, gloves, all colours and thicknesses and a few pairs of secateurs. She wasn't sure why someone needed so many, but she chose a pair that looked the sharpest and placed them in the barrow. She had negotiated with several spiders, the removal of these items, luckily, she wasn't the squeamish type and had ushered the creatures off what she needed and left the spindly creatures to their own devices. After all, this had been their home for a lot longer than it was hers.

She lifted out her father's spray watering bottle from the wheelbarrow. It was tall with a hand pump on the top. If you pumped it up and down the pressure built up inside, releasing the water from a small tube in a steady flow. However, she had another use for it today and pulled open the hardware store's carrier bag and brought out the weed killer. Madeleine had spent the walk home yesterday planning her assault. First, she would chop back some of the main pathways, not all, just a thin width down the middle to be able to move around. Just to make it more accessible. Then she would spray the sides of the pathways so that in a few days' time, when the allotment committee came to look, it would have died back, and it should be a lot less untidy. Hopefully, she won't face any possible fines or demands to come back and clear the lot. Then, when she can get to the greenhouse properly, she will collect up the glass, find as many metal stakes as she can and other bits and pieces and put them into the wheelbarrow. She will search for as many poly tunnel frame pieces as she can and leave them in the shed, someone may be able to fix it up and be grateful for it. Really, it shouldn't take too long at all. A couple of hours maximum.

It took exactly twenty minutes to realise her plans were not at all realistic. She bent down chopping with the shears at ground level, starting at the shed. When she stood up to ease her back, she fully expected an entire path to be clear. To her dismay, she had only gone a few metres and she had created a great pile of waste which would also need to be cleared, and so doubling the work to be done. She hadn't thought about where to put the old grass and weeds. Maybe in a compost bin? But there was going to be an awful amount. Still, someone will appreciate it.

She decided to change tactics, here she was chopping weeds and creating more work. Surely if she just soaked the weeds with weedkiller, they'll just die. No need to chop or remove anything. The weeds and grass were very long, admittedly, but if she flattened it all down with her feet, and the weight of the wheelbarrow, and then sprayed it all, it will be job done - easy. And her arms were killing her, from the scissor action and her back was feeling not much better. Madeleine read the instructions on the bottle. It was covered in warnings and symbols about how toxic it was, she had bought a good one, the storekeeper had said. "It'll get through everything, that one," he told her proudly. She had found clear plastic glasses in the shed, ideal, as the bottle said, 'protect your eyes.' It wasn't a windy day and she had gloves. All perfect. She filled the water bottle up to the right level from the standpipe and poured in several capfuls of weedkiller liquid, as the instructions said. The job will need a lot of the liquid killer, she perhaps hadn't bought enough. She decided on two main routes to start with and could always pop back and do a little more another day.

Maddie pumped the bottle and started spraying, walking forwards, swinging it left and right across where she was guessing the pathway should be. Quickly, she realised she was spraying and walking into its jet, getting her trainers soaked. Surely, it was better to go backwards. That way she was flattening as she walked and spraying where she had already trodden. No need to walk on it again. She pushed her way forward, creating a route through to the other end of the section. She started walking backwards, stamping firmly down and soaking in front of her as she moved. The smell was awful, it was stinging her nostrils and she daren't touch her face with her gloves. She wanted to wipe her eyes. the plastic glasses had steamed up from her sweat and she fumbled to keep the glasses from slipping down her nose. She twisted her shoulder to use it to push them back up again. She stopped to pump the bottle to build more pressure. Starting again, Madeleine took a step back but didn't feel the top edge of a thin board, marking out the side of an old vegetable bed, until it was too late. She slipped and fell backwards, the spray carrying on into the air in a fine mist, raining all over her legs and hands as she tried to grapple to control it and avoid it landing on her face.

Giant hands shoved underneath her armpits, yanking her up skywards as her feet left the ground. She dangled briefly before being dumped to the side and the water bottle was ripped from her hands.

"What the hell do you think you're doing?" the giant roared in her face, contorted and spitting in the air.

"I'm, I'm …."

"You're crazy, that's what you are! What the hell are you doing with weed killer? Don't you know the damage you are doing?"

Madeleine was grappling to speak.

"I'm clearing the weeds……"

"No, you're not! You're ruining the ground, not just this plot but mine and everyone else's in a five-mile radius." he shouted waving in all directions to demonstrate his point. "We don't use weed killer here, ever!" The giant stomped around collecting up the equipment and twisting the capped end closed. "This ground has been organically treated for decades and you've come along and poisoned it. Have you any idea the damage you have done? And that stench! I imagine you've overloaded the amount you are using. I can smell it on my plot.... if that has traveled over to mine and landed on my ground, I'll kill you."

"Look, I don't know who you think you are shouting at me like this...."

The giant grabbed her wrist and dragged her.

"What are you doing? Let go of me. You have no right to touch me, get your hands off."

He twisted the standpipe until freezing water poured onto the ground. He pushed her into the flow and splashed the water up her legs with his huge, cupped palms. He pulled hard on her hands, downwards into the streaming deluge, which now pooling around their feet, creating a muddy pit. He rubbed her hands into the water, ignoring her cries of protest, it was numbing and hurting both as he massaged her fingers roughly. She was drenched and so cold, she tried to speak but her teeth chattered, and she gasped for air.

He turned the tap off and the two of them just stood staring at each other.

"How dare you!" was all she could say. The indignation and rage muted her beyond this.

"I was stopping you ending up in hospital you silly cow," he raged back. "You've doused yourself with enough weed killer to strip your skin right off. I shouldn't have bothered. An eye for an eye and all that!"

She started to shake, uncontrollably. she wasn't sure if it was anger, cold or a mixture of the two.

"Hey, what's going on....You poor girl, you're drenched!"

The kind voice came from what appeared to be a denim flower. A vast, light denim dress fell shapeless to a pair of ankles beneath. Peeping out were the rounded toes of flowery Dr Martin boots. Around the waist, a carpenter's tool pouch, light pink with multiple cerise pockets, each with a hand painted flower. Layers of cardigans, each with floral stitching, piled over the top, one button on each stretched closed over an ample bosom. The largest floppiest hat with a knitted sunflower pinning back the front adorned a mopped head of bright, pink curls. Flowery gardening gloves, enamel flowers dangling from ears and the warmest eyes stood in front of them both. Madeleine could have rushed into the denim flower's body and buried her head into her bosom. At that moment she looked so warm, generous and friendly.

"She has only gone and sprayed Bert's patch with weed killer!" the giant gave a measured explanation.

"Oh dear, no, you mustn't do that sweetie, it's against the rules you see. As a committee we made a pledge to be organic and it's a key item on the conditions of having a plot here. We all abide by it. Hold on though, you're not Maddie, are you? Bert's Maddie?"

"Yes, I'm Madeleine."

"Well bless my soul, the last time I saw you, you must have been about ten or eleven. Such a lovely little girl. And your grandad worshipped you. Mind you, you've grown into a beautiful lass, hasn't she Tom? Oh no Tom, you probably won't remember her. You were both so young. But listen to me going on, you're freezing, come over to my caravan, I have spare clothes and a towel. Let's get you warm and dry and we can sort out the rest after that."

Gratefully, Maddie followed the flower across the central path to a plot just two further down. She could have guessed which one it was when she saw the caravan sitting proudly in the middle. It was daubed the required green but all along the bottom edge was a hand painted meadow. Bright dancing flowers on bended stalks, shooting up from blades of grass in various shades of lime and emerald. Here and there bright rainbows weaved behind the plants, a few balloons that had made their escape were added, as well as numerous suns, with smiling faces. Across the front edge, a cherry blossom tree had been sketched in full bloom and a CND symbol had been painted where the caravan badge would have once sat on the front bonnet. Under the windows, hand painted window boxes hung, stuffed full of glossy petunias and begonias. It was simply quite beautiful.

"Come on inside love, here pull this curtain across the middle and get those clothes off. I'll pass a towel round, let's see, here it is. Don't worry, it's clean. Right, what have we got to give you to wear? Ah here we are, I'm sorry that I haven't got anything as smart as you would normally wear, I'm sure, but at least they're dry."

Madeleine emerged from behind the curtain wearing an enormous pair of black corduroy dungarees, with silver buckles on the straps. Underneath, a white cotton blouse covered in yellow bees. The arms were so long she had to roll up the sleeves. Thick woolen socks replaced the £200 pair of trainers she would have to throw away. The flower lady handed her a donkey jacket to keep warm.

"How rude of me, I've invited you to my van and not even told you my name. I'm Filo, Filo Truebridge, short for Philomena but everyone calls me Filo, like the pastry! I'm always baking…. You'll not remember me, I used to have blue hair," she giggled as she talked. "I met you a few times when I first got a plot here, but then you stopped coming. I remember you measuring your sunflowers ready for the village show. I can't believe it, where have the years flown?"

"Actually, I do remember a lady with blue hair. Really, really blue."

"Yes, that was me! How long ago was that?"

Madeleine did a quick calculation. "About seventeen or eighteen years ago."

"Well I never! I've had a lot of hair colours in all of that time." Filo laughed again at herself. "So, you've come to do something with our Bert's plot? We heard he had left it to one of his family but wasn't sure who. Have you got it now?"

"Well, yes, technically. I was left it in his Will, but I can't keep it. I was just tidying it up ready to give back the keys."

"Oh, that is a shame. It would have been lovely to keep it in his family. I'm not surprised he left it to you. He talked about you all the time. He was very fond of his little Maddie. Are you sure you can't keep it?"

"No, she can't!" Tom's head poked through the open door. He looked Maddie up and down in disgust. "No wonder the air stinks, she has used enough weed killer to kill off half of Reigate's gardens and the North Downs too!"

"But I read the label…." Maddie protested.

"Look, 25ml per 5 gallons." Tom sneered, sarcastically reading from the bottle.

"Let me see," Maddie took the weed killer. "Oh, I thought it said 250ml, quarter of a litre. And I put it into 5 litres, not 5 gallons. I was just so keen to get started and get it all cleared. Have I really messed it all up? I am really sorry, I thought I could do it myself, that it would be easy. The last thing I wanted to do was to ruin granddad's plot. I just wanted to do something...... to make amends," she whispered the last part to herself.

"Look, we can sort it out," Filo soothed kindly, "I'm sure we can get Norris' little digger and dig out the bit that you've sprayed. We'll have to dispose of it over at the tip properly. It's best to do it quickly though, before any rain washes it all over the place. Tom, be a love and see if Norris is up the top end please?"

Tom grunted as he turned and left the caravan.

"Don't you mind him, love. His scowl is worse than his bite. Sorry about the donkey jacket, it was my husband's. I leave it here to keep me warm, inside and out." Filo smiled and turned to a wardrobe, "Here, shove your feet into these. They were his too, size 13. I'm guessing they'll be a bit big on your little feet."

Filo passed her some wellington boots and laughed her way through the caravan door, signaling that they were off to undo the mess that Maddie had made.

Filo grabbed some canes from behind her caravan, from a small potting area that lent up against the side. Maddie had not seen it from the front. It was a simple, homemade wooden awning, placed to make the most of the sheltered position. It had a sloping roof over a few shelves piled high with pots and trays. A bench held a tray full of soil. Various trowels and handheld forks dangled from hooks under the shelves and beneath stood bags of every type of compost and plant feed. Although it was open to the elements, Maddie could see the rain would not often reach it, making it a handy little workspace for Filo.

"Your grandad made it for me." Filo explained, sensing Maddie's admiring looks. "It's just perfect. I can potter and plant my seeds in the fresh air. Then I take them into my greenhouse. He was a very clever handyman, always wanting a project to do. Except, of course, you don't need me to tell you that!"

She did need Filo to tell her that. This world had been lost to her for a long, long time. A vital part of her granddad was here.

Clearly, people he knew well were here and who knew him, possibly better than she did in recent years. She found she wanted to hear more.

"Tell me more about my grandad."

A rumbling came around the corner and Tom arrived sitting astride a narrow digger, wobbling precariously on the uneven ground.

"Okay," he shouted above the engine, "I'll meet you over there."

Filo passed a pile of small plants pots to Maddie and carried the canes herself and led the way back to number 15. Maddie's request went unanswered.

After explaining the task to Maddie, Filo followed her around the area, planting a cane every few metres and sitting an upturned pot onto each one. Maddie pointed to the ground and Filo staked the canes. Soon the whole area, that Maddie could remember spraying, had been clearly marked out for Tom to see from the seat that was bouncing him like a baby on huge springs. As Tom lowered the bucket to start digging, a four-by-four truck arrived at the end of the plot.

"Bless my soul, it really IS our little Maddie!" An elderly man climbed down from the truck's cab and threw his arms open wide. Maddie stood slightly stunned as she was enveloped and squeezed tightly. "Let me look at you! I would have known you anywhere, even in Filo's clobber. You still have the most beautiful green eyes, my goodness I bet your grandad was proud." His eyes watered and a sadness fell across his leathery lined face. "Do you remember old Norris?" he asked, referring to himself in the third person.

"Yes, I do Norris. You're granddad's friend from here and the social club in town. I remember seeing you at both places, with your wife…. erm, Jean I think?"

"Yes, yes, Jean is well, at home with the grandchildren today. Your grandfather and I were friends for many, many years. I was really very sorry when he died. I miss him, we all miss him." Norris welled up again and patted Maddie's shoulder. She realised he wasn't as old as he first appeared. Weathered and nutty brown, he was healthy for his age and probably a lot fitter than she was. She guessed he was around 72 years old; her grandad had not quite reached his 80th birthday. He would have loved a party to mark it, but that was never to be.

The four began the task of clearing the ground. Tom dug down and scooped out buckets of earth and deposited it in the open back of Norris' truck. Norris pushed it to the back, into a pile with a spade, so they could get as much as possible in. Filo and Maddie walked around any areas that they could access, gathering up discarded objects, the broken glass and anything that could go to the tip on the truck. Maddie remembered her father would be meeting her, so she called him to explain the change of plan. She would walk home later once the job was done.

Tom and Norris volunteered to be the ones to go to the tip, so Filo suggested a cup of tea back at hers.

"I am really sorry for all of the work I've caused everyone, I guess I didn't think it all through well enough. I should have known I couldn't do it all by myself, it's far too big. I am grateful for all of your help." Maddie was also grateful for the hot mug placed in her hands, made from a kettle sitting on top of a small gas burner with a canister attached underneath.

"Oh, don't you worry, it's all sorted now, no harm done… well hopefully."

"You know, I actually enjoyed today after all, it's so much easier working as a team. I can't believe where the time has flown." Maddie checked her watch to see she had been at the allotment for five hours.

"Do you think you'll keep the allotment now?" Filo's hopefulness was thinly disguised.

"No, I really can't commit to it. I have a job in the city that takes all of my time. I just can't."

Maddie was adamant.

"I'll tell you what. Whilst you drink your tea, I'll read you your cards." Filo reached behind and retrieved a battered pack of Tarot cards from the dresser.

This came as no surprise to Maddie. The caravan could easily have belonged to an old Romany; the painted kettles and pots, the bunting in the windows, the shawls thrown over the furniture to make it homely. So, although Maddie thought it all a load of nonsense, she let Filo read her cards.

The bar was heaving. It wasn't really the type of place Madeleine felt comfortable in. It was designed to keep everyone on their feet, no seats except a few bar stools at high round tables, they were covered with the emptied glasses that had been left there, as people pushed past to get to the toilets or to the exit. She didn't enjoy being shunted by sweaty, suited men seemingly falling accidentally onto her, smirking an insincere "sorry." The music was loud with the same monotonous beat, booming out, electronic, with no beginning and no end. It just merged into the next similar sounding noise and made her chest thump. Dominic had gone to the bar, they had only just arrived but already she knew she would rather be home, in her pajamas, with her feet freed from the pinching stilettos that she'd worn all day. They had planned to go out after work, so she wore a dress to work that she wouldn't normally have worn during the day. It was a simple little, black, cocktail dress, with a twisted knot of material under the bust, accentuating her natural curves and highlighting her cleavage. It was entirely appropriate for work, not too revealing, but more than she would have normally allowed herself to wear. She was now sleeveless, having tucked the bolero jacket she had worn all day through her handbag, to stop it falling onto the sticky floor. Her dark waves were piled up into a deliberately messy bun, letting loose tendrils fall softly onto her perfect, bronzed skin. She was normally fairly pale but recently she had been exposed to the early spring sun and it gave her a healthy glow. She had reapplied her make-up, her green eyes were edged with smokey kohl, her lashes thick and her eyebrows full and dark. She didn't realise how beautiful she looked, she was natural and at ease with her own self. She didn't feel the need to judge herself against the other girls. She was pragmatic enough to know the world needs a variety of people, she had chosen to be studious and conservative, she didn't judge others for their choices. In school there had been the popular girls, who wore their skirts shorter than the rules, who clearly had mascara on although it was banned and who boasted that they had 'done it' with a boyfriend, whether it was the truth or not. Although Madeleine had not joined in, she was still friendly with these girls, and they respected and liked her in return. A few were jealous of her although she never knew. They admired her confidence in her own self, that she was actually an individual even though they were the ones fighting to be outside of the norm. Ironically, they all ended up being clones of each other and she, the original one.

Dominic returned with two cocktails. She had asked for a Pinot Grigio so was surprised to see a florescent orange drink in a martini glass.

"I thought you'd like one of these, they're gorgeous," Dominic handed one to her.

Madeleine didn't like to make a fuss, after all he had bought this round of drinks.

"Thank you."

It was far too sweet for her taste, she liked a crisp, dry white wine or a tart gin and tonic. Cocktails had never been appealing. It occurred to Madeleine, that Dominic often took it upon himself to decide on an alternative despite her asking for something else. When they had gone to the theatre after work, a couple of weeks before, he had pre-ordered alcoholic drinks for the interval even though she had asked for sparkling water. She felt he was probably just trying to impress her. He did seem to be keen that she liked him. He was attentive. At the theatre he had taken her arm and threaded it through his own, to lead her up the steps to their excellent seats, which turned out to be in a box. Throughout the show he had glanced across at her and at the exact moment of Jean Valjean's death he had produced a handkerchief for her to wipe her tears, except she wasn't crying. She dabbed her dry face in obligation and smiled back gratefully. In many ways she had enjoyed their first night out. Despite telling herself it was a work outing; they had spoken very little about C&B. In truth they had spoken very little at all, he had been late down to meet her in reception and by the time they took a black cab to the theatre, found the cloakroom for their coats and their seats, the curtain went up. During the interval, Dominic told Madeleine about his career journey. He too had been pushed into business and marketing, but it was obvious that he loved it. He told her that he had qualified through an apprenticeship and that the company he worked for offered him a permanent job. From there he quickly moved from company to company, building a portfolio that he eventually took to Claremont and Butler, they liked what they saw and offered him a post. Dominic oozed self-assurance. He was bold without being brash. He was confident without being arrogant. He had impeccable manners and liked to be a gentleman, treating ladies with respect and at times taking charge, which, he felt, was absolutely his role.

A few women and men passed by and gave him admiring glances. He was immaculate. His suit was blue herringbone with a matching waistcoat that scooped low at the front. He had a gold chain hanging from one pocket to the other and Madeleine assumed a pocket watch was on the end. His shirt was pressed - creaseless - despite it being worn all day. His dark hair slicked back on the shorter side and the other flopped to just the right point across his eye. His tan winklepickers matched the brown leather trimming across the top of each pocket. Madeleine couldn't help but see the beauty in this man, she guessed he had a weekly manicure and perhaps a whole range of beauty treatments. He had an air of Andy Garcia, his olive skin, long legs accentuated by skinny trousers. He was polished and despite her usual self-assurance she wondered, more than once, why she was there.

This was their fourth date. Madeleine was now sure these were actual dates. When Dominic had seen her to her train at the end of the show, his lingering kiss to her cheek, the palm of his hand in the small of her back pulling her towards him, were unmistakable signs of his intentions. A week later they had been to dinner after work to an Italian chain restaurant, chosen for its speed as Madeleine was tired and wanted an early night. They had also met for another lunch in San Martin's, when Dominic had suggested they go to 'their restaurant' she knew he was implying it was a special place for them both. She wouldn't have described it as that at all but didn't correct him.

It was Friday night. There was something about a Friday. This wasn't a casual get-together after work. This was dressing up, this was hitting the town, choosing venues that were intended to excite and make you want to party. Friday nights meant staying out late. No work the next day, so anything was possible. She knew this was taking things up a notch and she wasn't sure if she were ready for it. They had already been to a sports bar around the corner, packed and full of vast TV screens blaring out different commentaries from each one. They had had one quick drink and moved on. Now Madeleine was in this night club bar, with a cocktail in her hand, it was only 7.30pm and she feared this was going to become a long night. Despite the enviable company, the attention and the buzz, she suddenly found she really wasn't in the mood.

"Do you like it?" Dominic leaned in to make himself heard. The result was he shouted into Madeleine's eardrum, making her wince.

"Erm, yes it's fine, thanks" she offered, to please him.

"It's great here, isn't it? It's the place to be seen. Everyone who's everyone comes here."

"Have you been here before?" Madeleine shouted back, facing him fully, so he could lip read.

"Yes, I live not far from Camden Town Station, it's an easy ride and this is the best area to meet potential contacts." He leaned in further, placing his hand on her knee to steady himself as he spoke. "You look beautiful tonight" he smiled.

It threw her off guard. Apart from the kisses on her cheek as they said goodbye and the steadying arm here and there, there had been no intimacy as such. The compliment was genuine and warmed her. His touch was deliberate, an excuse to make contact. Her brain sent all its receptors down to her knee and as his hand remained there, it was all she could concentrate on. She had had the constant voice of reason telling her she was not allowed to be in a relationship with a colleague and up to that point she didn't feel that there was anything to answer to. But as his deep gaze sunk into her eyes, the deafening noise faded into the background and she found herself thinking, "Oh shit!"

The tarot reading had been a mistake. Maddie did not believe in mystical mumblings. She was practical and levelheaded and had no time for dream catchers, numerology, seances or mediums. She had pandered to Filo's quirks and had gone along with the game.

"I'm going to give you a three-card reading," Filo had explained. "You must remember, the cards will not give you specific answers, you must trust your instinct and be open to the possible meanings they bring. I can interpret them through my inner spirit, and you must do the same and between us it will all become clear. They will not tell you what to do, they will enter your energy field and guide you, but only if you allow them to. I will draw one card for your past, one card for your present and the third for your future. The symbols on the cards are not literal, so if I draw The Devil, it doesn't mean evil in the way you might think it does, it could be a chance to assess any negativity in your life and reevaluate it and learn from it."

"Ok, I understand," although Maddie really didn't.

"So, I'm now going to prepare the cards."

Maddie tried not to smile at Filo's theatrics. She pushed up her cardigan sleeves, and began to shuffle the pack, taking time to cut them and re-shuffle. She waved them around the air and gestured them towards Maddie. "Knock on the pack."

Maddie reached forward and tapped the pack with her knuckles.

Filo dealt the cards into three piles.

"Choose one pile, don't pick it up, just point."

Maddie indicated the pile in the middle.

"Now, I want you to close your eyes and think of a question you want the tarot to help you answer. It can be anything at all, keep it open, not too specific. It shouldn't be a yes/no type of question."

A question? Maddie wasn't aware she had any questions. She considered Dominic, her work, the competition and the possible promotion if they won but none of these, she thought were issues to discuss or decipher. Perhaps a question around the growing bond between her and Dominic, along with the implications if C&B found out, but then, she would simply pull the plug if it became something she wasn't comfortable with. So, no need to raise that as a question here. She thought she would keep it simple; she knew the answer to this question already so the silly tarot cards would be meaningless. So she asked…...

"What shall I do with this allotment?"

Filo pondered the question for a few too many seconds and then asked Maddie to cut the pile of cards three times. Filo took them and laid them, face up, in front of Maddie.

On top of the first pile was a man riding in a chariot. He held a sword or a wand, Maddie wasn't sure which. In front of him sat two sphinxes, one was black, the other white. They faced away from each other, they reminded Maddie of Janus, the two-faced god who looked both backwards and forwards. The namesake of January.

"Aha, The Chariot," Filo explained. "This is a Major Arcana card, one of life's big lessons. But if you can see, it is upside-down compared to the other two, this means it's reversed."

"Is that bad?" Maddie couldn't help but be a little intrigued.

"No, it just means the interpretation is a little different. It means rather than moving forward you are or have been blocked, up against a brick wall. There are obstacles in your past and you're not able to get around them. Hmmmm, there is also a warning…. have you always focused on your self-discipline, or have you let it slide?"

Maddie was a tiny bit incensed. Of all her traits she was proud of her self-discipline, she felt she had good values and had rarely been led astray. She abided by rules, she had never been in trouble with the law and even in school she had been a model student; not the brightest in terms of academic ability but definitely a hard worker and always gave everything her best.

"This really isn't my kind of thing Filo," Maddie didn't want to appear rude; she knew Filo was just trying to be nice to her.

"Look, the next card is also a Major Arcana, this time upright." Filo ignored her protests. "This is called The Fool. This represents your present."

Maddie really did think she was being a fool continuing and started to gather her handbag and keys.

"Can you see The Fool is stepping off a cliff? He is happy though, happy to be doing so. He is on his way to new experiences, meet new people who can teach him new lessons. He needs to step off before he can find where he is heading."

"So, you're saying that this is me, in my present time, a fool, stepping off a cliff?"

"I'm saying it's a possible present if your spirituality allows it to be. It's open to your interpretation of course. Let's just finish the reading, you may not see the relevance now but maybe in time......"

Maddie sighed, "Okay, but then I really should be going."

Maddie peered at the final card. She knew its name before even reading the small italic word at the bottom. A skeleton sat upon a horse, it was wearing armour, but the skull told her exactly what it was. The armour was black against a beautiful white stallion. A woman was on her knees in front of them, begging for her life.

Maddie stood up.

"That's enough. I have had enough of death this year and this is all nonsense. I'm sorry Filo, I do appreciate how you've helped me, but you can't go around telling people their future is death, I just don't like this sort of thing. I need to go; thanks again and please thank Norris and Tom for me."

Maddie grabbed her things and left the caravan as quickly as she could. She suddenly felt claustrophobic, trapped. She needed air and to get back home, where it was familiar.

"Maddie please don't go without me explaining the card to you…." Filo called out of the door. "It's three Major Arcana cards, that's important…"

Maddie held her hand up as a goodbye but did not turn around.

Madeleine's head hurt. She had allowed herself too many cocktails, each a different colour and each in a different bar. By the end of the evening, she was weaving slightly, and Dominic held her hand tightly as she walked. She remembered getting back to London Bridge Station and Dominic nuzzling into her neck. He whispered, "Overground or underground?" Was she going back home to Reigate or on the underground back to his home? His aftershave smelt musky, his warm breath on her skin inviting but she knew this was not the right time to make things even more complicated. She thanked him for the lovely evening and wobbled slightly to the barrier where she scanned her ticket. She looked back to wave goodbye but was surprised to see he had already left.

Now she was cross with herself for coming home drunk on a train, she was normally so careful with her personal security, letting her guard down could have had serious consequences so late at night. She remembered she had planned on going over to Queens Gardens again today to do a final few bits and pieces, ready to hand back the allotment. She had been over during the week after the tarot reading. Once she got home, she realised she had acted ungratefully and had taken Filo some brownies that she had baked especially.

"I know you are the baking guru, Filo, but please accept these as an apology."

"Don't be so silly, love, its ok, tarot isn't for everyone, and I should have been more sensitive. I want to explain what that last card means to you."

"Really, I'd rather just forget it all now if that's ok?" Maddie didn't wish to open up that conversation again. "I'm going to do a little more tidying up and maybe see what's in the caravan. I may need to empty some of granddad's things out of there, my dad can have some of it"

"Well, if you need any help or a cuppa, just shout." Filo had obviously not taken any offence to Maddie's previous visit and it was nice to put that all behind them.

Maddie never had the chance to unlock the caravan. As she left Filo's the heavens opened and the rain smashed down. Frustrated that she would need to come back yet again, she left for home resigned to the fact she would get soaked through and getting rid of the plot was going to take a little longer.

So that following weekend, despite the initial hangover, Maddie once more packed a small rucksack and set off. She felt a whole heap better from tea and toast and the fresh air was working wonders; by the time she arrived at the gate she felt ready for action. She pushed her way through to the front of the caravan but the thick brambles across the door barred her way in. She retrieved the gloves and secateurs from her bag and set about ripping out what she could. The thorns fought back, invading her sleeves and scratching her arms deeply. The gloves were not thick enough and she had to keep taking them off to pull tiny shards out of her fingers. Ignoring the blood, she built a large pile of weeds.

She scooped it up into her arms. Between her plot and the one next-door stood a compost bin. It was made entirely from old pallets, open at the top and easy to dump armfuls of waste into it. There were two compartments, one had waste in that was nearly ready to use, gloriously soft and brown. In the other she could identify vegetable peelings, cardboard and grass cuttings. As this was obviously the most recent side to fill, she heaved it over and dropped it in.

"You have to be joking me!" a familiar gruff voice shouted over the dividing hedge.

"Excuse me? What now?" Maddie felt her good mood plummet.

"Why the hell are you putting weeds into my compost bin?" Tom's head peered over, clearly in no better mood than the last time she had encountered him.

"To rot them down, I didn't know what else to do with them and I thought it could be useful, adding to the compost."

"You don't put weeds into there! You'll just be introducing weeds back into the ground, even if it's rotted, I don't want to run the risk. I've spent too much time getting my soil just how I want it, without you coming along and spoiling everything."

"Well, what do you suggest I do with them then?" she didn't hide her annoyance.

Tom looked at her, clearly thinking of many suggestions he could give her but settled on a more polite version, "Burn them…. and then put the ashes on the soil."

"Oh right, ok, I'll have to do that then." Maddie was exasperated, she was trying her best. Tom watched her as she struggled to lean back over into the bin and pull out as much as she could. She refused to wince as thorns pierced her arms. She felt Tom's disdain burning into her and miserably she dragged the pile back over to her side. She remembered the incinerator that she had found and went off to see if Filo had any matches. When she returned, Maddie lifted the dustbin incinerator onto a circle of bricks to allow air to flow into the holes that had been drilled into the bottom. She gathered small twigs from under the hedges and pulled a notepad from her bag. Scrunching up the paper into balls, she lit the corners of each and was elated that once she gently added the twigs, she actually made fire. She didn't feel so foolish and incapable after all. She let it take hold and then gathered up the pile of weeds before dumping it onto the fire. The smoke was instant. Thick and swirling it pumped out of the top of the dustbin at an alarming rate. The wind caught it and threw it over the hedge, far away from her own plot, she just knew what was coming next.

"Jesus!! I can't see!!" chocking and spluttering, Tom stomped around onto Maddie's patch and raised his arms up in surrender. "Ok, shoot me now," the sarcasm dripped from him. "You obviously want to see me off this planet, just get it over with, I give in."

"That's a bit over the top, isn't it?" Maddie thought he was now just trying to make a point and a stupid one at that. "You said burn it, so I am!"

"Yes, but there's a reason why fires are only allowed between 5 and 6 pm! I suggest you read the rules before coming back here again. People are here during the day working on their gardens, they don't want you barbecuing them. You obviously have no idea what you're doing so you really should just give it all up"

"But that's the point! I want to give it up, I know I'm not cut out for this sort of thing. But I don't need you criticising everything I do. I'm only here for today and then I'll be out of your hair. So you can rest easy, I won't be killing you anytime soon." she turned abruptly into the cloud of smoke and didn't let Tom see her momentarily lose the ability to breathe or her eyes filling with stinging tears. She held her head up high and found the keys to the caravan.

Monday arrived along with a cloud over Maddie that she just couldn't shift. She had opened the caravan and had not expected to find what she did. It had stayed with her all through the weekend and she found she was having trouble processing it all.

"Please all take a seat," Katrina Everett, the Deputy CEO, snapped Madeleine from her daydream. "Today, I'll be calling each of you in to present a ten-minute synopsis of your proposals for your Bittern Quays pitch. I can see from your faces this is unexpected and deliberately so. I wish to see how prepared you are at this point and the level of detail and commitment that has been put in from each of you. I must warn you that any pitches that are too weak will not go any further. I will be cutting the pack and only allowing the strongest to go through to present to the CEO. I will email your appointment slot; these will start in just over one hour to allow you to gather resources. Remember this is just an overview, I don't want to see a final product. But, be prepared to answer questions."

This was not the best start to the week! Madeleine knew she had not fully committed to the tasks she was preparing for the team. She had been using all her spare time to go over to Queens Gardens and her mind was not fully on the job. The team had only met a couple of times and not since Dominic had left her at the train station. Madeleine had wanted to see him this morning, just to check everything was ok between them, she didn't know why but she felt she had done something wrong.

Madeleine returned to her office. The corridors and rooms were cubes made entirely of smoked glass. Each had an impressive black glass kidney desk dominating the space with matching shelves, sideboards and a filing cabinet. The company policy was 'Neatness and order enables efficiency' so each working space was laid out the same, no clutter, just clean and bright from the vast windows that opened out to the city below. The only way to tell whose was whose was by the name plaque on each door and the few personal possessions allowed on show; a pen pot, one photo frame, personal stationery and your bag and phone. Post it notes around your computer screen or pictures of pets, blue tacked onto the walls, were strictly frowned upon. Being on show at all times made private conversations difficult. Relationships were maintained at work level only, there were little chances of corridor gossip or gathering around a kitchenette for a giggle. There was no shared photocopier to lean against for a natter, the limited items you were allowed to put onto actual paper were sent to the admin room directly, then delivered to you once a day. Everything was to be saved onto a digital format as much as possible. No, once in work you filled your corporate named insulated mug with a drink from the machine and took it straight back to your office.

Her PC pinged as her emailed appointment saved into her online calendar, 12.30pm, breathing space to gather her notes. The phone on her desk rang.

"Hi, it's Dom," Madeleine couldn't tell from the tone how he was or how she should respond. "I've just had my time slot, it's at eleven, so I've just got an hour to get ready. I'm all prepped of course, from my point of view. Nadir and Roseanne have emailed me every day any notes and updates but I'm not sure where I am with you."

The double meaning was not lost on Madeleine.

"Sorry, I've had things going on at home…." she trailed off, once again hearing her own pathetic excuses. "Anyway," she snapped herself back into work mode, "I've got the tracks for backing the videos, I have chosen five different versions and so far, really think the electronic dance has the right vibe. I'll zip them up and add them to the shared file as they're too large to email. I've set up sampling groups through Survey Monster dot.Com, they can set up face-to-face and digital opinion feedback on the tracks and then again once we have visuals to add. I've contacted some of the guys from Belbridge Inc, you know who arranged the models for my Rugby Aid campaign, they are sending over some profiles for us to look at. I've already seen what you have all added, the storyboards look great, we can finalise them after we have this morning's meetings."

Dominic sounded warm again, "That's great, I'll pick all of that up from the shared drive later. I think we've got enough to show Katrina, we have all of the background values and ethos sorted, the rest is just practical. Look, Madeleine, can we talk about the other day? I feel bad that I let you go home alone, I worried about you all night, in case something had happened to you."

"But you didn't call me to check," Madeleine silently questioned in her head.

"I think perhaps we had a few too many cocktails and I should have made sure you were ok. Can I make it up to you? Can we go out again, this time I'll choose a nice restaurant so we can really talk and get to know each other better?" Dominic sounded genuinely upset and before really thinking it through, Madeleine found herself agreeing to another date.

Madeleine arrived at Katrina's office early. She hated to be late to anything. If a bus was due at midday, she would be at the bus stop at 11.30. If she had an offsite meeting, she would get a train that arrived an hour early, rather than risk one that gave her ten minutes' grace. Katrina's P.A. pointed to the low, suede sofa in the corner as a signal to sit and wait. The office door opened.

"Oh hello," Roseanne towered above Madeleine, who sat with her knees higher than her lap in the absurdly small seat.

"Hi, how did you get on?" Madeleine felt the coolness but ignored it, as most staff at C&B carried an element of frostiness.

"No problems of course. I'm confident that my pitch, and Dominic's of course, will be fine. It's the team as a whole though, isn't it, so we'll just have to wait and see after you and Nadir have been in. We can't afford to have a bad apple."

"Don't worry, I have everything I need to sell our pitch." Madeleine couldn't believe the nerve of her, how dare she assume Madeleine and Nadir were not as good as she and that they were the weak links, incapable of holding their own.

"Well, see to it that you do." Roseanne hissed as she turned and left.

Fired up, Madeleine entered Katrina's office once the P.A. had given her the green light. Madeleine wasn't sure what she was expecting, a small panel of people around a table perhaps, but seeing Katrina in lycra, pedaling an exercise bike, wasn't it. Her face was thick with make-up yet not a bead of sweat could be seen. She didn't slow down as Madeleine entered the room, she just nodded towards the chair in front of the bike to instruct her to sit.

"Ok, so I've heard from Dominic and Roseanne so far, so I don't need to hear all of the content again. What I want you to tell me is where are the strengths and where are the weaknesses, as you see it. Give me a S.W.O.T. analysis of your team."

The S.W.O.T.s were relied on heavily at C&B and Madeleine was confident in using it as a framework to talk through.

"Ok, so Strengths, each member of the team comes with an expertise which contributes equally to the group and covers every element of the task. We don't have any gaps in skills, and we work well together." Madeline knew she was saying what Katrina and others wanted her to say and didn't really have the conviction in it herself. "Weaknesses.... timing. We have all been working on our respective areas but now need to clear our commitments to have quality time together to start to pull this into shape."

Katrina said nothing, just pedaled and nodded.

"Opportunities… this is a new venture for us working together in this way, already we are sharing contacts and broadening our capabilities. We have been able to tap into some of the best in the field, to provide us with services that are needed. There is no area of our presentation which we are not confident with."

"Ok, so Threats…..." Katrina stopped the bike.

"Threats…. Well, we are pitching to the theme of health within the digital arena, based on what we 'think' we know about Bittern Quay Investment Holdings. Honestly, there is a chance we may have not hit the mark."

"And Threats within the team?" Katrina stared hard at Madeleine.

"No, I really can't think of anything I would regard as a threat in that respect." Madeline lied. Although Roseanne had done nothing whatsoever to Madeleine, she hadn't experienced anything tangible that she could have described to someone else, it was simply the way she was spoken to by her, the insinuations, the slyness of her passing comments. Madeleine knew she was being petty; she knew in truth she probably felt intimidated by her and how ridiculous that sounded. Madeleine did know her stuff, she had proved it over the years, yet the imposter syndrome feeling kept creeping in and crushed her confidence.

"Hmmm," Madeleine felt Katrina was trying to get more from her. "Ok, I trust your analysis Madeleine. I would have liked to see your project further along by now, but I can see potential. I feel you are still missing a hook; you've got to find that niche, that originality, that surprise. I'll leave it with you. I'll let you carry on, but I expect to be more dazzled next time we meet. I'll see Nadir now and check over some of the online aspects but I'm sure they'll be nothing amiss there."

Madeleine was wordlessly dismissed and left feeling as though she had been used in some way. She checked back her answers in her head and felt sure she had stayed loyal to her team. Was Katrina trying to get more from her? Was she aware of something that Madeleine wasn't? She wanted to talk to the others about their experience. Nadir wasn't in the outer office waiting to go in, so she set off to her own office to set up a meeting.

The Starbucks on the corner was the easiest venue for Madeleine to arrange at short notice. They must have had a busy lunchtime as the tables were strewn with ripped up sugar sachets and soiled serviettes. She started to clear the cleanest one she could find of the half-emptied coffee cups.

"This is classy!" Roseanne came in and cast her eyes around the room in disgust.

"I couldn't get a meeting room, and this was the easiest place for us all to meet," Madeleine reasoned.

"I haven't brought my purse, get me a latte will you, with skimmed," The lack of warmth from Roseanne was not imagined.

Madeleine didn't quibble and returned a few minutes later with two cups and a selection of sugars and stirrers intertwined in her fingers.

"So, whilst it's just us girls," Roseanne began, "What's this I hear about you and Dominic?"

Madeleine was caught off guard.

"What do you mean, me and Dominic?"

Despite her every effort she could feel heat flow up from her neck to her face and knew the blush belied her.

"Oh, don't worry, it's not common knowledge…. yet. It's just you were seen out in Town the other night and apparently you were obviously not talking shop!" Roseanne smirked, enjoying revealing that she had something over Madeleine. She could see Madeleine felt uncomfortable and carried on. "Oh, I'm sure it was all very innocent, but let's face it, Dominic is quite a catch. I can see why you would want him on your arm, he won't do your street cred any harm now will he?"

"There isn't anything to know Roseanne, we went out a couple of times as friends, that's it!"

"Oh yes, I'm sure," the sarcasm wasn't hidden. "Look, I really don't care what you both do, but leave getting caught until after the competition, will you? The last thing I want is to have any chances ruined because you two can't keep your hands to yourself."

With no chance to retaliate, Dominic walked in, looking like he had stepped off the cover of GQ magazine.

"Hi," he looked only at Madeleine and smiled warmly. "So, how did everyone get on today with Katrina?"

"I outlined the project," Roseanne pushed in, "and talked through the research so far. She was obviously impressed with the level of detail I… we had. She appreciates if you want something badly enough you need to be ruthless."

Did Madeleine imagine it, or did Roseanne take a long, slow look at Dominic as she spoke?

"Well, I talked through the story line, the themes and sub-texts. It obviously touched a spot with her, I couldn't believe she was in there exercising, of all the luck, brilliant!" Dominic was like an excited puppy. "What about you, how did you get on?"

Madeleine explained how she hadn't been asked about the project itself but had to give a S.W.O.T. analysis of the team.

"Really, what the hell for?" Roseanne wasn't happy to hear that at all.

"I really don't know," admitted Madeline, "It did seem strange and I felt she was trying to get me to say something more."

"It's me she's after," Roseanne was clear. "She was never in favour of me joining the company and she's trying to find a way to test me. She's looking for faults but I'm sure you didn't have any, did you Madeleine? I mean we are a team and no matter what we know about each other, we stick together."

Madeleine couldn't believe the blatant threat, in front of Dominic. She was hinting at revealing the two of them. Be nice about me or I will ruin you. I know something that can destroy you, so don't be negative about me. This was blackmail and Madeleine knew it.

"I don't know if all of that is true Roseanne, but I didn't say anything negative about any of us. I want to come through this competition in the winning team and I'm not going to jeopardise that." Madeleine realised she was contradicting herself to Roseanne, she was jeopardising things if she kept seeing Dominic, but hopefully she had convinced her she was willing to stick on her side…. for now.

The door flung open and Nadir rushed in, unusually clumsily he bumped into a pushchair, apologised to the mother and sat down.

"I'm sorry I'm late. I was a long time in with Katrina. What have I missed?"

They filled him in with their summaries and deliberated again over Madeleine's curious meeting. Nadir agreed it probably had nothing to do with Roseanne and he was sure every team had the same questions asked. He told them he had gone through the draft website and some of the 'spoilers' he had set up to drip feed into social media over the next few weeks. Fully caught up and finishing their coffees, the four made their way back to work.

Madeleine had only just sat down at her desk when the phone rang. It was Nadir.

"Look, I won't put this in an email, and I wanted to see you alone to tell you, but I feel I need to warn you about Roseanne."

"Why, what has she done?"

Nadir continued, "It's not what she has done, yet, but I am sure she is planning something. One of the guys in my team used to work with her and apparently, she destroyed a woman who she took a dislike to. She thought this woman was competition and found a way to bring her down. I don't trust her. I have seen the way she looks at you and the way she talks, I just have a bad feeling about her and wanted to warn you. I hope I'm wrong, maybe it's not true, but you had better keep your wits about you just in case."

Madeleine was shocked. She had never been a target. Even with others who she had little in common with, she still enjoyed a pleasant level of friendship and respect. She had nothing that Roseanne could want. They worked in different departments, had completely different roles, they didn't spend time in each other's circles. Madeleine was genuinely surprised to find she was suddenly the object of someone else's dislike. If Nadir had spotted it, she was sure it must be true. He didn't normally get involved in gossip, she was surprised that he had, but she appreciated that he had told her. That must have been hard for him to do. All Madeleine could think of, was that Roseanne liked Dominic for herself. She had seen a strange look towards him in Starbucks, when she said she wanted something badly. Of course, she hadn't seen it before, but it made sense. That could be the only thing Roseanne could be jealous of, her and Dominic. It was all getting too complicated and nothing really had happened between the two of them. Madeleine knew she had to stop anything going further, she couldn't risk her job and her career reputation. She couldn't see Dominic again outside of work and would tell him so.

At the end of the day, Madeleine crossed the main reception marbled floor and headed to the revolving door.

"Madeleine, wait," Dominic was behind her taking only a few strides to catch up. "Where are you going? I have a table booked."

"Oh tonight? I'm sorry, I didn't know you meant tonight. I'm not sure Dominic, I'm not sure it's a good idea."

His face darkened slightly. "You said yes! I've booked the table. I had to pull a lot of strings to get it, it's at Muse, you have no idea what I had to do to get in."

Muse! Madeleine was taken aback. She had longed to go there but the waiting lists were forever. She had no idea how he had managed it but now she was torn.

"It's a tasting menu night, it's rumoured to be amazing. You can't let me down, you CAN'T!" Dominic took her elbow and ever so slightly pulled her back from the door. "Look, we have time to pop out and get something else to wear. I'll meet you at Sally's Wine Bar in one hour for a drink before the meal."

He turned and walked off. Madeleine was left genuinely confused. What had just happened there? She had decided she wasn't going to be led into a situation she didn't want, yet here she was going shopping for an outfit for a meal at Muse. She couldn't get out of it now but to be honest, she wasn't sure she really wanted to. She was hungry and the thought of eating at the Belgravia restaurant was just too tempting. She headed off to the underground for a spot of speed shopping.

Madeleine's dress had cost a small fortune. She hadn't had time to shop around so had grabbed a beautiful crimson silk dress from Ted Baker, it had a high neckline and bare arms and wrapped around her body softly, swinging slightly as she walked. Her work clothes were tucked away in the clothes bag. She wore a pair of gold strapped sandals, heels higher than she would normally wear, but she had to admit, she felt very glamourous.

She found Dominic at the bar waiting for her on a stool.

"I thought you were going shopping?" she asked him, as he sat wearing the same suit as earlier.

"Why? I didn't need to." his reply slapped her. How rude! She always presented herself well at work and would have been comfortable going out in her trouser suit and blouse. The pleasure she had in her new outfit disappeared in that instant and she resented how it felt on her skin. "But you… look at you, you look beautiful." The compliment had lost its impact and Madeleine managed a stifled thank you.

As expected, the meal was amazing. As each course arrived, Madeleine forgot the earlier criticism and began to enjoy herself. Dominic had chosen the wine, making a show of discussing each one with the sommelier. To be fair he was obviously quite knowledgeable, but Madeleine was sure, after a while, even the sommelier was getting a little bored with it. Dominic asked Madeleine about herself and listened intently. She described her brother, James, not holding back her annoyance at his lack of direction and aspiration in life. She told Dominic about her relationship with her mother. They had a respectful bond, not particularly close but polite and almost businesslike. She told him about their house in Surrey, beautiful and traditional. Her father, she had little to say about. He was fairly quiet until he had something to say. By that she meant he didn't get involved in anything, allowing the ladies to do all of the talking but when he felt something strongly enough, he spoke up. Normally aimed at Madeleine. Normally a veiled criticism. Never about James. She told Dominic she would like to have her own business one day. He didn't fully understand the appeal and questioned her more about why.

"But you'll have years of no money and struggles." he pointed out.

"But I'll have achieved something of my own." she really didn't see why this needed pointing out.

"But who will really see that achievement, who'll give you the rewards and recognition?" Dominic was not seeing it at all.

"I'll have my own rewards and I'll know what I've achieved. I don't need a trophy." She felt as though she were talking to her parents. Why was it so hard to understand that self-gratification was also a good thing? The sense of purpose and achievement that came from within and not from outside.

"Well, I would stick with C&B if I were you and don't risk losing everything. You'll just end up looking a fool."

The meal was sensational, she felt content and had only a small amount of wine to make her feel warm and a little fuzzy, but not drunk. Dominic walked her to the tube and bought tickets. She asked him for her ticket, but he kept hold of it and led her to the turnstiles. He motioned for her to pass through, letting the ticket zip through the arm of the barrier. She went through first, as a small crowd were waiting behind them, but as Dominic joined her, she questioned him.

"This isn't my train, Dominic. I should really be getting back."

"Look, don't spoil a great evening. I have an XO Brandy at home that you'll love, it will round the meal off just right. C'mon, I'll get a cab for you afterwards back to London Bridge."

Despite a small voice in her head, she didn't want to make a big thing of it; they had had a lovely meal and he had taken care of the bill. It must have cost a small fortune. She nodded and clarified it was just for a drink.

The padlock to the caravan wasn't even locked. It had been hung over a large hook, screwed straight into the caravan side, to give the illusion of being secured. She pulled the door but only the top half opened. She peered over the lower part of the stable door and found a latch. Once fully opened she stepped into the doorway and found the floor felt spongey and soft. She looked around and took it all in.

To her left was the remains of a kitchen. It was once light oak veneer but was now mostly bare chipboard. The sink held spiders and dried leaves. The doors on the cupboards hung loosely on their hinges, she could see inside housed a variety of bottles and sprays. Beyond the kitchen area were two parallel seats, thin board again but topped with slabs of foam that was covered in orange and brown flowers, seventies style. In between the seats, under the front window, a small dresser with drawers sat still in fairly good condition. On top a brown vase with dried flowers, so dried you could not identify what they once were. The water long since evaporated. Along one seat lay rolls of black fabric and a windbreak. In front of the main door was a wardrobe and a small bathroom. The wardrobe had two camping chairs and some clothes hanging from the rail. Maddie took a jacket from inside and pulled it into the light. It was one she knew so well, a light cream puffer jacket, padded for warmth but lightweight to wear. It sent her straight back, it felt like no time before that she had seen her grandfather wearing it here, in this caravan. He would wear a proper shirt underneath, often chequered, long or short sleeved depending on the season. In winter, he topped the shirt with a jumper, the collar pulled inside, and then the jacket zipped up tight. In the bathroom stood some tools, a hoe, a rake and a couple of spades. In the small bathroom cabinet, she found hand cream and a range of simple first aid items, mostly rolls of plasters and a small pair of scissors. There was no toilet, the caravans were not plumbed in. Allotment owners could use a communal port-a-loo that got emptied once a week. At the back end of the caravan another set of parallel seats, shorter than the front but with a table in the middle. Madeleine pictured herself there, with a board game or cards on a rainy day. Granddad played games with her often or she was equally content playing a game of Patience alone. He taught her how to play Cribbage and never let her win out of kindness. If you play a grown-up game then you play like a grown-up, he would say. She soon held her own and beat him fair and square by the age of seven. She slid into one of the seats tucking her legs under the table and gazed out of the window. The panes were plastic and green from moss. Cobwebs hung in every corner. A small gap had appeared next to the bathroom, she could see daylight out of it and a plant had coiled its way into the hole to escape the winter frosts.

She didn't see the need to spend too much time here. As soon as she has collected anything that her father might use, she would leave. She had done all that she could and would drop the keys straight off on her way home.

She laid the tools outside but didn't know what the fabric was for, so left it on the seat. She didn't think he would want an old striped windbreak, the wooden poles were spilt from years of bashing and after all, when did they ever go to a beach? There really wasn't too much to take, she could easily carry everything under her arm, so began to gather her things.

As she turned to leave, she remembered she hadn't looked under the seats. They were designed to hold a lot of the storage in a caravan, sitting low to the ground to keep the weight near the axle when you were towing. She lifted the first and saw it filled with plastic boxes with lids. She held the seat up with her shoulder and pulled the first box out. Inside she found five pairs of wellington boots. All different sizes. She lined them up on the table like Russian Dolls, largest to smallest. One was stripey, another spotty, one had Thomas the Tank Engine on and one covered in pink butterflies. The final and smallest pair were a complete rainbow covered with a glittery sheen. She remembered each one perfectly. She had loved her boots, she would have worn them all day if allowed, even to school. He had kept them; she hadn't given them a second thought but here they were in front of her and ridiculously she realised she had missed them.

The next box was full of paper, all sizes and colours. Each adorned with treasured artwork, saved lovingly even if the art was not very good. Some pieces were collage, torn from magazines. Some were painted, with brushes or dabbed with fingers. Many were scribbles, the work of a very small child, up to illustrations of flowers and vegetables, more advanced and carefully observed. She recognised most of them, she was convinced she could actually remember doing some of them. She pictured where she was in the caravan, facing which direction, what she was wearing, where her grandfather was standing as she had created each piece. He had kept them all.

Each box revealed more and more of her childhood. The seats were a shrine to Maddie, she found jumpers and jackets of all sizes, trinkets that she had collected over the years. Handmade jewellery from twisted twigs still with clumps of glitter and beads, pressed flowers in-between pages of granddad's books, bottles of homemade perfume brown and moldy from rotten rose petals, she had been so creative, so content in a little world of craft and imagination. Where had that Maddie gone? When did she stop enjoying all of that? Where was her memory box in her parents' house?

The last box was wooden. It had a sliding lid and was painted with flowers, this time she suspected by her grandfather. She was surprised to see it held some letters, still in their envelopes that had been carefully cut open with a sharp knife along the top. They were not addressed or stamped, just a plain envelope. She expected they were between her grandfather and grandmother, who she barely remembered. She hesitated as they were personal, not intended for her to see. But curiosity found her sitting down and she pulled the first one out.

'Dad......' the opening line read. 'I am having to write this as we don't seem to be able to talk without arguing lately. I have always been happy for you to have Madeleine whenever you wanted, I would never deny you that, but her teachers are saying she must work harder on her studies, she is slipping behind and she needs to have better grades to get into Grammar School. She has every opportunity to get in and go onto college and university but for now she must concentrate. I can't have you taking her away all the time. She has her head stuck into that garden of yours and won't make friends or put her mind to her work. I know you love her but please look at the big picture and understand. Love Fiona x'

Maddie pulled out the next.

'Dad, I tried to explain last night to you again, please don't pick Madeleine up from school without asking me first. She has homework club and sports club. If she is to get into Grammar School she must show she will take full part in the school life. She needs recommendations from her teachers. Please try to understand. love Fiona x'

The next.

'Dad, I know you were home last night, please answer the door when I come round. I asked you not to collect Madeleine from school. I got to school a few minutes late and how do you think that makes me look to the teachers? They are worried about her; she is not showing any interest in her work and they are struggling to assess her at the levels she needs. For the last time please consider her needs. Fiona.'

The last.

'I have no choice; you cannot see Madeleine unless it's by arrangement and planned a week in advance. She won't be able to come to the allotment, she needs the weekends to work with the tutors I have found to support her. You can see her when you're invited round for dinner but until she gets a place at school and starts to work hard, I must put my foot down. Fiona.'

Madeline released her breath; she hadn't realised she had been holding it. This was all completely new to her; she had no knowledge that this had happened. She tried to cast her mind back to the year, the age she would have been. She recalled the torture of the Eleven Plus exam. The hours in her room being monitored and watched over. The atmosphere at home. No one could come round to visit, no one could distract her. She hadn't realised at the time that included her grandfather. She thought that was simply the way it was. You had an exam at eleven and spent time away from everyone. When she emerged, she was not a butterfly, she was a miserable academic with the weight of the family on her shoulders. Her brother was going to the local comprehensive, she didn't remember him taking exams, she was sure he didn't. She wasn't a naturally academic child, why had they assumed she would find it easy? Why push her like that? And worse, how can anyone stop their own family from seeing each other, that was unforgivable. Maddie had spent the last years, especially as he became ill and died, thinking that she had let her grandfather down. That she had abandoned him. But that wasn't the case. He was told to stay away and by the time Maddie was well into her schooling she had become a teenager with teenage needs. The bond had been broken. But not by her hand. By her mother's. And at that moment she hated her!

"Knock knock!" a sharp rapping on the caravan wall was followed by a head poking through the door. "Anyone home?"

Esther Quinn looked like she had stepped off a Dad's Army set. Khaki trousers were tucked into thick brown socks. Brown walking boots were laced up high. A baggy khaki jumper had leather patches over her collarbones and on her elbows. Several woolen scarves coiled around her neck and a knitted hat was pulled low over her ears. Curls of salt and pepper hair escaped around the edges.

"Hello there, I'm Esther, Esther Quinn, one of the committee members here. I heard you had been here to look at the allotment. Well, what do you think?"

Esther was clipped and direct and spoke to Maddie like a sergeant.

"What do I think?' Maddie repeated.

"About the allotment of course! I take it you've had a good look around. What do intend doing then? Are you going to keep it?"

Maddie couldn't decide if Esther was being curious, nosey, interfering, or rude. She was being interrogated by a woman she had only just met.

"I am leaving it and giving it back today. Can I leave the keys with you?"

"Why would you do that?" Esther reprimanded her. "There's people waiting for years on a list. You have got this as part of the family inheritance clause. People are dying to get their hands on a plot, excuse the pun! To just give it back would be disrespectful, after all the work your grandfather put into it over the years. He would be devastated if he ...... what's the matter? Are you alright?"

Maddie couldn't help it. She sat on the bench seat and sobbed. She hadn't realised what had taken place behind her back, how she had been manipulated and how she had been denied the special time with her grandfather. She could see now how she had been pushed against her will and presumably against her grandfather's. The memories here, the treasure boxes, it brought everything back. Was this the treasure she was meant to find?

"Coooee…... is this where the party's at?" Filo took in the tableau before her and realised something was wrong. "Ok, budge up a bit and let's get you sorted. Whatever it is we can help. Don't you listen to Esther here, has this old bat made you cry?" Filo laughed and to Maddie's surprise so did Esther. "Esther here has no tact, but she has a heart of gold, don't you, you old goat." They clearly were at ease in each other's company and Maddie felt safe to tell them all about it.

Maddie showed them the store of memories, the boots, the pictures and finally the letters. She wanted their perspective; from people you knew her grandfather but were distant from the situation. They listened carefully and looked at each other several times throughout.

"We know all about this Maddie." Filo's soft response was as gentle as she could be. "Your grandfather told us all about it. I had only just joined here but Esther, you had been here a while, hadn't you?"

"Yes, you won't remember me, but I used to come up with my husband and son, Thomas. He has the plot next to yours. You may have met him. He got the gardening bug and now has his own. I saw you here from time to time, but I knew your grandfather very well. He was devastated not to see you anymore. We knew your mother and father wanted you to go to the Grammar School, but he couldn't understand why it was all or nothing. It looked like, to him, you had been taken away from him. It broke his heart."

This wasn't what Maddie was hoping to hear. She wanted to think that he had been alright with the decision, that he hadn't been happy but had understood. To learn he was so upset just added to her angst.

"So, what do you think you're going to do?" Esther was pushing her once more.

Maddie sat quietly, deep in thought. They gave her the time and space. Eventually, she looked at them both.

"I have to make amends. If I could rewind time I would have stayed here, with him as I grew up and my life may have taken another direction. I don't know what that would have looked like, but I wasn't given the chance. He loved me and I loved him. I have missed out on years of knowing him and although I saw him when I had grown up, it was never the same. It could have been though. No one has the right to deny family seeing each other. I left a different version of me here and I want to see if I can find it again. It's the least I can do for him. I have no idea what to do, I have no idea where to start. I'll need some help and will ask a LOT of questions. Will that be okay with you? I think I'd like to keep it after all and give it my best shot.... for my grandad."

Esther and Filo clapped they hands in applause and delight.

"You see!" Filo exclaimed. "The Fool, this is your new present, meeting new teachers, moving towards a new future."

"Yes, I do see," Maddie agreed, "Okay, I'm ready to step off that cliff!"

Chapter Four - APRIL

Esther had suggested the best place to start was at the weekly committee meeting. Maddie had no idea what she was joining but agreed to go along as a guest, with a view to being signed up at the full meeting at the end of the year. Committee meetings brought images of Dawn French and Co, sat in a dusty church room, each talking in riddles and achieving very little. The Queen's Gardens Allotment Committee were meeting in Norris' house. They took turns to host each week and she found herself in one of the cottages in the village of Buckland that she had often admired. She stooped to go through the tiny front door and stepped down straight into the large kitchen with a flagstone floor. The kitchen was at a lower level than the outside and it came as surprise how spacious it was. In the centre was a huge farmhouse table, gnarled from knowing a thousand stories. She already knew Filo of course, who was busying herself at the kettle and setting up mugs on a tray. She seemed very much at home and familiar.

"Hi Petal, so glad you came. Tea? Coffee? Wine?"

"I'll have a wine thanks, that's the advantage of not driving. The bus driver can take me home." Maddie was struck at how cosy the kitchen was, it was obviously the hub of the house.

Norris came through an archway at the back of the room carrying a bottle in each hand.

"Well hello again, Maddie, lovely you could join us. Would you like a wine?"

She nodded and smiled at the other two who sat her the table.

"Hi, I'm Alice," a girl about Maddie's age grinned at her. Her blonde dreadlocks were piled up high and anchored by a red paisley head wrap. She wore a multicoloured striped jumper over a pair of baggy jeans. Her basketball boots were cherry red with a white plastic star on the ankle.

"And I'm Ranweer," the tall man, sat next to Alice, stood and leaned across the table to shake Maddie's hand. His turban was white, and he wore a grey jersey tracksuit. Maddie guessed he was probably around thirty-five years old. "It's very nice to meet you. I've only been on the committee for about a year now, you'll like it, everyone here is really friendly."

"I'm new too," added Alice, "I joined around the same time as you Ranweer, I think?"

He nodded in agreement and sat back down.

Norris passed Maddie a wine as Filo gave the other two a hot drink.

"I'll join you in a wine," Filo pulled up a chair next to Maddie and leaned in to deliberately bump shoulders in a friendly gesture. Maddie tasted the wine had been handed to her, it was a little too sweet and still at room temperature, but it had a pleasant floral taste.

"What is this?" she asked, raising the glass to explain what she was referring to.

"That's my elderflower, from three years ago, a pretty good vintage that year!" Norris was clearly proud. Maddie felt it instantly warming her and guessed it was probably pretty powerful stuff.

The front door opened without a knock; Esther came in followed by Tom. Maddie had forgotten how tall he was, as he filled the room in his corduroy jacket, which hung squarely down from the width of his shoulders. As he took his jacket off to hang on the back of a dining chair, Maddie noted his T-shirt had been bought at a concert a few years before. A drawing of a motorbike with a band name was faded across his chest and as he turned the date and list of gigs could be read down the back. He moved from one side of the room to the kettle in just a couple of strides and started to help himself. It seemed everyone felt at home in Norris' house. Esther unpacked a notebook and laid it next to her car keys and phone on the table and apologised for being late.

A lady walked into the kitchen from the rear and kissed Norris on the cheek.

"Evening everyone, don't let him bully you into drinking his wine unless you've booked the day off work tomorrow. Right, I'm off to meet the girls, have fun everyone," Norris' wife, Jean, smiled as she left them to their meeting.

"Right, I think we're all here. Shall we start?" Esther was obviously chairing the meeting and everyone obediently stopped talking and turned to listen.

"Apologies first. So, I've heard from Steve and Gail but nothing from Rob, has anyone heard anything at all. It's not like Rob to not let anyone know?"

"I saw him in Sainsbury's yesterday, he didn't say he couldn't come tonight." offered Alice.

"Okay, well let's move on. There was nothing to update you with from the last meeting, so we'll move onto the main agenda. First up, let me introduce Maddie to everyone. Maddie is Bert's granddaughter and is taking over his plot."

Welcomes were given and Maddie nodded and smiled back.

"We need to support Maddie in getting started. We can all remember our first year and how hard it is, so I wanted to ask everyone for your help and perhaps we can make a rota. We are now already in April and unless she gets going quickly, she will miss the boat on some of the key planting times, that would put her back a whole year." Esther forged ahead in a very businesslike manner. Maddie was impressed, she had expected dithering and disorder, but Esther obviously ran a tight ship.

"The important thing is to keep it manageable," Norris offered wisely. "If you take on too much to start with you will fail. Start small and build up as you get more knowledge."

Maddie took out her notebook as she had a feeling the tips were going to start coming thick and fast - and they did.

"Lay carpet on half the beds to start with and look at them again next year."

"Get cleared and mulched as soon as possible."

"Don't try and grow everything, choose a few things that you'll enjoy eating first."

"Don't forget succession planting to last the season."

"Oh, and plant flowers for companion growing."

Maddie stopped scribing; she had no idea what they were talking about, so it seemed senseless to note it down.

"Oh dear, we are going to swamp her with our tips," Norris was sensitive enough to see the glazed look on Maddie's face. "I will join you on Saturday and we will make a start. I'll point out what you already have growing there, and we will soon get you up and running."

"I am more than happy to join you too," Ranweer offered. "I just need to do the weekly shopping with my wife first and then I'll be over."

Esther pulled together a rota for the following few weeks of who was available to help. Maddie realised she was committing herself to every Saturday and Sunday and even an evening or two. She began to regret her decision.

Esther moved the meeting on, "Now, agenda item two, our Harvest event. I would like to propose something a little different this year. As you all know, we lost two of our longest serving members this year,"

Filo clutched Maddie's hand and squeezed her fingers briefly.

"Both Bert and Grace were looked after in St Anne's Hospice and I think we should thank the staff in some way. I would like us to open our Harvest event up to the public as a fundraiser, to raise money for the Hospice. What do you all think?"

There was instant approval all round.

"Maybe we could cook from our own produce and serve food and drink? Ranweer and I can run a vegan stall, can't we?" Alice turned to Ranweer who was clearly very happy with the idea.

"I can run a craft stall and give tarot and aura readings," Filo added.

Tom, who had remained silent throughout the meeting, eventually smiled, "I'll add the brawn and the DJ skills, we'll need tables and chairs, a gazebo, lighting and music. I can sort all of that out."

"Maddie, is there anything you can do to help, don't feel obliged of course," Esther urged.

"Actually, I *can* help. I will do all the advertising. I can arrange the local radio to publicise it and create posters et cetera. It will be my pleasure. Thank you for thinking of my grandad, and the other lady of course. That means a lot."

The rest of the meeting settled everyone's roles and jobs for the event. A few 'Any Other Business' items were discussed, stock for the shop, tidying the compost bin area and the lack of bark clippings from the local suppliers. As Maddie gazed at black night sky from the bus window, she realised she felt more energised and positive than she had for a long time. She had been welcomed into the group and straight away was made to feel valued and part of a team. There was no doubt, there was a lot of hard work ahead, but she relished it, she wanted the challenge. She compared it to her normal working day, there she didn't feel the same sense of excitement or anticipation. She felt more alive tonight, to which she smiled to herself, to feel more alive amongst a group of gardeners talking mostly about plants and vegetables…... who would have thought it?

Norris was already at Maddie's plot, lifting great clumps of grass out with a garden fork. He deftly threw them into his wheelbarrow and had already cleared a small bed. He had exposed the wooden planks that sat upright on their edges, marking out the rectangle.

"Good morning, Maddie. What a beautiful morning!"

"Morning Norris, I'm sorry, I didn't know what time you would be here. I've bought a flask of coffee if you'd like some?"

"No, no, I'm fine thank you. So, look, I've started with this bed as it's nearest to the shed with the tools and gets the full sun throughout the day. We'll prepare a few beds and not to worry about the pathways for now. We'll be treading them down and we move around anyway. So, you grab that other fork over there and make a start just here, can you see? Dig down a good six inches and lift, try and get as many roots out as you can. But don't tug and snap any thick roots, it's best to dig down deeper and try to get the whole lot out." Maddie was thankful that Norris was taking charge. He had a lifetime of knowledge, that was easy to see and she knew he could teach her so much." Maddie started to dig and lift and was surprised how tired and aching she was after just a few minutes.

"You'll soon toughen up, this is the best exercise," Norris spotted her flagging.

Together they worked, Norris pointed out two small gooseberry bushes before she dug them up and Maddie was delighted that she spotted and recognised the huge leaves of rhubarb, hiding thick stalks that were already turning pink. By midday they had three beds cleared. Norris was right, the pathways between were now flattened grass and they were able to move around the area quite freely. She looked up at the expanse still left to do and felt a little disheartened, there was still so much. She took a photograph to document her achievement and sat down with her packed lunch on the plastic chair.

"Hi there," Alice and Ranweer arrived together waving their tools in greeting. Alice was wearing army green overalls tucked into bright orange welly boots and layers of jumpers underneath, so many that she couldn't do up the overalls. Ranweer was more conventional in jeans and a jacket covered in buttoned down pockets. "Wow, you've both done loads!" Alice was impressed. "Has Norris gone?"

Maddie had insisted Norris stopped before he did too much and exhausted himself. Despite being much fitter than Maddie, she was aware he was a lot older and didn't want him to overdo it.

Ranweer popped back to his plot to fetch a bag of compost and some plant pots. When he returned, all three headed for the greenhouse to make a start there. Alice and Ranweer told her that a greenhouse should be washed before each year's new planting, to avoid any contamination. They dipped buckets into a freezing open topped water butt and used rags found in the caravan to wash the glass inside and out. It came up sparkling and looked like new. They lifted the staging back inside (Ranweer explained these were the shelves to hold the seedlings in their trays and pots) and positioned them against one length. The other side was exposed to the ground, Ranweer took charge of clearing this, as he pulled old, dried tomato plants out he pointed to the beautifully soft soil in envy.

"You have amazing soil here; your granddad must have conditioned it really well."

"What do you mean," Maddie had to double check everything she was told to fully understand.

Ranweer was very patient. "He would have added plenty of new compost and fertilisers each year. As the plants grow, they use up all the nutrients, so we must put goodness back in. That's why we use compost, especially our own that we all add to, over there by the front gate, it's free to help yourself to. Nothing in my house goes to waste, my family put everything into a big bucket in the garden and I bring it over each time, peelings from fruit and veg, eggshells, even the cardboard egg cartons. You need a good balance in your compost, dry things like shredded newspaper, cardboard and twigs, wet things like grass cutting and peelings. Give it a little water now and again and turn it over with a garden fork. In a year's time you'll have wonderful compost."

Alice gave Maddie a pile of seed packets to look through.

"Take your pick. Check the back to see which month to start them off. Look for the 'sowing indoors instructions. We're in April but we can still get some started that say March too."

Maddie chose broad and runner beans, peppers, carrots, courgettes, leeks, various types of lettuce, peppers and sweetcorn. Alice had gently dissuaded her from cauliflower, saying perhaps leave that for next year as it was a bit more advanced to grow. Maddie listened as Alice talked about the different varieties, explaining to her that the Lady Di runners are stringless, that Sugarsnax carrots are ideal for eating raw, to try the Defender courgettes as they have a good reputation for being resistant to disease and crop before some of the others and definitely Sundance sweetcorn as it was very reliable to grow. Maddie carefully read the depth to push each seed into each pot, watered them gently with the watering can with a rose on the spout and Alice wrote labels onto wooden lollysticks and pushed them neatly into each pot that Maddie filled.

Ranweer dragged a wooden trough, held high off the ground with scissor legs, from the side of the shed.

"You can get some salad things started straight away in here." He lifted a bag of compost into the trough and patted in gently flat with his hands. Showing Maddie how to do it, he laid a small piece of wood along the top and used it as a ruler to drag the edge of his trowel along, carving out a neat groove in the soil. He chose rocket and pak choi for salad leaves and packets of radishes with all types of multicoloured varieties, some were blue and some even had rings inside, like a cut open tree truck. Maddie spread the tiny seeds carefully into the trench and them covered back over.

She looked around. It was amazing how much had been achieved in just one day. Every bit of her ached. She took a photo inside the greenhouse and said goodnight to the pots as she slid the door shut.

"We heard you!' laughed Alice. "Talking to your plants already."

Maddie laughed, yes, she had, they are already her babies and she was determined to look after them.

"Madeleine, why have you taken the soundtracks off of the shared drive?" Dominic strode into the office without knocking.

Madeleine looked up from her computer and tried to catch up with his thought processes.

"What do you mean?" she was genuinely confused.

"Well, I've got the visuals guys here with me this afternoon and we wanted to start to layer the video and sound, but you've moved it from the shared drive."

"I haven't, I put them there when we had the meetings with Katrina, I've not touched them since. Have you asked the others? They may be using them for something?"

"I've checked with them, and they haven't touched them. The file history says you deleted them." Dominic was trying to stay calm but was beginning to pace across the front of Madeline's desk.

"You must be looking in the wrong place, look, I'll show you...." Madeleine swung her screen around so they could both see it and opened the shared files. "That's odd," she clicked in and out of various folders, "I definitely put them in here, look, this folder," she began to feel a rising panic.

"I've got the guys here now, waiting for me. How the hell can I go back and say we can't find the soundtracks? You must have deleted it by accident, it says you were the last person on the folder. What have you done Madeleine? How the hell can I explain this without looking a total prick?" Dominic's anger was clear, and Madeleine felt total confusion. She knew she hadn't even been to the shared drive for days. She had no need to look in it. She sat thinking back, trying to retrace each day's work activities and think if she had missed something.

"Don't just sit there staring!" Dominic's face showed utter contempt.

"Look, there's obviously been a mistake," was all Madeleine could offer at that point. "I'll get onto IT and the sound company that we used, we can either lift it from our own file history or the sound guys will have a copy of everything. Don't worry, we can get it back."

Dominic looked a little less fierce, just a little.

"Ok, I'll go and grab the visuals team a coffee and delay them a bit," he conceded. "Can you go and find a copy then and call me when you have it?"

He left her office and left her in complete shock. It's probably an innocent mistake, a computer glitch, files disappear and reappear for no reason. She hadn't been prepared for Dominic's attitude and lack of empathy. It could happen to anyone. She grabbed her handbag and went to the lift to find someone from IT to help.

"No, I'm sorry Madeleine, usually we can backdate the system and find deleted items, but we had a new server for your floor this week and due to incompatibility, we had to lose the history. We are now using the Cloud for everything, but your floor still had the in-house servers. That's why we had to update you see." The IT manager was being very helpful in his manner but totally no help at all in finding a solution. Eventually she left to go and call the company who had created the soundtracks for her, they would definitely have a copy.

"But Madeleine, you called the other day and asked that all versions were destroyed. You said they were too similar to a rival's advertising campaign and you couldn't afford to be accused of plagiarism." Madeleine couldn't process what she was hearing.

"Called you? I haven't called you. Why would I do that? You must have a copy? You know me, you know I didn't call? Madeleine was panicking and confused, her head felt light as she struggled to think straight.

"There was a message left with the receptionist, she took all of your details and message. She said it was you. She had all of the information; we had no reason not to do as we are asked. You are the customer, it's your property and you asked for it to be deleted." The sound engineer quickly covered his tracks, he knew there was every chance this could blow up in his face and he started to protect himself and his company. "You signed the paperwork, the files are your property, not ours to keep."

Madeleine couldn't breathe. Her heart was thumping so hard she could feel it in her neck, throbbing. She put the phone down and immediately rang Nadir. He confirmed he hadn't touched the files. She called Roseanne.

"Roseanne, it's me, Madeleine. Look, if you've accidentally deleted the files, or moved them, or anything, please just put them back. It can happen to anyone, please just put them back."

"Let's get one thing straight Madeline," Roseanne's voice was measured and calm. "I am not sure why you think of all the people in the team, that I am the incompetent one. You can think again. I have made it abundantly clear I am only working with the three of you to win this competition and if you thought beyond your tiny brain, you would ask yourself why, why would I sabotage my own chances? That *is* what you are actually accusing me of, isn't it? Sabotage! Not only am I now stuck with a team who have no idea where the project is but I am also being accused of foul play. Brilliant, just brilliant!" The click on the phone was obviously created by force.

Madeleine had been sure it was Roseanne. The file had been deleted in Madeleine's name, but she was absolutely sure she hadn't been near it. There was a high level of trust in C&B

amongst the staff, it was encouraged as part of professional ethics to keep office doors unlocked. Roseanne could easily have popped in and deleted it from her computer. Nadir had warned her that she was capable of anything to get her own way. But Roseanne was right, what would she have to achieve? Surely, she has shot herself in the foot. If Roseanne wanted Dominic for herself, what would deleting the files achieve? Maybe to force Dominic into seeing Madeleine as incompetent and useless. Well, if that was the case, it seemed to have worked. She picked up the phone to tell him the bad news.

"What's with the long face?" Madeleine's father walked into the kitchen to see her sat up at the breakfast bar nursing a mug of tea.

She looked at him and balanced whether to tell him about her day. She had never had a problem at work before, well not a big one that impacted so hugely on other people. She hesitated, she wasn't sure he would listen properly or be very understanding. She couldn't bear him to side with Dominic and say she must have done something wrong, that accusing Roseanne of sabotaging was just nasty and aimed at getting herself out of the situation. Dominic had not been kind when she had called him, she offered solutions, many of them good ones, but he was too angry and felt let down by her. She felt useless, she knew she hadn't done anything wrong yet thought bad of her and she didn't like that feeling. And now, her father would be disappointed too. The day really couldn't get any worse.

"Ok, so you say you didn't delete it, but the history was in your name?" Henry Richards recapped what Madeleine has explained to him. "And you think this woman, Roseanne, had something to do with it?"

"Yes, that's it," Madeleine confirmed. Her father had listened surprisingly well and hadn't given her that look of disapproval she was expecting. He had made himself a cup of tea and joined her at the bench.

"Firstly, you must be very sure not to actually accuse her of anything, you know that could be seen as slander. And definitely don't do it as a written email or anything, that's libel. Secondly, there must be a way to find out what has happened to the files. It could all be very innocent, a technical hiccup, but you don't want people to think it is your fault, that wouldn't be fair, if you didn't do it that is."

There it was, just as she thought he was backing her up and really taking her side…. 'if you didn't do it, that is'…. meaning she may have done so, in his eyes.

"Yo, sis!" James strode in and greeted her warmly. "What's going on?"

Madeleine and James did have a good sibling relationship. Yes, his lifestyle annoyed her but if she was honest, it was probably more like jealousy on her part. He was affable, you couldn't help but like him. He had been a good older brother as they grew up, had not been mean to her, no tormenting that she could remember, in fact they had been very close when they were small. They had grown apart during secondary school, she had gone to the Grammar and he to the Comprehensive. They never seemed to be in the house at the same time, they never fell out, just drifted a little apart. She outlined briefly what had happened, now too tired to repeat it with all of the details, but just enough to give him an idea of her day.

"Well, you know what you should do?" James seemed to see things very clearly. "Every keyboard record key presses, get the timings of when your keyboard went to that folder and then track back where you were at the same time. If you were somewhere else, with other people… bingo!" He laughed and grabbed a can of cola from the fridge and sauntered out chuckling.

He had a good point. It wouldn't get the soundtracks back, but it would clear her name and reputation. She already felt she wasn't as sharp as the rest of the team and at times she felt inadequate, but she wasn't incompetent, she hated to be made to feel like that and wanted to clear herself of this terrible mistake. Whatever had happened to the files, she wasn't part of it, accident or sabotage, she wanted to have it made very clear that she was too good at her job for it to be her.

Lewis, in IT, was the apprentice. He couldn't have been more than 17 years old but was an absolute whizz with computers, Madeleine had no idea what he was talking about and wondered at the speed of his typing as he completed beta instructions in the background of his systems. He relished the challenge she gave him, problem solving was his forte. She felt sure he would make a great codebreaker or worse, hacker! Anyone else on the team would have said they were too busy, but he was bored and ready to be stretched. He identified the precise date and time that the folder was accessed and then deleted from the keyboard strokes. He printed out a list of computer actions in the three-hour period around that time and handed it to Madeleine.

"Ok, so this column shows you the time, it has hours, minutes and seconds and just looks like a long number, can you see? This column is the keyboard strikes and I have highlighted here and here where the folder was accessed and deleted. There are only a few seconds between those two things happening to it, so it wasn't looked at for long, or read and edited. It was literally opened and deleted. Hope it helps." Lewis grinned, feeling very smug yet Madeleine guessed this task had been small fry to him.

"Thank you so much, I'll go and compare it to my diary and try and remember what I was doing that day." Madeleine was so grateful, she felt sure she could solve the mystery. Back in her office she pulled up her online calendar. She had been in a health and safety training session most of the morning, but she needed to remember what she had done after that, her calendar was empty of meetings or appointments. That was it! After the training she had met Dominic for lunch. She met him at 1.30 pm (she could remember precisely as he had text her) and they had tried the new pub around the corner. It was supposed to be a short lunch, but the new staff hadn't had very good training, and everything went wrong. They had ended up waiting an hour for their food and she was definitely still there at 2.47 pm, the time her computer was accessed. Madeleine felt sick. Someone had been into her office to deliberately set her up. It had to be Roseanne. Roseanne had probably realised both she and Dominic were out of the building, got jealous and seized the opportunity. Maybe it had been an impulse, that would explain why she did it, risking her own place in the competition. She hadn't had time to think it through. Now all Madeleine had to do was show Dominic the proof. She couldn't bear for him to look at her with the same look of contempt as yesterday. She had been hurt at the way he reacted to her, especially as they had kissed so passionately at his flat after their meal at Muse. She hadn't let it go further that night, although he had tried to persuade her to stay but he had eventually got her the taxi he had promised. She thought they were close enough for him to trust her when she said she hadn't deleted the files. Perhaps it was just the stress of it all that made him flare up like he did.

Dominic studied the print outs.

"Oh Madeleine, I'm so sorry, you're right, this was definitely when we were out of the building. I feel awful, I should have listened to you. I was just so worried and had people waiting for me to play them the soundtrack. I thought you had deleted them, and I couldn't understand why." Dominic looked around to make sure no-one was watching and pulled her quickly towards him and squeezed her gently. He brushed her ear with his lips, so briefly it couldn't have been seen. "Let me make it up to you, let's have a day together this Sunday, we can do whatever you would like to do. I'll treat us to a nice country pub meal, one with a real fire and a great wine list."

Madeleine was satisfied that Dominic believed her. She was still put out that he hadn't in the first place but was prepared to accept his apology.

"I would like that, a Sunday outing. Oh no, I'm sorry, I've just remembered it's my mother's birthday and we have family and friends coming for lunch. I've promised to help."

"That's ok, maybe I can come too and meet your family?"

Madeleine was not prepared for that suggestion and wasn't sure that was what she wanted. It was far too soon to meet parents. She hadn't yet worked out where their relationship was or was heading. It still wasn't too late to revert to being simply work colleagues. She wasn't sure she wanted the questions from her family, they would assume the relationship was far more than it is, after all she had never taken a boy or a man home before, they would definitely think it a sign of something more serious.

"I really don't think you'll enjoy it; it will just be food and questions and I'll be busy in the kitchen," Madeleine reasoned.

"Don't you worry, I can look after myself in these situations. Just tell me when and where and I'll be there," Dominic wasn't picking up on the hints.

Madeleine reluctantly gave him the details and he added it to his calendar. She wondered how many 'situations' he had practiced on but pushed it to the back of her mind.

Fiona Richards was enjoying herself. Her birthday had landed on her favourite day of the week this year, a Sunday meant most people were available to come and celebrate with her. It wasn't a special birthday, but Fiona and Henry loved to entertain, any excuse to show people their lovely home. Madeleine had to admit they did always make their guests feel very welcomed and looked after. Fiona was helping to put champagne glasses onto linen covered trays in the kitchen. She carried them through to the conservatory where canapés were to be served. Madeleine was finishing filling vases and glasses with a variety of daffodils, all different shades of yellow, orange and cream. Some were simple trumpeted blooms, others frilly with several layers. She arranged them very simply, but they looked wonderful, lifting the room up and bringing the spring indoors.

"So, tell me again who this Dominic is…." Fiona set down the tray on the bar counter.

"He is just a work colleague, we are working together in the same team, you know, on the competition. We can catch up on work whilst he's here."

Fiona wasn't going to let it drop, "No one talks shop on a Sunday and especially not at my birthday party. Well, I'm glad you have found a boyfriend at last Madeleine, I was beginning to wonder if it will ever happen."

Madeleine took a deep breath; it was her mother's birthday and she didn't want to start an argument.

"I've had boyfriends, mum, I just haven't brought them home…. and Dominic is not my boyfriend." So, what is Dominic? How would she describe their relationship? He is certainly persistent and absolutely gorgeous, but she is still very aware of the company rules, she mustn't take it further. She wasn't looking forward to him coming today, she liked to keep her work and home life separate, she was independent at work, she made her own decisions and carved a work life for herself. She didn't have to explain herself to her parents about it, she enjoyed having the separation. Also, she had had so many years with work colleagues who didn't enquire into her home life, so it worked both ways. Her mother dropped the subject and went to check her make-up as the doorbell rang.

Madeleine busied herself in the kitchen. They had decided to make a birthday buffet, with hot and cold selections so guests could help themselves. Although they had large enough dining tables, Fiona didn't want a sit-down meal, she wanted to mingle with her friends and make sure she talked to everyone. Auntie Irene and Uncle Michael had arrived early, Irene was helping Madeleine with the finishing touches with the food and Michael was happily sampling the box of beer that Henry had on the bar.

"Do you think this Coronation Chicken needs a bit more salt?" Irene sipped the yellow sauce from a teaspoon.

"I think it's just right, what about this Bourguignon? We can keep these hot in the slow cookers on the dining table. I've made rice and already put the dishes of chutneys in the other room. We just need to take the prawns and salads out of the fridge, and I think we're nearly there." Madeleine was extremely able in planning and organising and was a very good cook. She was enjoying herself spending time chatting to Irene whilst sipping wine and almost forgot that Dominic was due to arrive.

"Madeleine, someone's here to see you," Her father sang through the kitchen door.

Why did she feel a small bit of disappointment? Surely seeing Dominic again should give her a bit more excitement. She took off her apron and smoothed her cotton tea dress. She was wearing bright yellow to match the daffodils and had her hair loose down her back, it shone in soft waves. Her choice of bright white plimsolls made her outfit young and quirky, she looked comfortable, fresh, and healthy. She followed her father into the conservatory, where most of the guests were gathering. She spotted Dominic immediately. He was at the bar with James both deep in conversation. Dominic looked exactly as he usually did at work, she recognised his grey pinstripe suit and pink shirt. His paisley tie matched a neatly folded handkerchief in his breast pocket.

"Hi, you found us then?" Madeleine crept up behind him.

Dominic turned, smiled, and lent forward to kiss her on the cheek. Whilst standing close he whispered to her, "I thought it would be more formal." He appraised her, the briefest of glances up and down.

Was it her imagination or was he disappointed in her weekend 'look?' She had thought she looked just right for the occasion and she had expected perhaps a compliment or at least a warmer greeting. She decided to ignore the remark.

"I see you two are getting to know each other," Madeleine looked at her brother.

"Oh, we know each other already! Dom and I used to play in the same Saturday league, we haven't seen each other in years, have we?" James looked at Dominic for confirmation.

Dominic was relaxing into the conversation, "Yes, years! I lived in Kingswood for a while and joined the local football team, when you said you had a brother called James, I didn't put the names together until just now. A small world!"

"Are you going to introduce me?" Fiona joined them at the bar and looked at each person in turn to see who would start.

"Mum, this is Dominic from work, who I told you was coming today, Dominic this is Fiona, my mother."

"Very nice to meet you," Fiona spoke in what Madeleine called her telephone voice, "I'd like to say I've heard everything about you but I'm afraid she has kept you very quiet. I can see why; she wants to keep you all to herself and I can't blame her!" Fiona had had a few glasses of Prosecco already and was almost flirting. "You're rather gorgeous, I didn't expect that!"

Why wouldn't her mother think she were able to have a good-looking partner? Madeleine wasn't sure but she knew she didn't want to stand there and listen whilst the conversation got any worse. Dominic was clearly happy standing with James and her mother was on the verge of embarrassing someone, probably her, so she made her excuses to go and finish up in the kitchen. Dominic didn't respond. It wasn't the way Madeleine had always imagined bringing a man home. She had expected butterflies and to see the glow of pride that her date gave her as he looked at her across a room. She escaped and found some wine in the fridge.

"Aren't you going out there to mingle? Aunt Irene brought some dirty glasses into the kitchen to wash.

"I think I'll just hang out here for a while." Madeleine sat on the stool at the breakfast bar.

"So, is that your man out there?" when Irene asked a question it seemed natural and non-judgmental, Madeleine was always happy to explain things to her.

"I really don't know!" Madeleine answered honestly. "We've had several dates, just drinks and meals, you know. He is always keen to ask me out but when we are together, I just feel there is something missing, I can't really explain. He is a gentleman, attentive, mostly, but there have been a few times that I have felt he has…. I don't know what…. disapproved maybe, been disappointed in something I've said or done perhaps. I can't even give you a proper example. He has such high standards and as you can see really looks after himself. He wants to succeed, and I just sometimes wonder…... wonder why he is going out with me."

"Now, you look here! You are gorgeous, kind, funny and smart and anyone would be proud to be with you. It doesn't sound right, you know, if he makes you feel like that. You should feel like a Queen. You can never be a disappointment to anyone. Don't put up with second best, if it's not right then walk away." Irene was incensed and wagging her finger at Madeleine, kindly.

"I know, I know, but these feelings are just fleeting and then he is lovely, really lovely and it's all forgotten about." Madeleine felt she needed to defend her decision to have him there, at the party. She realised she must be looking quite rude, sitting for so long in the kitchen. She slid from the stool and squeezed her aunt's arm.

"I'll be okay, don't you worry," she reassured her, as she left to find the boys at the bar.

The party went well. After the buffet food was eaten, Henry brought out a cake with just a few candles. He protected the flames as he walked, starting the happy birthday song and everyone joined in. The guests divided themselves into activities, charades in the dining room, small talk in the conservatory and a few who wanted to talk loudly, and drink stood in the kitchen. They say the best parties are in the kitchen. Madeleine was enjoying herself much more, Dominic had been charming to her family and several had complimented her on her catch. They hadn't held hands or even touched, it was all polite and correct. Eventually, he placed his hand on the small of her back and talked gently into her ear.

"I must go, I have train to catch and as it's Sunday they can be a bit temperamental. I've had a really nice time; it was great to catch up with James again."

"Oh right, yes of course, I'll walk you to the door." Madeleine led the way.

She opened the front door for him, and he kissed her gently on the lips. She felt warm again, close again to him. She was disappointed that she hadn't felt like that all afternoon. This was the closeness she had expected, and it felt nice.

"I'll see you tomorrow at work, take care." Dominic left her in the doorway and passed through the archway in the hedge and out of sight.

It was still early, and the evenings were lighter now the clocks had gone forward. Madeleine still had time to pop over to the allotment to water her seeds. She glanced through the glass door and could see everyone was busy and wouldn't miss her, she would help to tidy up when she got home.

When she arrived at her plot, she was surprised to see a large bed had been cleared and dug over. Long deep trenches had been prepared, the soil looked crumbly and totally weed free. Norris must have been there today; she must thank him when she sees him at the committee meeting. This would have taken him all day to dig.

She looked around. She could see a large straw hat and a bottom stuck in the air, she guessed they belonged to Filo. Maddie walked over to her friend's plot.

"Hi, how are you Filo?"

"Hey, I'm very good thank you. We've missed you this weekend."

Maddie explained to her about the party and asked after Norris.

"No Petal, I've not seen him today, it's been pretty quiet, just me, Ranweer and Tom and a couple of nurses who have a plot at the top end. They work shifts so we don't see much of them."

It must have been Ranweer, he had said he would try and get over this week to help. She made a mental note to bring some vegan treats to the meeting on Tuesday, as a gift for him. Maddie stopped by her own greenhouse and filled the watering can from the water butt. She was delighted to see the tiniest shoots appearing in most of the trays and pots. She watered as gently as she could, using the rose attachment on the end, avoiding flooding the little seedlings out of their beds. She remembered the salad leaves in the raised tray outside and looked around the plot. It was already looking vastly different from her first day there. She took a few photos, as a log, said goodnight to the plants and went home to help clean up the party.

Tuesday night meetings were a part of Maddie's new weekly routine that she particularly looked forward to. This week the host was Filo, Maddie was anticipating where she lived. She had tried to imagine what her house would be like, she assumed very much like the caravan, quirky and fun, a little chaotic and full of interest. She was not wrong. Filo lived on the outskirts of Reigate, in a Victorian terraced cottage that looked impossibly thin from the outside, just the front door with a small sash window to the side. The door had a wooden porch, that sat just on the top of the frame, like a party hat. It must have been added later as no other cottages had one. It gave the house a country cottage look, complete with dormant twists of a climbing rose, just budding its new leaves. The front garden was small, it only took Maddie a few paces from the gate to the door, yet it was stuffed full of pots and plants that only the narrow path was visible. There was no bell, only a gargoyle door knocker. Except when Maddie looked closer, the gargoyle was actually a strange creature winking. She knocked and was pulled inside by Filo grabbing her hand excitedly and hugging her tight.

"You're the first, I can show you around if you like?"

Maddie didn't need asking twice.

They had stepped straight into the lounge from the front door, Maddie could see the house was narrow, but it went back very far, with several rooms leading onto another in a straight line. The living area was painted a deep burgundy, Maddie would have painted it cream or white to brighten it, but the bold, dark colour looked cosy and actually suited the house. The side table lamps were covered in shawls to mute the light. One small two-seater sofa and one wing backed armchair was all the seating the room could hold. Both were shrouded with crocheted granny square blankets. Maddie wondered how the meeting could take place, perhaps sitting on each other's laps! On every inch of carpet were piles of books, magazines, knitting bags, a Persian lampshade hung from a ceiling rose and crystals dangled across the small window next to the door. The walls were filled with pictures in frames of every type of wood and size, they had no order, a random selection which altogether gave a spectacular impression. There was no theme to the pictures, dancing elves playing flutes, dragons, finely detailed sketches of plant anatomy, cartoon dogs, rainbows and copy prints from master artists. You could gaze at the walls for hours and still not see everything.

In the centre of the house was a beautiful kitchen. It was galley style, with cupboards running along each wall with the walkway through the centre. The units and worktops were made of heavy wood, left very natural, the handles were unpolished nickel. Dainty lights ran under the wall cabinets throwing downwards warm glowing fans. Maddie would never turn on the long strip light on the ceiling if she lived there, she would always cook in this room in this snug cosseting ambience. The kitchen was sparse and tidy, in complete contrast the living area, it looked as though it had just been photographed for a magazine. To the rear of the kitchen, slightly to the right, was a door leading to a downstairs toilet. The rest of the back wall was open to reveal a surprise, a huge wooden conservatory with a towering glass roof and windows that stretched the entire width of the house.

"They open right up," Filo proudly explained. "So it brings the tiny bit of garden that's left, right into the house. I had the outside lights put into the garden walls, here you see?" Filo flicked a switch and the small garden lit up to reveal a U-shaped bench, with seating and planters alternated all around. Large heaters stood in the centre, a small brick barbecue in the corner and lots and lots of herbs. "On a nice evening like this we can all sit in the conservatory and outside, with the doors open, it stays really warm as it's sheltered."

"It's stunning, it really is," breathed Maddie. "As lovely as it is, why did you take up all of your garden with it?"

"My husband, he was poorly for a long time and loved the garden, but with British weather there were just so many days that it was too cold for him. So, we created a way for him to have as much daylight and warmth as possible. Anyway, I couldn't look after him and a big garden too. We had the allotment together before he was ill, and I kept it going to get my gardening 'fix' and now I'm happy to keep things as they are. I don't need a large garden; I can come and see friends at the allotment and enjoy this space at home."

A knock on the gargoyle head signaled the others had arrived. Filo bustled off to let them in and Maddie stayed to enjoy the lovely space. How lucky Filo was to have somewhere to call her own, to fill with her personality and fill with good friends.

Ranweer and Alice turned up together, they didn't live far and had walked. Alice rushed through to find Maddie.

"How are your plants coming along? I peeked in the week and saw what looked like little shoots!" Alice was a bundle of enthusiasm, her dreadlocks were looser than usual, she just had one plait on each side pulled to the back to hold the rest in place. Her hair was long down to the bottom of her back. She was tiny and full of energy.

"Yes, I watered them Sunday evening, they are definitely growing!!" Maddie was equally excited at the prospect of achieving her very first crop. "Hi, Ranweer, I have brought you these to say thank you for all of your hard work. I didn't know you were doing it, it looks great, although I don't know what to do with it," Maddie grinned and grabbed her rucksack, pulling out a round Tupperware pot. "It's maple, date and hazelnut tart, I followed the recipe from a vegan website exactly, so I know it will be okay for you."

"Well, thank you Maddie, that's so kind, but I'm not sure what you're thanking me for? I'll take the tart though of course, I'm not that gracious," Ranweer laughed at himself.

"Oh, I thought you had dug my allotment bed, the big one?"

"That would be me!" Tom stood filling up the doorway. "I dug it over for you, you need to get your potatoes in, you're too late for earlies but you can get main crop in now. I've prepared the trenches for you and have left the chitted potatoes in a bag under one of your baths." He turned back to kitchen without another word.

Maddie turned to the other two.

"I didn't understand a word he just said!"

The three giggled as the conservatory filled with Esther, Tom and two others who Maddie did not know. They were Steve and Gail, who hadn't been able to make it for a while, both nurses, they sat quietly outside talking to each other. Filo passed around her legendary cakes and biscuits and placed a tray in the middle of the room with teapots, mismatched cups and saucers, a milk jug and a sugar bowl. The front door knocked again and Norris walked through with a carrier bag clinking with the unmistakable sound of wine bottles. This week it was damson wine, dark and syrupy and very strong.

Once everyone had a drink in their hand and had sampled the cakes, Esther took up her position at the top end of the garden, looking in at the circle of chairs and expectant faces.

"I want to dedicate the whole meeting to the Harvest charity event if I can, we won't worry about other formalities." Esther launched straight in and didn't wait for anyone's agreement as usual. "The first thing to do is to agree the name of the event, that way Maddie can start getting posters printed and social media what-nots out to the public."

"I have already made a start," Maddie interjected, "I have been posting little teasers onto the Reigate Forums, you know, things like 'watch out for a new and exciting event coming soon' and 'two more weeks until you can get your early bird tickets."

"Oh yes, I've heard about this," Filo excitedly recognised something, "Some of my tarot clients have mentioned it to me, funny, I didn't realise it was *our* own event. I joined in with their guessing game. Although Angela Higson is hoping the countdown is to that male stripper group coming to town, she may be disappointed!"

Hilarity unfolded with everyone suggesting what Norris, Tom, Ranweer and Steve could wear and what routine they would dance to.

"Norris, you could be like one of the Wurzels, all dressed in countryside garb with straw behind your ear!" Alice giggled.

"Ranweer, you could be a Bollywood film star, you would really look the part." Filo offered.

"Tom, well you could be…. you could just be Tom, that's handsome enough!" Gail the nurse sprung to life and then instantly looked embarrassed, as if she had said out loud what was in her head.

"Okay, okay, yes that's all very funny," Esther had a secret smile, "name suggestions please everyone."

It took a while to rein in the suggestions to be even vaguely sensible but at last they settled for the obvious title of 'Queens Garden's Charity Harvest Event - raising money for St Anne's Hospice.' It was perfect, there was no doubt what people were going to expect. Even though it wasn't going to be male strippers.

Tom had pulled in some favours from friends and managed to get a large DJ deck and the lighting system to sync along with the music. Everyone offered to loan him a range of CDs, cassette tapes and even Norris' 45 record collection but Tom politely refused all offers and said he would mix a digital playlist instead. Maddie was secretly impressed, she had assumed he was not into technical things, more of an outdoors only sort of man. He was making simple trellis tables for anyone running a stall and was working on creating signs on wooden posts, that could be driven into the ground, to direct the crowds to the First

Aid, Lost Children and most importantly, the food areas. Norris was helping Tom, but he was charged with the painting of the signs and pleading with the local Indoor Bowls Club to get them to offer their car park for the day. It was only over the road from the allotments and was huge, it made complete sense to have that as the main car park and not have traffic onto the allotments, it would make it very safe for families.

Filo had been building her collection of craft for sale, she was very talented. She showed the group a sample of soft furnishings, cushions, throws, arm covers for chairs, silk scarves, soft shoulder bags and men's' handkerchiefs. They fell into two themes: countryside pursuits, majestic deer, foxes on the run, cute rabbits and less cute hare alongside a collection of mystical images with goblins, glamourised witches, dragons, stars and moons. She has hand embroidered most of them or used printed materials to make attractive accessories.

Alice and Ranweer were spending as much time as possible encouraging their produce to grow, designing menus to match what they were confident would be easy to do, with whatever was ready to harvest. They were hoping to offer a range of vegan wraps as well as sell excess produce that may be left over. They were growing unusual varieties to showcase what a better range you can have if you grow your own and to interest the children and get them wanting to start producing their own food. They would have a selection of pots with a range of salad items that customers could choose their fillings from. They were hoping to also cook hot fillings such as vegan chili, plant Bolognese and tofu curry. Ranweer's wife was making a range of chutneys and will make yoghurt dips on the day. It all sounded delicious.

Gail and Steve apologised that they couldn't commit to anything too big but promised to book the day off and help man the stalls to give everyone a break and a chance to look around the event too. Esther noted everything down, they settled on a date, Saturday October the 18th and the meeting was called to a close. Filo offered a free reading to anyone who wanted to stay and Gail and Steve took up the offer gratefully.

Once again, Maddie left the meeting feeling warmed and content, the wine helped but the new friendships were beginning to have a real effect on her. She hadn't realised how long it was since she had friends with commonalities. It was possibly in school when this last truly happened, she kept in touch with some of her friends from there, but lives take people far and wide and she couldn't say she had many people she could just turn up and say hello. She had friendships that needed planning, "Shall we go to the theatre next month?" "Do you want to try the new wine bar out when you can get a babysitter?" Her new friends seemed less complicated and genuine and a far cry from the people she was surrounded by all day at work. Maybe they were the treasures she was destined to find? Whatever the deeper meaning, tarot readings or her grandfather's voice, she was glad she decided to keep the allotment as she weaved, ever so slightly, home.

Chapter Five - MAY

Madeleine felt sharp and determined. She had set her alarm half an hour early and had taken the extra time to put her hair in rollers, press her new silk blouse free of the marks left by the hangar in the shop, put that little extra attention to her make-up and brush her suede covered emerald stilettos that would match her skirt and jacket perfectly. She glanced at her own reflection in the glass offices as she walked past on her way to Room 43L and was pleased with what she saw. Today, she was in control, today she was well rehearsed and prepared for the meeting with Gregory Alford, Director of Human Resources, who had sprung a surprise email to her yesterday requesting she see him to discuss a possible new opening. He hadn't gone into much detail, simply asking that she bring herself along and be prepared to discuss her own self-evaluation S.W.O.T with a view to a promotional role. He had asked that she prepare a ten-minute presentation to support her appraisal. She clutched a good old-fashioned memory stick, no longer trusting the reliability of the company IT for such an important task. She had not seen an internal advert, which was the usual route to promotion and opportunities, perhaps there was a secondary route that only those who get an individual invite get to know about? Whatever the role is, she had analysed her skills and strengths and presented them in a generic enough way that she could be seen to be suitable for most tasks. She was working blind so tried to cover all eventualities. She was well aware of the offer of promotion to all those who secured the Bittern Quay contract, but there was stiff competition and the odds of winning were decreasingly rapidly with the fractured relationships in the team. If something came up separately that injected more interest, then she would definitely consider it and she had spent many hours into the night preparing for today.

"Come in," Gregory called towards her knock on his door. "Ah, Madeleine, thank you for seeing me at such short notice, I appreciate it very much. Please take a seat, I just need to finish this urgent email, I'll be with you in just a tick."

He finished tapping on his keyboard and then pushed it back to show her that he had finished.

"Okay," he started the meeting off, "I glad that you wanted to come and see me to talk about your next steps."

"That's fine, it's a bit of a surprise but I have a presentation here for you."

Gregory looked briefly confused.

"Here it is, if you want to pop it into your computer, I can talk you through it," Madeleine passed the memory stick over and laid it on the desk in front of the Director.

"I really don't think we need to make this formal," Gregory left the stick where it was. "I just want to get an idea from you why you are looking to move out of the department you are in. I thought you were happy and working on the Bittern Quay project. I thought we could have an informal chat to find out what's going on, has something happened? Is there a problem?"

It was Madeleine's turn to look back confused.

"Erm, I thought you asked me here to discuss a promotion?" Madeleine instantly heard alarm bells in her head.

"Promotion? I'm not sure what you're talking about. I asked you here to talk about the email you sent me, giving in your notice." Gregory stumped her.

"What …. what….?

"Well, I was very surprised Madeleine, you always seem to be happy and settled here and I would like to think you'd come and see me to talk about your plans before making any kind of decision."

"Gregory, I have no idea what you mean? You emailed *me* to say there may be an opening for *me*. I spent hours on the presentation you asked for too! I didn't hand my notice in, why would I do that? I don't have another job!" Madeleine was panicking, there was some serious mistake being made here, she couldn't afford to leave C&B, she didn't want to either. It may not be the job that fully stimulates and excites her but it's stable and well paid and what on earth would her parents say!

"Look, here it is," Gregory turned his computer screen to show her an email which was definitely from her email address, sent two days before. It was short and to the point, three months' notice as per the contract. No explanation, no nice words thanking the company for their support, nothing! This was not the sort of email Madeleine would ever have typed, it simply wasn't her style and more than that, she didn't want to leave the company. She felt sick.

"Look, no harm done. Maybe you had a bad day and if you want to retract it then that's great for both of us," Gregory didn't believe her and why would he, the email was from her email address.

"Please believe me, there have been a few strange things happening lately and most of them to do with computers, I really didn't send this, I don't want to leave. Please look at my presentation and you'll see I created it last night, I wanted to show you that I'm ready for promotion. Why would I have done that if I had handed my notice in?" Her plausible explanation connected with the Director, he took the memory stick and opened her file.

"Well, it's a shame there is no promotional role as this is a very good piece of work, Madeleine. You're right, you wouldn't have gone to this trouble if you intended leaving. So, what do you think is going on then?"

Madeleine explained to him all about the lost soundtrack folder and what that meant to the team and the project. She told him how her colleagues had viewed her badly as a result. She described how the IT apprentice discovered it was her own computer that had been used whilst she was offsite. And now this email, it must have been sent from her computer too. She told him about Roseanne and her sly threats about being seen out with Dominic. Madeleine knew she risked a lot, telling her Human Resources Director that she was out with a colleague, but she trusted him and hoped he saw that she was genuine.

"So, you think Roseanne is behind all of this?" Gregory had listened and didn't appear to think Madeleine was crazy.

"She must be, she is new to the company, I've worked here all of these years and no-one has been mean to me. It's since she joined that this has happened and the way she talks to me, she definitely doesn't like me." Madeleine was forgetting her father's advice and laying her cards recklessly on the table.

Gregory paused, tapping his pen on the desk. "Okay, I've heard enough to take this further. If you are saying your computer had been compromised and there is maliciousness at play, then we have good reason to turn this into an official investigation. I'll appoint a neutral member of my HR team to complete the investigation and feedback to me. I'd appreciate it if you didn't talk about this further with anyone, so the case can be investigated with an unbiased view. Everyone will be interviewed who may be connected and we will be able to access CCTV on the back of this becoming a formal process. Is there anything else you need to tell me?"

Madeleine considered telling him again that she and Dominic are not involved, at least she could honestly say they were not having an affair as such, but she decided protesting too much and making an issue out of it could look even worse. She shook her head, thanked him and left Gregory's office.

Maddie was up and out of the house before anyone else was awake. The sun had streamed into her bedroom window, still low in the early spring morning and it looked like it was going to be a glorious day. She had planned a whole day in the allotment, things were shooting up so quickly that she was having trouble keeping up with it all. Her backpack had enough supplies to keep her going, snacks and a flask of coffee and a bottle she could fill from the water standpipe. She had taken to writing down notes in a little book to remind her of what she had planted. She sketched a small spreadsheet to show when she had sown seeds, when to plant them out and when they could be harvested. Everything was still so new to her, she kept notes and diagrams on what she had planted in each bed and if she turned the book over and viewed the pages from the back, there she had lists of jobs which she prepared before each visit and ticked off when they were done. She had photos and videos on her phone to match each day's entry, so she could look back next year and remember what she had done. One day she hoped to throw the book away but until she became more experienced, she kept it close by. Despite the lovely start to the morning, Maddie still made sure she had plenty of clothes, she had been caught out enough times to know that until the summer warms the air then the cold could strike at any time. A few weeks earlier she had treated herself to a thick pair of wellingtons, they weren't the most comfortable footwear to walk in but once she reached her plot, they were a godsend, it made all the difference not worrying about ruining her shoes.

It was a peaceful Saturday morning; the supermarket shoppers weren't yet on the road and the playing fields were not yet filled with footballers. Madeleine thought back to her work and tried again to fathom why she was attracting such nasty and spiteful attention. She had had jealousy before with previous boyfriends. One ex-girlfriend had spotted her in town and had confronted her, telling Madeleine he was still going out with her and that she needed to 'Keep her hands off him!" The girl's friends were standing behind her, crossed armed, forming a protective wall of support but not uttering a word. The encounter hadn't bothered Madeleine, she had heard the previous girlfriend could be particularly unpleasant. As it turned out, Maddie broke off with him anyway a few weeks later when she found he had been seeing a third girl; at the tender age of 19 Madeleine had cried for days. Not because she had liked him that much but because it was the first act of betrayal she had experienced, his lies were replayed over and over in her head, the sick feeling in her stomach when she found out her friends had known before her and the crushing dawning that she wasn't good enough, not even for a low-life boy who still had acne. She wanted to sit down with Roseanne and talk like adults, she would tell her she liked Dominic but was taking things slowly. She would point out that he was his own man who would make his own choices, not have his hand forced through her scheming and plotting and that a man wouldn't want to be with a woman who was capable of stooping so low. But for now, Madeleine had to keep away from Roseanne, there was going to be an investigation and she had promised not to interfere with it. She hadn't told Nadir or Dominic about the HR incident, Nadir would back her up that is was Roseanne, but she would leave him to tell the investigator. She wouldn't tell Dominic, she didn't want him to think she got involved in office conflicts, that she was above all of that, so for now she would just have to wait and be patient.

Her mind wandered to Dominic. She was so confused on how she felt about him. He was courting her in the old-fashioned sense, taking things slow, a stolen kiss here and there, holding hands when they went out, but she couldn't read him, wasn't sure what he was thinking as he dropped her in a taxi or said goodbye after a day at work. Did he want her to say she will stay with him overnight? Did he want to move things on further? Their relationship was mostly a Monday to Friday arrangement, she reasoned it was because she was already in London, less travel for her. She didn't yet feel they were at a stage where she could really be herself, let her guard down and be silly, act a fool, make mistakes that they would both laugh at or giggle at shared jokes that only they knew the meaning. They were a long way from that type of relationship. How long until she felt comfortable in that way? Should she be concerned that it's still so polite and serious? And there's the nagging voice in Madeleine's head, that sometimes Dominic takes the role of gentleman a bit too far, it's sweet that he chooses their food, their wine, where they go and when but occasionally she has felt criticised by him, or judged, or is it just her paranoia that someone as handsome, successful and aspiring wants to be with her, out of all of the women on the planet, why her? She needs to push him a little more to test where the relationship is heading to, she just needs to think, how?

Madeleine wasn't the first at the allotments. In fact, as well as Norris' pushbike leaning just inside the gate, Esther's battered Defender and Filo's classic Citroen 2CV were there and also a police car sitting silently but with its blue light circling around needlessly.

"Maddie, oh Maddie, it's just awful!' Filo rushed to Maddie and gently pulled her into the main car park. "Look, look what they've done! I just can't believe anyone would do this...."

Maddie scanned the site and soon understood. Daubed across the shed shop were huge words spray painted, multi-coloured, artistic, like the words you see on motorway bridges, graffitied and stylised so heavily you must carefully decipher what it says. Maddie made out the words, 'Hoes have hoes' and 'Grow weed not weeds.' The double doors were smashed and there was little left inside.

'But that's not all," Esther joined them, "Look at all the allotments, poor Alice, her's was hit the worst. Everything has been destroyed, all her hard work gone. Who could do something like this?" Esther's eyes watered, she looked bereft. "Norris' is not too bad, he is up at the other end, yours and Tom's have had some damage but nowhere near as bad as these front four."

Maddie looked at Alice's plot, it was as though an army of moles had chosen her patch to crawl up out of the dark, pile high great mounds of earth and party late into the night. The arches of canes, she had built for her selection of beans, were ripped out and discarded along the edge, like javelins, the beans pulled out and ripped apart. The perfect rows of onions disappeared, each tugged from the ground and flung like throwing hammers in the Celtic Games. Alice's greenhouse was peppered with holes, air rifles possibly, the policewoman was scouring the ground around it, probably looking for ammunition. The contents all emptied, hundreds of plant pots littered the ground, the delicate baby shoots ripped from their beds and lay drying and dying on the flagstone ground. Tomato plants snapped, courgettes also, there looked to be nothing left to save. The soil in the beds was dug over and the contents spilled out onto the pathways.

"Alice is on her way up now," Tom came down from higher up the path where the phone signal is better, "She's understandably very upset." He put his phone away and nodded towards Maddie. "I haven't checked yours yet, I've had a quick look at mine, there's a few bits of damage but the police don't want us trampling around yet, until she's had a good look herself."

"Okay, thanks," Maddie couldn't think of anything more constructive than that. "How did they get in?"

"Over there," Tom pointed to a small gap near the communal compost bins, the green fence had been cut low down, big enough to crawl through. "It's been done with professional equipment; they must have been in a van to carry it. Norris was the first one here and called the police and then my mum.... bastards." Tom was livid, it was the most he had actually said to Maddie, but she could tell the depth of frustrated anger in his voice. "Filo, don't bother," he called across, "it's too much to sort out now, let the police take care of things first." Filo was busying lifting discarded pots and gathering strewn plants from Alice's garden, in a bid to make it less of a shock for when Alice arrived.

"But we have to do something," Filo implored, "This is just so sad, why would anyone do this?"

For just the fleeting moment, Maddie felt Deja vu, that sense of something vindictive happening again. Surely this vandalism has nothing to do with Roseanne, that is just too much of a leap of imagination, she doesn't even know where she lives, let alone that she has an allotment or where it is. Maddie discarded the thought as absurd.

"Okay everyone, gather round." Esther's practical tones called out to the group. "The police lady would like a quick word with everyone and then we can go onto our plots. Tom and Maddie, why don't you both go first as she's over on your side now. She can see Alice when she arrives. Filo, please stop clucking about, you're making me feel dizzy watching you!"

"But I feel so bad, "Filo explained as she juggled with an armful of brown plastic pots, "My plot wasn't touched so I must help everyone else."

"I know, but let's wait until everyone is here and we can make a plan of action." Esther's organisational skills were kicking in and she was taking charge.

As Maddie approached her plot she felt relief, nothing was touched apart from the plastic chair being thrown into the hedge. She felt a little guilty that she had escaped the worst of it, after a quick check in the shed and greenhouse she could see everything was still there, intact. She was about to join Tom and the policewoman when she remembered the caravan. She could see the lock dangling as she approached it. She knew before she opened the door that they had been inside. She edged the door ajar, almost as if they were still inside but instead saw her worst fears, the seats had been lifted, the boxes inside were turned upside down and she could tell immediately that things were missing.

No, oh please no, not her treasures. She had only just found them, her grandfather had kept them for all these years and now someone has taken them, just like that! They were worthless to anyone else. Doing a quick inventory in her head, Maddie saw the little wellington boots had gone, some of the boxes of games, compendium of card games, some tools and the beige jacket. Why on earth would someone want the jacket? She ran to Tom's garden.

"This is Maddie," Tom introduced her to the policewoman, who looked like she had barely left school herself.

"Hi, have you had a chance to look over your property?"

Both Tom and the policewoman looked at her and waited. Despite herself, she started to cry.

"They've been in my caravan; they've stolen some things." Maddie hiccupped her way through.

"Oh really? Ok, can you describe what has been taken?" the policewoman turned to another page in her notebook.

Maddie listed what she could see had been taken, the jacket, yes it was about fifteen years old, the boots, yes they were over twenty years old, the games, yes, they were used and older versions than in the shops now and a few packs of cards with a book of card games. She could hear how trivial it all sounded, she could see she must look ridiculous and selfish being upset over such items but the policewoman and Tom didn't laugh, they looked serious and at one point Tom reached out and touched

Maddie's shoulder to console her, just a quick tap, almost a pat, but she appreciated the gesture.

"I know these are just silly things, but they mean a lot to me. They are sentimental. My granddad kept them as a reminder of when we were close and now I have them back, to remind me. I don't know why anyone would want to take them. They are worthless but are priceless to me." No-one disagreed with Maddie, they could see on her face and in her anguish the meaning behind these belongings.

"You have given me good descriptions, Maddie. I can't promise anything, but we will do everything we can to track who did this and when we do, I'm sure we'll find your belongings." Maddie believed the policewoman's commitment.

"Thank you, I appreciate it very much." Maddie was grateful to her as she closed her notebook and went to question some of the others.

"Did you have any damage?" Maddie turned to Tom, feeling a little foolish for her tears.

"Just some of the structures have been broken, the netting around my fruit bushes, some of the stakes have been taken out and thrown but I think I can string up what's left. I've been lucky." Tom scanned around as if to check if he had missed something. "I'm sorry about your caravan." Tom looked embarrassed to say something nice to Maddie, this was more obvious as he turned and hurried away.

The group sat in a circle. After gathering up a few chairs, they arranged themselves into an impromptu committee meeting, in the car park, at the front of the shed shop. Alice had arrived, she had sprinted in through the gates to her plot and sunk to her knees in distress. Alice, lovely, happy, smiling Alice sobbed. This was the first year that she had started right from the beginning of the season, knowing a lot more of what she needed to do than when she had first begun. She had thrown herself into developing a beautiful allotment plot, it was the perfect balance of serious allotmenting along with unusual areas of interest to reflect Alice's passions; rotated beds to ensure the crops were healthy and given the best start, additional guttering for maximum water conservation, combination planting of stunning dahlias, nasturtiums and marigolds to encourage the natural destruction of aphids and entice the pollinating bees but also quirky areas to sit and relax, made from reclaimed furniture and donated wood. Alice had made an insect hotel from tubes, bricks and sticks but this now lay decimated. Alice was dedicated to the natural, organic cycle of life, she encouraged it with hedgehog houses which would provide her with resident slug eaters. She had buckets of soaking comfrey and nettles, which stunk in the heat of the sun, but gave her nutrient rich free plant food, this was now all overturned and soaking into the grass. She even had a pile of horse manure behind her shed that she would scoop up off the road and allow to rot and mature before mulching her beds in its glorious goodness. She had spent extra time and care building up a supply of produce ready for the Harvest event, all of this now looked lost, she wouldn't be able to run her stall. Alice had not only given a considerable amount of time to her projects but her beliefs, her passions and a part of herself were integral to her plot. It was heartbreaking to see it ripped away.

Ranweer arrived shortly after Alice, along with his wife, Janalee and their two sons. The boys were ten and eight and instructed to go and play football on the other side of the car park whilst the adults talked.

"We have been given the go ahead to start clearing up by the police." Esther took charge. "I propose we look at our skill sets and team up to tackle the same task across all of the plots. Norris and Ranweer, can you both look at everyone's structures? I have called the reclamation yard and explained what's happened, they are happy to help us with any wood that needs replacing. Look at fences, arches, canes and stakes et cetera."

The men nodded, that worked well as Norris had his pickup truck and all of his tools were untouched in his shed.

"Maddie and Tom, you are both on clear up duty. The graffiti on the shed shop and also over on the wall at the side of the allotments needs to be cleaned off or painted over. Whatever you see fit."

Maddie felt that was a good delegation of task, she could do that easily.

"Filo and myself will make a start helping Alice collect up as many plants as we can salvage and get them re-planted or re-potted. I'm sure we can save a lot of things Alice; the key is to get started soon before the sun dries it all up too much." Esther smiled at a very grateful Alice.

"And me and the boys will do whatever you need too." added Janalee, "Please give them as many jobs as you like, it'll help wear them out! I'll pop home and get some refreshments for everyone; I'll be back shortly." Janalee took the car keys from Ranweer and went off for supplies.

The circle dispersed like dandelion seeds in the wind and went to their allotted task. Maddie retrieved an old bucket from her shed and a long-handled broom, Tom came back from his with exactly the same items.

"Snap!" he laughed. A wide, warm, generous, and easy laugh transformed his face and took Maddie by surprise. He looked an entirely different person and she blushed when she realised she must have gaped.

"Well, I couldn't find a graffiti blaster in my shed so I just figured this will do." Maddie grinned and almost ran to the standpipe to hide her pink neck.

They started to scrub on opposite faces of the shed shop, the sprayed writing was huge, almost the length of each side.

Maddie noticed the yellow, purple and red shades were running off nicely but the black outlines were too stubborn and already too seeped into the planks. She was finding it hard to reach the top of the letters, even stretched high extending the broom as far as she could reach. Tom poked his head around the corner to see how she was getting on.

"I can't quite reach the top either, I'll fetch a ladder," he offered.

He set up Norris's step ladder in front of Maddie in a triangular shape, shaking it gently to test its' stability on the ground.

"If you climb up that side, I'll stand on the bottom rung this side to make sure you don't topple over," he instructed.

"Why don't you climb up, you're stronger than me?" Maddie wasn't sure why she was arguing, there was something about Tom that had made her defensive.

He sighed, "Because, if I'm up the ladder and you support me, what do you think will happen if I fall, hhhhmmm?"

Maddie had the grace to apologise and say she hadn't thought of that.

She climbed the ladder as Tom held onto the sides and stood on the bottom. She became aware they were facing each other and standing very close. She hadn't had the chance to really look at him before and saw he had the bluest eyes, watery blue with flecks of silver, his light brown hair had natural golden highlights from the spring sun. His hair flopped about his face, an attempt at a sweeping fringe had been long abandoned. It curled at the nape of his neck, ready for a trim. His face was healthy, nut brown with the hint of lines which could tell a hundred stories. His teeth were bright and very slightly crooked, no false crowns or aesthetic dentistry, Maddie doubted the thought would even occur to him. Tom was stocky, his shoulders were broad and neck thick set, but he looked fit and toned, except for the slightly rounded belly that his T-shirt couldn't hide.

They looked at each other for what was probably just a fleeting moment, but it felt like time stood still, taking the chance to inspect each other and analysing what they found. One of them had to break the moment.

"You need to pass me my bucket and broom," Maddie went first.

Tom laughed again, his mood now light despite the awful events, as he bent down and picked up her things. He offered the bucket up to her; she dipped the broom and began scrubbing at the higher parts of the shed. She felt his eyes on her as she pushed backwards and forwards, arms raised up, knowing that parts of her body were swaying right in front of him. She had never been so aware of someone taking her all in before, without glancing down she knew he was stealing this chance to appreciate the view he had, looking up, as she pushed and pulled the broom with water running down her arm, past her armpits and soaking her cotton blouse. She was glad she had tucked her blouse into her jeans, a baggy T-shirt could have been far worse. Each time she stopped to dip the broom, he just looked at her with a knowing smile, she knew he was watching her, and he knew that she knew. It was a game of no words. He didn't look away, teasing her to be the first to stop, cat and mouse, the first to break. Maddie wasn't going to let him win, she dipped and stretched and grinned knowingly back at him, testing him, would he look away first?

"Hi there, how are you both getting on?"

Janalee had returned loaded with supermarket bags for life. She looked from Tom to Maddie quizzingly. They both jumped to the ground and muttered fine, fine.

"Oh, that's good, I'm going to set up some food and drinks over on Ranweer's plot, as he has plates and things there and a trestle table. Pop over when you're ready and help yourself. Maddie, you're pretty wet, you know!"

Maddie looked down at herself as if she hadn't realised.

"Oh yes, don't worry, it's a nice day, I'll soon dry out," Maddie laughed as Janalee left them with the feeling she may have interrupted something. "I think I'll finish the rest after a drink, I'm thirsty." Maddie muttered to Tom, as she followed Janalee, so she didn't need to think of anything else to say.

Maddie found Filo helping to collect up Alice's plants from the ground and re-plant them into the raised beds. Alice was explaining to Filo where everything should go but it didn't look like Alice trusted her to get it right, as she was following her and repositioning as she went. Filo was oblivious, singing to herself old New Seekers folk songs, teaching the world to sing. Esther was in the greenhouse re-potting.

"Can I help?" Maddie offered, "I need to rest my arms from all that cleaning for a while."

"Of course, here," Esther lifted two plants up as a demonstration. "If you can put anything that's about this big into these pots here and if anything is this size, or larger, then use these pots. I'll stick the labels in."

Maddie wondered at how Esther knew which label went in with which plant.

"Well, Alice has given me the seed packets that she has kept, they remind her which variety she has sown and how to care for it. These plain envelopes are her own seeds, that she saved from plants last year. And the good girl has written all the details onto the envelopes… see. And then it's just a case of me knowing my carrots from my tomatoes. Look, these are definitely tomatoes, very familiar leaves. The trouble is the varieties can all look the same at this stage, so there will be an element of surprise this year, some will be large beefsteak ones, some cherry tomatoes, she won't know until they fruit but the good news is she will have tomatoes…. of some kind!"

Maddie understood and set about sorting the seedlings and plants into the right pots. There was a lot of soil on the ground that had fallen out along with the plants. Esther told her that there were seeds that have not yet germinated in the soil too, so she was using fresh compost to re-pot the plants and would then scoop what was on the floor and divide this into new pots and label them with a big question mark. Something may be inside ready to grow, or it may be empty. It will be another surprise. She said it had given her an idea for the Charity Harvest Event, they could plant some seeds in pots and nothing in others and it would be a lucky dip, 10p and you take your chances on whether you have bought something. Esther explained there was plenty that could be sown in a pot in late September or October, like poppies, aubergines and cornflowers. It was a fun idea.

Maddie worked companionably alongside the girls, chatting to Filo about her passion for mystical stories, but not mentioning her own dabble with the tarot. She helped Alice rebuild the bug hotel, all the time learning from her the theory behind the piles they were creating. Her stomach rumbled and she realised it was lunchtime already.

Janalee's food was delicious. The trestle table served as a self-service buffet, plates and forks at one end and you walked a conveyor belt of dish after dish of vegetarian delights. Soft, oozing silky aubergine tapenade on crusty rye bread, couscous and bulgur wheat salads, drizzled with oils and garlic, a Russian salad that Maddie hadn't eaten since she was in school and this version was nothing like it, it was a revelation of potatoes, carrots, pickles and peas, vegan friendly mayonnaise and no less tasty with the omitted ham. After lunch, everyone sat around chatting and letting the food digest. Maddie was talking to Norris but as soon as he left to go and 'sort some things on my allotment' Tom replaced him next to her.

"So, you've dried out then?" he was twinkling today and it was beginning to unnerve Maddie.

"Yes, thank you, did you manage to finish the shed?" Maddie had busied herself at Alice's so that she hadn't needed to go back to help him.

"Yes, all done, except it will still need a coat of wood stain to get rid of the black lines." Tom sat with his knees apart, balancing a plate of salad in the air where his lap should be, using his elbows on his thighs for support. He hunched over slightly to eat.

"I never thanked you for the potatoes you gave me," Maddie had found out what chitted potatoes were and had googled how to sow them into the troughs. "And I didn't realise it was you who dug my potato patch, I thought it was Norris, thank you, it was really nice of you and helped me a lot." Maddie felt calmer near him, less defensive than earlier and definitely less aggressive than the previous weeks. She felt they had turned a friendship corner.

"That's okay, I could see it needed doing and it's not fair Norris taking it all on, you have to watch him, he's like your granddad, he won't say no and will just keep on going until he breaks." Tom looked down at the floor.

"I don't ask Norris to help me, he takes it on himself," Maddie needed to justify herself. There was silence for a while. "Did you know my grandfather well?"

"Yes, very. I've known him since I was little. I used to come up here with my mum and dad. My dad, Bert your grandad and Norris were all the best of friends. When my dad died, I was only about ten and I started to come up with just mum. Bert and Norris kind of took me under their wings. I remember you a little bit, you were five when I started to come up, five and a bit annoying! I started to help your granddad doing odd jobs, he taught me all about the allotments, I loved it, I loved him, he was a really good man, Maddie."

Maddie felt the familiar heat in the back of her eyes as they whelmed up.

"I didn't realise you knew him so well," Maddie didn't want to cry in front of him again.

"I was five years older than you, well I still am of course, but back at that age it's a big difference. He loved having you with him here but when you stopped coming, I guess I was probably about sixteen or seventeen and so me and Bert were like good mates, very good mates. I guess I helped fill a gap for him."

"I can see we probably didn't have much to do with each other back then, I don't really remember you, sorry." Maddie wanted to tell Tom it wasn't her fault she had stopped coming, that it wasn't that she didn't want to, well not at first anyway. She wanted to say she hadn't abandoned Bert, that she still saw him at home. But she hadn't yet processed the events at that time, she hadn't spoken to her mother and father about why they sent her to Grammar school, why she couldn't see her grandfather or the letters from her mother. Until she had a chance to work it all out in her head, she didn't want to discuss it with him. Up until this morning she thought he detested her, she wasn't going to start opening up her soul to him just because he laughed with her once or twice. She didn't know if she could trust him with her truths and questions. She didn't want to hear how close Tom was to Bert, she didn't want to know the missed years had been filled with someone else, that Tom knew things about him that she didn't, that they had shared experiences that she didn't know about. Tom possibly knew her granddad better than she did at the end, and she pushed that truth to the back of her head. She left him to finish his lunch and returned to the sanctuary of Alice's plot.

As the sun dipped below the tree line, the early spring chill crept in. Maddie put her many layers of clothes back on as she was beginning to shiver. It was the longest day she had spent on the allotments and couldn't believe how much they had achieved. Looking around her, it was hard to see the damage that had been caused overnight. Tom had stepped in to help Ranweer and Norris finish the fences and posts and had strung up the small broad beans securely again on everyone's plots. A few other allotment holders had been contacted and there had been a lively buzz all day, working together across each other's gardens, meeting new people, stopping and having a cup of tea and a biscuit and getting to peek into each other's caravans. Maddie hadn't been on her plot all day, she knew it was all watered and safe and didn't want to go back into her caravan yet, not today. Even though the day had started so awfully, it may be the start of something new, friendlier exchanges, seeking each other out, taking time for each other, helping each other more. Up until today Maddie had often not spoken to a soul all day, even when she could see others bending down weeding and planting, walking around to the compost bins, she had kept herself to herself. She had a feeling this is about to change. She will make more of an effort, she will push herself more to be part of this community.

They are lovely people here, genuinely lovely people and today she started to really feel as though she belongs.

"C'mon, were off to the pub!!" Filo shouted to anyone who cared to hear. "Last one to the Swan buys the round."

"Are you coming, Maddie?" Alice called over, "I'm going to buy the first round, it's the least I can do." Alice pulled the long strap of her hessian bag over her head and across her chest.

Maddie had no plans, she was tired and cold but had been hot and sweaty all day, she thought she must smell pretty unpleasant, but the thought of a cold cider was too tempting and she followed Alice up the path.

The Swan was a bit of a dive. But it was a happy dive and one that was very popular. It hadn't been decorated for at least twenty years; the floorboards were still sticky from last nights' live band. The wood smoke soaked into it from the days when smoking was allowed. Every inch of wall and ceiling had faded beermats stuck on to it with a drawing pin, hundreds of breweries, beers and ciders were represented here. Locals had brought beermats back from holidays to pin up, some were Belgium beers and a few Australian lagers, transported from a surfing trip by a group of guys, now all married, with children of an age to go surfing themselves. Simple wooden stools surrounded the bar and a few tables and chairs collected around the edge. The centre was left for dancing, day or night, to the jukebox or a singer or to a jamming session if anyone had brought along their guitar or harmonica. In a side room, a pool table always had coins lined up along the edge, reserving the next game. The beers changed every time you visited, witty named pale ales, comical stouts. Televisions were banned, the landlord refused to have one in the bar and said to stay at home if you want to watch the football, his bar was for meeting, talking, laughing and drinking. A few times he had tried a 'no phone' amnesty day, but everyone just snuck out to the toilets to send their texts and check their messages, so he gave that idea up.

Accepting a lift to the pub, Maddie had jumped into Filo's 2CV which had been hilarious. The tiny French car had a gear selection stick poking out from the dashboard, there was no carpet in the footwell, the original striped seat covers were frayed, and a spring was sticking into Maddie's bottom. They bounced along the road, feeling like they would tip over at each roundabout,

Maddie squealed with laughter as Filo sang along to the radio, with the windows rolled down. The striped fabric roof flapped where it was sagging with age. Filo pulled into the car park at the front, parked and linked her arm through Maddie's to lead her through the wooden door which was propped open by an iron beagle door stop.

Some of the group were already at the tables, Esther was rearranging, pulling two together to make a larger area to sit. Alice was at the bar with Tom, calling back over her shoulder to double check everyone's drinks requests. Tom had one foot on the brass pole at the base of the bar, leaning slightly over to read the labels on the hand pumps.

"Ladies, what will you both have?" Alice called over to Maddie and Filo as they arrived.

Filo ordered a cider with a shot of blackcurrant whilst Maddie stuck with a plain cider. After a few minutes of reshuffling chairs and handing out the drinks, the group finally settled down.

"Cheers!" Esther was the first to raise her glass into the centre of the table. Alice, Tom, Filo, Norris, Steve, Gail and

Maddie all raised their glasses in a collective cheer. Ranweer and his wife had taken the boys home, both lads were filthy dirty from "helping' through the afternoon and had spent more time rolling in the dirt and playing hide and seek.

"I'd like to say a few words," Alice cleared her throat and waited for everyone's attention. "This morning, when Tom phoned me, I felt awful, like someone had gone out of their way to attack me, not physically, but it felt like that. I know you all had terrible things happen too, poor Maddie has had things stolen, but I felt just dreadful, like my world had been invaded and it was personal, which I know is silly. But, if it wasn't for all of you, I don't know what I would have done, I would have run away from it all, I think. I just want to say thank you, you are all my friends and I love you all for helping me today. Thank you so much."

Tom pulled Alice into him, stretching his arm around her shoulder and gently kissed the top of her dreadlocked head. Alice patted his thigh in return.

The move surprised Maddie. It hadn't occurred to her that any of the group may be in a relationship and especially not Tom and Alice. She wasn't sure why, but she wouldn't have placed them together. Both were fairly quiet, not loud, or brash. Both had an obvious love of the outdoors and their gardening but looking at them side by side, Maddie couldn't see them as a couple, not that she was an expert at all, her own love life was hardly straight forward. It seemed strange that Tom had been quite upbeat all day when his girlfriend had had a terrible shock and would have needed his support. It didn't make sense to her, but she put the questions to the back of her mind and turned to finish her drink with Filo and Norris when her mobile phone rang in her bag.

"Hi Dominic!" Maddie was surprised, she didn't expect to hear from him over the weekend.

"Hello Madeleine, where are you? I'm at your house but your father says you've been out all day. I've come down to see you but you're not here."

"At my house? Are you? I didn't know you were coming. I'm in the pub with friends at the minute, I'll finish up here and come home." Maddie was enjoying herself; she hadn't been out with a group of friends for a long time, the company was easy and she felt relaxed. She was loath to leave but if Dominic had made the effort to come all the way down to see her, she should get back quickly. She would have preferred a bit of planning, Dominic had often taken it upon himself to arrange things on their behalf but he had only been to her house once, she didn't feel they were in a relationship where they simply turn up at each other's houses.

"No, don't do that. I'll come and meet your friends. Which pub?" Dominic didn't give her the chance to argue.

"It's the Swan, down near Queens Garden Allotments. Are you getting a taxi, they'll know where?"

"Your father said he'll give me a lift, so I'll just be a few minutes." The phone went dead as Maddie wondered at how her evening was changing so suddenly. She looked down at her clothes and realised she was caked in mud at her knees, where she had been kneeling to plant. Her blouse, which had washed-out paint all over it, was covered by an old striped jumper with frayed cuffs. She hadn't bothered with make-up, Saturdays she just didn't. She already knew she probably smelt strong from her day's work and her hair had foliage in it. She turned to Filo quietly and asked if she had anything in her bag she could use to freshen up. Filo looked puzzled so Maddie was forced to explain she had a friend joining them.

"Oh, who's coming to meet us?" Filo asked too loudly, so that the rest of the table all turned to listen.

"He's just.... he's just my friend," Maddie couldn't define what she should call Dominic, friend felt a safe explanation. Filo passed her a huge denim sack with handles and said she was welcome to anything she could find in there. Maddie scurried off to the toilets, embarrassed that everyone now knew she was cleaning up for a man. Pulling everything out from Filo's bag, she found a brush and a small bottle of eau de toilette. It wouldn't have been a fragrance that she would have chosen but she was grateful it was better than manure. She washed herself as much as she could and took off the striped jumper. She had a choice between the jumper, or the blouse and the blouse just edged ahead. By the time she emerged from the toilets Dominic was just walking in. She was relieved to see he wasn't wearing a suit; she was beginning to think that was all he wore. He was no less smart though in mustard chino trousers, brown leather brogues, and a thin beige cashmere jumper with a shirt underneath, the collar sticking up slightly at the nape of his neck. Dominic greeted her with a kiss on the cheek and a protective arm around her waist.

"I've been texting you all day," he muttered sulkily.

"Have you? I haven't checked my phone; I've been busy all day." Was that why he had turned up out of the blue? Was he checking up on her? "You don't normally text me on a Saturday, so I didn't think to check." Why does she always feel the need to explain herself to him, she could hear herself doing it but somehow couldn't stop.

"I wanted to spend the day with you, I had some other plans cancelled so thought it would be nice to be together today. I came to your house to make sure you are alright. I was worried about you." Dominic eased her towards the bar. "I didn't expect to end up in a place like this though, I've got to be honest I had slightly better ideas in my head." Clicking his fingers at the barmaid, "I'll have a red wine please, make it a Shiraz.... and you?" he motioned to Maddie to offer her a drink. She accepted a white wine. They both took the house wine that the barmaid selected and looked at each other. Maddie realised she was still clutching Filo's bag. She hesitated, suddenly she felt torn. On one side of the room sat a group of new friends who knew nothing about her day job or the Madeleine she was Monday to Friday. With them she could escape, she could be herself, no judgement, no expectations, just Maddie who was learning, Maddie who was growing. She didn't feel judged or held up to a criterion that was a daily struggle to meet. She was building a new world, one that she felt comfortable and was enjoying immensely. On the other side was Dominic, who she couldn't deny continually made her flustered, that she wanted to please and wanted him to like her. Dominic who represented all her career achievements, success in her field, financial security, a good solid prospect that could be relied upon and definitely had pleased her parents. They had fed back to Madeleine how much they liked him after the birthday party; they had approved, and her father must like him to bring him down to the Swan to meet her. But did she want her worlds colliding? Was she ready to blur those lines? The decision was made for her.

"C'mon Maddie, come and introduce us to your friend," Filo was calling and waving like an excitable puppy. Of all the other faces now looking up from the table it was Tom's she noticed, she couldn't describe his expression but gone was his easy smile of earlier today, replaced instead with an intense stare.

"Dominic, this is the allotment group, we were vandalised yesterday and we've been putting it all back together again today." Maddie introduced each person in turn, Norris leant across and shook his hand amicably, Alice was staring open mouthed, not hiding the fact that she thought Dominic was possibly the most handsome man she had ever met. Esther was polite but Tom just grunted an inaudible greeting.

"I didn't think you actually did anything over in these allotments, Madeleine, don't vegetables grow by themselves?" Dominic's opening question was embarrassing. It was true Maddie had been unsure about how to start when she first took over the plot and she had to ask a thousand questions but she wasn't ignorant, she knew it would be hard work. Dominic's lack of taking any prior interest, when she had told him each week about her previous weekend, was evident. She had dropped into conversations what she had achieved each visit to Queens Gardens, surely in a relationship you share these things? She had realised he wasn't fully interested but that had suited her, she didn't want him too involved in her weekend world, but what did he think she did each week…. hire someone to do the digging and weeding? Madeleine tried to retrieve his dignity and move the conversation on.

"Steve and Gail are nurses at the local hospital and Filo reads tarot cards and gives psychic readings."

"Oh, mumbo jumbo stuff," Dominic taunted. Maddie saw a flicker of annoyance on Filo's face but she replaced it quickly with a smile.

"It's an art form. To be able to read and explain phenomena is a powerful thing. I support people, I can help coach them and guide them to make better choices and be fulfilled, to be their best selves." Filo looked briefly from Maddie back to Dominic.

"Okay, so will you read me mine then?" Dominic asked, surprising Madeleine. Filo willingly pulled out a pack of tarot cards from her bag and began to shuffle them. She followed the same routine that she had done with Maddie but this time with an audience, the group around the table stopped their conversations and leaned in. She guided Dominic to make three choices and began to read them out. Too soon, Maddie realised he wasn't asking from genuine interest but as a chance to belittle Filo's interest in the supernatural. She couldn't interject.

The first card was the Ten of Wands.

Filo interpreted, "This represents your past, it is one of the wand suits, they are associated with energy and ambition. This one symbolises accomplishment and responsibility but with it brings burden. This has brought you to this point in your life."

"Hhmm, like I said, so far it sounds like mumbo jumbo. I'm not burdened, I have goals and I will accomplish them, but it's true, I do have energy and ambition." Dominic sounded defensive.

Filo looked at the next, and explained it represents Dominic's present.

"This is the Devil. Don't worry, it's not as scary as it sounds, however it is sometimes linked to addiction, not harmful perhaps but addicted to something you want, sometimes it's materialistic. It can also mean temptation." Filo also knew the Devil card was a warning to look at unhealthy relationships, but she was already sensing this was not the time or place for such a revelation. Dominic just sniffed as a response to his present card and downed his wine in one gulp. He put his glass down a little too heavily. "What a load of rubbish…..."

"Your final card is your future, or a possible future," Filo continued regardless and was careful to explain. "This card is called The Lovers." There was a giggle from the spectators and a smile from Dominic at last.

"Sorry, I have to go, I'll see you all tomorrow, do you want a lift, Alice?" Tom pushed his chair back, pulled his jacket from the back of it and left with Alice, waving goodbye as she followed him out.

"Well, I think I may start believing in the tarot cards a little now," Dominic declared happily. "The future sounds much more positive. Thank you, Filo, that was enlightening. I've finished my drink Madeleine, shall we go? Nice to meet you all." Dominic stood and gave a little bow to the group and lingered by the door waiting for Madeleine to join him.

"But I haven't interpreted the last card for you yet!" Filo looked anxiously from Maddie to Dominic, as Maddie finished her drink quickly and gathered her things. As she leant over to pick up her jumper Filo touched her hand and whispered, "It's a reversed card, Maddie, it's reversed." Maddie had no idea what she was talking about, said her goodbyes to everyone and followed Dominic out of the pub.

"Let's go to a decent place for a meal. You're not exactly dressed for it but maybe we can sit in a corner?" Dominic was serious.

"No wait, I'm sorry Dominic but you were really rude to my friend, it made me feel uncomfortable." Madeleine found her voice.

"I was only messing with her, she must get it all the time from her customers, they all know it's not real, it's just a laugh. She wasn't bothered, she's heard it all before." Dominic dismissed any effect that Madeleine had felt, she had been embarrassed by his behaviour, yet he wasn't seeing her point of view.

"But she is my friend, and you had only just met them all. If you think its mumbo jumbo, then why bother to have a reading?"

"Are you telling me you believe in all that stuff?" Dominic asked incredulously.

"No, I don't, of course I don't, but I would remember my manners. Look, I'm sorry Dominic but I've had a really long day, I'm tired and I'd just like to go home."

"Are you serious? I've come all the way to see you!" Dominic's face shut down.

"Yes, I know, but you didn't let me know beforehand." Madeleine was tired and not prepared for a fight.

"I've been texting you all day, check your phone. If you bothered to look, you'd see I've been trying to get you. It's your fault if you don't check it, how am I to know you're not in some kind of trouble? Of course I'm going to make sure you're ok." Dominic was twisting his reasoning and she was beginning to accept he may have a point. "If I can't always reach you then I need to do something about it, your father agreed with me, he thinks it's perfectly reasonable that I came. I'm looking out for you and you don't seem to be appreciating it at all. Madeleine, I'm trying here, I'm here for you, why are you pushing me away?" Dominic was gripping Madeleine's arms tightly, he spoke urgently into her face, almost shaking her, just almost.

"Okay, I guess I am hungry but nowhere too posh, or far away, a meal and then I'd like to go home." Madeleine conceded out of hunger, despite an inner voice nagging in her ear. They left to find the nearest restaurant in silence.

Chapter Six - JUNE

Nadir had really pulled this one out of the bag. It turned out that his partner, Giorgios, worked as an insurance advisor; his role was to calculate risk in any business decision as part of change management policies. He would then advise the company of any potential pitfalls before they implemented their changes. He was currently working on a commission for a health club chain and had made a contact that he thought would be useful to Nadir and the team.

"So, explain who this is to me again." Roseanne didn't feel this meeting had any useful purpose at all, after all she knew every link and contact connected with the Bittern Quay development project. She was doubtful Nadir could unearth anything that she wasn't aware of.

Nadir was losing patience with her, "I'll explain again, I have invited Earl Williams to meet us here today. Earl is working with my partner, Giorgios, on a change management investigation for Konnect Health Spas, the chain of spas owned by Nobuaki Ito. As you know Mr. Ito is one of the Bittern Quay Directors. Earl works for Mr. Ito and oversees making sure all the risk measurements are accurate, ready to present to Mr. Ito. Mr. Ito will then decide whether his changes are a good risk or bad risk. Earl hired Giorgios's company; you see.

"Okay, so I understand who he is but what is the link to us?" Roseanne was getting bored.

"Apparently, Mr. Ito is bringing about changes to his health spas to include a focus on the environment and the natural world. Giorgios isn't allowed to give me all the specifics, he signed a confidentiality paper, but he said he thinks Earl would be happy to talk about it to us in general terms, just no details. Apparently, it's something Mr. Ito is keen to include as a core value in his business ventures. Any insight must be helpful, surely!" Nadir looked smugly at Roseanne, knowing that this was potentially an important lead.

"It sounds good Nadir, well done," Dominic slapped him on the back gently. "We know we need a hook; we are almost there with our advertising campaign, but we need a specific angle, something to pin everything onto. Earl may be able to help us with that."

The internal intercom flashed on the desk. Nadir picked up the receiver and spoke to the receptionist.

"He's here, I'll go and greet him." Nadir was enjoying himself.

Earl Williams was not at all what Madeleine was expecting. As he shuffled behind Nadir into the meeting room, wiping a smudge from his glasses with a greyed handkerchief that he foraged from the depths of his trouser pocket, he didn't look up and seemed to forget he was there to meet actual people. His baggy, cream linen trousers were hung low under an enormous stomach, pulled in tight by a brown belt. The matching linen jacket was dreadfully creased. He looked as though he had just returned from an African safari. Nadir pulled a chair out for him and smiled an invite to sit down.

Nadir, sat next to Earl, contrasting in his pink candy-striped shirt with a dark green herringbone waistcoat and a superhero tie, deliberately tied so it was as wide as possible. Nadir's closely cropped beard was perfectly outlined under his jawline, making him look dark and powerful. Nadir took the lead.

"Earl, thank you so much for seeing us today, we know your time is limited so we will keep the meeting to an hour, if that suits you?"

Earl nodded silently.

Nadir carried on, "Please help yourself to refreshments that are at the back of the room. If there is anything else you would like, that's not there, please just ask. We can arrange most things. Giorgios has explained to me that you are not permitted to give us the details of the changes that Konnect are hoping to bring in, but that you may be able to answer some of our questions, is that alright with you?"

"Yes, that's fine," Earl's voice was so high pitched, he squeaked. "I'm not sure if I can help you much, but I'm happy to, within my limits of course."

Madeleine opened the discussion, kicking into her day job mode. In these situations, a hidden person inside her steps outside of her body and takes over. She can almost hear herself talking, outside looking in. She is not controlling her body and voice, it is an automatic reaction, she steps up a gear and throws a cloaked mantle over herself, becoming the person she should be. It is easy for her, she doesn't have to think too hard to be that person, but is it really her, is her heart and soul behind the narrative? She hears her own words coming out of her mouth and for a few brief moments is impressed with herself.

"Hello Earl, my name is Madeleine Richards, I am one of the Marketing Managers here in C&B. We will be pitching to Mr. Ito and the Board of Directors for the new Bittern Quays development, possibly around September time. We are currently working on the themes and key messages we want to deliver, to underpin the new area of London. I'm sure you know a new large development such as Bittern Quays can be hugely influential to the demographics, the growth and the future of so many people and businesses, we want to get the culture right. We want to tap into the Board's own passions and vision and bring it to life."

Roseanne was not happy now sitting on the edge of the action, she jumped in, interrupting Madeleine's flow, "So you see, it's vital we understand more about what Mr. Ito is looking for in his companies. We have only been given the simplest of briefs, we know the Quay will be a hub for digital advancements, it will showcase the best of British in the digital world but we want to inject more innovation and need your insights into where we need to be heading. What can you tell us about the Spa developments, it may lead us in the right direction?"

Earl continued to nod to no-one in particular, removed his glasses once again and pulled the dirty cloth from his trousers once more. He rubbed vigorously, carefully measuring his response. A word popped into Madeleine's head as she looked at him, 'slimy,' yes, that was the perfect word for him, 'slimy,' she realised now he would want something in return for his time and information.

"I can tell you that Mr. Ito is investing a significant amount of money into conservation and global warming companies and charities. He has expressed to his team that all existing business contracts of his must be reviewed and if there are any associated businesses that don't meet his exacting criteria then they are to be phased out. All new conglomerates will only be sealed if all parties sign a commitment to the same levels that Mr. Ito has set out. He is committing to lowering his personal and professional carbon footprint to such a low level he is exceeding all nationalities' targets; he is setting a high bar for sure. He has commissioned a team to look into how this can be achieved in all of his enterprises; my team are charged with his health spas and sporting outlets."

Madeleine was shocked at how Earl was singing like a canary; she had expected to barter for his knowledge.

"Earl, can you tell us the types of changes Mr. Ito is making, what are the risks you are looking at? Madeleine was intrigued, this was visionary and sounded extremely positive, she felt already that she would like Mr. Ito. If Earl is telling the truth, he sounds a man of high principles and values, there are not too many of those in the high business stakes.

"I can Maddie, I can give you an example but not all of the specifics, as I said before. The risks are financial. If he converts to hydro, wind and solar power in every aspect of energy, if he insists on all transportation being electric, if he replaces the carbons to match the losses, if he gains the commitment from every one of his employees to sign up to do the same in their personal life, he risks an outlay that is too high to be able to reap the financial rewards, in the time frames that he has set. It may be that he can only concentrate on one area at a time until it becomes financially viable and then move onto the next change."

Madeleine thought Earl was either incredibly stupid or very smart. He had basically told them everything they needed to know, whilst saying he wasn't. She also noted he had abbreviated her name, no one here ever did that.

"Now add to this," Earl hadn't finished, "His further quest that every member of his staff, around the world, has access to the best wellbeing and positive mental health policies in the world. He wants to proactively ensure his staff have everything they need to promote positivity and he will give everyone the best quality support if anyone needs it, such as a life event, you know, death… or something. He lost his own wife you see, I won't share the details but the effect has been Mr. Ito has looked at himself and the impact he has on the world and his staff and he has pledged to do better."

Dominic had been listening intently. "Why isn't this splashed all over the business news? Surely a shake up like this, where he may just ditch companies and businesses because of their environmental policies, would be common knowledge?"

"Because we are still in the investigation stage, the feasibility stage and Mr. Ito has strict confidentiality rules."

"But you are talking to us and have given us quite an insight, why?" Roseanne spoke up.

"That's easy! I respect Mr. Ito and admire him for his innovation but more than that, when *you* get the contract, you will be paying me for my services." Earl sat back smugly and cleaned his glasses for the third time.

So, there it was, out in the open.

"Nadir, did you know about this?" Dominic launched straight into his colleague.

"No, I didn't, Giorgios just gave me Earl's name and contact details, that's all." Nadir looked ill, he was a company man, always sticking to the rules, he had spent most of his working years with C&B and upholding their values. Earl had played it well, he had already given them information, he didn't ask about the money first as he knew he would have been shown the door. They now possessed a great insight into where one of the main Board of Directors was heading and how could they not use it to their advantage? They were bound to use his information so why shouldn't he gain?

"We could use the information you have given us and not give you a thing!" Roseanne was thinking the situation through.

"This is true," Earl was squeaking like a strangled mouse. "But, there will be a calling off period in-between the winner of the contract being announced and when it is finalised, this will enable me to investigate the risks with Claremont and Butler, as per Mr. Ito's instructions. In that timeframe, I get paid. If I don't then C&B won't come out favourably, you'll lose the contract before you have even started and probably also your jobs!"

The four, looked from one to another. There was silence.

"…a..a..and if we don't win the deal in the first place?" Nadir asked.

"Well then all arrangements are off, however I have looked at your competitors and done a little risk assessment of my own, if you don't win the deal then you have really blown a dead cert and that will only lead you to the redundancy pile too. So either way, you take what I've told you, win the contract and pay me what is due." Earl passed something across the desk to Nadir, stood and waited for a reply.

"Leave us with this, we need to discuss it between us," Nadir was crestfallen. He had thought he had given the team something huge, that he had outshone them all, so that he stood out and would be recognised but all he had done was brought a whole heap of trouble to their door.

As soon as Earl got into the lift, accompanied by a passing colleague who was also going down to the reception area, the rest gathered around Nadir and demanded to look at the figure Earl had already scribbled on the back of a London tour bus leaflet. Anger erupted!

"How the hell are we supposed to come up with a figure like that?" Roseanne was incensed. "We are not winning a prize fund, we aren't going on 'Who Wants to be a Millionaire,' we will just win a good step up our career ladders and lifetime passes to the very health spas that are landing us in this mess!"

Dominic joined in, "This is unacceptable, we can't use anything that he has told us, we can't bring in even the slightest environmental slant or he will say it was due to him, we can't even use what we have prepared so far."

"I don't understand how this has happened," Madeleine was genuinely confused and uncharacteristically angry. "In the last few minutes we have gone from a confident position to now being part of a bribery scam, which will lose us our jobs, potentially owing some slime ball a vast sum of money - from our own pockets - or not using his information and losing our bid and therefore losing our jobs or winning the bid and then C&B lose every link they already have with the companies and we also lose our jobs! We are well and truly stuffed, thank you Nadir! Brilliant job, thank you very much!"

The rest of the group looked at her, she was attacking Nadir, one of the few people she would have considered a friend in the company, her voice was dripping in sarcasm which was not her style at all. She was not happy with the situation and had not been backward in showing it.

"Okay, okay, let's all calm down and take a break to think this through," Dominic's suggestion was for reason and clarity. He stepped in to take control and this time it was welcomed, no one argued that it was probably a good idea to step outside for a while. "Let's meet back here at 2pm, go and grab some lunch and we'll work on this together. Nadir, I'm sure you weren't to know what Earl was going to pull out of the bag, don't worry, we are a team and we are stronger together." This was the side to Dominic that Madeleine admired, he could be so empathetic and caring, a good leader, thinking about his team and getting the best out of people. It was when he takes it too far, making decisions and controlling a situation that she feels disappointed in him. When he takes it upon himself to make an arrangement or set something up and then just announce it and then become hurt if it's not received well. Then you feel guilty because he said he was only thinking of you. It could send her spinning, asking herself if she is a bad person for not welcoming his good intentions. Should she be more grateful and let him take charge? Silently they left the meeting room.

At 2pm sharp, the group returned dejected. Each had sat in their office, checking emails, shuffling papers, and watching everyone as they walked past their glass fronted divisions. Was everyone looking at them as they walked by? Did their colleagues suspect they were about to embark on one of C&B's most notorious bribery deals? Was Janis, Stephan and Lee aware they were in a competition that was now tainted and rigged, as they strolled past clutching iPads, hopeful and eager? John Murray, the Procurement Director, walked by putting his thumb up at Roseanne who weakly smiled back. Jennie, the cleaner, popped in breezily to empty Madeleine's bins, was she aware she was in the presence of a cheat? By the time they all met they felt like condemned criminals, the weight of guilt already eating them alive before anything had actually been done.

"Look, I just want to say I had no idea what this Earl chap was like or what he intended. I've called Giorgios and told him what happened, he is really upset. He had no idea he was being used, to get to us. He feels dreadful, he's asked me to tell you he is sorry." Nadir spoke to his feet, not meeting the distain emitting from the faces before him.

"I'm sorry Nadir," Madeleine felt she needed to clear the air. "I didn't mean to take it out on you, it's just that I have never done anything bad in my life, I have worked for everything I do, not cheated. I don't like that I've been forced into a situation against my will. I feel I am trapped now, I've been put in a very difficult position that I don't want to be in."

"That's fair enough," Nadir conceded.

"Has anyone figured out what we should do now?" Dominic looked hopeful.

"Well, yes, I think I have," Roseanne sat at one end of the room alone, quite separate from the rest of the team, and spoke quietly, not her usual force of arrogant confidence.

The rest looked at her and waited for the full explanation. It came slowly.

"As much as it pains me to say it, we go to Katrina Everett and explain what's happened. She met each of us in turn and knows the background themes we have already started on. She knows we were already working on health and lifestyle. We tell her exactly what's happened and leave it to her to decide what happens next. I am not happy with the suggestion; I'll look a complete and utter fool and she already wants me out. We will all look stupid and incompetent but if we go any further, we will all be accomplices and be in deeper trouble. There is no way I am giving that snake a penny of my money and if it means I ultimately must leave here, then so be it. I have a reputation to consider, and I am not prepared to risk it. This is the right thing to do. We go in together and face whatever the outcome is together."

Madeleine looked at Roseanne and saw her in a completely different light. She had assumed, especially as she has already tried to damage her reputation with the lost files and get rid of her with the fake resignation, that she would willingly see Madeleine and the others go down in a heap of destruction and that she would find a way to separate herself from them, coming out clean and unscathed. But this suggestion of her's seemed fair, that she was putting herself in with the group and finding a solution that they would stand by together. Madeleine was surprised and strangely full of admiration. She should despise the woman, who sat alone and unexpectedly vulnerable, at the opposite end of the table yet she felt an unexpected warmth, that she couldn't explain.

Nadir spoke first.

"Would you really do that? You could have just gone to Katrina and laid the blame on me; told her I was trying to get you all involved in bribery and corrupting the competition. Would you really do that for me?" He looked tearful.

Madeleine reached across and clutched his hand. "Nadir, it could have been any one of us who invited that creep here today. It just happened to be you. You have always been a good and honest person; you have a solid reputation here and no-one would doubt you had any bad intentions in all of this."

Nadir stared at Madeleine. Just stared. She could see he had a million thoughts hurtling past the back of his eyes, he clutched her hand back.

"Madeleine, Madeleine, you don't understand, please forgive me."

She quietened him with a shush and patted his hand back. She had been a little harsh to him earlier, but she didn't need his pleading eyes and tears, that was a little over the top and she felt uncomfortable, embarrassed even. She wanted to move this meeting on quickly and stood up to change the mood in the room.

"I agree with you Roseanne, I think it's the only solution, it's the right one and it may not end up very well for us, but every other option will end up far worse."

"Agreed too," Dominic stood up in a gesture of solidarity. "I'll send Katrina an email asking to meet with us and sign it on all of our behalf's."

Roseanne nodded quietly and Nadir stayed sat, looking down at his knees in silent agreement. The meeting was over.

"So, your boyfriend seems, er, nice." Filo was helping Maddie weed the never-ending green army that marched each night, wrapping themselves around every stalk, strangling the life from all in its path, muscling in on every root, drowning every inch of space to suck up the air and block the sun. Filo was speaking into her armpit as she bent down in front of Maddie, pulling and filling a large, green trugg full of sticky weed, bind weed, thistles and dandelions.

"I'm not sure I'd call him my boyfriend," Maddie confessed. "He is more of a date that I see at work, I don't really know what we are, to be honest."

Filo stood and gave Maddie a curious look, squinting her eyes and furrowing her brow in a silent question mark.

"What does he do?" Filo was keen to find out more about the person Maddie chose to be with but was also careful not to make any judgements out loud. She had become very fond of Maddie, she observed how her friend had taken on her grandfather's plot with an honesty and openness, she wasn't confident, she had vulnerabilities, but so far had proved to be a tough young lady who took advice well and appreciated the help but also got stuck in. She was a hard worker and Filo saw a lot of her grandfather in her, he had also worked hard. One of his sayings was, 'If a job's worth doing, it's worth doing well.' Maddie seemed to live by this rule and Filo felt she deserved the best in every part of her life. Filo had seen the cards, she had interpreted the tarot on Maddie's behalf and wanted to warn her, to guide her, but they didn't have that relationship yet. Filo didn't want to rock the boat on their early bond. She remembered Maddie's reaction to the tarot and wasn't keen to open the awkwardness again. So, she let Maddie just talk.

"He has the same job as me, we work together, we have our own clients and wouldn't normally work so closely but we're in a competition, in a team, so are spending more time together than we would normally. I'm just going with the flow, I guess."

"He's certainly a good-looking man, quite a catch!" Filo tested the water.

"Yes, he is smart, successful, very popular too. He knows what he wants from life and works hard to get it."

"Does that include you?" Filo immediately thought she had overstepped the mark.

"What do you mean?" Maddie looked up.

"Oh, I just mean does he work hard at getting you, you are a real catch too Maddie, someone would be very lucky to have you."

"He is very …." Maddie struggled for the word that put Dominic in the right light. "Insistent! He has set up some lovely dates and is very thoughtful."

Maddie thought she heard Filo give a small sigh or was it a 'hhhmmmm' noise but ignored it. She hadn't wanted Dominic to enter this part of her world just yet and she didn't really want to discuss him with Filo. He had embarrassed her in front of Filo and the others, he hadn't appreciated why she was upset, despite her trying to explain over dinner. She had agreed to go for a meal although the long day after the vandalism had exhausted her. She had tried to explain that they were her friends. He dismissed them, dismissed the importance of being there with them and he felt she was ungrateful for his turning up, out of the blue. He told her he had gone out of his way to check that she was alright, others would have seen what a kind gesture it was, romantic even. It had been a terse meal; she should have stuck to her original refusal to go. They had parted with the briefest kiss and he told her she was just tired and she'd feel better in the morning.

Maddie changed the subject.

"Oh, I forgot, I met Esther the other day in the supermarket and she had a great idea about holding a plant sale mini-event, to raise funds for the charity bash. I think it's a really good idea. We'll need a bit of money for the local newspaper adverts, we need to buy refreshments and ingredients for cakes and bunting and possibly a hundred other things. Has she told you about it?"

Filo nodded, "Yes, she's going to bring it up at the meeting this week, I can't see it being a problem, we all have plants to spare which we can sell. We need to do it quickly whilst we have young plants that people can buy and grow on."

Maddie had bumped into Esther in the bakery aisle in the local supermarket. She had spotted her straight away, the familiar khaki work trousers and a chequered flannelette shirt topped with a man's sports cap. Maddie realised she had never seen Esther in anything other than work clothes. She pondered if she owned anything else, anything a little more flattering. Esther couldn't be much older than her own mother, in fact someone had mentioned she had Tom when she was quite young, so she would be younger than Fiona. She didn't look it though, her strong, brown arms held up rolled sleeves, she never wore make up and her hair was kept practically short. Her footwear was always wellington boots or army type boots which Maddie was sure had steel toe caps inside. She spoke with an assertive tone, clipped, sergeant major style, she was both warm and friendly and a little over-bearing and scary.

"Maddie," she had called her over loudly despite only being a few feet away. "Just the girl, you can be my guinea pig ahead of the next meeting. If I were to suggest to you that we hold a plant sale, what would you say? Is it too much? Does everyone have too much to do? It will be for the Harvest event funds; we need more coffers in the pot to run the event, but I don't want to over-burden everyone. What do you think?"

Maddie had been flattered that she was chosen to run this through, however she suspected it was just because she happened to bump into her and not someone else in the shop.

"I think it's a great idea. I'm sure everyone would be happy to do it. It won't need much preparation, just advertising which I can do and a few tables to set plants out. We could charge a small fee for seed swaps too."

"Aha, you see, that why I asked you, you're the 'ideas' girl! The plant swap is a very good idea too, I like it, I like it. Thank you, Maddie," and with that Esther had trotted off down to the end of the aisle to pick up a French baguette with salt and pepper encrusted on the top.

Just two weeks later, Maddie stood behind a meagre looking trestle table of items she had donated to the sale. She hadn't sown too many seeds, on the advice of Norris, Alice and

Ranweer. They had been right. She had wanted to sow every variety of tomato, at least three of four of each. But now she was seeing her five successful tomato plants filling up the greenhouse, she was already concerned she soon wouldn't be able to get in to water the furthest ones. Norris had taught her how to create cordons, snipping off their bottom shoots to grow the tomatoes tall and strong. She already had to tie them up with string, dangling from a pole across the roof, holding them up steady as they still had weeks of growing time to get through yet. She didn't have anywhere to plant the rest of her tomatoes, so the remaining ones now sat on the tabletop, alongside a few courgette plants, a few bundles of rocket that she had already grown and had bagged up, she had some strange named squashes that she had sown from packets found in grandfather's caravan; Uchiki Kuri, Harlequin and Spaghetti and that was about all she had to offer. She had baked some carrots, not real carrots, but fun little finger cakes using flexible silicone moulds in the shape of fruits and vegetables. She had iced the tops green and the roots orange and painted a smiling face on each. They had nearly all been sold, a few were left remaining on a plate, children had begged their parents to buy one, so she already knew what else she was going to do for the main Harvest event in October. She'd bake a whole greengrocer's store; she knew already it will be popular.

"Hi, are these going begging?" Tom ambled over to her stall.

"Not begging, no, but you can buy them for five pounds for the lot." Maddie chanced a high price.

"Blimey, you're harsh!" he laughed and took out a folding wallet from the back pocket of his jeans, he handed her a ten-pound note. "Keep the change."

"But that's far too much, they really are only sponge cakes," she protested.

"I am willing to gamble you have good baking skills, I saw that young lad come back and buy a second one, so my market research tells me these are good!" when Tom laughed his eyes came alive, they shone and creased around the edges. His cheek skin bulged into two round dumplings, his chin a hint of a dimple. He was wearing another rock band T-shirt, this time a low-profile chopper motorbike was heading out of his chest, sat astride it, a skeleton wearing a top hat, laughing with his head back. It reminded her of something, where had she seen that skeleton before? She couldn't quite place it.

"So, you know about market research?" she tested, knowing she could outsmart him on that subject.

Her summer cotton dress had been the perfect choice for the warm weather. Its scooped neck was elasticated so she could pull it down on her shoulders to avoid strange suntan marks. It was lime and white chequered gingham, pulled in at the waist with a thin white belt and flowing loosely to the knee. She looked like a dancer in a country and western musical. Her flat white sandals meant she had to look up to talk to him, she wasn't short by any means, but he stood high above her, even across the tabletop.

"I know enough, I've had to do my fair share," he didn't elaborate willingly.

"What is you that you do, Tom?" she realised he may have a job, she had only really thought of him being at the allotments every day.

"I'm a garden designer," he wasn't giving much away and she felt like she was grilling him a little.

"What type of gardens? Domestic ones? Large ones?"

"All sorts really, I went to horticultural college and took landscape design qualifications too. So, if you and your boyfriend ever need your garden revamping give me a call," he eyed her carefully, the smile faded slightly.

"Oh he's not….. we don't live together. I live at my parents. I know that sounds pathetic, it's a financial arrangement really, as soon as I have a deposit, I'll be getting a place of my own. I think it will have to be a flat though and I could probably manage to design my own balcony by then." It was Maddie's turn to laugh out loud at her own joke. Tom saw her wide, open smile with perfect, natural teeth. Her emerald eyes had a tiny black line around the outside of each iris, making them striking, like a High-Definition picture. Her dark hair was loose, he usually saw it scrunched up into a ponytail or bun for ease when digging or weeding in the wind, but today it shone down in soft waves below her shoulders and down her back. She wore small, simple silver hoops in her ears and a thin silver chain and locket, in the shape of a leaf.

Tom smiled when he heard her living arrangements.

"Well, if you ever need balcony advice then you know where to come. That's a pretty locket by the way."

Maddie's hand shot protectively to her neck, "It was a present, from my grandfather, I don't have any pictures inside, I don't have anything small enough. It was a birthday present when I was very small. I've had to buy a longer chain as the original was for a small child, of course. But I've kept that one safe."

"Maybe you can give it to your own daughter one day?" Maddie was sure she saw Tom blushing slightly as he spoke, or maybe it was the early summer heat. They looked at each other, the gentle conversation had seemed to run its course.

"I hope you enjoy your ten-pound carrots," Maddie concluded.

Tom nodded and grinned, clutching the paper bag that Maddie had given him with his cakes inside. As he walked away, Maddie realised she was admiring his swagger for just a little too long, she remembered Alice had Dominic and quickly turned away. She hadn't been the only one watching Tom, Filo had been glancing up at their exchange, from her stall on the other side of the car park, with amusement and curiosity. She watched as

Maddie gazed at him and she spotted him turning back to look at Maddie from a safe distance behind his mother's car.

The plant sale had been a mild success, they had sold out their stock and had made about £150 but Maddie knew that with the right sort of planning, they could have made a lot more. It had all been rather rushed, so it was no one's fault. Everyone else was thoroughly pleased with the profit but Maddie's head for business knew what they could achieve if they planned for it well.

During the sale, she had spoken to a young family, keen to start gardening but wanting to start small, just one tomato plant and one runner bean planted in a grow bag on a balcony. And the family who have moved into a new home with a huge garden who want to grow their own vegetables and teach their children about healthy eating. There was also the barrister, a lovely man about Maddie's age, with his husband, who want to turn their small yard into an edible kitchen garden. Maddie's ideas were racing in her head with how they could have supported these people, given advice and supplied exactly what they needed, a bespoke service that large garden centre staff can't always take the time to do. She could see potential and possibilities but for now they were all happy they had some funds to put towards the Harvest Charity Event. For now, she had to be content with getting on with designing an advertising campaign to post in the local newspapers and on social media.

Madeleine's office was as usual, calm and tidy. Company rules, no clutter. Her outfit was coordinating the furniture, a black pencil skirt with a caramel silk blouse tucked lightly into the waistband. Her stilettos matched the shirt and she looked every inch a business executive. She wore her work outfits like a mantle, cloaking her original self with a costume to disguise and fool the unsuspecting audience. As she stepped into the foyer every morning, she tilted her chin higher, pushed her shoulders back further and placed one foot ever so carefully in front of the other, in a straight line, as if on a New York cat walk. Her stance would take her through the main entrance, across the marbled floor, greeting the security person on duty and into the lift. In the lift she would check out her appearance for any commuting damage and step out into her corridor with a greeting smile ready set on her face. Once in her goldfish bowl office, she couldn't allow herself to slump, she remained upright in her office chair with the constant knowledge that she was on show, expected to be actively engaged and remain animated, dynamic and interesting at all times. It exhausted her. She could do her job easily; she knew it inside and out. She had a set of current clients who she was working with on their advertising campaigns, they were happy with the results, she never received complaints. It was the theatre that she felt a fraud within, the clothes, the attitude, the persona that everyone was expected to mould to. When she first started, just like all new employees, the staff handbook stuffed full of expectations, the induction days, the paper weight engraved with company values were all exciting, she embraced them, but gradually over time they stunted her, confined her into a model which no longer seemed to be her at all. She didn't recognise herself, but it had been so long happening that she couldn't remember what the previous version of Madeleine was like.

Seeing the memory boxes in the caravan had reminded her that she was creative, wasn't that an attribute C&B praised her for in her interview? When was she last really able to show her creativity? She had thought as a Market Manager she could fly with her ideas, push the limits, and innovate. But the reality was the opposite. She created an idea and watched it being torn apart by each department who needed their input, changed and altered to fit policies until there was very little that she could identify as her own any more. The final product was always a success, but was she proud of it? Did she really own it? Madeleine sat looking around her office and not for the first time asked herself what she was doing there.

The phone made her jump.

"Hello, Madeleine speaking," even her work voice didn't sound like her.

On the end of the phone, Gregory Alford asked if she was available.

The Human Resources offices clearly came under a totally different policy model. Black lever arch files flopped over on shelves, piles of photocopying awaiting sorting were stacked high on the floor. Cardboard wallets that held paper notes on all staff were strewn across the desks. What happened to the electronic only guidance everyone was issued? The waste bins, designed for recycling only, had apple cores and drink cartons thrown haphazardly in together with discarded coffee cups, some still with half their contents spilling out. She chose to ignore her irritation; she was more intrigued with what Gregory had found out.

"Please, come in, come in," the Director called Madeleine in from his desk, wiping his bacon sandwich from his lips and stuffing the wrappings into his drawer as if to hide the evidence. "Thank you for being so prompt, I have quite a lot to share with you."

"Anything you can tell me will be welcomed, it's been playing on my mind a great deal, especially why Roseanne has done this and what she hoped to gain. I've not been able to have a proper conversation with her whilst I've waited for you to call me."

"I need to stop you there," Gregory held his hand up like a policeman on traffic patrol. "The first thing to tell you is it was not Roseanne."

Madeleine lent forward, as if to focus Gregory clearer in her vision. "I don't understand, if it wasn't her then who did these things to me?"

"We have been through the CCTV for both incidences. We watched all activity across the three days when the files were deleted and we could clearly make out someone coming into your office, sitting down and doing something on the computer. We checked against the times that the keyboard strikes were recorded and they matched. We did the same for the day and time that the email was sent, with your letter of resignation, oddly there was no one coming into your office at that time. There was also no record of your keyboard being used for the email, however, it was definitely sent from your email address."

"So, who was the first person?" Madeleine was getting impatient now.

"I'm really very sorry to tell you, both incidences were done by Nadir."

"What? Nadir? But he and I are friends, well not friends but as friendly as anyone is working here. Why on earth would he do that? I thought it must be Roseanne, she was the only one who doesn't like me, or so I thought. Oh my god, Nadir? And I've sat with him, talked to him since then. Yes, I had a sharp word with him recently but that was after the files and the email. Before that, we've never had a cross word." Madeleine felt as though she had a fist pushed into her ribs, it was thrusting her lungs up, squeezing the air from them, making it difficult to breathe. It had never occurred to her that Nadir would be behind such horrible activities, she thought they were allies, the thought of spending time with him the past few weeks and talking to him, and all the time he knew what he had done, made her feel physically sick.

Gregory continued, "He was able to hack into your email account to send the resignation email. We traced the origin of the email to an I.P. address, it was his own computer in his office. If he had done it from home, we would have struggled to get the evidence but we matched the time the email was sent with his own keyboard strokes, once we had seen him sitting at his own desk at that time we knew the email was him too. He confessed when we showed him the evidence. There was little else he could do. It's conclusive."

"I am honestly shocked; did he say why he did it?"

"No, he would not discuss it at all. He said he did it and said he had his reasons but has asked to talk to you. Now, I understand that you might not want to talk to him, that's perfectly understandable, but he is refusing to give details to anyone other than you. You can have a third person sit in the room with you, if you feel uncomfortable in any way."

Madeleine didn't know what to think or do. She sat quietly, Gregory waited patiently, whilst she processed what she had been told. Why would Nadir deliberately try and sabotage the team's work by deleting files and jeopardising his own chances of winning the competition? It didn't make sense. Why did he want to make her look incompetent? And the resignation? Did he hate her so much he wanted to get rid of her? She knew she had no choice, if he would only talk to her then she had to meet him. The thought of that made her feel ill, to face someone who had plotted against you and gone to such lengths to hurt you, she didn't want to be in the same room or look at him but how else will she ever know the truth? It would haunt her forever if she didn't find out the truth.

"I will meet him. I need to see him alone so that he can be honest with me. Can it be in one of these offices though please, so I can call someone if I need any help?"

She knew what she had to do.

"Of course, you will be visible and we will keep an eye on you, I don't think for one moment he is malicious in a violent way, we would never put you in that situation, he just wants to explain to you why he did it. He has been suspended, pending a disciplinary process, so we will need to invite him in. When would you like to meet him?"

"I would like to do it today please because if I have to wait another day, I'll lose my nerve. I just need to find out what's been going on and the sooner I can do that the sooner I can move on, hopefully."

Gregory agreed to try and set the meeting up for later that afternoon. He was also intrigued why someone would do these things to their colleague. Madeleine had always had a good reputation; he had never heard negative comments about her from other managers or staff. She held an impeccable record, always hit her targets each year, had positive appraisals and was destined to move upwards one day with promotion. Yes, he was definitely keen to find out what drove Nadir, an equally well respected and hardworking man to do such a thing. Nadir has probably killed off any chance of staying with the company and to receive a good reference. He would now just get the bland version, with simple dates of employment and very little else, that any new firm would know was because of a disciplinary issue arising. The sooner they could meet, Gregory's own questions would be answered. He had been an HR adviser, then manager and now Director of the whole section for over twenty years and had never come across anything as malicious as this between staff. He had to find out what had driven Nadir, for his own development of understanding what make people tick.

The day dragged. Madeleine couldn't concentrate on anything else. She didn't have any face-to-face meetings so had to try and look busy in her office for several hours. Dominic was locked away with a new company he was supporting, outlining ideas and establishing what his client's needs were. She would never go to Roseanne to talk to, she didn't talk to her about anything other than business and she felt dreadful that she had accused her of something she hadn't done. She should have listened to her father and kept her suspicions to herself. Even though Roseanne probably didn't know anything about the events and that she had been in the frame, Madeleine knew, and she felt that just by being near Roseanne it would somehow creep out of her pores and reveal itself to her. No, she would continue to avoid her for the time being. That only left Nadir, it would have been Nadir that she talked to about any problems or issues. He was her confidante. That's what made this all so strange.

An age later, Gregory called down to Madeleine and told her Nadir was waiting in one of the small rooms on his floor. He said his secretary was in direct eye line of the room and that she knew to stay there during the meeting and then escort Nadir off the premises when it was concluded. Madeleine knew in her heart that she had to go through with it but would have done anything at that point to turn the other way and just go home, forget it happened and hope it all went away.

Nadir glanced up from the glass office as the lift opened and Madeleine stepped out. He watched her walk towards his door and open it. Only when she entered did he look down. Madeleine sat opposite him and put her hands in her lap and waited.

Nothing was said.

She felt compelled to start. "Why did you do it? Why do you hate me so much?"

Nadir looked up at her slowly, his usual assuredness gone from his face. His eyes no longer bright but clouded and dull.

"You have it all. You have it all, yet I have nothing, and I work so hard, so much harder than you. How is that possibly fair?"

Madeleine had expected an explanation but one that made sense. One that described a time that she had done something wrong, a concrete explanation, but this was so open ended she didn't know what he meant.

Without realising, she shrugged, "Ugh, what are you on about?"

"Oh, so you think this is nothing. Trivial?" Nadir snapped out of his reverent demeanour and went straight into the defensive. "You let me do all of the work on the Tradestorm account and you sat and took all of the glory, the reward and not once did you think to mention all of the work I had put into building the package for you, and getting you the deal. You stood up at the End of Year Awards ceremony and bare faced received the Highest Achievement Award, when most of the donkey work was sat next to you, on the same table and you never said a word, nothing. So, who gets the glowing reports on their record then? Not me! And then what about the time you needed help building media attention for Givency's Shoes, who was it who sat up most of the night creating a media noise? Who sent them to the top of every search engine and probably made them extremely rich? Me, that's who, me and when did you ever stop and think how I might feel?" Nadir was shaking and despite himself tears filled his eyes.

Madeleine knew that she had taken advantage of his helpful nature, but she had no idea that he had felt so deeply wronged in any way.

"Nadir, I am so sorry, I had no idea, I truly didn't. I always came to you for help because you're so good at your job."

"Don't flatter me now!" he spat.

"I'm not, I'm telling you the truth, you are good at what you do, and you always seem so willing to help me, I thought we all worked together for the same company, I didn't realise I hadn't given you the full credit for the work you do."

"We do work for the same company, but you know as well as I do that we all have commissions, we all have clients and targets and you found a way to use me and be the only one with the rewards."

"I didn't do that on purpose! I can see now how you feel, and I do understand but why didn't you speak up before? I didn't do anything intentionally. Each time I came to you, you seemed happy to help. I didn't think there was a problem. If you'd told me I would have understood. What I don't understand though is why did you do such terrible things to me? It's been horrible, I've felt so targeted, why do it Nadir, why?"

"Because I could! I have the technical skills far beyond what anyone here can imagine. I sit every day getting on with my job, good ol' Nadir, reliable ol' Nadir, everyone takes a piece of me, I won't say anything or rock the company boat but I deserve to be noticed, I can do far more than any of you could possibly imagine but I don't get the chance or the glory." Nadir was crying openly; Madeleine had no idea how things had got to this stage without her having any clue.

"Nadir, I am honestly and truly sorry for any part I have played in making you feel like this. I wish you had spoken to me. I thought we were friends. I would never hurt a friend intentionally. I'm hurt too, that you plotted against me, but I can see how deeply this has hurt you and I feel awful that I made you feel that way. What can I do to make amends?" Madeleine spoke gently and quietly. Nadir's nose was running and she had never seen him any less than perfectly presented, she didn't like seeing him so vulnerable.

"Nothing! I've well and truly stuffed everything up now. I'll lose my job and my reputation. I'll never work anywhere like this again. I hope you're happy now."

Madeleine felt that was very unfair. She hadn't intentionally done anything to him, she would have listened if he had talked. He decided to plot against her, that was his doing, not hers'. She couldn't be held responsible for him losing his job. That was his fault. What a mess, what an awful mess.

Gregory tapped on the glass and came in. His secretary had called him and said Nadir was very upset and maybe the meeting should be ended. He dismissed Madeleine gently and said he would take it from here. At the door she turned.

"I don't hate you for this Nadir, and I will be telling Gregory I don't think you should lose your job. I just wish people here were able to talk more openly and honestly, this environment doesn't lend itself to people letting their guard down. We all have the sense of having to be the very best at all times, none of us feel we can show our vulnerabilities, our weaknesses. But saying we are struggling or not happy isn't a weakness, we should all learn to speak up more. You have now, but I just wish you had done it in a different way."

Nadir was a victim here not the villain. Madeleine saw him sob because of a deep-felt issue that he didn't feel he could be honest about. That wasn't right, it was unfair on him. She didn't blame him. She blamed the culture around her. For all the inclusivity policies, for all the tightly bound visions and ethos on how everyone should act, be and think, it didn't allow for error or simply getting something wrong once in a while. The pressure to be perfect was just too high.

As Madeleine was putting her coat on ready to leave her desk phone rang.

"I'm glad I caught you before you go Madeleine," Gregory sounded rushed. "I just wanted you to know that I have requested Nadir is given some garden leave to step back and recuperate and seek help. He is having a total melt down and it's not right that we wade in at this point. I want to give him time to recover and then we'll talk to him. I just wanted you to know. Also, I did take onboard your points at the end. I'll need to write a report and it would be extremely helpful if you could give me your insights, that I can take forward to the Board. I'll contact you in a few days for feedback."

"Yes, of course, thank you Gregory, thank you for your help. I hope Nadir will be okay, I feel so responsible."

"Don't be! Nadir told me of other factors things that are happening in his personal life and I think that all contributed to his meltdown. It wasn't just you at all, you were just the vent and the way to be angry at someone. Don't take it as personally as it all seems, honestly, he has an awful lot on his plate."

Madeleine knew better than to ask for details. What Nadir had told Gregory was obviously personal and therefore confidential. It did help though, to know it wasn't all about her, that he was troubled in other ways too. It helped to ease her mind a little as she picked up her bag and left, feeling utterly drained.

The house was empty. Madeleine peered in the fridge and found an opened bottle of wine and poured herself the remains. It was gloriously cold on her lips as the late June evening was humid and heavy. Her body seemed limp and sluggish, she struggled to pull herself onto one of the kitchen stools and she sat staring at her glass to help the day melt away. She knew the conservatory would be a hot house so was happy cool off, kick off her shoes and let her throbbing ankles start to deflate on the coolness of the slate tiled floor.

"Penny for them? Mind you, what does a penny get you these days? A tenner for them instead please!"

James had come home without Madeleine hearing the door. He was always cheerful, she couldn't remember a time when he ever got uptight or cross, he was a perpetual grin on legs and as frustrating as he could be, she couldn't help but love him and enjoy his company. She welcomed his upbeat intrusion into her thoughts.

"Hi there, where have you been?"

"Just out and about, you know," his flippant response was the usual one, you never got too much information from him. He opened the fridge, as he did every time he came into the kitchen and stared in. It was a habit, years of being forever hungry, a growing lad, inspecting the goodies and deciding what was the quickest and easiest thing to eat; a chicken leg, half a pork pie, a chunk of cheese, milk drunk straight from the plastic bottle, anything to have a quick fix in-between meals.

"International man of mystery," she teased.

"What about you? How was your day?" He didn't imagine at that point the oncoming outpouring of events that Madeleine spewed. She had sat silently all day awaiting the meeting with Nadir, she had travelled home on the train in equal solitude, she needed to offload and James was the first person in line. She described her weeks of worry about who was stabbing her in the back, her shock at Nadir's confession, the frustration she felt at work, the way she felt day after day, going through the motions of getting her job done but feeling nothing, feeling empty inside. She didn't talk about Dominic, this had nothing to do with any relationship they might or might not have. This was about her, her career, her future and what she wanted at this point for the rest of her life. She had watched a well-respected man today crumble and fall apart. It wasn't right, something was wrong and although she did accept she hadn't treated Nadir as well as she should, there was a bigger picture, it had made her look at herself and made her openly question for the first time what she really wanted to do. She had often queried to herself how on earth she got to where she was, but today it stepped up a whole new level. Today, she asked herself the actual question, "Is this what I want for the rest of my life?"

Chapter 7 - JULY

The two-week stretch of wet and warm weather had catapulted the allotments into Jurassic sized proportions. Courgettes crawled and slivered across the ground with umbrella sized leaves like webbed hands splayed all over the paths. Broad bean plants bent over with their weighted bounty, garlics and onions with purple flowered tops desperate to be pulled, some already sticking up out of the ground in anticipation. Wooden archways with groaning string, threatening to snap under the weight of tomatoes, many still green but many turning black, purple and red of every variety, shape and size. Greenhouses stuffed with foliage pushed up against the glass, packed in, pressing its cheek tightly against the panes. The grass around the edges of paths and caravans waved in the welcoming breeze, nettles that had been trimmed and pulled daily were piled high, or left in old baths soaking in water, stinking and ready to use as plant food, so full of nutrients that no one minded the smell. Potatoes that had been earthed up into little mounds were now left to allow its foliage to emerge into the light and whither, yellow, ready for digging up its golden nuggets. The constant changes amazed Maddie, the speed in which she could see results was satisfying and spurred her on. Some things had taken a long time to fatten, the chilies she had sown at the start of the year were now oozing fruit from the dried flower pods, like squeezed toothpaste pushing out a little each day. She was envious of the garlic that others were pulling and laying by the side of their plots, she had been too late to plant any, but this year would be different. She had planted on the shortest day to harvest on the longest. It was one of Norris' sayings. He had taught her so much, as had the others.

Norris was a quiet plodder of a gardener. Every day he slipped in unobserved and pottered on his patch. He didn't force his wisdom onto Maddie, but drip fed her little treasures of knowledge through his stories and recollections; she could spend hours with him in easy fellowship. Alice had been a good friend, she brought Maddie the modern shortcuts, the ethical reasoning behind decisions that she made, environmental understanding and an awareness of issues that Maddie hadn't considered before such as using plants to create an eco-system, rather than human interference. Some plants help deter weeds, or attract certain wildlife, her knowledge was vast and Maddie felt she learnt something every time they met. Ranveer was the scientist and inventor. He used recycled household items all over his plot; his children made birds scarers from old CDs and used foil. He had engineered an irrigation system from old pipes, from the community recycling centre, by boring holes through them and laying them in open channels. Master tubes led from huge water bins filled by the shed and caravan guttering. These dripped and flowed out from the bins to form a network of dikes and junctions which in turn watered the patchwork of raised beds. It was rudimental and needed a lot of developing but the principles were ingenious. Tom remained an enigma. He kept himself to himself, occasionally seen chatting to Alice on her plot and often seen helping Norris mend or build something. But the friendly flirting after the vandalism and at the Plant Sale had stopped, which Maddie thought was right, now she knew he and Alice were an item. She liked Alice very much and was not prepared to create any rifts, no matter how innocent.

Maddie started the day's visit as she always did, with a walk around the allotments to look at everyone's plots. The day after the vandalism had showed her what real camaraderie could be like, that morning had been so awful, yet she had loved working with everyone, pulling together as a team and immersing herself into shared activities, whilst chatting and getting to know each other. She made a pact with herself that day to push herself more and take the time to talk to everyone. Nadir's breakdown had made her evaluate her relationships. He hadn't been able to talk to her, to share his frustrations about her or to confide about his troubles at home. She questioned whether she had become too remote, too distant from others. She had accepted the one-dimensional relationships with her work colleagues too easily. She had been so frustrated with her colleague's inability to show real interest in each other, yet she had become the same. She knew in her heart that wasn't her at all, she loves people, she loves to laugh and have fun, yet where had that gone from her life? She realised that she had lost the art of gentle pleasantries and banter. She was always so professional at work that she found it difficult changing that level of communication even when she was home.

Her parents were good people but not known for their silliness and ability to goof around. They were great hosts and gave parties that everyone enjoyed but they were always too aware of what impression they were giving, what others thought of them and their appearances. It stifled them and in between the hosting and bon viveur, their day-to-day relationships with their children and family was polite and respectful but rarely filled with honest or in depth emotionally charged discussions. She couldn't remember the last time they played around, acted daft, teased each other, or simply enjoyed being together for enjoyment's sake.

Maddie decided to do better. Her new friendships at the allotments filled her with warmth and a sense of belonging, even as new as they were, she knew theirs was the type of relationships she craved. She felt, for the first time in such a long time, that she could truly be herself there. She didn't need to have a persona, she didn't need to be aware of what she was saying, selecting her phrases so carefully to avoid tripping over some politically taboo topic or letting her guard down and not be seen as a serious professional. She was finding that it was a relief to admit she didn't know so many things. The freedom of saying out loud, 'I'm not sure, can you help me?' was almost exhilarating to Maddie. For so long she hasn't been able to be anything less than at the top of her game at work. And at home, the level of expectation to always be a successful adult was unspoken but tangible in its silence.

Maddie stopped off at Alice's plot.

"Hey there, how's it going? I can't believe your sweetcorn; how tall they are already! Mine aren't anywhere near that size yet."

Alice beamed. Her sweetcorn had been ripped out on that awful day but were a replanting success. Esther had plunged the roots into water for a good soak and replanted them with fresh soil and a good nettle feed and they were magnificent already.

"Hi Maddie, you're looking lovely today, is that a new hat?"

Maddie had learnt the value of wearing a good hat and sunglasses on the allotment. The first few weeks she found her eyes were stinging at the end of the day from straining against the sun. She chose a wide brimmed hat to cover her neck whilst bending down weeding and planting, she found she could stay outside for far longer without the heat beating her down. She had started to wear a soft, white cotton over-shirt too, covering her bare arms and shoulders. Esther had helped treat her insect bites with medicated cream and advised she cover up at this time of year. Maddie took the advice on board after a night awake clawing at her own inflamed skin.

"Thanks Alice, yes, it's only a cheap one from the market but it fits just right. I'd never have thought I'd be wearing this outfit a few months ago, how times have changed. How's Tom, I haven't seen him for a while?"

Alice looked surprised, "I'm not really sure, I haven't seen him much myself. He came round earlier this week to fix my kitchen sink for me, he's such a sweetie, he'd only take dinner as payment, so he had to pretend to enjoy my tofu skewers."

Maddie would have thought he would do it for free anyway but knew better than to question other people's relationships. She could picture him in Alice's garden, with a beer and a barbecue, just perfect this time of year.

"I'm going to try and tackle the weeds in my salad plots today," Maddie explained. "I really didn't know that gardening was ten per cent sowing, ten per cent harvesting and all the rest weeding!"

"A common misconception, yes. Next year I'll help you with the benefits of combination planting too, have you seen the glorious nasturtiums that are out on everyone's plots? They seem to be huge this year, absolutely stunning!" Alice always threw in an extra layer of support, always finding a way to up level Maddie's skills and knowledge.

"I've seen them, my area looks so boring compared to everyone else's, I will definitely add flowers next year. The dahlias everywhere are magnificent, I would love some to cut and take home."

"Don't beat yourself up. You've achieved so much. Look back at your photos and you'll see the difference you've made already!" Alice grinned, her flowing cheesecloth smock dress and steel toe capped boots looked like she was in a festival field. She had unplaited her blond dreadlocks and her hair hung on each side of her shoulders in two loose pigtails, tied with a ribbon on each end. It looked lovely and made her look like a young girl. Maddie could easily see why Tom would like Alice, she was like an urban doll, streetwise yet innocent, smart yet caring. She exuded independence but had a warmth that was beguiling. Maddie liked Alice and hoped they could be friends for a long time, like Filo and Esther.

"Pop by on your way out later and cut some from here, you are more than welcome to some of mine to take home." Alice was always so generous, Maddie wanted to find a way to thank her, she'll give it some thought.

Maddie followed the path up and away from Alice's towards the top end of the allotments, to where Norris had, not one, but two full sized plots. One of them was to solely grow flowers to use around the town and villages. Norris's wife was part of a volunteer group called the Surrey Urban Gardeners, or S.U.G.S. They were often seen planting up underneath road signs, benches and little corners of common land that was otherwise neglected. They asked nothing for it except donations for seeds and canes. Norris grew the flowers and shrubs for the ground features and also for window boxes and baskets for small businesses who paid a small fee for the ladies' work.

His other plot was the epitome of excellence. His lifetime of trial and error gardening had provided him with a wealth of knowledge and his plot gave him an annual yield that fed not only himself and his wife but also vegetable gift boxes to their children and neighbours and frequent donations to food banks in the area too. His was the allotment plot that everyone aspired to. Tom's was pretty close, as was Esther's but you could see Norris was the one who would lift the Gold cup to everyone else's Silver.

Norris was nowhere to be seen so Maddie wandered around the top end of the path and back down the other side towards her own plot.

"Hi," she saw Tom kneeling on a plank of scaffolding board lying across an empty bed.

He stood up and removed his gardening gloves and wandered towards the edge where Maddie stood.

"Hi yourself," he remained on his side of some invisible barrier.

"How's it all going?" Maddie realised she didn't have anything specific to say, to warrant his coming over.

"Fine, fine, I'm just sowing some leeks and brassicas to get me through the winter," he offered. "How are you, I've not seen you for a while?"

"I have been here a few times, I've been making the most of the light evenings to come after work, rather than at a weekend." Maddie explained.

"I guess that gives you more time at the weekend to see your boyfriend!" Tom fished.

"Not really, we don't see each other too much," Maddie didn't feel the need to explain to Tom that she didn't know what was happening between her and Dominic. The truth was she hadn't seen much of him lately, she had avoided everyone at work whilst Gregory conducted his investigations and Dominic had been busy anyway. She was enjoying the late evenings in the low sun, she found it quieter in the allotments and peaceful, it helped her to stop the working week become overwhelming.

"Well, I'm glad I've seen you; I've got something here for you," Tom smiled and turned towards his caravan.

"Hey, there you are……" a familiar voice boomed from behind the hedge that divided Maddie and Tom's plots. "I've been here ages waiting for you!"

James' head popped up and over the hedge, grinning.

"Hi James, I didn't think I'd see you here. What brings you to Queens Gardens?" Maddie was surprised but delighted to see her brother. "Tom, this is James, I don't think you know each other."

Tom stopped from heading off and reached over the hedge to shake James' hand warmly.

"Hi James, I can see the family resemblance. Are you as hopeless as Maddie with a spade?" Tom obviously felt comfortable enough to tease Maddie and she found she liked it.

"I don't have a green finger on my body," James was quick to establish, "I'm just here for a free cuppa and a bit of quality sibling time."

Maddie was taken aback; she hadn't heard James speak of 'them' for a very long time. They have been living in the same house but almost as strangers. The longest conversation was the other evening in the kitchen when Maddie told him all about her troubles at work. She felt warm at the sibling reference and suddenly proud he was there, her brother.

"Well, that's really nice. But you'll be hard pushed to get a cuppa out of Maddie, she doesn't even have a gas burner." Tom grinned, relaxed in James' company. "But if you pop over to my mum's plot at midday, she is having her aura read by Filo. They're not here yet but check back in an hour and the kettle will bound to be on."

Maddie and James agreed to that as Maddie joined her brother around the other side of the hedge; whatever Tom had for her was long forgotten.

"This is a nice surprise, I never expected to see you up here James." Maddie was genuinely pleased to see her brother. "How did you know which plot was granddad's, well mine?"

"That rather nice young lady over there told me, she let me in the gate." James grinned at his accomplishment. "I saw her at a compost bin and called her over, charmed her with my smile and she let me in. What's her name?"

Maddie laughed at him, "It's Alice and she's spoken for, with him," as she gestured across towards Tom.

"That's a shame, I could have sworn she gave me a second glance."

"Not every girl falls at your feet, James, despite what you think!" James seemed to always be out with a girl, never really bringing any home and Maddie's lighthearted mood allowed her to tease him for it. "Let me get the chairs out of the caravan and we can sit down."

Maddie pulled out the two fold-up chairs that she had bought from the supermarket when they had opened the seasonal garden aisle. They were cheap but she didn't need anything more robust. She looked at James and tried to see what a girl would see in him. It's hard for a sister to judge their brother, there is a natural block that prevents you from seeing them as a partner, as a husband or a boyfriend. They are always just your brother. She guessed that he was good looking. His hair was not as dark as Maddie's, hers' was the darkest brown just before it could be called black, his, a tone or two lighter, if it were a dye she would call it chocolate. She detected the smallest wisp of grey in his unkempt sideburns, she had pulled one or two stray ones from her own hair, so it was only reasonable, that at nearly thirty years old, for him to be going grey too.

James was tall and slim, bordering on lanky, but had just enough muscle across his chest and shoulders to give him shape. His tatty t-shirt had an indistinguishable picture on the front, faded from many washes over the years. It had a few tiny holes on the stomach that looked like moths had been eating it but was more likely to be wear and tear. His jeans were faded and shapeless, pulled in with a leather belt, fixed by an oval metal buckle, adorned with a Harley Davison motorbike. His hair flopped forwards, as he talked, he ruffled it, so most of the time he had parts of it sticking up. She decided girls would like what they saw and maybe even wanted to tame him, to show him that the structure of a good woman and relationship was good for him, but he had avoided that so far and seemed extremely happy to be mostly single and having a good time.

"To what do I owe this pleasure? Not that you need an excuse obviously, you're welcome here anytime, especially if you grab a hoe!"

Maddie's mood was upbeat as the sun shone down and she realised she was happy to share her little plot one of her own family. She was proud of her achievements but didn't speak much about her weekends' toil with her parents. Ever since finding the contents of the caravan, her old memory boxes and the letters from her mother to grandfather, she hadn't wished to venture into any conversation about it until she had learnt more about her grandfather's life. The more she came to the plot, the more she felt she knew him. There would be a time that she felt equipped to face the hard questions and not accept any less an answer than she deserved. Up until now she had enjoyed keeping the allotment to herself, it was her project and her's alone. She didn't want her parents, mother in particular, making comments and disguised criticism, when she herself felt she was succeeding as things were. She already knew her mother thought she was spending too much time here. Regular comments about not focussing on work or not seeing Dominic at their house anymore had to be batted back unanswered.

"I was worried about you. The other day, you seemed so unhappy with work. It's not like you to say you're not happy, I always thought you were loving your job, the success and everything," James came straight to the point.

"Oh, I don't have success, not like that anyway, I just feel as though I am at a crossroads and several things have happened lately that are making me question everything."

"Can I help?" James surprised her.

"That's really kind, but I honestly don't know how. I'm not sure what it is that I want yet, I need to figure it all out. Anyway, since when did you become a life coach? I wouldn't have you pegged as a guru. You've hardly got your own life together, have you?" Maddie said it nicely but meant every word.

"Ouch!" James joked. "I beg to differ. My life is ticking along very nicely, I don't have worries or conflict, no one is chasing me for anything. All's good in the hood." His fake Bronx accent made her laugh.

"But seriously, how do you manage it? You come and go, no questions from mum and dad, you do as you please and they never comment. I have every aspect of my life analysed and commented on and I never seem to clean up good enough. No matter what I do, I can always do better. Why are they never on your tail?" Maddie felt her mood changing. She was being honest now and asking questions that have been bottled up for years. She didn't want to vent at the wrong person, so kept what she wanted to say reined in, it's not James' fault he's treated differently but he is the one other person who may recognise that he is.

"I guess it's just the first-born son thing," James didn't seem to match Maddie's concern and his flippant joke wasn't welcomed.

"I mean it James, there is a definite difference on how we are treated and I have to be honest, it does sometimes really get me down. It's not fair and you seem to get away with things that I can't." Maddie heard herself and knew she sounded pathetic but what she was saying ran deep, years of annoyance and injustice. She knew it sounded petty out loud but living the reality was difficult for her.

It dawned on Maddie that James hadn't seen any differences. Being on the better side of the receiving line may have kept him blinkered.

"Yeah, I guess so, but I don't encourage it. I think they just want you to be the best you can be, you have so much more potential."

"But why is that?" Maddie asked. "Why is all of the expectation loaded onto me?"

"I think it's just because of the illness thing, mum and dad haven't pushed me too hard in case I break." James shrugged.

"What? What do you mean illness thing? Are you ill?"

"Not now, no, but I was, wasn't I? As a baby. Surely you know all about that?"

Maddie was confused. "As a baby? No, I don't know anything at all about this. What was the matter with you? Are you okay now?"

"I had meningitis Madeleine, I nearly died, I thought you knew?"

"No, that's the first time I've heard about it. How old were you?"

"I'm not sure, very young, a few months old. Mum told me about it once or twice, but I didn't see the need to keep bringing it up, it was years ago and I'm all better now."

"How ill were you?"

"Very! Mum said they brought me into the doctor with a high temperature and blotches that were sprouting all over my body, really quickly. She said I was floppy. Apparently, I was taken to a London hospital and put in an induced coma, I had a blood transfusion and everything. I was in there for a few months, she said. I was really lucky, I came out with no side effects, it wasn't the case for many of the others in there. The vaccination came out soon after, so I think you've had that and now I have too obviously. I really thought you knew!"

"I had no idea, no idea at all, that must have been so scary for everyone. I would have been too young to know what was going on. How strange I don't know about it. It's not been mentioned as far as I know. But that does explain a lot. Maybe they didn't push you because they thought you were delicate."

"Hey, do I look delicate?" James laughed.

"No, you know what I mean. I was coming up close behind you in months, only eighteen between us, so if you were still weak or they didn't want to push you too hard then I was only just behind you to take over. It does make sense, don't you think?" Maddie's mind was racing, piecing together what her parents had gone through and how they may have reacted. But look at James now, he is a big strapping man, no reason at all to take the foot off the parenting pedal. It didn't excuse the years that have come afterwards, of letting James get away with everything.

Maddie was feeling like a detective, piecing the jigsaw pieces of her life together. Why is she in the dark? James' illness, her mother and grandfather's relationship, their own breakdown of communication and Maddie's estrangement from her beloved grandfather. Still so many questions. Just when Maddie thought she was getting somewhere, solving, and sorting her life, another thing was thrown into the pot and stirred around.

"Look sis, I've gotta go, I can't stay for that tea as I'm meeting a mate. I just wanted to check you're okay, you are okay, aren't you? This hasn't changed anything has it?"

"No, I'm fine honest. As long as you promise you're okay now. It all happened years before I could even walk so really it hasn't changed anything at all, but it may well explain a lot. I'm going to have to talk to mum at some point, I think. I want to address the imbalance between us. I'm not looking forward to that. It wouldn't be so bad if we all talked openly about things but how do I open a conversation about something that has clearly been brushed under the carpet? Oh, I don't know, I'll have to pick the right moment, I guess. It was really nice seeing you here, next time come for longer, meet the gang and help me with my weeding please"

"I will, I promise. That bloke Tom looks like a nice guy, shame he has a girlfriend hey and shame it's that very nice Alice who definitely fancied me!" James waved laughing all the way down past her runner beans until she couldn't see him anymore.

Maddie couldn't help but smile, as annoying as James was, he didn't mean any harm to anyone. He ambled through life without a care and she was touched that he had come to find her today. She must have seemed really down for him to do that. It made her even more resolved to finally get some answers and then make some decisions about her life. She needs to move on in some way, she just needs to work out how.

She remembered Tom was going to give her something, probably some of the seeds he was sowing. They can wait to another day as she set about pulling the weeds from her potato beds.

Madeleine felt like a schoolgirl, sat in front of the headteacher, explaining her naughty actions. Katrina Everett, the Deputy C.E.O. had been busy for days and unable to meet with them. They had faced an agonising wait to tell her about Earl Williams and his attempt to extort money from them. Today she had a cancellation and summoned them to her.

Madeleine had taken Dominic and Roseanne aside the previous day, to tell them Nadir was no longer working in their team, or even for C&B for the foreseeable future. She confided to them about his attempts to derail her and explained that she couldn't discuss it before as Gregory had asked her to remain confidential. They had been, as she expected, truly shocked at Nadir's actions. Dominic openly reached out and held

Madeleine's hand across the cafeteria table as she told them how she had not trusted colleagues. She admitted that she had suspected Roseanne but didn't elaborate why. Dominic was sat there, and it wasn't fair to discuss Roseanne's possible feelings towards him in front of him. She opened up about how awful the events had made her feel, how she thought they had all found her to be incapable when the files went missing. Dominic apologised, saying he never doubted she was good at her job. Roseanne had the good grace to agree. They decided they were able to continue as a group of three and to put the events behind them. Madeleine felt lighter than she had for many weeks but knew they still had another hurdle to face.

"Well this is an unholy mess, isn't it?" Katrina was not impressed and the three sat before her accepting the scolding. "We will never know if Nadir was part of any set up, I suppose. He may have been in with Earl from the start? Either way, Nadir can't defend his actions today so we must try and solve the issue."

Katrina took notes as she spoke. "So, let me get this straight. This Earl Williams has divulged to you that one of the key members of the Bittern Quay Board is overhauling his own companies to bring in line, and even be a leading example, in environmental compliance?"

The three nodded silently.

"And now you are in the position of not using any references to this in your bid for the Bittern Quay contract, or else he will say you obtained the information from him?"

Dominic went to say something but Katrina raised her hand to silence him.

"And your original market campaign does already veer towards the health and well-being aspects, so now you can't even use your own ideas that you had before even meeting him?"

"That's correct," Roseanne spoke out.

"What I don't understand, Earl is putting his own neck on the line…if the Board hear of his actions, then he is sacked, surely." Katrina was working things through.

Dominic managed to speak, "He had already thought of that, he suggested if we tried to contact his company then C&B would never be involved in any business with Bittern Quays, or any associated deals, because he has the power to say C&B's policies are lacking the required levels of environmental commitments that are needed. If we say nothing, then C&B will sail through regardless. He will see to it that it does"

"This goes against every value that we have here in our company. The fact that we are having this conversation saddens me deeply." Katrina was visibly angry. "Our own policies are based on truth, integrity and honesty. I am shocked that you have allowed this vile man to infiltrate us and put us in this position. By rights, all three of you should be suspended immediately whilst we sort this mess out."

Madeleine couldn't help herself, she started to cry. The past few weeks at work had been bad enough, but being told-off, like a child, for something she had not instigated or done, felt grossly unfair. She felt miserable and wanted to collect her things and leave the building forever.

"However," Katrina hadn't finished. "I can see that you three were not aware of the real purpose of Earl's visit and Nadir's issues are unravelling each and every day. I'm prepared to give you the benefit of the doubt and help you."

Madeleine glanced at Roseanne and was shocked to see that she too had wet cheeks.

"I stand by our company's stance, we will not tolerate anything less than an open and honest approach, therefore I will go to Mr. Ito myself and talk to him about what has happened. You need to understand, that this may jeopardise the chances of not only your team's pitch but also that of all the teams we are putting forward for this deal. There's every chance Mr. Ito will embargo us from it completely. But I have no choice. For us to come out with any kind of integrity, I can't see any other option."

"Thank you so much, we…." Dominic was stopped short again.

"I don't want to hear it Dominic, I am so disappointed in you all, I'm not doing this for you, I'm doing it to unravel the mess you have put us all in. That's all, this meeting is over."

The three stood in unison and left the room.

Once out of sight and sound of Katrina's suite, Roseanne lent against the wall and bent over as if in pain.

"I left a fantastic job to come here as I thought it was a move up the ladder, but Christ this is a joke, an absolute joke. I'm tarnished now, whatever happens, I'll never be taken seriously."

Dominic moved towards her to touch her arm, she shrugged away from him viciously.

"Look Roseanne, we're all upset but we've been given a lifeline here. We still have every chance of coming up with a great campaign and now we can use the health, well-being and environment issues freely. Mr. Ito will know we are aware of his passions and we can now tap into them. Look at this as an opportunity. We can turn this around." When Dominic was placed in the leadership role, he really did do it well, he showed compassion and fairness. Madeleine looked on in admiration.

"Okay, yes I can see that," Roseanne composed herself. "But it's job and finish as far as I'm concerned. We finish the job and then I look for other work elsewhere. But that's between us, I don't want it banded around thank you very much!"

"That's fair enough," Dominic agreed. Madeleine nodded and felt a wave of sadness flood over the little cameo in the corridor.

"How was your day? Fiona was arranging cut flowers into a huge china jug. She spent most of her day in-between the garden and the conservatory, yet the garden activity was restricted to deadheading roses and selecting fresh flowers from the limited borders to brighten up the room. She paid a gardener to come once a week to weed, mow the lawn, trim the conifers and water the baskets. Madeleine wasn't sure why the gardener was necessary. The garden was simple and low maintenance, but it did provide enough colour to regularly fill the jug that sat upon the end of the bar.

Fiona's week ran like clockwork. Predictable and efficient. She shopped on a Thursday, always the same supermarket, mostly the same list of food but with a good eye for special offers. Monday was Bridge Club with the girls, Friday night was Cricket Club with Henry; they enjoyed the live singer and the half-time bingo. Saturday was friends' night, sometimes at their house or at a rotation of each of their wide circle of friends. Sunday roast was served at home at around 3 o'clock and Madeleine and James were expected to be there. Madeleine usually was, but James was a bit hit and miss.

"It's been very stressful to be honest," Madeleine didn't have the energy to fabricate her day into something wonderful for her mother.

"Oh, and why's that?" the suspicion already creeping Fiona's voice, assuming Madeleine was to blame in some way for her bad day.

Years of practice told Madeleine that at that point she should have said it didn't matter, that she was just tired or blame the train system, but weariness caught her off-guard and she told her mother of her day, of the lost files, the letter of resignation and of Nadir's part in it all. Her mother was still clutching the china jug as Madeleine expanded to Earl's attempt at bribery and the Deputy C.E.O's intervention.

It was as though Fiona had not heard a word. Or just heard single words that she rearranged and made new sentences from, sentences that said, 'Madeleine has brought shame and trouble to the door of her employer.'

"I just don't understand how you can get into so much trouble; this will look terrible on your record, they won't promote you now."

"Mum, I didn't do anything to get into trouble."

"How do you know these dodgy people? Swindlers, extortionists, and the like. I can't believe you mix with these types of people!"

"Mum, I don't know him, a colleague invited him into work to see us."

"But you didn't have to meet him, did you?"

"But mum, I didn't know who or what he was did I? You don't understand, I shouldn't have said anything to you."

"I understand more than you know. I may not have worked for a few years, but I know about these things. I know that what you're telling me is not right, it's just not what should happen at work." Fiona was indignant.

Madeleine had heard it before. Fiona knows best, her wealth of experience in the few weeks work she did, a quarter of a century before, meant she always had the upper hand in advice and judgement. Exasperated, Madeleine said she was going out.

"I suppose you're going to run away to the allotment again. That's not going to solve anything is it? You can't hide there indefinitely!"

"Mum, I am not hiding, I am watering. I need to go over and water my greenhouse, it's been a hot day and I don't want to lose anything now, not after all of my hard work."

"Well, it's a shame you don't apply that same principle to your paid job, isn't it?"

There was no reasoning with her mother when she had everything worked out in her head, as she sees it, so Madeleine muttered 'I'll see you later,' as she grabbed her bag from the side and left her mother angry and yet again, disappointed.

The truth was Maddie hadn't planned to go to the allotment that evening but she needed to escape. Why couldn't her mother have a reasoned, well-balanced conversation? Why couldn't she take her point of view, just for once and empathise with her daughter? Maddie was running away in one sense; she was going to the one place where she felt calm and at peace. She wasn't judged by her allotment friends; she didn't feel any need to pretend to be anything other than what she is. There's an honesty amongst them, a sharing of skills and openness to advice and support. She feels accepted and appreciated despite any of her failings. As she pushed open the gates to the allotment car park, she felt she could once again breathe.

Henry came home to find his wife ripping the leaves off long stems of roses and tearing her fingers on the thorns. He gently pulled a tissue from a box on the arm of the sofa and wrapped her fingers to stop the blood dripping onto the furniture.

"What's happened now?" he sighed, not really wanting to hear whatever drama had unfolded this time.

"She's throwing her life away! The silly girl has got herself into trouble at work and she's going to lose everything I've worked for."

Henry checked under the tissue and saw it had already stopped the bleed. The smallest scratch can create the greatest flow.

"What kind of trouble, what do you mean?" he already knew the explanation would not match the frustration that his wife was displaying.

Fiona repeated the tale told to her earlier, she omitted much of the important details, of how events had happened to Madeline without her knowledge or understanding. She didn't relay the hurt and confusion that Madeleine had said she had been feeling and she didn't describe the way her daughter looked exhausted and defeated.

"I'll talk to her," Henry knew his role, he would find the truth out himself and smooth the waters. He would find the midway balance of supporting his wife and backing her up whilst also showing his daughter that he cared. He understood often the balance didn't happen, he had to back up Fiona's stance on each situation, she was his wife after all.

They had married young and she was a good wife to him, he had a lovely home, good friends and a social life he enjoyed. Fiona's views could be blinkered, once her mind was made up there was no reasoning with her, but he had learnt to cope with her single-minded attitudes and adapted to keep the peace. Perhaps he should have challenged her more in the early days, he had made a rod for his own back, but they were young and he wanted to please his new wife, her early tears had cut him deeply and he had been at a loss of how to make her happy. She no longer cried, she had a pit of anger and contempt always bubbling just under the surface. He didn't understand why. She had a life that others were jealous of, a beautiful home, two well-adjusted grown children who never brought real trouble to the door, good friends and a good husband. She didn't need to want for anything, yet she always carried a satchel of resentment wherever she went and he couldn't get her to put it down.

James's illness had altered their marital path, there was no doubt in that. He was born healthy and for a few wonderful months they lived the life they had talked about and planned for. Fiona was a loving mother and built a welcoming home for them all. Henry's work consumed him, dealing with complex legalities and preparing for each day's work the night before. But Fiona loved being the attentive housewife, ensuring everything ran like clockwork, their lives were perfect. And then that awful day, James had woken unusually late and Fiona called first the doctor and then her husband at work. His secretary interrupted a meeting to tell him to meet his wife at the hospital; they were arriving by ambulance.

When he arrived, he was ushered into a room with James's tiny little form in the middle of a bench bed, tubes already inserted into his little arms and groin, pumping liquid into him as fast as they could. A nurse took them both to one side and said he will be having a blood transfusion and 'if' he stabilises they will transfer him to St Mary's in London. Henry remembered just standing there, staring at the orderly chaos of the staff, so many busily doing their part, surrounding their son, all doing their best to keep him alive.

Fiona stayed with him in London for weeks. She refused to come home and they gave her a bed in an empty room in a closed off ward. She became quite practiced in reading the charts as the bleeps, buzzers and pumps kept him asleep and restful. The only times she left his side was to shower in her own ward shower and get a cup of tea from the family room or grab a sandwich and piece of fruit from the volunteer's shop. Occasionally she stepped out to walk around the streets, she stumbled on Oxford Street and it made her jump. She hadn't realised she was so near to normal life, thousands of people going about their day, excited tourists, London workers on their lunch break. She had wanted to scream at them, to tell them what her world is like, that they had to stop for a moment and appreciate the awfulness of what was round the corner. She had hurried back to James and felt safe once more.

Once they finally brought James home, Henry sensed the change. Fiona was no longer the laid back and calm mother that she had been. She was nervous and tense and worried about every noise James made. She constantly took his temperature and washed his clothes over and over, even if he hadn't worn them. She didn't want them sitting unused in the drawers and cupboards so she would 'freshen them up' continually. Henry had to wash his hands before and after holding James; if he even sniffed then James would be snatched quickly from his arms.

As James began to toddle, every room was emptied of sharp furniture. Everything smaller than a tennis ball was squirrelled away in case he choked. Play was clean and structured. Henry would try and encourage James into the garden, to dig in the dirt and get wet with the hosepipe but Fiona had put a stop to all of that, it was too dangerous, too fraught with germs.

James didn't go to playgroup or the mother toddler groups. He didn't have small friends, so when Madeleine had arrived, Henry was pleased to see him given the chance to interact at last.

Fiona remained focussed on James. It was as if he was going to break at any moment. If he cried, Fiona would scoop him up. If he looked tired Fiona would wrap him and rock him. It was too much to apply the same attention to Madeleine and she was left to watch and learn and become increasingly independent even at such a young age.

By the time Madeleine started school, aged five, James was still being collected every day at lunchtime to go home with Fiona for a home cooked meal. Madeleine stayed in school with her sandwich box. James would be met at the end of the day, Fiona standing at the classroom door, despite the teachers requesting daily that parents remained on the playground. Madeleine would stay for after school clubs, it helped Fiona have extra time to get James's spelling tin out and pay him the extra attention, learning his words and his times tables. Other mothers would drop Madeleine off later at home and after tea, Madeleine would take out her simple homework in her bedroom and finish it herself.

Aunts and Uncles would start to praise Madeleine for being such a strong girl, independent girl, smart and intelligent. They would sigh and smile at James as he still had his meals cut up small, by Fiona, at the age of six. "Bless him, we need to look after James, don't we?" It became a self-fulfilled prophecy, James was weak, James was needy and no one must push him hard or he will break and so he didn't push himself. Why would he? He had learnt that he could sit back and everything would be arranged for him, he didn't need to worry, to think, to challenge, to discover. It was all there. James simply lapped it up. He didn't have to tidy up after himself, choose clothes, dress himself, make early decisions. His days were stress free and happy.

Madeleine's achievements were a constant source of enquiry and veiled criticism. "Why did you only get 19 out of 20 spellings?" "You didn't get a Level 3 in your year two SATs, did you try hard enough?" Did you get your 5 Star Gymnastics Award today?" "How come the other team won the math's quiz challenge, when you're so good at maths?" When did Madeleine begin to spot the difference? When did the resentment start to brew?

And then there was the time Fiona got a job. Henry saw his wife crumble with the weight of guilt at leaving her son. He tried his best to help around the house but on her workdays, he came home to find her crying until he couldn't watch her anymore. She had wanted *him* to suggest she leaves the job. He did so willingly, but secretly doubted if it was the best thing for her. She hadn't made any new friends since having the children and he thought the companionship of adults in a workplace would be healthy. But it wasn't to be.

And where did that leave them now? Henry wasn't allowed to push James into work or paying rent. "He will find his own way eventually," Fiona had said, "when he's ready." Henry watched his daughter go off to work each day, smart and educated. He saw the look his wife gave her as she left the house in her designer suits, longingly wanting a taste of her daughter's life that had somehow passed Fiona by.

It was hard to see over the tops of errant hedges and fences full of spent Montana. The nettles clustered around the ramshackle sheds and towering corn lined up in regimented walls. Cages packed with netted fruit shielded the hidden treasures of each person's plots from view. It was quiet except for the returning birds, tired from their day's soaring and now jostling for their places to sleep overnight, the best spots already taken amongst the canopies of the elder. Maddie loved this time of the day, the summer warmth hung in the air despite the lowering sun, the land was rich and bursting and she felt calm once more.

She heard laughter. Throaty laughter was a sound not often heard at home. It wasn't an unhappy home, not at all, but no one played in a happy or frivolous way, finding humour in ridiculous situations and anecdotes. If Maddie tried to retell a silly story from the news or from her day, it was unpicked seriously, and academia squeezed the life from it until it was irrelevant. She had learnt not to bother. So, what was left was polite conversation, easy and unchallenging, monotone and safe.

She followed the sound until she arrived at Alice's plot. Through the gap in two pallet compost bins she saw Alice and Tom spraying water at each other with two children's water guns. They were dipping them into the open butts for refills and chasing each other, Alice squealing as Tom's cold jets hit his target every time. Alice's aim was random and feeble. Tom dominated the match, determined to win and relentless in the soaking. Alice knew she was beaten, she held her hands up in surrender, drenched and giggling uncontrollably.

Maddie suddenly felt uncomfortable, she shouldn't be watching, she was intruding in a private game between a couple who probably thought they were alone in the allotments. She didn't want to be seen, let alone as a spy, so crept away quietly without calling out.

Once safe on her own turf, she unlocked the caravan and sat quietly looking out of the window. She now loved the idea that this little patch of earth, a tiny piece of the universe, belongs to her. It was ramshackle, it still needed years of developing but it is her's. Her achievement. She felt pride when she looked out over the roughly laid raised beds, nothing was square or neatly finished but they held overflowing vegetables and salads of a greater variety than she ever thought possible in her first year.

She had started to take home a trugg loaded with produce at the end of most days. Her mother just said, 'Pop it in the pantry'. It would get used eventually but not commented upon or appreciated. Maddie would ask if the carrots were her's on the Sunday platter, her mother would seem disinterested and affirm they were, but it was rarely celebrated. Maddie had started to invent recipes so she could use her vegetables for her packed lunches at work, beetroot cake was a current favourite, her fingers would be purple for days after baking a batch, but she didn't care. At first. she didn't mind what happened to the things she grew but recently she questioned the purpose of her toil. She was growing to love the act of gardening, the pride and the sense of achievement but she wanted to make sure her hard work was put to a good use. She didn't want her freshly pulled, healthy crop to wither in a cupboard or fridge. She wanted them to sing, to receive the praise and appreciation they deserved. As she sat quietly in her caravan, she took out her notebook from her bag and started to plan.

"Hey stranger," Dominic lent on Madeleine's doorway, his brown tailored suit had the faintest orange tartan pattern, barely visible, with a burnt umber handkerchief sticking out from his breast pocket. Madeleine thought he looked stunning.

"Hi, I've been meaning to call you Dominic, but things have been so busy. I'm sorry."

"It's fine, I understand, I've been busy too. I've missed seeing you though. I wondered if you'd like to come to lunch with me today, my treat." Dominic's smile was easy and relaxed.

Madeleine mentally checked herself over before she answered, she didn't know why but she felt she needed to match his appearance, she couldn't let him down. She was glad she had chosen a beautiful silk dress to wear that morning, knowing it was going to be a hot day. It shimmered as she moved, olive green fabric with a loose dark ginger belt, she couldn't have known but she complemented his earthy outfit perfectly. Her dark hair was pulled back in a sleek ponytail to keep her cool. She was wearing large, gold hooped earrings which set off her long neck beautifully. Confident that she was looking suitably smart, she accepted and realised she was looking forward to seeing him alone again.

Seeing Alice and Tom together had made her feel lonely. She had sat in her caravan contemplating what she wanted from a relationship and wondered if she had been blocking Dominic somehow, keeping him at arm's length although she didn't understand why. Part of her didn't believe that a man like Dominic would have any interest in her, outwardly she may look the part, smart, glamorous and heading for success but inside she feels a fraud. She feels a dowdier or more simplistic person than she portrays. Her first choice is not the wine bars, theatres and nightclubs, she is happiest in a cosy country pub with a dog in front of the fire. But has she been selfish? Has she been looking for a man to be too much like her and not been prepared to meet anyone else halfway? She should spend more time in Dominic's world, and she could open up her's to him more willingly. Perhaps some of the times he has irked her were down to her inability to accept he is different from her. She should accept his criticisms more readily, they could help her develop as a person perhaps, maybe she needs to change in some way, and maybe he will match her halfway, there was only one way to find out.

Dante's was a simple Italian restaurant, elegant with white walls, white linen and beautiful white china, created so thin the bowls and plates were almost translucent. Italian staff served efficiently and quietly on the restaurant floor but behind the open kitchen counter a torrent of passionate instructions boomed out, for all to hear. Madeleine thought they sounded angry with each other, but the smiling faces belied the noise and created an emotion driven and heightened dining ambience.

Dominic pulled Madeleine's chair out slightly for her to sit down. He brushed the back of her neck ever so gently and she felt the impact down into her feet. He wordlessly smiled at her as he sat opposite and took her hands in his. His eyes scanned her face, starting with her forehead, moving around her jawline, her eyebrows and nose, her upper lip, taking in every line, every pore. Eventually he spoke.

"Madeleine, you are a very beautiful woman. I've neglected you lately and I am going to make it up to you," he reached his face across and kissed the back of her hand.

"Oh, and how are you going to do that?" she joked, his seriousness was unexpected and she felt a little awkward.

"I am going to spend more time with you and perhaps we can go away together, for a long weekend. We can book a couple of days off and get a flight from Gatwick maybe. How about Barcelona? What do you think?"

It was years since Madeleine was last abroad. She had one trip to Budapest with friends from her business course, it had been cold but beautiful. They had walked miles admiring the architecture and hung out in the ruin bars all night drinking cheap wine. The thought of a little holiday was very appealing, but she was aware it was loaded with a sub-text. A holiday together would take the relationship to another level for sure. They still were not meant to even be together. If they were found out at work that would surely be the final straw. Katrina would end their time there immediately.

As tempting as it was, Madeleine thought she had no choice but to say no.

"Dominic, that sounds lovely, I would like to, but can we wait until after the competition is over? There has been so many things threatening to jeopardise it, I don't want to tempt fate, we shouldn't really be seen to be together. Let's wait until after September."

Dominic's face dropped.

"Are you saying you don't want to?"

"No, no, I'm saying I do want to but now is not the right time. We have work, I have my allotment to look after and I would prefer to wait, that's all."

The waiter arrived at the table and asked for their orders. Dominic requested the veal ravioli and just looked at Madeleine, waiting for her to order for herself. Usually, he would order for her or relay her order to the waiting staff on her behalf, but he just sat looking at her. She felt uncomfortable and quickly glanced down at the menu and picked the first thing that she saw.

Madeleine was confused, surely, he could see her reasoning made sense.

"So, you want me to book my holiday around your little allotment? Don't you think your priorities are all a little.... hhhhmmm skewed? I'm asking for us to go away for our first holiday together, I expected, hoped for, a little more enthusiasm Madeleine."

She'd done it again. She had promised herself to be more open to Dominic and had shut him down at the first opportunity. Was it so bad what he was suggesting? Was she being ungrateful? Why didn't they ever seem to be on the same page?

"Of course, you're right. You just took me by surprise that's all. A mini break is just what I need and it's a lovely idea. I'm sure I can ask someone to look after my allotment just for a weekend. I'll ask around when we sort out the date."

"That's my girl," Dominic brightened instantly and gave Madeleine's hand a wiggle. "Now, let's just enjoy our lunch, shall we? Oh, by the way, Katrina has asked for us to go up and see her at four o'clock, she wants to update us about Mr. Ito. Roseanne is meeting us there.

Katrina had managed to see Mr. Ito, she wasn't happy as she had been made to look incompetent herself, going to a fellow professional and telling him her own employees had been involved in a situation with one of his employees. She didn't enjoy telling him how his staff are behaving behind his back, Mr. Ito is a proud man and he wouldn't want other people to think he doesn't manage his staff and business properly. The meeting had been awkward for them both.

Katrina didn't disguise her disappointment in the team stood in front of her. "So, although it was a meeting that I never want to have again, it did end positively for our company. Mr. Ito said he respected my honesty and willingness to risk so much for the sake of openness and truth. He is prepared for our teams to still put bids forward for Bittern Quays, including yours. He knows you are hoping to align with his environmental stance and expects you not to let him down. So now your task is much harder, you have a great advantage, so you'll look extremely inadequate if you don't match what he is hoping to see. So now it's up to you three to put a bid forward and take your chances. I'll just finish with this message to you all, this will go down on your records and will be taken into consideration if there were ever to be a need to bring it up again in the future. Do you all understand?

Roseanne, Dominic and Roseanne stood meekly, hardly looking like the power team they aspired to be. When the silence extended to a few seconds they realised they had been dismissed.

As they left in their own thoughts, Madeleine could only wonder how she can possibly avoid going away with Dominic. That was the last thing she wanted Katrina to find out about. As much as she wasn't enjoying her job anymore, she wouldn't want it to end in that way.

As Roseanne turned the corner ahead, Dominic pulled Madeleine into the cleaning cupboard that had been left ajar. It smelt of bleach and damp mop heads. He pulled her roughly into his chest and bent to breathe deeply into her neck. He clutched the tops of her arms and squeezed them into her sides. Her arms dangled from the elbows, unable to bend.

"Fuck them, we'll book a week off and go off into the sun together, just you and me baby. We'll drink cocktails and you'll look sexy as hell in a tiny fucking bikini and… you… will… be… covered… in …slippery… oil. I'll smear it all over you, every inch." He breathed heavily into her ear in between each word and licked at her ear lobe.

She was shocked, he'd never talked like this to her before. He was panting into her face, pushing himself into her, forcing her back against the racking that stored a multitude of sprays and bottles. The force knocked some over and a few fell to the floor. He ground himself into her thigh and she was in no doubt how much he was turned on. His face was sweating, it was damp on her cheek, she tried to pull away, but he held her arms tight.

"We'll show that bitch Katrina, we'll show everyone, so get packing, I'm gonna be showing you who the winner is here."

The door flew open and one of the cleaners stepped back in surprise. She clutched a long-handled broom in her rubber gloved hand and stared at the two of them, not knowing what she should do.

"Okay, so I'll see you at the meeting...." Dominic walked out quickly and threw the invented parting comment over his shoulder towards Madeleine.

Madeleine, looked around her, she had no idea how she came to be in that position, she looked at the cleaner and gave her a small smile, hoping she wouldn't say anything to anyone if she was nice to her, in some small way. Madeleine scurried out of the cupboard and ran into the first ladies toilet she came to. She clutched at the silver taps, one in each hand, squeezing them until her fingers were white. She hung her head low into the basin, breathe Maddie, breathe, she muttered to herself. She could still feel Dominic's fingers on her arms, the weight of him against her leg. Her face felt clammy from his damp breath. She filled the sink with cold water and washed her face. Looking up, her eyes were black from smudged mascara, she took a palm full of liquid soap from the dispenser and washed her face again. This time as she looked up, a shiny confused face stared back.

What the hell just happened? Was it lust? Anger? Was it her, Madeleine, he was squeezing or any woman in the company? He had been angry after the meeting with Katrina, she could tell, but the change in him.... yet, they are a couple aren't they? Shouldn't she have enjoyed it more? Surely by now a secret bit of passion was expected. But if so, why did she feel dirty and why were her hands shaking so much?

Chapter Eight - AUGUST

When did August stop being a summer month? The rain was torrential and there was no sign of a break. The allotments were piling high with weeds and grass, thriving in the warm and wet conditions. Maddie wasn't getting over there as much as she should, and she found it was becoming overwhelming. Dominic was demanding more of her time and she had promised to make more of an effort to spend more time with him. He had booked a holiday for them both, but she was yet to ask for the time off of work, she had been too busy, or was she putting it off deliberately? They were working hard trying to finalise their bid for Bittern Quays, the team were aware there was only a few weeks left and they all felt there was still a huge element missing from their presentation. Nothing was said about the incident in the cupboard. Dominic had returned to his gentle and well-mannered self, chaste kisses and holding of hands were the most he pushed her to. They stayed late at work, Roseanne would leave at six o'clock and they would stay on to finalise prints or run through presentation scripts. They would sit in a bar after work for one or two drinks at the most and she would leave for home on a late train.

He would talk about the geography of the resort he had booked, the excursions they could take climbing the peaks to the most elevated churches or kayaking the coves, the expected climate and latest weather report but they never talked about any hidden agenda or referred to anything he had said to her that day. She would have to find a way to let him down as she simply didn't feel ready, a small voice held her back. She wasn't sure why. She wants a relationship, to feel loved, passion and everything that comes with it, but why can't she step over that line with Dominic? Perhaps she just needs to take a leap, just like Filo's tarot cards had told her to. Step off that cliff!

Normally Maddie looked forward to the Tuesday evening allotment meetings but this week it was an intrusion and an extra activity she could really do without.

"Hi sweetie," Filo's call to her during work was unexpected. "Just calling to see if you want me to pick you up later, for Tom's house?"

"Hi Filo, thanks but I really don't know if I'm going to be able to make it tonight. I'm snowed under here and just really tired."

"Oh Maddie, you must come. The whole meeting is for the planning of the Harvest event, if you're not there you'll not know what's happening. Anyhow, we need you and your ideas. Please come, Tom makes a mean quiche, what was that booked called? Real Men Eat Quiche... or was it that they don't eat it? Either way, I'll be outside your house at six thirty."

Maddie had no idea what Filo was talking about and sighed as she placed her mobile back on the desk. Perhaps she should make the effort and a small part of her was intrigued about Tom's house. The address on the email reminder said 6, Hennessy Way. Maddie didn't know the road and tried to imagine what the house would be like. So far, all the hosts had lived in cottages and homes with real character and all with small or non-existent gardens. She assumed that was the typical allotment keeper's style of dwelling, countryfied and homely. Ranveer lived in a Victorian terraced house with his family. It was set out over three floors with his children enjoying their own level right at the top, with small look-out windows, one to the front and one to the back. They were lucky to still have so many of the original features, they had decorated it tastefully to show off the picture rails and amazing staircase. His wife had served the most sensational selection of savoury and sweet pastries, little filo triangles of curried vegetables, vol-au-vents stuffed full of oil soaked aubergines and artichokes, jars of pickles filled with Ranweer's finest produce, soaked in vinegars and exotic seeds all washed down with homemade lemonade.

Alice's flat had been a surprise. Maddie had imagined her to have a house with a large garden, but she found her living on the first floor of a Victorian converted house, very similar to Ranveer's. The only edible things she could grow were balanced precariously on the kitchen shelves, vying for the sunshine that only grasped them for the last few hours of each day. The shelves were stacked with green, red, yellow, purple and black chili plants held neatly in a wooden tray, tin pots with basil, coriander and parsley enough for a feast. Alice had made everyone vegan biscuits using spelt flour and molasses, they were delicious. Her flat had a modern ethnic twist, huge Indian throws were pinned up on the walls, an enormous canvas frame filled almost an entire wall, Alice had created it herself by dipping leaves of all shapes and sizes into paint and slapping the canvas until it was almost completely covered. The effect was dramatic, yet she proudly told everyone how cheap it was to create. Houseplants stood proudly in large pots that had been bought in local car boot sales. The group had sat on huge bean bags on the floor and high kitchen stools, as Alice only had one small sofa. They laughed at themselves scattered at all different heights, cozy and cuddled up together, especially Norris and Ranweer with their knees up to their ears and Esther trying to take notes in her notebook whilst clutching a mug of lemon balm tea.

Maddie pictured Tom, in his tiny cottage, hitting his head on the beamed ceiling, stoking up an Aga and hanging his socks to dry above it. She guessed he has a large shed or workshop, to tinker with wood or dismantle greasy engines and store his tools in a messy heap. She imagined him to be messy and Alice forever tidying up for him. Tom hadn't been to the meeting at Alice's flat, a good job as he would have filled the room but she would see for herself how much Tom had prepared for the meeting tonight and how much Alice has had to do for him.

Yes, I will go to the meeting, she thought, I need to touch base with everyone and get Dominic and the holiday out of my head.

Maddie ran through the rain and leapt into Filo's car, which sat ticking over on the main road, its lights on despite being in the middle of summer. Filo sat, a vision of yellow plastic, in a fisherman's oilskin coat, a stiff peaked hood flopping down to her eyebrows, with a few wisps of hair escaping around the collar.

"Hi Filo, thanks so much for picking me up, what awful weather! Hey, you've changed your hair, it's blue again, I love it!"

"I thought it was time for a change, I looked at the browns for all of two seconds and thought I'm not ready for that yet!" Filo's laugh was easy and Maddie was glad already that she'd made the effort to come out. "I haven't seen much of you Maddie and I'm happy to come and fetch you. Watch the drips though, there's a tear in the roof just above your head."

Maddie looked up at the canvas roof just as a large drip landed on her forehead. "Ha, ha thanks! Good job I haven't bothered to redo my face and hair tonight."

"You always look lovely Maddie; you don't need make up. Hey, did you hear Norris' wife and her gardening group have won first prize for the best dressed shop front? Well, the shop has won the prize, but Jean and the group did all the hard work. I think they're all going to be in the local paper, isn't that great."

"Yes, that is pretty cool. I hope Norris gets a mention for his growing skills too. How are you Filo, I've missed seeing you too, sorry I've been so busy at work, Dominic and I are having to stay late most evenings."

"So, you're still seeing each other then?" Filo walked a careful line when she spoke about him.

"He has booked a holiday for in a couple of weeks' time….. Filo, can I be honest with you?" Maddie had a sudden urge to seek advice, feeling Filo's warmth, she realised she trusted her new friend more than anyone else to talk to.

"Maddie, you are my friend, we can say anything to each other."

Maddie had always tried to keep her two lives apart, she didn't want Madeleine's world to stain her newly found alter-life, but seeing Filo tonight she realised how much she missed her new friend and how much she needed to confide in her.

"He's booked this holiday and I don't know why but I just don't want to go. I think it's the thought of being together twenty-four hours a day and the shared room and all that that means. We haven't been together like that yet and it seems a big leap from dating to full on relationship stuff. I don't know what's wrong with me, he's gorgeous, you've seen him, plenty of women would love to be in my shoes, but there's something stopping me from being keen to go and I don't know how to let him down."

"Yes, he is certainly a looker, not that he's my type you understand. But looks aren't everything. It's how he makes you feel, how he treats you." Filo took a sly look sideways to see Maddie's face

"In so many ways he's charming. He is a complete gentleman. At work, he can be so kind to his colleagues, but…."

"Aha, so there is a but…..?"

"He can make me feel a little stupid sometimes, no, not stupid exactly….. less worthy I guess."

"Less worthy? That's not good! How do you mean?"

"He'll off-guard me, like book a restaurant without checking with me first, or like the day he turned up at the pub and then if I don't appreciate it, he'll get…. Oh, I don't know… he'll get upset, well, more like sulky and he'll make me feel bad."

"You are allowed to voice your opinion Maddie, you mustn't be closed down by anyone."

"I know and that's the crazy thing…. I am a grown woman, very capable and able, so why does this man make me feel like a child sometimes, like I should apologise and tiptoe around him?"

"Maddie, this doesn't sound good at all! Listen to what you're saying, please. Let me tell you what Dominic's tarot said, I know you think I'm foolish but please let me tell you." Filo swerved a deep pothole and the two of them flew sideways, Maddie's head colliding with Filo's shoulder.

"I don't think you're foolish, Filo. It's just I can't lead my life based on a pack of cards."

"Do you remember, his first card was the Ten of Wands? It shows his ambition, what he has worked towards and he has his sights set on achievement. It can weigh heavy though, it's not always a positive thing. It's a burden and can overshadow more important things in life. And then his second card was The Devil. It's his present Maddie, where he is now and it's not healthy, it can be an addiction to material things or to a relationship. Don't you see Maddie, there's a picture building here?"

"Oh Filo, I know what you're trying to tell me but I'm a realist, this is all just imaginary."

Filo ploughed on, taking the opportunity to tell Maddie what she believed whilst she had her full attention in the tiny car. "And then, his final card, his future. It was a reversed card, upside-down, it was The Lovers. That's not what it sounds like, Dominic didn't let me explain. The Lovers in reverse means he is not in tune with his partner, he has conflicts. It means he has relationship issues, infidelity even. It's not a good sign at all, Maddie, it's a symbol for bad choices, breakdowns in communication.... you get the idea, don't you?"

"Are we talking about work relationships or love relationships?"

"Both Maddie, it can be either or both. I'm worried about you. I really think you should listen to these signs. It's a warning." Filo knew she was pushing it, but she genuinely felt the tarot was giving Maddie a message. Filo knew she had no place interfering in Maddie's personal life but the more she got to know Maddie, the more she liked her and wanted her to be truly happy.

The rain was hammering down, the early evening threw an eerie purple and orange blanket over the fields and villages passing by. The sun was still visible behind the milky cloud, yet rain contradicted the brightness and the small windscreen wiper blades swept across at top speed as the windows steamed up, creating a cocoon inside the little car. Maddie and Filo sat in silence for the rest of the journey, Maddie occasionally wiping the drips from her face. She had listened to Filo and she had to admit, it all sounded too realistic to simply dismiss. Filo let her digest the points she was trying to make, she knew from the years of reading people's cards that you can't push too hard, you can guide and advise but it's up to each person to decide if they're ready to listen or not. Eventually, the messages drip feed into people's psyche over time, Maddie will be considering what she had heard, of that, Filo was sure.

6, Hennessy Way was a newly built semi-detached on the Woodcroft Estate. The small parking space for only one vehicle was already filled and Tom's guests had left their cars littered up and down the road on the curved pavements. New estates never seemed to cater for the number of parking spaces needed and it was difficult to distinguish between each person's front garden and property, where one ended and the next began. Filo risked the wrath of a neighbour and left her 2CV outside a house just a little further down the road.

Heads down against the rain, the two ran to the tiny porch that overhung the matt black door, inset with stained red poppies set into silver lined windowpanes. On the left of the door was a small opaque window, Maddie assumed a downstairs toilet and to the left of this the garage door with Tom's truck parked outside. The next-door neighbour's front door was only a few steps away and Maddie felt either door could open at the sound of the doorbell. The house was cramped and devoid of any hint of the owner within.

The front garden was an immaculate square of lawn enveloped by shallow borders, each filled with low ground cover, dwarf chrysanthemums, Busy Lizzies and wild geraniums which were just dying over and needed chopping back. It was straight, neat and regimented and a complete surprise to Maddie. The whole front garden was only double the size of the parking space. She would never have picked this as a house for Tom, it didn't seem to have his personality at all.

The door opened and Alice ushered them in. The house was brightly lit, despite it being summer, the rain had dulled it inside and every sunken ceiling dimmer light was turned on full. The laminate floor pooled rainwater from their shoes as they entered, Alice grabbed a towel from the radiator and threw it onto the floor to soak it up. "He needs a carpet runner!" she raised her eyes in mock exasperation. They removed their shoes before any more damage was done and slid into the living room in their socks, trying to avoid slipping over completely on the polish.

The room was sparse, a black corduroy corner sofa filled most of it with a large flat screen TV set upon a black glass unit along the opposite wall. A token pot plant sat on the floor; Maddie reasoned it was a yucca of some type. One small MDF coffee table sat at one end of the sofa and thick long curtains trailed on the floor in front of sliding patio doors. Through the glass she could see a small patio area directly outside the doors, then a low brick wall, just about five brick layers high and beyond this what looked very much like fake grass. Surely not! It was just too green, too neat, to be real. Maddie stared and realised Alice was asking what she would like to drink.

"Oh, sorry, can I just have some water please? It's quite muggy today, isn't it?"

"Hi ladies," Norris was enjoying the corner spot on the sofa, Ranweer was next to him and Steve and Gail completed the longer section of the seat. Filo had removed her yellow rainwear and was settling in next to the other side of Norris, Esther came out from the kitchen with a tray of mugs and glasses and sat it on the small tabletop and started passing them around.

Offering her the glass of water, Alice insisted Maddie sit down next to Filo and then squeezed in next to her, filling the last space.

Esther went back into the kitchen and came out with a pine dining chair in one hand and her notebook tucked under her armpit, holding a mug carefully as she walked. Tom followed, with a matching chair and a pint of cola. They set the chairs down either side of the TV unit, facing the group. The room was full and intimate, everyone squeezed up together tightly, sunken back into the sagging sofa. Maddie felt slightly claustrophobic knowing that in order to stand up someone else would have to move, she was wedged in tightly, directly in front of Tom's gaze.

After a few minutes of welcoming chat and placing mugs carefully down on the floor where they couldn't be kicked over, Esther opened her book to signal the start of the meeting.

"Hello everyone, thank you for coming tonight in this dreadful weather. Still as we all know, it's good for the gardens!"

Everyone nodded in agreement but secretly wished it would go away.

"I would like us to start picking up pace for the Harvest Charity Event for St Anne's Hospice. I'll start off with an update if that's okay with everyone." Esther continued regardless, knowing full well no one would stop her and challenge the order of the meeting. "I have talked to St Anne's and they are happy to supply us with their printed bunting and feather flags. They're those fabric flags that stand on the ground with a weight at the bottom with things printed on them. They also have a whole host of things that we can give away as prizes, with the Hospice logo on, like mugs, pens…. you know the sort of things. The manager has offered us some of their long trestle tables, they are lightweight aluminium and wipeable, so will be ideal. Tom and Norris, can you arrange a time to collect these please? It will need to be in the morning as they need them for dinner service the night before. Right, next, the Bowls Club have offered their car park again which is very kind of them, we know we can fit everything into the allotment car park, just like the Plant Sale."

Maddie spoke up. "Esther, don't you think we need a bigger space, the Plant Sale was small scale and we just about managed, this is going to be far bigger so we may struggle to fit it all into Queens Gardens?"

She could feel the silence whilst Esther looked at her. No one usually interrupted Esther when she was in full swing, let alone challenge something she was saying.

"Just how big do you think our Event is going to be Maddie? We're not planning the town carnival here you know; the allotments will be plenty big enough."

Tom looked at Maddie with a look that said, 'I'd drop it now, if I were you.'

Maddie ignored his eyes. "It's just that if we are charging an entrance fee, we need to be putting on more than a few tabletops. We want to raise money for the Hospice, don't we? So, let's make sure there are things there for all the family. We don't want to limit ourselves due to space."

"Let's move on, shall we?" Esther wasn't keen to discuss it further, as far as she was concerned this was her event and she was in charge. "Ranweer and Alice, can you update us on your plans please?"

"Well, it's still too early to finalise the menu because we'll be using produce that's at its peak in the first week of October." Ranweer was excited about their contributions, he thought of little else. A chance to show how exciting Vegan food could be, and how it could be fresh and organically grown. He was researching menus, reading cookbooks every night and trying out ideas on his family. "The final menu decisions will be made a week before, won't they Alice?"

"Yes, we have painted some boards in blackboard paint and will write up the choices, just like in a Bistro. We'll do cold food as much as possible, street food which can be eaten standing up. We will do a couple of hot dishes too and will need to buy recyclable takeaway pots and wooden forks from the funds if that's okay?" Alice was just as excited as Ranweer, they checked in with each other's allotment plots most days to guess what food would be ready in just the right time. Ranweer had an impressive range of squashes that were sure to be just perfect. Alice was hoping her sweetcorn would be ready for a perfect vegan chowder and some of the colourful squashes would also be at their peak.

"Just a thought," Maddie had to interject again, "Do you have a food hygiene certificate? You need to have one to sell food you have prepared yourself."

Ranweer looked crestfallen, "No, I didn't know that. We don't have one do we?" He turned to Alice hoping that she would miraculously say she already did.

"No, we don't. Do we need to go to college? We don't have time to do a course."

Maddie knew all the details, in marketing and business it was her job to keep abreast of all legalities, she had seen many people get unstuck out of ignorance or just not looking into things properly. "It's fine, you can do it online. It shows you can demonstrate that you know how to store and prepare food safely. You just print it off and display it near your stall."

Ranweer and Alice looked relieved. They were confident they could manage that, so disaster was averted.

Maddie looked at Esther, to signal she should continue. Esther's face was set hard and Maddie could have sworn she looked piqued at Maddie's interference.

"Filo, how about you?"

"I have lots of craft things to sell but I thought I would do it in a wellness tent, I can give tarot and aura readings, perhaps some Reiki. I'll have the craft on display in the tent too."

"Steve, Gail, do you have any updates for us?"

Gail leant forward, happy at last to be able to contribute. "Good news, we have both booked the day off so we can be there all day. Also, we have permission to bring the Resusci Annies with us, the children will love to have a go at saving lives, it will be fun and could prove really important to someone one day. We'll also show them how to do simple dressings and bandages, take blood pressure, you know, all of that kind of basic First Aid stuff."

Steve joined in, "We can bring everything, like antiseptic wipes and all of the dressings and slings. We will just need a couple of tables and chairs."

Esther's face brightened, "That's fantastic, thank you both. Have a think about how much you can charge for the experience, don't forget this is all about raising money too. Tom, can you start making a list of what each person needs for their stall? Norris…."

"Yes Esther, Jean and I are going to give flower arranging tutorials." There was a collective murmur of appreciation around the sofa. "I'll also have a lot of produce to sell, I will box it all up attractively, so people can just by a box of mixed vegetables for the week. I'll do different sizes for different size families. Jean will lead the flower arranging, she'll charge a small fee and they can take their arrangements home with them. I'll donate the flowers from my plot and Jean's friend is donating the foliage. Janis from The Flower Shop is donating ribbons and floristry oasis, you know, the green stuff you poke the flowers into."

"Norris mate, that sounds great!" Tom spoke for the first time and looked at his old friend kindly.

Esther smiled at Norris warmly, they had been friends for many years, and she knew he was getting a little slower and finding things a little harder, so his effort was really appreciated.

'Yes, it does Norris, it sounds really very good, thank you and please thank everyone who is helping you too. Tom, do you have anything to add?"

Tom leant forward resting his arms on his knees and hanging his hands down between his legs, "I've been able to get a couple of generators from my mates who run Mikes Bikes in town, they have a few extension leads too but I need to source some more. Remember Patsy, the school patrol lady? Well, she is on the school PTA and they have some free-standing floodlights that we can borrow. What I need to know is what equipment everyone wants and then I can collect it and have it put up in time. Does anyone have any gazeboes?"

"My parents do," Maddie offered. "I think they have a few of the pop-up ones that are quick to erect, and they may have the side panels too, that you can add to them if the weather's not great. I'll ask them for you, I know they won't mind."

"Thanks Maddie, I can come by and collect them nearer the time, if they don't mind. I think that's all for now, I'll start a list when the meeting's finished, so before you all go tonight can you come and see me? All I ask is you don't leave anything to the last minute, its only me and Norris and my truck and I'll need time on the day to set up early in the morning, so I can't be running around. Thanks everyone."

"Thanks Tom, Maddie have you got an update for us?"

Maddie felt she had little to contribute compared to everyone else. "Yes, I have given the designs into our printing department for the posters and leaflets, they are all ready to run. They need a week's lead time, so I'll need to give them the go ahead soon. I've held off until the last minute in case of any date or venue changes. I can get one lot of posters printed through work, but I think I'll struggle to get another batch done if something goes wrong. My boss has kindly said I can use the facility for the charity, but I don't want to push my luck."

Everyone agreed the date and details were now set in stone and she could order the printing to be done.

"I have given the local radio all of the details and they will start dropping in name checks from about the middle of September. I have set up a Facebook page and an Instagram account, I've already started adding to these and now I know some of your planned activities, I can add even more. We have a few likes already, but I need you all to 'like' the page and then encourage your friends and families to do so too, that way it will spread out and get the word out there."

"And what about those of us who don't have Facebook?" Maddie felt Esther was deliberately being a little bit negative towards her this evening.

"That's fine, we will have the posters and leaflets and if you can help deliver these instead, that would be great." Maddie remained cheerful but had a small impression she was being challenged; she didn't know why, surely everyone was working together.

"Okay, that's really good progress everyone, let's take a break and then we can do a few more agenda items and Any Other Business." Esther stood and headed for the toilet, followed by Norris who had had quite enough tea. Maddie realised she needed the bathroom too so headed upstairs whilst everyone put in another order for drinks.

The stairs and landing had no carpet, just bare floorboards which had been painted gloss white at the edges. Maddie opened the first door and saw it was possibly a spare room. It was carpeted a child's shade of pink with mauve, pink and yellow unicorn curtains. There was a single bed covered in piles of folded bedding and towels, a fishing chair and a few storage boxes with lids and a guitar. On the floor, stacked up against the wall were hundreds of cardboard tubes filled with rolled up posters. Tucked behind were several loose sheets, curled up at the edges but she could see instantly that they were paintings or drawings. She picked the first one up and pulled it open, her arms stretched out wide. It was a garden design, painted in delicate water colour.

In the centre was a sunken garden set inside a stone Amphitheatre, but instead of steps going down, it had a spiral path coiling around to the lowest point. A beautifully carved oak handrail followed the pathway down and in between each sweep of the path, planting was added, low lying lavender and soft herbs to soften the edges and taller shrubs of every colour. Together it created a dramatic dish. The seating on the bottom was sheltered and anyone who sat on the benches would have the perfect position to smell the lowest level of scented plants.

Dotted around the central painting were carefully sketched studies of some of the elements of the garden, a wide water wall pooling gently into a trough of lilies, hollow steel poles of various heights with holes drilled all the way through, the handwritten caption read 'Steel Reed Pipes - the music of the wind.' Low slung wooden carved swings were covered with blankets, big enough for two people to sit together and talk beneath the apple trees from where they hung. The seats of the swings had been carved and smoothed to form small hollows so each person could sit snuggly without sliding off.

The ideas before her fascinated Maddie, the painting was beautiful, it was so delicate and the care taken was obvious to see.

"Are you lost?" The voice behind her made her jump. As she saw Tom standing in the doorway, she felt ashamed, she hadn't meant to snoop. The painting hadn't been hidden as such, but all the same she shouldn't have been in the room looking at his belongings. She felt her face heat up with the rising blush.

"I'm so sorry, I was looking for the bathroom and then saw these. I wasn't snooping, honest!"

"Let me give you a little hint," his eyes smiled despite his serious mouth. "Bathrooms have these things called baths in them, usually a toilet and a sink and if you're lucky, a shower too. They're quite easy to spot once you know what you're looking for."

"Oh, very funny," Maddie knew she was being teased and he wasn't angry. "But bathrooms don't have beautiful paintings, like these, in them, they'd get damp and run."

"This is very true; you are more of a bathroom expert than you're letting on!"

"I may have been in one or two, now you've described them to me…. a few years ago, perhaps." Maddie was enjoying the banter, Tom had shown his playful side to her once before and now again, his whole face lit up, he was gentle and considerate, pushing his luck just enough without being hurtful.

"Did you paint this, Tom? It's really beautiful."

"Yes, it was a design for a care home in West Sussex. They'd been left a private donation with the request it was used to set up a garden sanctuary. You see here, this sunken area is protected from winds and it's wheelchair and stumble friendly. I have added something for all the senses, the planting is highly scented, lavender of course for calm but also chamomile in the lawns, white star jasmine for height over the walkways here and the smell is amazing as you walk through. The steel pipes are positioned on the corner of the building where the wind clips around and through them, they have a low pitch, gentle and relaxing, not like some of the wind chimes you can get that just get on your nerves." Tom's enthusiasm was animated, he pointed and waved his fingers over the painting to draw out each element. "The garden has lighting all around that's operated by remote control and the staff link it to their smart phones to blend with music. There are hidden waterproof speakers all around. They use it for outdoor tea parties and themed evenings, like Burns Night or the Summer Solstice picnic."

"Did you actually get to build it?" Maddie was seriously impressed; she had no idea this was the type of design that Tom did for a living.

"I did indeed, about two years ago now, I loved doing it, lots and lots of tea and cake on the job."

"I didn't realise you...."

"…. could do anything like this?" he teased her.

"No, well, yes I guess, the painting is beautiful, and the ideas are so thoughtful, you're very talented."

"Thank you, but I don't really do it anymore."

Maddie was just about to ask why, it seemed such a waste, he was truly talented but Ranweer was calling upstairs to gather everyone back together.

"I'll let you go and see if you can find that bathroom," he gently removed the paper from her hands and rolled it up and placed it carefully on the floor. Maddie hesitated, she had so much she wanted to ask him but Ranveer called again so she wandered down the corridor knowing Tom was still smiling at her as she opened each door and peered in, until the last door at the end. She entered and turned to close the door, smiling at him knowingly and gently closed it tight.

By ten o'clock the Harvest event plans were well and truly in place, decisions had been made on a new rota for the allotment shed shop, Norris had told everyone the wood chip supply would be temporarily stopped whilst the local wood merchant was sold and Filo had held a tarot reading for everyone, collectively telling the group they were on track to make lots of money for the hospice.

Both ladies were contemplative on the way home. Maddie had tucked her legs up in the passenger seat, hugging her arms around her knees to stop them falling back down into the footwell. Filo concentrated ahead, the rain had slowed but the night had drawn its curtains closed and she found the sparkle of the raindrops through the streetlights disorientating.

Maddie was pleased she had gone to the meeting. If she hadn't, she would not have seen Tom's house or his talent. She puzzled at the lack of warmth in his home, she had assumed he would be a home maker with homemade furniture, interesting nick-nacks, Norwegian style blankets and evidence of countryside pursuits, not hunted or stuffed animals but perhaps wall paintings, bits of farm machinery or a dog. And why was there a child's bedroom? As far as she knew there were no children in his family or perhaps, he had a child that no one had mentioned?

She puzzled at the way Ranweer had grabbed Alice early in the evening to give her a lift home. Ranweer missed seeing his children go to bed on meeting nights, but he liked to spend some time with his wife, so was keen to leave. Alice just called out goodbye to everyone and didn't talk to Tom, as far as Maddie could see. She guessed it was easier for Ranweer to drop her home on his way than Tom getting his truck out again to take her home.

Esther had definitely seemed a little odd this evening. At first Maddie thought it was aimed at her, but she noticed a few other jibes and clipped comments towards some of the others, it seemed very unlike her to be unkind.

Filo had her own thoughts. It was only when Maddie turned to ask her about Tom's home that she realised, unusually, Filo hadn't said anything at all for the whole journey and they were nearly back at her house.

"Are you okay?" Maddie furrowed her brow.

Filo snapped from her trance. "Oh yes, yes, don't you mind me, I'm okay, I'm just thinking…. oh damn, you confided in me so it's only fair I do to you. I didn't only see positive things in tonight's tarot, I saw something else, I didn't want to share it, but it was very clear to see."

"What on earth was it?" Maddie could see whatever Filo had seen was bothering her deeply.

"I saw an accident, or someone hurt, it was definitely health related but more of a sudden thing, like a trauma. The specifics weren't given to me, so I didn't say anything, I don't want anyone to worry, the tarot isn't for that purpose. But now, I'm worried that I had a personal vision, I am very in tune with the spiritual world and perhaps I've seen a sign. Supposing a member of the public gets hurt at our event? Or one of us? If I saw it and didn't do anything about it, I would feel dreadful."

"Oh, no Filo, you can't think like that! You said yourself everything is open to interpretation, it could have meant a hundred different things, you are absolutely not having a premonition, no one is going to get hurt." Maddie's practical tone spoke firmly to Filo.

"But it felt so strong!"

"No! No! No! Listen, you must forget this, you are tired, we all are, it was a long meeting tonight. Please get yourself home and go to bed, it will seem insignificant in the morning." They pulled up outside Maddie's house and left the car windscreen wipers to scrape on the now dried glass. Maddie lent over and squeezed her friend's shoulders. "Honestly, everything always looks better in the morning." She got out of the car wishing Filo would leave the tarot readings for charity events and parties. She took too much store in what she read in those pictures and Maddie didn't have the patience to deal with it tonight. She bent down and waved through the small window at Filo and pushed open the garden gate.

Her phone rang at six thirty in the morning.

"Filo, what on earth are you doing calling me at this hour? What's wrong?"

"It's Esther, she's had a heart attack!"

Maddie flung the phone still connected across the bed and swung her legs out. On the floor last night's underwear and clothes lay still turned inside out. She struggled to get dressed and grabbed the phone from the duvet, Filo calling out if Maddie was still there.

"Yes, yes, I'm here, oh my god, what happened?"

"She went home from Tom's. She had told me earlier that she wasn't feeling too good. I didn't connect it with my readings, Esther is always complaining, she's my good friend but boy can she moan sometimes! Anyway, she called Tom to say she felt unwell, she was having trouble breathing. Tom called an ambulance and by the time he got to her house there were blue lights outside. She's okay, well she was half an hour ago when Tom called me, but I'm not allowed to go and see her until she is on the wards, whenever that may be. I did it, I did this to her, I should have told her what the cards said...."

"Filo! Just listen to yourself. If someone says they don't feel well, you can't tell them they are going to have a heart attack because some cards told you so. This had nothing to do with you or those cards. Where are you now? I'll call into work and say I'll be late."

Maddie had a quick shower and pulled on her fleece jogging bottoms, a T-shirt and a hoodie top. She had called work and left a message to say she would need to book a day off due to an emergency. Finding her trainers, that still had mud on from her first visits to the allotment, she jogged down the road to wait for the early commuter bus.

Filo stood in her doorway wearing striped flannelette pyjamas that were several sizes too big. Huge fluffy duck slippers nodded and wobbled as she opened the door wide to let Maddie in. The house was dark, thick curtains were still pulled tight against last night's rain. Filo grabbed Maddie and pulled her into a bear hug.

"I can't thank you enough, I couldn't bear to sit here by myself just waiting for the phone. Tom has promised to keep me informed but it's the not knowing."

Maddie busied herself opening the curtains and collecting up the dirty novelty mugs that littered the shelves and coffee table. She sent Filo upstairs to shower, telling her it could be a long day and took herself into the kitchen to wash up. The home phone rang as she heard the boiler start up, Filo would be in the shower, so she grabbed it.

"Tom, how is your mum?"

"Is that Maddie? Sorry I was expecting Filo."

"Filo called me first thing, I'm at hers, well of course I am, I'm on the phone…." Maddie heard herself rambling.

"Look, I can't be long, can you just tell her mum's stable, we managed to get her to East Surrey Hospital in really good time, so they saw her straight away. They said it was a mild attack but a warning sign to slow down. They will keep her in, they're still doing observation tests and she won't be allowed visitors for a little while. I'll let Filo know more when I do. I think she will go up to the wards once the day doctor sees her, later this morning hopefully."

"Oh Tom, I'm so glad she's okay. You must have been so worried."

"Yes, it was pretty scary. I thought she was invincible, a real tough cookie, but it just goes to show you, any one of us could get ill at any time."

"Yes, that is so true. Is there anything I can do to help?"

"That's really kind, Maddie. No, thanks, I think I'll be okay. If you could just let the others know for me, please, I called Filo as they are good friends, but I haven't gotten around to telling anyone else."

"What, even Alice?"

"Alice, Norris…. everyone. If you can let them know I'd really appreciate it. And please ask them not to call the hospital, the staff are so busy, they can't have everyone calling them. I'll update Filo and then she can pass messages on."

"Of course, it's not a problem. If there's anything else just ask!"

There was a pause for a few moments, "It's just been nice hearing your voice, comforting."

Maddie didn't know what to say. She had lost her grandfather recently, but they had been prepared for that, he had been ill. Esther was strong, or so she had thought, and Tom only had his mum in his family, Maddie wanted to reach out and touch him to know she was there.

"I'd better go," she heard Tom hang up but she still held Filo's phone to her ear, trying to send positive thoughts down the line, trying to stay close.

"Was that Tom?" Filo stood wrapped in a towel with her hair tied up in a turban. Maddie relayed the messages and the two spent the rest of the morning at the kitchen table staring into their mugs of tea.

It was two more days until Tom called and said Esther could have two visitors at a time. Maddie had stayed with Filo; she couldn't leave her alone worrying. She had plenty of days annual leave to use and her boss had been very kind in letting her take some at late notice. Filo had run Maddie home to pack a small bag of clothes and toiletries. Fiona started to protest at Madeleine taking time out of work for 'someone that she hardly knew' but Maddie felt this was the right thing to do. It was the only place she wanted to be. Dominic had left endless text messages and voicemails. She didn't want to explain herself, the protests from him demanding that she called became weary. She had texted him a few times on the first day and said a friend was very ill and she was staying at home until everything was okay. She had hoped for an understanding response, some kind words, empathy of some nature but as each day passed, she felt his anger pour through down into her phone until at some point she didn't care anymore. She would have turned it off except Norris had taken to calling her on behalf of the others, she became the communication chain and she couldn't risk not being there for everyone.

"I am going to be out of meetings between three thirty and four o'clock, call me, I will be waiting," today's first text.

"Don't let me down, I am arranging my whole day for you to call me," second.

"It's just after three thirty, why aren't you calling?" third.

"It's three fifty, this isn't good enough Madeleine, I am waiting in a corridor for you to ring."

"This had bloody well not ruin our holiday, how well do you know this person anyway? It's gone four, I've got to go back to work, thanks Madeleine, thanks a lot!"

Maddie looked at Filo packing a bag to take to the hospital. Her heart went out to her, she had been beside herself that Esther's heart attack was somehow her fault. Filo piled in packets of wet wipes, several gardening magazines, a bottle of lucozade (because that's what everyone drinks when they're poorly), a homemade lemon drizzle cake, an old hairbrush, an old nightie, a photo of Alan Titchmarsh cut of out a magazine and stuck into an old photo frame and a packet of cashew nuts that she had found at the back of a cupboard.

Maddie was going with her. They told Tom he could have a proper break, go home for a while knowing Esther had friends there with her. Tom had barely left the hospital since she had been admitted. Depending on the staff on duty he was either banished to the empty canteen throughout the night or allowed to doze in the armchair next to his mum's bed.

When they arrived, Maddie was shocked at Tom's gaunt face, his long stubble was greyer than his hair, ageing him considerably. Filo flung herself at him, wrapping herself around his chest. Maddie hung back, she didn't feel she had the same familiarity and suddenly felt she shouldn't be there. After all, she and Esther hadn't known each other for very long. Seeing someone in hospital, at their lowest and most vulnerable was a privilege left to those who are close. Now she was in the hospital, she felt she was intruding and taking the place of someone else, someone who knew Esther for longer. She stood awkwardly.

"Maddie, thank you for coming," Tom strode the few steps between them and put his arms around her. He bent his face down and laid it briefly on top of her head, breathing in deeply the fresh smell of her hair. Her own face pushed against his him, she felt the shape of his chest, firm but soft enough to cushion her cheeks against his tight squeeze. "It's so good to see you, both of you."

He released her gently. Maddie felt the space between them heavy with unspoken words. She had never been so aware of another person's closeness to her, she wanted to reach out and pull him back into their embrace, she could easily do it, just reach out and pull. He stood just an arm length away, yet he was untouchable, she could smell his musty clothes, she still felt the imprint of his chest on her face, her desire to hold him made her arms ache but she stood still, watching Filo clucking around her, her voice sounding like it was somewhere in the distance, all Maddie heard was her own breathing.

Maddie snapped out of her own thoughts as Tom was pointing down the corridor, with hurried instructions on how to find the ward. He smiled at Maddie as he left, promising not to be too long.

Esther lay behind a drawn curtain, in one of six bays in the ward. Two other beds were surrounded by visitors, mostly standing up as the blue, vinyl armchairs were piled high with coats, bags and clothes. One patient lay alone and was calling out, she wanted to go home and was making her views very clear to anyone who walked past. Two beds were made up ready to receive the new intake. Esther's hospital gown had slipped on her shoulder revealing a thin wire attached to her chest with a suction cup. A machine on wheels, next to her, beeped rhythmically.

"She won't shut up!' Esther exclaimed; her eyes still closed but knowing she had new visitors standing there. "All day and all night, shouting her head off, I can't stand it, take me home!"

"Oh Esther, I was so worried!" Filo flung herself across the thin form that lay beneath the cotton sheet. "I knew something bad was going to happen, I should have warned you…"

Maddie sighed inside. They had talked about the tarot reading in the car and Filo had promised not to bring it up with Esther.

"What are you dithering on about, you silly old fool?" Esther squinted as she opened her eyes to see her friend bent over her with her head lying on the invalid's knees.

"Hi Esther, I hope you don't mind me coming too," Maddie changed the subject quickly and gave Filo a stare that forbade her to say another word about it.

"It's lovely to see you, of course I don't mind, it's really sweet that you did." Esther looked genuinely pleased through her tired and grey smile.

Filo emptied the contents of her bag on the bed, the cake had been packed at the bottom so now resembled a flan, Alan Titchmarsh was soon propped up next to a water jug on the bed trolley and the cashew nuts got opened and Filo's fingers were instantly stuffed inside the packet. Esther watched wearily but her smile was warm and the fondness of her friend was heartfelt.

"How are you feeling?" Maddie felt a little conspicuous standing there, looking down at Esther. "We've been so worried about you."

"Oh, I'll be fine, I just had a funny turn that's all, don't know what all of the fuss is about. I have to stay here listening to this bloody machine and that bloody woman, *she* wants to go home apparently, well we all do because of *her*."

"Are you getting any sleep Esther, you look worn out," Filo was now sat side saddle on the bed clutching her friend's hand.

"Of course I'm not, what with the nurses waking me every time I fall asleep to prod and poke me and then someone keeps pulling the emergency cord instead of their light switch. I've asked for sleeping pills, but they won't let me have any. Filo, bring some in for me, would you?"

"I really don't think you should," Maddie felt she had to intervene as Filo started to take out a notepad to write a list down. "They may interfere with something else you've been given. You can't risk your heart being overloaded."

The curtain swished back and a nurse strode up to the bed. She pulled the clipboard from the foot rail and flicked a few pages backwards and forwards, without saying a word. She silently took a small gun type machine from her pocket and placed it in Esther's ear until it beeped. She unwrapped a stethoscope from her neck and placed it on Esther's chest whilst grabbing her wrist, gazing at the second hand on the clock above the head of the bed.

"Well, it seems you are doing very well, Mrs. Squires. The doctor will come and see you shortly and if she is happy, then you are going home."

"Thank goodness for that! I can eat a decent meal at last." Esther's bluntness did not impress the nurse who roughly pulled the curtain back as she left the cubicle.

"You must come and stay with me," Filo was overjoyed and beamed broadly. She looked at Maddie apologetically, "I'm sorry, I only have one spare room."

"That's fine, of course it is, now Esther is getting better I'd be heading back home anyway." Maddie had enjoyed staying with Filo, they had shared stories of each other's lives and had swung from laughter to sadness as each tale was told. But Maddie needed to get back home and to work, she couldn't stay away any longer. She had almost forgotten about work and Dominic. Being happily cosseted in a Filo bubble, she had found herself truly relaxed and was surprised at how easily she was able to abandon the other side of her life, it was liberating and it would take all of her will to get back on the train to London on Monday.

Shortly after a good catch-up and the tea trolley coming round, a young woman peered around the curtain, "Mrs. Squires?" Esther nodded and the doctor smiled at her and picked up the notes and spent a while quietly reading.

"So, what we have here is a little voice from inside telling you a very serious message. It is saying to you, if you don't slow down you are going to make yourself very poorly. It is saying that you are not the young person you think you are anymore, and you need to take things easier."

Tom pulled the curtain around his shoulders and across his back like a cape and stepped into the small space now full to capacity.

"Hi, I'm the son, Esther's son, sorry I was late and missed the start of what you said."

"That's okay, Mr. Squires. I was just telling your mum that we have concluded our tests and this has been a little scare, nothing to go home and worry about too much except there needs to be some lifestyle changes. There is to be no stress and worry, gentle exercise, healthy eating and not too much of that!" pointing to the flat cake on the bed.

Esther was indignant, "But I do eat healthily, I grow all of my own fruit and vegetables. I exercise by keeping the allotment and I don't have any stress."

"Mum, you are taking on too much. There is the Charity Event, you insist on leading all the meetings and won't let anyone take minutes for you. You help at the scouts and guides; you volunteer in the charity shop as well as run around checking on all the neighbours. You do need to slow down; you may not think it's stress but just take it a little easier."

"There you are, listen to your son please. Make an appointment to see your doctor in the next two days and they will continue with ongoing checks. You can go home as soon as you are ready." Indicating to the tubes and leads, "I'll send the nurse in to disconnect you." The doctor left with a nod to the group.

"She's coming home with me," Filo insisted. Tom didn't argue, his house was not set up for another person and as much as he loved his mother, having her under his roof full-time would have been challenging.

Maddie made her excuses to leave, she said she could get the bus home as Filo wanted to fuss over Esther and take her home herself. As she gave her goodbyes, Tom jumped up. "I'll give you a lift, you don't need to get a bus. Filo and mum will need a bit of time before they can go home anyway, so I'll just get in their way." Maddie was grateful, the buses to her end of town ran very infrequently and it looked like the wind had picked up outside. Without a jacket she would be cold. Tom collected a few things that he could carry for his mum, gave her a kiss on the cheek and said thank you to Filo. Together they left for the car park pay booth.

"What will you do about your bags at Filo's?" Tom pulled himself up into the pick-up's cab.

"It's only one bag with a change of clothes and my pyjamas, they can wait until I next see her." Maddie had her handbag which was all she needed for now. "Thanks again, I really appreciate the lift." She looked across and studied his face from the side, as he maneuvered out of the car park to join the main road. He hadn't shaved, he had only hurried home to shower and change his clothes before rushing back. She looked at his forearms stretched out to the steering wheel, soft downy hairs covered his well-defined muscles, he had a collection of plaited leather bracelets around one wrist, with the sleeves of his chequered over shirt rolled up. He looked like a rugged lumberjack, handsome in his roughness. His default face was surly and serious but when he turned to her briefly and smiled, she could see the warmth and kindness that only those in his inner circle could know about. His eyes drew her in, connecting in a secret, knowing bond. She felt safe, without saying a word she trusted him, she was calm and cocooned in a world cut off from the outside. She relaxed into the leather seat and closed her eyes, suddenly tired.

"How long have you and Alice been together?" it just came out. It had been unplanned, but the silence seemed to require a question and Maddie had asked it before thinking it through.

"Me and Alice, I'm not sure what you mean? Like friends?" he kept his eyes straight ahead as she kept her eyes closed to avoid the chance of her face giving anything away.

She curled herself up into a ball as if to sleep. "Oh, I thought you two were an item. I'm sorry, I must have made a mistake."

He flicked his eyes towards her, his glance felt by her, but she remained in a half doze. It provided a screen between them, making it easier to talk. "No, we are just good friends. We have helped each other through our break-ups and she's like a little sister to me. We get on really well but it will always only ever be good friends." He felt the need to make his position clear to Maddie, he wasn't sure why, but he wanted the honesty to be laid out, no confusion, no lies.

Maddie's confusion sat silently in her head. She had been sure they were together, Tom was always at arms' length because of Alice, her lovely, new friend Alice. She realised she had kept a distance from Tom, even as a friend, because of Alice's gentle nature, she would never have hurt her. But then, surely, she should have been keeping away from him because of Dominic. Didn't she owe Dominic that much? What did this revelation mean now? Has anything changed between her and Tom? She hadn't allowed herself to consider him anything more than a neighbouring gardener. So why has this news made her heart lift? He may not see Maddie as anything more than an annoying novice, was she so conceited to think that he had feelings for her? This news meant nothing had actually changed between them, only in Maddie's head. She opened her eyes to come back to reality and shift from her daydream within.

"I'm sorry, I jumped to conclusions, Alice is lovely, I just assumed that's all."

Softly he spoke. "Don't worry, there's no harm done, as long as you know now." Tom glanced at her again and this time looked deeper into her, it was the briefest moment, but they both felt it. The silent, unspoken knowing.

The rest of the drive was in silence. Maddie gazed out of her window to avoid having to speak next. She only spoke to tell him where to pull over, she grabbed her handbag and slid off the leather seat down onto the grass verge. As she went to close the door, he stopped her.

"Maddie?"

"Yes."

Silence.

"Can you ask your parents about the gazebo for me please?"

"Oh yes, of course, thanks I had forgotten. Bye."

As Maddie walked through the hedge archway, she didn't see Tom hitting his forehead on the steering wheel in frustration and telling himself what an idiot he was.

Why are there more people on the tube on a Monday than any other day? Surely most people will also work on a Tuesday and a Wednesday? Or was it simply Madeleine's mood that meant the bodies pushing up against her were heavier and sweatier than normal. No one glanced up or nodded a smile. Everyone stood swaying from the ceiling ropes avoiding the fact that their armpits were closer to a stranger's face than any member of their family had the pleasure of. She had snoozed her alarm so many times as if to dare herself to miss the trains, she had willed the phone to ring, to say work had been shut down due to a burst water pipe, a gas leak, the River Thames rising to a dangerous level.... nothing where anyone was actually hurt, but just as a precaution. No call came.

For years she had walked into Claremont and Butler with a sense of anticipation and pride. She had seen people glance at her as she stepped through into the vast atrium from the street, their envious gaze at the smart businesswoman, with her life in order, all set out, healthy and successful. But today she carried a dark cloud above her, she couldn't put her finger as to why. The last few days she had only thought about her new friendships and with this she felt content and at peace. As she walked towards the lifts, she felt a rising angst of what lay ahead for her, the endless emails to catch up on, the unfinished task of forming some type of credible presentation for the competition, Roseanne must think she has fallen off the edge of the earth and Dominic, most of all she couldn't face Dominic. She pushed the button to take up to her to her floor.

"Wait, Madeleine, hold the door!"

Dominic stepped into the lift in a cloud of aftershave that Madeleine knew would have cost at least £200 a bottle. The four other people in the lift stepped back to let him in, he lent in towards Madeleine and hissed in her ear.

"Where the hell have you been?"

"I told you, with a friend in hospital."

"Why haven't you called me? It's been nearly a week!" Dominic was seething, spittle sprayed her ear from his clenched hiss.

"Not here, Dominic," the force surprised her, but she was in no mood to put up with his tantrum today. "Come to my office in an hour once I've sorted some things out."

The door opened as someone pushed forward to get out. She stepped out too and although there were still a few floors for her to go, she made her way to the stairs to avoid getting back inside.

Exactly one hour later Dominic walked into her office. He sat across her desk; his arms folded across his chest. His side fringe had grown long and he had to keep flicking his head to keep it off his face. Eventually he unfolded his arms to push his hair back and then didn't seem to know what to do with them.

"Well?"

"Well what? I told you I wouldn't be in to work, I told you where I was and why. I don't know why you are acting like this and I'm sorry Dominic, but I don't have to explain myself any further."

"I thought we were closer than this. I thought we were in a relationship and when two people are in a relationship they keep in touch. I expect to be able to call you when I want."

"Expect? Expect? That's the point Dominic, you do a lot of expecting and I have been too quick to jump."

"What the hell does that mean?"

Madeleine had started and she was prepared to see it through. She didn't need to analyse what was happening, all she knew were the feelings she had had over the last few days compared to those of today were poles apart. She knew she hadn't missed Dominic; in fact, she had been relieved not to see him. Absence can make the heart stronger but equally it can give you clarity. She hadn't stood back far enough before today to see things clearly, but the recent space had allowed her to see what was happening in Dominic's arena and she didn't like it, she didn't like herself and what she was becoming. She was strong person, not a doormat. She had a voice and opinions and wasn't prepared to allow Dominic's ego to crush her.

"Exactly what I have just said. You do things and expect me to be there, to agree, to change my plans and to do things your way. For months I have found myself following you, being there when you want me to be and always at your beck and call, your bidding. When I have done things for myself you sulk, like a child."

"So, there is someone else, isn't there?"

Madeleine couldn't help the laugh coming out loud. "I am telling you the reasons I don't want to be with you, and you are assuming it can only be because there is someone else? You still don't recognise that I have my own mind at all do you? It is possible, Dominic, that someone doesn't want to be with you. I know you probably haven't come across this phenomenon before, but it does exist." She didn't like the way she was resorting to sarcasm, but the annoyance and rage was building inside her and she couldn't help it.

"And what about the holiday? We are supposed to be going in a couple of weeks."

"I am not going away with you, Dominic. I didn't want to in the first place, but you didn't listen to me."

"So, what do I do with the tickets? I have paid for it all. That's just brilliant Madeleine, you can pay me what you owe me."

"That's fine, if that's what you want, I'm happy to pay my part of the holiday. Just give me a copy of the receipts and I'll transfer the money to you."

Dominic stood up.

"You have no idea what you're giving away. I could give you success and money that anyone would be envious of, there are plenty of girls who would give anything to be given that opportunity."

"Dominic, I am quite capable of giving myself the success and money or whatever it is that will make me happy, thank you. I don't need you to do that for me. I want a partner who will want to be happy and successful in whatever shape that comes for themselves first and foremost and only then will they be mature enough to share their lives with me. I hope we can remain professional about this; we have a lot of work to do and I need to concentrate on that. I'll see you at tomorrow's staff briefing and we can meet with Roseanne to discuss next steps."

Madeleine could hear her own calmness and measured reaction to Dominic. She felt more powerful and confident that she had for many months. She was cleansed, free and the dark cloud drifted out of the door as he closed it behind him.

It was all so surprisingly easy. Dominic avoided Madeleine for the rest of that day and at the staff briefing the following day he sat with some of the team from the print office. He emailed a meeting request to both her and Roseanne for later in the afternoon which turned out to be respectful and professional and apart from a few quizzical glances from Roseanne, no one would have known there was anything amiss. Just before she left, an email came from Dominic with an attachment of scanned receipts and his bank details; the flights and hotel were all separately booked, along with a few excursions. She winced as she added them up and halved the total amount but once she transferred her funds, she knew that was the end of it and she felt only relief.

As she walked through the London streets to the tube, she asked herself, "What next, I wonder?" As if it heard her, her phone vibrated in her bag.

"Hi Filo, is everything ok?"

"Yes luvvy, everything is going really well. Esther won't eat any of my food and is insisting on getting one of those delivery things from the supermarket. She has been on Tom's laptop for hours trying to work it all out. He lent it to her to keep her out of trouble, but it's opened up a right ol' can of worms!"

Maddy smiled, she could just picture the two of them bickering fondly.

"I'm glad it's all going well. I must collect my things anyway at some point, no hurry though."

"I took the liberty of washing your clothes, I hope you don't mind but I thought they might be festering in a bag for so long."

Maddie giggled and wondered at how she really didn't mind this strange act of kindness.

"Anyway sweetie, Esther wants a word with you!"

"Ok, I am early for the train, but I only have a few minutes, if that's ok?"

"Maddie, is that you?"

"Hi Esther, how are you feeling? I'm so glad you're on the mend."

"I'm fine thank you or at least I will be when I can order my favourite biscuits. Filo is baking these awful healthy options and they don't dunk into my tea properly! Look, Maddie, I know you're in a hurry, but I wanted to ask you something…."

Maddie was curious, Esther had never asked anyone for anything as far as she knew. She was an extremely capable lady and prided herself on being so.

"Both Tom and Filo have been nagging me and I have realised they may be right, I need to let some of my activities go, at least for a while and I wondered if you would take on the Harvest event for me, I mean the organising of it. You are so good at all of that kind of thing; I know I will be handing the baton over to the best person."

"I don't know what to say. I would be honoured; I know how much it means to you. I will do it of course and I'll do my very best for you. I'm surprised though, I thought you didn't like some of my ideas?"

"Don't listen to this old fool! I'm sorry about the allotment meeting, I wasn't feeling well and didn't want to raise the alarm or be a burden to everyone. You have the best ideas and you know what you are doing, I was ungrateful as I wasn't feeling my best and I hate to not be running on all cylinders. I'm sorry if I was rude to you. Filo has told me I was rude to everyone, but she has forgiven me."

"Of course I forgive you too, it's perfectly understandable, you must have been feeling awful. You really should have told us you weren't well."

"Thank you, Maddie, that means a lot to me and I'm relieved now to let it go. Honestly. it's your baby from now on and if you want to change anything then please do, I really won't mind."

They finished the call with a fond goodbye. Maddie realised she was beaming, another good friendship just getting better and better, a new challenge, being recognised to do her job well and appreciated. She had asked 'what next' and she thinks she may have just been given the answer.

Chapter Nine - SEPTEMBER

Name: Madeleine Richards

Re: Extraordinary meeting for the Harvest Charity Event

To: 'Allotment Owners'

Hi all, just to let you know Esther has asked me to step in to lead on the Harvest event organisation. I know you all join me in wishing her a speedy recovery. Can I ask that we have a short additional meeting this week, on Thursday at 6.30pm? As we are enjoying an extra mini heatwave, it will be lovely to hold it at the allotments. Please bring a drink and nibbles. Can you pass the message on to those

without email please?

Thank you and hope to see you Thursday, Maddie

Maddie had been busy since taking on the role from Esther. She had kept her in the loop of everything she was planning, the last thing Maddie wanted was to make Esther feel excluded. She had been surprised at how much Esther really had taken a back seat, Filo said the heart attack had frightened her more than she admitted, so when Maddie told her the changes she was going to make, she expected a little resistance but there was none at all. Esther just told her it all sounded wonderful. She closed her office door and left for the station.

September was glorious so far. Maddie loved the early autumn. For some, the tiny signs of changing leaves, from green to burgundy, made for sadness and a sense of loss but to her the colours and food that autumn provided were a source of great delight. Of all the times she had spent with her grandfather, it wasn't the hot and sultry days of summer that she remembered, it was the harvesting of food, the pickling and bottling back in his kitchen, the laying out of potatoes and onions to dry, the collecting up of apples falling too early from the trees and finally picking them once they were ripe to slice into crumbly apple pies. They would gather blackberries and she would wash them and pop them into the bottle tops of cheap brandy ready for Christmas. Her fingers stained purple. She would be on sloe watch; they knew the best places to collect the sloes for gin and each season they would be ready at slightly different times of the year. They were at their best if a good frost caught them as they ripened. But if the autumn was mild, she would pick them and put them in her grandfather's deep freeze for a few days before squeezing them, juices oozing, into gin to give as presents to family and she knows now, to Norris and Esther too. She had already spotted some in hedgerows, still green and not yet the ideal dusty purple; she was ready to pounce once they were ripe.

Maddie's allotment was still going well. She accepted it was only yielding a fraction of what was possible, but she knew her limitations. Norris had told her to start small and he was right! She was still learning every time she visited. She had some successes but also a lot of failures. A whole set of outdoor tomatoes had caught blight, the stalks and fruit all turned into brown mush and the whole lot went into the bin. The leaves on her runner beans were eaten by slugs or snails and the few beans she had were covered in silver sliver juice which put her off eating them. But her sweetcorn was standing tall and proud, like a tortoise formation in a Roman army. Each stalk had about six cobs wrapped tightly up in their blankets. She watched for the fronds at the ends to start turning brown, then they were ready to be harvested. She couldn't wait to unwrap them and savour their sweet bounty; her favourite way was simply steamed with a knob of butter and a sprinkle of salt. One of her greatest pleasures was to see her queue of sunflowers dancing happily along the edge of her plot. They had been a gift from Ranweer, he had grown them from seed and gave them to her once they were strong enough to stand a good chance of survival. They had, even better they were admired as some of the best in Queens Gardens.

Fiona was standing in front of the oven, peering into the glass. It was set at head height, recessed into a cupboard along with various drawers filled with pots and pans. The hob was at the other side of the kitchen. The room was old-fashioned, the units were dated in shiny dark oak with a flowery pleated pelmet over the kitchen window. The sink was a creamy beige with brown plastic taps. The worktop had ring stains from many cups of tea over the last few decades. But it was cosy and homely and familiar. Maddie came in from work and pulled herself up onto the kitchen stool and asked her mother how her day had been.

"Not too bad, I've been shopping, Thursdays always have good bargains. I think they empty out ready for the weekend rush. I've made Shepherd's Pie for tea." Fiona was a fairly good home cook. She had a collection of tried and trusted dishes which were cooked on rotation. If she entertained, however, she would buy things in ready prepared, she wasn't confident in the more adventurous menus that she saw on her daytime cooking channels. "How was your day?"

"It wasn't too bad actually; I've got a few clients who I'm working with, and I'll be quite glad to get the competition done and dusted. It's been an extra layer onto my days that I could really do without." Madeleine waited for the comments. She wished she could talk honestly to her mother without the instant negativity and challenge. Why couldn't she just accept what Madeleine had said and be sympathetic, empathetic, or supportive?

"But surely that's the one thing you need to be putting your energies into, Madeleine? You won't get far if you regard it as a hassle. It should be your priority. What does Dominic say about this? Why haven't you brought him to see us again anyway?"

Madeleine took a deep breath. "Dominic and I aren't seeing each other anymore, only as work colleagues."

Fiona put down her oven glove and took a sip of her wine before asking.

"Well, why is that then?"

"It just didn't work out, that's all. We want different things."

"Well, I thought you were perfect for each other, you don't often get a man like that, successful, handsome and obviously liking you a lot. You can't go around being too fussy Madeleine, what is it you want anyway? What *is* better than Dominic?"

"I don't want a man who bosses me around for a start!" Madeleine heard herself snap at her mother, but she hated the way she had to explain herself in everything she did. It made her feel like a child.

"I'm sure he didn't do that, Madeleine. Did you try hard enough?"

Madeleine had heard enough. She wasn't prepared to sit and justify herself and convince her mother that Dominic's attitude and behaviour wasn't just in her imagination. She shouldn't have to do that. She could see yet another initially congenial conversation quickly sliding down the drain, so she took herself upstairs to get ready for the evening's meeting.

As she came downstairs a short while later, she heard her mother telling Henry how she had let another opportunity slip through her fingers. "I really must try and get my own home soon," she muttered to herself as she slipped her head around the kitchen door.

"Hi dad, can I borrow the gazeboes for the Harvest event at the allotments on the eighteenth of October?"

"Hi love, yes I don't think that will be a problem. I'll have to get them out of the back shed and dust the cobwebs off. Remind me a week before, will you?"

Madeleine thanked him quickly before she was drawn into a second interrogation for her father's sake and left the house to enjoy the last of the evening's warmth. There was a buoyancy in her step as she cut through the new housing estate towards Queens Gardens, she wasn't sure why but she felt more excited about the forthcoming Harvest event than that of many of the projects she has led for years. She knew a lot of the allotment owners would be here tonight, she was strangely nervous about taking her first meeting which was ridiculous, she had led many hundreds of meetings with very important people, but this was personal, this bridged her everyday world with her newfound friends; they would see her strengths rather than always being the student. Most of all she didn't want to let them down.

She spotted Alice behind the lean-to shed on her plot. Alice was waving madly at her, wearing a pair of dungarees made up of patchwork squares with a bright yellow T-shirt underneath. Her hair was back in tight dreadlocks piled high on her head with some strands coiled round in a large bun. She wore John Lennon sunglasses with bright red lenses. Her smile was broad and welcoming. Maddie thought she looked stunning.

"Hey you, I hear you've married me off to Tom!" Alice's laugh was deep and genuine. "I couldn't stand his rock music all day or his passion for a rare steak! No way, he's all yours!"

Maddie was embarrassed, is that what Tom had told her? That she wanted him for herself?

"No, god no, what makes you think that? He is definitely not my type either. Don't you worry, I've got no designs on him either. Far too grubby for me!" Maddie started to laugh but quickly realised Alice wasn't joining in. "Oh god, he's behind me, isn't he?"

"Yep, the grubby one is right behind you!"

"Tom, I am so sorry, I was only teasing, we were having a laugh that's all." Maddie wanted the earth to swallow her whole and quickly. So much for starting with a good impression, her confidence plummeted, and she would have given anything to turn the clock back, just one minute.

"It's okay, you're not my type either, so we're all fair and square." He gave a weak smile but Maddie could see the damage she had done, she was never usually cruel, it wasn't in her nature to be unkind. She was only covering up a feeling that if she spoke about Tom out loud her body would belie her and tell a different story. He was a friend, that's all, well he was until one moment ago. They stood looking at each other. "We'd better get this meeting started then," was all she could think to say. He didn't hear her muttering 'stupid, stupid, stupid' to herself as she went to round up the others.

Maddie would have enjoyed the meeting, had she not been so conscious of the things she had said. The others were relaxed, sat in a circle near to Norris' patch, drinking wine and cider and munching on crisps and cakes. She had led the meeting well, everyone contributed, more than usual she noticed, she saw that as a good sign.

She told them of her plan to move some of the venue to the Bowls Club car park. She had spoken to the club and they were happy to cordon off the top end, nearest to the allotments.

By extending the space Maddie wanted to bring in more activities and give visitors plenty of things to interest them as well as bring in money. She reasoned that if people were making the effort to attend then they should be rewarded with a great time. She had notified the local cadets who were more than happy to help out with car parking and a crossing patrol on the road. She would get them high-vis jackets to identify them as marshals. She explained how the day could be broadened with a programme of events. She had a local singer and the school brass band already lined up with more people getting back to her. She explained the music license would cost money, but the local Garden Centre had offered to sponsor the event in exchange for some advertising and a hedgehog awareness stall. They were launching a hedgehog campaign in the store, so they wanted to set up a pop-up version at the event too. No-one objected to the plans and she could see a growing excitement about how the day was shaping up.

An idea sprang into Norris, "What about the Morris Dancing Troupe? My Jean knows the leader, I'm sure they'd love to do a routine for us."

"I could put on a demonstration for cider making," Craig, one of the new allotment owners, who had been working on his plot, had asked to join the meeting. "I have a press and equipment; I'd be happy to do that. I could sell some of my cider from last year?"

Maddie felt the ideas were flowing well but wanted to make good decisions without being rushed. "Yes, to the Morris Dancers, they fit the Harvest theme as I think they celebrate fertility and let's face it, Harvest time is all about fertility. And the cider demonstration is a great idea, thank you Craig, but I am not sure about selling the cider this year, we would need a license for that too and we already have the Bowls Club offering to open their bar to non-members in exchange for their car park. Can we see how it goes this year and maybe plan for an alcohol license next year?" Everyone seemed to think this was a sensible decision and Craig didn't look too disappointed.

"Okay, so I'll adjust the leaflets and radio and social advertising with the new extended venues and parking availability. That should bring in more people. So now, I wanted to explain my last idea to you all, to see what you think...."

Maddie gave a pause to make sure everyone was listening, Filo and Ranveer were discussing his wife's syrup-soaked pistachio cake which had gone down a storm.

"At the Plant Sale in June I remembered I had so many people asking me for gardening tips and advice. I hadn't a clue, of course, and had to keep sending them over to you all to fill in my knowledge gaps. At the time I thought we should have offered a service, a gardener's forum, like a Q and A or something like that. And then it hit me, why don't we have a small tent with a few seats in it and hold demonstrations and themed talks? After all, this is an allotment group's Harvest Open Day as well as raising money for St Anne's. People would expect there to be people here who they could ask advice. We could publish the times of each talk or demonstration and charge a small fee to go into the tent to watch it. What do you think?"

No one spoke. They all just kept looking at Maddie as if she was still talking, no one wanted to go first.

"Oh, come on guys, this would really turn the event into a great day, but I do understand I'm asking a lot from you, I know you may not have done anything like this before. Norris, you and

Jean could bring your flower arranging into the tent, Craig, you can do your cider making demonstration, this way we will be sharing tips and getting some money for the charity."

Maddie was on a roll. Her enthusiasm was beginning to spread its magic.

"One of the sessions could be a Q and A, just like on Radio 4. At a certain point, probably at the end of the day, we all leave our stalls and come into the tent together, so there will always be a panel of experts for any question that gets asked."

Ranweer was the first to speak out.

"I think it's a great idea. I'll be happy to do an Asian Vegan cookery demonstration if Alice doesn't mind me leaving her on the food stall for a while? I can bring my little stove in and do something simple, a one pot meal or stir-fry."

"You know Jean and I were already happy to do our flower arranging, we can still do that throughout the day but I'll think of something special for our time slot in the tent, maybe with a Halloween theme for the kiddies."

"Norris that's inspired!" Maddie was delighted that they were warming to the idea. "Halloween will only be a couple of weeks after the event and we'll have squashes ready to carve or use as props for the stage. Well, I say stage, I mean tabletop! I'm getting carried away now too."

"It looks like I'm going to need bigger list then?" Tom sulked. "We're going to need a tent and chairs, a microphone for the entertainers, an easel with a board to show the times of the talks and lighting to make it look a bit professional...." he looked exhausted.

"Thanks Tom, I appreciate it will be more work, but we can all help, I'm going to be running around on the day and I'll book off a couple of days before it too, to help set it up. I won't leave it all to you." Maddie was desperate to make amends and although she wasn't sure Tom would want her around him, she didn't want him to feel over-burdened or used. His grunt spoke volumes.

Maddie set a deadline for a few days' time to tell her the name and content of each person's topic for their tent appearance. She would get everything printed and published early next week.

She was worried she was pushing them too far with her ideas. They had started the whole charity event with just a few stalls selling their produce but now she had elevated it to a community event that could easily become an annual fixture. She was taking them out of their comfort zones in the demonstration tent but they seemed to rise to the challenge, even Filo was prepared to leave her Tarot stall to give a talk about the healing power of crystals. There was going to be a wide variety of things on offer for everyone, that was for sure.

The party drifted off. Maddie saw Tom skulk off towards his allotment plot, so she followed him quickly. He ducked into his caravan which doubled as a shed, full of tools and bits of wood. Most of the compost cages dotted around were Tom's work, Maddie's grandfather had made the originals but over time Tom had replaced and repaired them. He didn't hear her come up to the caravan door.

"Tom, I just wanted to say sorry again. You only caught the end of the conversation, we really were only having a banter, I didn't mean what I said, and I feel terrible."

"What part didn't you mean? I'm too grubby or I'm not your type?"

"Well, both, I mean the grubby part, no both, oh now you're making me confused!"

"That two of us then. I thought we were getting along okay. I didn't realise I was that repulsive."

"You're not, you know you're not. Now you're just trying to get me to give you compliments. Alice had been teasing me so I was throwing it back at her, it was all a joke but I can see how it wasn't nice to hear. I'll keep saying sorry if that will help?"

"No, you're okay. I've been called worse, usually by my own girlfriends, so don't worry about it." Despite his serious face Maddie laughed, he was teasing her now, so she knew they were going to be okay again.

"Friends?" she asked.

"Yeah, alright, friends. In fact, that reminds me, I have something for you. I meant to give it to you a while back, hang on and I'll find it."

Maddie had forgotten he was going to give her something on the day James visited her. She couldn't think what it could be.

He returned from the back of the caravan, stepping over piles of wood on the floor. In his hand was a small brown envelope, folded over several times to stop whatever was inside falling out. She unfolded it; it weighed no more than the envelope itself. She looked inside to see two tiny pieces of paper, no bigger than the nail on her little finger. As she pulled them into the light, she saw they were photographs, or rather two cut outs from actual photographs. Despite having to screw up her eyes to focus, she knew instantly what it was. On one was her grandfather, exactly as she remembered him here in the allotment, at the age she would have spent most of her time with him as a child. He was smiling at the camera and looked healthy and younger than she took him for back then. But there was no doubt it was taken around the time of their closest days together. In the other was a young girl, she didn't recognise her at first but then it dawned, it was herself aged about eight or nine. She hadn't seen the picture before but now she could see it was definitely her.

"Where did you find these?" she held them as if they were the finest treasure.

"There were some old photos in mum's photo box. I found them. The one of your grandad was taken by mum here in the allotments, there were a lot of other people in the original photo who I didn't know, so I cut it up to take your grandad out, mum didn't mind. And the other one, that was a photograph taken here too, I think on the same day. I spotted you in the background. You told me you didn't have any photos for your necklace, I thought they looked the right size."

Maddie stared at the images in her hand. She had very few photos of herself and her grandfather together. There were plenty separately or together at family events but as far as she knew there were none of the two of them here, at the allotments. She stood speechless, overwhelmed.

"Tom, that's the kindest thing ever, I don't know how to thank you, I'm so touched that you thought of it, I think I might cry!"

"Here, let me see if they fit," Tom stood in front of her and lifted the locket up from her throat. His large fingers struggled to open the clasp. She felt his breath on her face as he lowered his head to see the locket closer. He gently lifted the tiny frame from one half of the locket with his nail and picked the first photograph from Maddie's open palm. He laid it in and replaced the frame on top of it. He did the same with the other picture on the other half.

"Perfect fit!" he beamed.

Maddie took the locket from his fingers and wrapped her hand around it protectively. Impulsively she threw her arms around Tom's neck, standing on her tiptoes she stretched up and with the briefest hug breathed 'thank you' in his ear.

"It's my pleasure, Maddie. I told you, I was very fond of your grandfather and now…."

"Now?"

"Now, I have to go home." He took the caravan keys from the padlock dangling from the door latch and began to lock up. "I'll see you later."

As he left, Maddie stood for a while holding the necklace in her hand before running to Filo's to catch her before she left. Filo had a mirror to look at the locket for herself. She knew she was well and truly forgiven by him for the earlier incident. For someone so surly at times, Tom surprised her often. She would treasure the necklace now even more.

The evening light was drawing in as she walked home. The sun always seemed exhausted at the end of the summer, choosing to bed down earlier and earlier at such a speed. One day the sun sets at ten o'clock and the next blink it is seven thirty. And in the spring, the sun seems to take its time rising from its hibernation, taking so long to get lighter each evening, endless days of waiting for the chance to sit out in the garden for a drink or a barbecue. Maddie felt suddenly tired, the day had been a strange one, sending her in peaks and troughs of emotions. She had the anxiousness of leading the meeting, the excitement of sharing her ideas, the plummet of her error with Tom and the joy of his forgiveness, his gift had overwhelmed her.

She turned the corner towards a stretch of main road where a few local shops lined the path. Two Chinese takeaways (Maddie always wondered why a second one would open in a row of only ten shops in total), a late-night newsagent who also sold convenience foods and a whole wall of little sachets that held everything from tap washers to hinges, wood screws to coils of electric wire. There was a launderette, an Indian restaurant (small from the front but opened up to be vast inside), a flower shop, a Spar, a cut price Booze Emporium, a chemist and at the far end Janie's Hairdressers. She was about to cross the road when a familiar man and woman came out of the newsagents and walked the same direction that she was heading. She recognised the back of James, her brother, instantly. His flared jeans a little baggy around the bottom, a slightly creased T-shirt and his floppy dark hair long to his nape, messed up and sticking up in all the wrong places. His companion was unmistakable. Her patchwork outfit suited his perfectly, they looked bohemian, relaxed and as they looked at each other and held hands, very much smitten.

Maddie hung back. She didn't want them to see her. It wasn't that she was spying, she didn't wish to intrude but she needn't have bothered, they weren't aware of anyone around them, they were talking and laughing, James bent down and gently bumped his forehead on Alice's as he grinned at her and tried to snatch a bite of the snack she was eating. They were playful and so happy in each other's company. Maddie remembered James had asked about Alice when he came to the allotments, he must have gone back at some point to find her. They looked made for each other and Maddie was over the moon. She was so fond of Alice, she wouldn't mind her being around at all, she would bring fresh air to their stuffy household. She hoped James would bring her home soon so she could enjoy her company more. He had only brought one or two girls home and they never lasted long enough for a second visit. She hoped he would look after Alice and not treat her the same. Alice was too kindhearted, and she felt protective over her. But she wouldn't say anything to either of them yet, let things take their course and if it all worked out, then Maddie, for one, would be delighted.

"Hi Tom, it's Maddie. I was hoping to catch you, my father is clearing out the shed and has kept the gazeboes out for you. He's found some outside lights and bits and pieces that may be useful too. Did you want to come over at some point to collect them? Give me a call or a text, ok thanks, oh it's Maddie by the way, or did I say that? Of

course, you know that, how many fathers are lending you gazeboes? Anyhow, let me know...... " BEEP

What is it with answerphones that make people lose the ability to speak? Maddie was about to go and run a bath when the phone rang back.

"Hi Maddie, sorry I couldn't get the phone out of my pocket in time. Are you okay?"

"Hi, yes, I've just left you a message. My dad has the gazeboes. He's having a clear out of the shed ready to bring some of my grandfather's tools over. His old house has been sold and the exchange date is soon, so they need to clear it out. Anyway, are you able to store them until the charity day?"

"I should think so, yes, I've got space in my garage. When does he want them gone by?"

"As soon as possible, I think. Sorry for the short notice."

"How about now?"

"Yes, great thanks. You remember where we live don't you?"

Tom confirmed he remembered where he had dropped her once before and she swapped her planned bath for a quick squirt of deodorant and a fresh swipe of lipstick.

"Dad, this is Tom."

"Hello son, how are you? How's your mum getting along? Madeleine told me she's been ill."

"Hello Mr. Richards, nice to meet you again. Mum is doing really well, you can't keep her down for long, she is tough. Thanks for asking."

Maddie was surprised they were so familiar.

"Come through and I'll show you what I've found for you. There may be a few spiders in the gazeboes so watch yourself when you open them out!"

The two men went through to the back of the house where a pile was ready for Tom to collect.

"Who's here?" Fiona came home carrying two bags of shopping with her handbag slung diagonally across her body. She gently kicked the door closed behind her. "I don't recognise the truck outside the front."

"It's Tom from the allotments. He's come over to collect some things for the Harvest event. Dad's showing him the pile, out the back."

"Tom? As in Esther's boy?"

"That's him, he's doing all of the equipment for us. He said he'd collect it early as dad needs the space."

Fiona's face set hard. "Oh, I see. Is your brother home, I've got lamb chops for tea?" Madeleine looked at her mother puzzled but helped her unpack the food into the fridge and cupboards.

"I've not seen him today, but that's nothing new."

"He's been quite evasive lately; I think there may be another girl around? Who knows, maybe one day he'll settle down. And talking of settling, have you seen anything more of Dominic lately?"

Madeleine sighed. Fiona had brought up Dominic at every opportunity. Despite Madeleine making it very clear it was all over, Fiona held onto some hope that it was all a mistake. The fact that Madeleine had told her he was possessive and controlling made no difference, Fiona had decided Dominic held the key to

Madeleine's success. How could she have let such a good man go? Hadn't she tried hard enough; a partnership is a two-way thing? You're too independent Madeleine, you need to give and take. Madeleine was tired of explaining.

"That's it, all loaded." Henry came through into the kitchen from the back door, followed by Tom, his T-shirt now covered in stripes of thick cobwebs with a smudge of dirt across his cheek. Fiona looked him up and down. His hands were covered in dried black oil from where he had tinkered earlier with his engine, his jeans were green around the knees where he had knelt in the allotments to fix Filo's fence post, his old trainers were filthy.

"Hello, Tom." she couldn't hide the disapproving sneer. Madeleine winced; her mother was capable of being highly rude even when being nice. It was quite a skill.

"Hello Mrs Richards, nice to see you again." Tom continued with Fiona warmly, ignoring her look of distaste as he grabbed her hand to shake it.

"I'll come with you if you like, to help you unload at the other end." Madeleine saw an opportunity to leave, she knew there would be an analysis of Tom and she couldn't be bothered with the ensuing comparisons with the dashing Dominic. She already knew the rhetoric, her mother was a snob, a blinkered snob. She had her view on the world, what people should look like, their career, their homes and if they didn't measure up to her ideal then they were damned. She loved her mother, she knew she was lucky and had a good life still living at home with her parents but increasingly she saw the limited world Fiona had built around herself and the scorn she held for others. She judged and disapproved. Madeleine saw the world differently, she embraced difference, she was curious about others and welcomed the chance to learn more about them. Where Madeleine was warm, Fiona was tepid. Not cold, not openly rude but she had a disdain deep inside and Madeleine couldn't understand why.

"But we've got lamb chops for tea Madeleine, what time will you be home?"

"I'm not sure mum, if you could plate it up for me, I'll heat it up later, like you do for James, that will be lovely, thanks."

Fiona watched her daughter leave the house. Plate up her dinner? Not stay and help? Is this Tom the reason for Madeleine's lack of direction lately? The frown remained until after Henry had listened to Fiona's berating and had passed her a glass of wine.

In the car Maddie felt she had to ask, "Do you know my mum and dad then?"

He flicked a glance at her, a little confused, "Yes, of course, through your grandad." He didn't elaborate and drove the rest of the way in companionable silence.

Tom's house was even more sparse in the daytime without the warm lighting to cheer it up. After off-loading the equipment straight into the garage, Maddie joined him for a coffee. The small kitchen felt too intimate to stand in whilst the kettle boiled so she wandered around the living room, trying to find something to look at and open a conversation with. "This vase is beautiful. Is it hand crafted?" "I love your wall print of the trees of Britain, where did you buy it?" "Your candles smell amazing, which flavour are they?" Instead, Maddie stood awkwardly gazing at the soulless garden.

"Awful, isn't it?" Tom stretched out a mug towards her.

"I didn't want to be rude and say it first but, yes, it's not what I expected." The daylight revealed the full extent of the garden's lack of character and lack of anything resembling a living organism. It looked like someone had picked up a garden display from inside a DIY shop and plonked it outside Tom's patio window. The space was perfectly square with a new fence all the way around. Bright green plastic grass touched each edge, tucked in like a wall-to-wall carpet. Perfectly spherical lime balls dangled from wall brackets on every fence post, fake topiary bobbing in the wind. The only respite was a flagstone patio with small wall and a green tarpaulin cover over what she imagined was a table and chairs. Apart from that, nothing! No plants, no pots, no trailing climbers,

"There's no point me doing anything to it, it's not mine," Tom explained simply.

"Oh, isn't this your home then?"

"It's my home I guess, but not my house, I rent it."

It made perfect sense now. "Oh, I see, I couldn't see you creating a garden like that, you're far too organic. Now I see why you spend so much time at the allotments."

"I try and escape the house and the garden; I don't like either really."

Maddie was now intrigued. Why be in a house and garden that you don't like?

"I do have a house. Well, I did have a house but my ex bought me out of my share when we split up. I stayed at mum's for a while but no adult child should go back to their mum's, it's embarrassing and as much as I love my mum, I couldn't deal with her treating me like her little boy again."

"So, you found here to rent!'

"Yes, there was nothing on the rental market at that time, I was lucky when this came up, I just happened to be in the estate agents when they took the call and I took it without even viewing it. I knew the area and the new builds so I knew it wouldn't be awful. It's not awful, it's just not really me."

"No, it's really not that bad but as you say, it doesn't reflect you at all. So is the children's bedroom for your daughter?" Maddie was sure she would have seen Tom's daughter, or he would have mentioned her. He was always at the allotment alone so maybe he didn't get to see her often?

"I haven't got any children. The bedroom was already decorated like that. I never use the room so there's no point in me decorating. I don't intend staying here too long anyway. Although I said that a couple of years ago and I'm still here, us men are so lazy!" Maddie laughed with him as she thought of James. She wondered about telling Tom about James and Alice but it wasn't her business, she had no right in spreading their relationship as gossip.

"Can I see some more of your garden designs?" Maddie had been intrigued about the piles of drawings in the spare room and wanted to know much more about this man and his talent.

Upstairs, Tom made space on the single bed for Maddie to sit down whilst he juggled the tubes of drawings, reading the descriptions he had written on each side. He pulled out one or two for her to see. The first was not painted but drawn using coloured pencils. It gave a soft, springtime tone to what looked like a cottage garden, huge deep borders of plants with a key written down the side describing the choice of planting. The detail of a winding brick path was enlarged on the other edge of the paper, forget-me-nots tumbled over the edges, moss creeping along the cracks. It was a small garden, just visible was an outline of fences through the archways and tumbling rambling roses. It was pretty, really pretty but Maddie couldn't see the significant design element like she could in the painting she had seen the previous week.

"Did you get to create this garden, in real life?"

"I certainly did, look out of the window."

It was then that she understood the skill and imagination. A few doors along from Tom's house sat a sumptuous garden overflowing with colour and interest. The contrast between it and its neighbouring shells of emptiness was incredible.

"I was commissioned by my neighbours to do something with their garden. They bought their house and couldn't stand the plainness of it. They love gardening but didn't know where to start. It's only two years old so there's still a lot of growth to happen but you can see what it will look like in the drawings. It took a lot of digging; I can tell you! These new builds have so much rubble in the garden, we dug it all out completely and filled it with good soil. It was hard work but worth it for the future. It was better to start with really good preparation than work around the stones and bits of bricks forever more."

"It looks fantastic, who would have thought that you could turn a garden like yours into something like that, it is so clever."

"The trick is to go large, in a small space don't fill it with small pots, give it big statements, big curved borders and bold structures like the wooden arch and pergola. Then fill it with plants."

"I'm impressed, you are very clever!'

Maddie handed him back the paper and picked up the second one from the bed. This was different again, it showed a block of flats, only three stories high, with small balconies and children playing outside on the grass. Attached to each balcony was a wide window box that extended along the front and side and continued out onto the wall. Running down the length of the walls were aluminium rods which drove down through each window box, leaving each box with three rods sticking out of them. On the enlarged detail, Maddie could see the rods were designed to act as climbing poles for plants, they were thin and allowed the homeowner to plant taller plants to grow upwards and not interfere with the balcony above them. The wall boxes weren't too long, so no-one would need to stretch out too far and the overall effect was each balcony had wraparound planting, if they chose to use it. The flats looked so much prettier than if they were kept plain.

"This is a design I did for a housing company. They build homes for people needing social housing. Many of their tenants would have loved a garden but this was the next best thing. The company didn't have much scope, or money to do anything too extensive. They asked for a simple idea that was easy to erect. The window boxes are wider than normal and have a special fixing and drainage system, so you don't get dirty water running down underneath. Look, the small tubes running underneath go to these drainpipes, all the way down to the ground. I loved doing this project. When I met the tenants, they wanted to believe they had a garden, they wanted colour and to show their children how to grow plants. I've been back a few times to look and some of them have created amazing spaces, it's so much healthier for the families to be able to do this."

"I bet that was so satisfying to do, to help families who needed colour and gardening in their life? It's so important for the soul, isn't it? It's all about well-being and being positive."

"I like to design for a purpose, one that impacts on people in a positive way. It's the relationship between the spaces and the people that intrigues me, how a well-designed space can influence how we feel, our mindset... even our health."

"I can see why you loved doing this design so much, I'd like to go and see it one day, if I can?"

"Of course, it's in London, so I'll give you the address and you can go and have a look one day whilst you're in Town."

Maddie was looking at Tom intently, he could see she was thinking about something, computing it in her head before letting it spill out.

"Do you still do commissions?"

"No, I haven't had a chance, my relationship broke up, I moved to mum's and then here. I did the neighbours' garden to keep me busy and the allotment takes up a lot of my time, so I haven't really been out looking for work. I'll need to soon though, as the pot is beginning to run dry!"

"Tom, pop the kettle on again, I'd like to talk to you about something."

"So, this guy is a friend of yours? You don't know his background or qualifications and you're recommending him?" Roseanne was bored, she didn't see the relevance in anything Madeleine was telling her. She wanted to get away early today, she was meeting a friend in the bar down the road and her lipstick shade said she wanted to make a night of it. Her right leg crossed over the other bouncing up and down with impatience. Her shoes were, as always, impossibly high and the heels were covered in hundreds of shiny silver spikes, if she accidentally rubbed her ankles together, she would have ripped her skin open. Her dress was, in Madeline's opinion, not suitable for office wear, it was a tight black dress, so shiny it looked like plastic or indeed rubber! Her whole 'look' today was of a dominatrix.

Madeleine had called Roseanne and asked if she was free for just a minute, she had something to run by her. She thought she had hit on a brilliant idea but didn't want to take it to Dominic just yet, he was still prickly with her, polite and businesslike but very distant and not very cooperative. She didn't blame him. In his eyes they were in a relationship, it just didn't match her image of one. It was never going to work between them. What had shocked Madeleine was how easily she had become submissive. She always regarded herself able to stand up for her beliefs, self-assured and able to have difficult discussions in order to put her opinions across yet with Dominic she became a pathetic, people pleaser. She didn't recognise herself when she was with him. She didn't like herself when she was with him. She was disappointed in herself for even starting any kind of relationship with him. She had known it was against the rules and there was a very good reason for that, because when it all falls apart (as it was bound to) what happens next? A cold, working relationship that is strained and not productive, that's what!

Roseanne was as cool towards her as always when Madeleine walked into her office. Roseanne had recently freshened herself up and her office smelt overpowering in a fog of deodorant and Millionaire perfume. Roseanne continued to tidy away her desk and packed her handbag as she invited Madeleine to say whatever it was that she had on her mind. "I've only got a few minutes," she warned as she clicked off the power to her PC.

When it became clear Madeleine had a lengthy explanation, Roseanne pulled out her chair and crossed her long legs with her arms folded across her chest unimpressed.

"Look, I know this has come out of the blue but if you saw his work you'd understand. His values sound just like Mr. Ito's. He wants to blend working and living spaces with health and well-being. He has proven himself able to take his designs through to completed projects, we can go and view some of them. He has a portfolio with excellent feedback from his clients. I really think this is our missing link. We're running out of time, and we need to bring in a concept, something that draws everything together. Tom's ideas can do just that. I think we should invite him in to meet us and see what comes out. At the very least he can give us a few ideas, or if the Board like what they see maybe he'll get commissioned for the work too."

"I think you're getting a bit carried away," Roseanne had heard enough. She picked up her bag and headed for the door but turned as she opened it, "But what's to lose? Invite him in and set it up with Dominic too. Ask him to bring some of his work and we'll see what he's like, if he's any good." Roseanne didn't wait for Madeleine's response. She had left already.

Maddie spotted him instantly, he stood dangerously close to the edge of the platform clutching a huge, leather portfolio case. A non-stop train smashed past him sending the case sailing up into the air, he held onto it but took a few steps back into the safety zone. He looked up and saw Maddie coming towards him. She looked different. Groomed. Less natural. She had a full-face of make-up, a long ladies' trench coat, open, with the belt tied behind her and a smile. Underneath the coat, she wore beige, flared slacks with a tight crease down the leg, stiletto court shoes and a silk blouse. Gone was her usual rucksack, replaced with a tan leather briefcase.

"I almost didn't recognise you," Tom stepped towards her, as if to kiss her cheek in greeting, but stopped himself. "You look very clean."

"Thank you very much," Maddie laughed. "So, you're saying I'm usually dirty?"

"I prefer the dirty look," as soon as he said it, Maddie saw he regretted his choice of words and looked embarrassed.

To spare him, the train pulled in. Most of the seats were reserved, little tickets stuck up on the headrests indicating a passenger was going to sit there. Maddie expertly prowled the aisle scanning the tickets quickly and grabbed Tom's arm to pull him into a pair of seats.

"These people aren't getting on until East Croydon and even then, the chances are they won't show up. We can sit here for now at least."

Tom heaved his case up onto the luggage rack and took his overcoat off. Underneath Maddie saw he was wearing a beautifully fitted suit. It was dark navy and she guessed woollen. The trousers were an intentionally tight fit down his legs, the jacket was open to reveal a perfectly pressed white shirt, the cuffs poking out at his wrists held together by two cufflinks, blue stones set into silver casings. His tie was dark, burnt orange which matched his suede shoes, tied through a single eyelet with a simple brown lace. She noticed the hint of his round stomach, not enough to stretch his shirt but she fought back an urge to pat it.

"Well, talking of not recognising people, where did you come from?" Maddie teased him with a curved smile.

"I have been known to have a wash from time to time," he retorted, settling into his seat next to her. Maddie was instantly aware of their thighs touching. The seating arrangements were sparse on the train and many times she sat squeezed up against a stranger, yet she never noticed before today how intimate the feeling was, to be almost laying against the person in the next seat.

"How do you feel about today?" she asked him.

"Okay, it is just to meet these people isn't it and chat about your project? It's not an interview or anything is it?"

"No, no, honestly. It will just be me, Roseanne and Dominic. You've seen Dominic before; he came to the pub once with the allotment gang. Roseanne can be a bitch, but she's like that with everyone, don't take it personally. Dominic isn't talking to me much so he may be a bit frosty but none of this is anything to do with you. They'll just want to hear some ideas for the Bittern Quays development, how to bring in garden spaces to give the workers a sense of nature and calm. Have you had any ideas about it?"

"So, it's definitely all over with this Dominic guy then?" Tom ignored the work-related question.

"Yes definitely, it never really started I guess, I felt it was wrong from the start. His ego didn't take it very well though."

"I can see that would have been a problem for him, he looked like the trophy girlfriend sort of guy."

Maddie wasn't sure how to take that, but the conductor saved any more talk about Dominic as she came through the carriage for the tickets, singing a reggae tune to cheer up the early commuters. The journey flew by, talk turned to Esther's health and how amazingly well she was recovering. Tom was finding it difficult keeping her resting but as she was still staying at Filo's house it had taken the pressure off him a lot.

The underground journey and the early autumn stroll through the streets of London was so much more pleasurable with two. Normally Maddie kept her head down, pacing out the familiar route but this morning she looked around seeing her commute through new eyes, Tom's eyes, and she appreciated it all over again.

As they entered the foyer together, Tom stood and whistled. His gaze travelled up the vast, glass atrium which glistened with a thousand hidden lights. The marbled floor shone so much it looked wet.

"I had no idea you worked somewhere like this?" he whispered.

"I'm used to it after all these years but I had to pinch myself when I first got the job, it is amazing isn't it?"

They went through the signing-in procedures, Tom clipped his visitor's badge onto his lapel and looked a little less confident than before. Maddie squeezed his arm in reassurance and nodded her head towards the lifts.

There was no time to get nervous as Dominic and Roseanne were already sat in the glass meeting room. Tom and Maddie stepped from the lift. The look of surprise from the room wasn't disguised. Moments before Roseanne had been giving a monologue in a West Country accent, mimicking Tom's introduction to himself. Dominic had called him The Country

Bumpkin. The sharp, handsome man who towered above them was the exact opposite of what they expected. Dominic immediately went into defensive mode in what Madeline recognised as a sulk.

Roseanne dived straight into flirt mode and unpeeled herself from her chair to greet Tom with a warm smile and clasped his outstretched hand in both of her's. "Really lovely to meet you, Tom. Please come and sit." She pulled the chair out next to her own and motioned for him to join her.

Maddie introduced everyone, although it was obvious who everyone was.

"I'll start," Dominic looked a little uneasy but wanted to take the lead. "Madeleine has told us that you design spaces to bring gardens and plants to the people who most need it, is that right?"

"In a nutshell, yes, but there is more to it than that." Tom exuded confidence in the room. Maddie felt a rush of pride. "I design spaces to maximise the sense of well-being to anyone who comes into it, it could be an outdoor space or an indoor one. I use horticulture as a medium to link our natural infinity with the environment. Nature is the human race's source of power, of nurture, of health and the basic roots of our physical and emotional cycle of life. Add to that, the sense of fulfilment and pride that people can get from growing and looking after a living organism, not only to prevent it from dying but to give it everything it needs to thrive and live and reproduce. I design spaces where people can do as little or as much as they need, to make them feel healthy inside and out and above all happy."

"Fascinating," Roseanne was leaning in closely watching Tom's face intently.

"Tom, show them some of your work." Maddie should have felt jealous about Roseanne's sudden interest in Tom, but she was making herself look a little ridiculous and Madeleine just felt sorry for her. She knew Tom wouldn't have noticed the sad attempts at flirting.

He unzipped his case and spread out a collection of sketches, paintings and photographs onto the table in the middle of the room. He matched the photographs with its drawing to demonstrate a 'before and after' story.

"I'm sorry, I didn't have time to put these together into a presentation but I'm happy to talk you through any of them." Tom proceeded to talk through the design briefs, the concepts, and key aspects he wanted to achieve from each and then the final results along with his customer's feedback and recommendations.

"Has Madeleine told you about the competition we are working on?" Dominic was impressed with the work and could see why Madeleine had brought him in. He watched the two of them closely, looking for clues of anything else going on between them but he hadn't spotted anything to make him think this man was the reason she had left him.

"Yes, she has. I have had some ideas. Basically, I envisage the Quays being loaded with areas inside and outside where people can interact with the natural environment but more than that, I would take it to another level and have the staff actively take charge of the planting, including the care and ongoing design. I would expect any staff who wants to work in the Quay to commit to taking ownership of their working environment. As a member of staff, they 'own' a piece of the space and must keep it alive. If I was the boss, I would have it written into their contract along with time in their working week to do it. It will keep them moving, keeping fit, getting them away from their desks and all the digital stuff that they do all day. Active and motivated and that way, they'll be more productive. Even better if they can produce items to eat, sell, put into the canteens and such like…."

Roseanne jumped up and slapped Tom on the shoulder. "You've hit the nail on the head, I love it! We're not sure if the Quay designers will take it on board but we can certainly add it to our marketing, it fits the brief perfectly. It may not actually get created but it will make Mr. Ito sit up and look at us as his marketing company."

"I have to agree," Dominic added reluctantly. "It is the kind of thing that Mr. Ito wants to hear. We're not sure about the whole Board, we have only tapped into his likes and dislikes, but he is a key member of the Board. Madeleine, where do you want to go with this, as this was your idea?"

Of all his faults, Dominic was always a good team player. Madeleine appreciated his thoughtfulness and turned to Tom. "Do you think you would be able to draw us some images of what some of the spaces could look like? Even better if there are staff members in the spaces, working, creating, exercising and so on. What do you think? We'd be able to commission you obviously, we have expenses for the project."

"Yes, I don't see why not. Just give me a time frame and I can do something for you."

"We'll work out the timings. We'll need to take your drawings to the design team here to work their magic, so we will need the drawings pretty quickly. I'll call you later once we've had a chance to work it all out, is that okay?"

Tom nodded this was all fine, he was relieved they liked what they saw and even more relieved he would be getting some income from it too. Dominic shook his hand and thanked him for his time. Roseanne held onto him again in an extended goodbye, pressing his hand into her abdomen as she shook it gently. He packed his things away and Madeleine walked with him the door.

Once safely in the lift, Tom turned to Maddie.

"Bloody hell, do you have to spend your whole day as uptight as that room was?

"What do you mean?"

"Well, Roseanne, the man-eater, was enough to stress the hell out of me in just a few minutes and Dominic is so slippery, I'd have to strap a mirror to my shoulder to keep an eye on him slithering up my back."

Maddie laughed; he had summed them both up perfectly after only spending a few minutes with them. "Yes, I do feel a total fraud when I'm at work. I don a sort of cloak, become a superhero and step out of my own self and turn into someone else. It's how I cope. Do you know, the only time I really feel like Maddie, like myself…?"

"Yes, I do know. I can see the difference in you, I can see where you want to be. I know Maddie, I know you…." His soft tone so close to her and his understanding of her soul shook her. She felt warm tears fill her eyes. She shook her head to rid them.

"Thank you for today, I really appreciate it was a lot for you to come all the way here for me. You did really well in there, really well."

"You asked me to do it, Maddie. Of course, I was going to come."

He kissed her gently on the cheek and unclipped his badge before dropping it on the reception desk and signing out in the visitors' book. He raised his hand to say goodbye and left the building. The urge to go with him, to run after him and never come back was overwhelming. She stood and considered it. She realised her bag and coat were still in the meeting room and by then Tom would have gone too far down the road. The moment passed and she pressed the lift button once again.

Chapter Ten – OCTOBER

"Mum, would you like to come for a walk with me and do a leaflet drop? I've got the Harvest event leaflets from work and want to post them in the streets around here."

"No, I'm too busy Madeleine. Why are you doing it anyway, surely there are other people who can do it?"

"It's a team effort Mum. I've given everyone a bundle and we'll all do our own areas, where we live. Filo is going to use it as part of an exercise regime for Esther, to get her slowly active again. It's going to rain later so I need to go out now. I thought it would be nice to have a stroll together."

"Not today, thank you."

"Could you leave a pile of leaflets in the Golf Club tonight then?"

"I really don't think so, you have to have permission to advertise and it's not really the sort of thing we have up there."

Madeleine didn't know why a hospice charity event wouldn't be acceptable but didn't press the point. She had tried to draw her mother into taking an interest in the event. She'd asked if she would bake cakes to sell, talked to her about the running order of the demonstrations in the tent and if she would like to go up and help set it all up. Each time there was an excuse and a sly comment about it is obviously taking up too much of Madeleine's time.

Halfway up Tilbury Lane her mobile phone rang. Surprised, she saw Dominic's name on the screen. He never called her on a Saturday, in fact now he never called her at all.

"Hello Dominic, is everything okay?"

"Madeleine," not even a greeting she noted, "I've just seen an email come into my inbox, the date of the final part of the competition has changed as some of the Bittern Board will be in China apparently. It's now the eighteenth of this month and the first part of the presentations to C&B are going to be held this week. Has Tom finished his drawings? We need them now, to get them processed into our pitch."

"I don't believe it! The eighteenth is my charity event day. I can't do both."

"There's hardly a choice is there? You don't need to be at a charity thing, you'll have to be in London that day."

"You don't understand, it's really important I'm there, everyone is counting on me. They're following a lot of my ideas and I can't just dump it on them!"

"Not my problem, I'm afraid. If you can just get hold of Tom and tell him, we need the drawings now." The line went dead. Madeleine couldn't believe it. The rudeness of the man and now the dilemma of the date. There's no way she can abandon all the of the preparation, the setting up and leading the events on day. She had taken so much of it onto herself, so she didn't overburden the others. But what about work? If they progress through the first stages this week and go onto the final, she will need to be there too. On the same day. She couldn't believe the bad timing. She had started the day so positively and now with a single phone call she was in turmoil.

Maddie found Filo in her caravan.

"Hey, you, you'd better get in here before the rain starts. Do you want a brew? I've left Esther at home for a while, she's getting better as she's driving me potty. It may be time for her to go home soon but I think she's more nervous about being by herself than she is admitting."

"Tea would be lovely," Maddie slumped down with a sigh. "It's good she's getting stronger. You'll miss her when she's gone home though." She slumped her elbows onto the table and put her chin into her cupped hands. "Filo, I've got a real dilemma!"

A cup of tea and some walnut and coffee cake later and Filo was fully in the picture. Maddie spilled out the call from Dominic, the clash of dates and her divided loyalties. They hadn't had much time to talk about Dominic, so Filo took the chance to find out if it really was all over.

"He took it well in the end then. I'm surprised, I thought he would make a big song and dance of it. What about that holiday he booked?"

Maddie told her she had paid half back.

"I wouldn't have! He chose to buy the holiday and all the excursions. He didn't ask you first. It would have been a lesson to him not to do it again. I'm glad he's out of the picture, he wasn't right for you. Sorry, I know it's none of my business and don't get back with him now you know I don't like him! That would be awkward." Filo laughed easily, by the sounds of her friend's story there was little chance of a reunion.

"What do you think you're going to do about the Harvest event and work? I'm sure we could manage if we had to. You'd have to explain it all to us fully, but we can sort it all out, I'm sure."

"I know you're all very capable and I know that if I wasn't there it would still be a great success but that's not the point. You see, if I'm to have a choice I would rather be with all of you at the event. My work leaves me cold, I never thought I would say that but I've no hunger for it, I don't really think I want the prize of promotion, so the importance of being in London that day is only to not let the team down. Also, I have a really good name at work, a good reputation. I don't want to spoil that at the end of my career there." She hesitated, "If I choose to move on, that is." Maddie surprised herself. She hadn't even said that in her own head, let alone out loud. Would she really consider leaving such a good job? Should she even consider it? What would people say? What would her parents say?

"Do you think you *will* leave? What will you do?"

"I don't know, I can't leave, it's my security and all I really know what to do. I haven't any idea what I can do anymore. Or who I am anymore. There was a time I was creative, really creative and I loved it. Finding the things in my grandfather's caravan reminded me how much I loved my art and craft and the imaginative worlds I would conjure up. Somewhere along the line that has disappeared. My days are corporate and restrained, I want to feel free and not under scrutiny for being perfect at all times."

Filo reached across the table and lifted the knitted dolly dress up to reveal a teapot underneath in the shape of a peacock.

She lifted the tail feather handle and refilled their mismatched china cups. She allowed Maddie to talk freely, knowing not to interrupt as her friend summarised her thoughts and worked things through for herself. Filo had once trained as a coach and had learnt the art of listening and letting others speak first, formulating their own paths and conclusions without being misled or judged.

"You see, I can't really pinpoint when it all changed. I was happy to be a Marketing Manager. I was thrilled to be working in London, in a huge, prestigious company. But somewhere along the line things have changed. I really don't feel like that person anymore, I'm not Madeleine the businesswoman, I'm Maddie.... but this is the dilemma.... I'm Maddie the I-don't-know-what! I know I have a duty to complete my work competition, I would never let the team down, even if I don't have any real connection with them. It's the professional integrity, I guess. But the thought of letting you all down makes me even more sad. It's personal. You all mean so much more to me and you don't let your friends down, do you?"

The pause was long enough to know Maddie had finished; she was spent.

"When I'm at a loss, Maddie, I turn to the cards. I know how you feel about them but when you can't see things clearly, they can be a comfort, a form of guidance. Please let me finish your reading. You never let me explain your future card."

Maddie had no fight left in her to complain or resist. She watched as Filo shuffled her bottom along to the end of the bench chair, stand up and find her pack of Tarot cards. She watched her friend billow in an oversized smock dress, burgundy fake velvet from top to toe. Maddie secretly wished she had the confidence to wear whatever she wanted, no matter how crazy. She admired Filo for her individual style and the strength to carry it off.

Filo rifled through the pack of cards, locating the three that Maddie had picked out, back in February when they first met. She turned The Chariot around to face Maddie and placed it in front of her.

"So, if you remember, this is The Chariot. It was reversed when you picked it, so rather than moving forward it told me your past was the opposite, it was stuck, blocked somehow and your inner discipline was wrapped around it."

"Yes, I can see that now. I haven't been moving forward, I'm still at home, I'm in a job that I just go through the motions with every day, I have no real love life, I am actually no further on now than I was years ago. I'm living the life others want for me. And that is a very sad fact!"

"We use our reflections in a positive way, Maddie. If you can see that clearer now, then it's a good thing. It's what you choose to do with that information that's key. Now here is your second card again, remember it was The Fool?"

Maddie took her time this time to study the card.

"I've thought about this card a few times," she admitted. "The 'stepping off a cliff' metaphor is very strong, and it does explain how I feel right now. I feel on the edge of something, whatever it is, it's into the unknown, like jumping out of an aeroplane, into mid-air. It's not natural and makes my tummy flip over inside just thinking about it."

Filo laughed as she recognised the sentiment but became more serious as she laid the last card down in front of her friend.

"Death. Not as scary as you may think! Not scary at all in fact. Maddie, this card is all about new beginnings. Yes, it means something must end and that's the part people worry about but it's the end of one era and the start of a new one, it can be exciting, liberating and positive. The white horse, that Death sits on, cleanses everything, wipes it clean ready for literally a clean sheet. It also means you're released, set free, your chains and shackles are unlocked, and you can have a fresh start. You see, it all makes sense, doesn't it? You couldn't see it at first but now, you see, don't you? Your past and present cards are absolutely true, on the button. So, it makes sense the future one is too?"

Filo leant against the back of the chair, her hands flat on the table and the largest, smug smile on her face. Her eyes twinkled in a 'told-you-so' kind of way.

"Okay, okay, so I admit, a lot of this seems to match my life. I'm not saying I believe it *all*, but I can't deny there *are* a lot of similarities. I won't be so quick to dismiss your mumbo jumbo from now on." Maddie squeezed Filo's hand to reassure her she was teasing. "It doesn't tell me what to do about the 18th, but it has given me lots to think about. Thank you, Filo."

"Good. Now young lady, I have tomatoes still growing out of my ears that need picking and I need to do it before the rain comes, so shoo, off you go." Filo ushered Maddie out whilst grabbing a large bowl to fill with her bounty.

She heard Tom chopping something back before she actually saw him. The swish of dried foliage and the soft grunt from the effort told her she would find him there. He stood up when he heard footsteps, placing the scythe carefully on the ground where he wouldn't tread on it. It was hot work, clearing a large patch of overgrown grass that had dried over the summer. Tom wanted to tidy it ready for planting in the spring. With his jumper off and his T-shirt with small patches of damp across the chest, he looked strong and Maddie had to admit, quite sexy. He wiped the back of his hand across his forehead, leaving a grass stain streak. Maddie pointed it out with a miming motion on her own forehead. He wiped it clean, not taking his gaze off her. His eyes drew her in with their warmth and growing familiarity.

"I'm here on a mission and I really hope you have good news for me. Dominic called me and said we need the designs for Bittern Quays, like today. I know that's no notice at all but please tell me you have started them…. please?"

Tom could see the desperation in her face.

"No, I'm really sorry, I thought I had much longer to finish them."

"Oh crap, I was hoping for a miracle."

"Aha, now you didn't say anything about a miracle, now miracles I can do, I have done them really, I was just teasing you."

Maddie launched herself at him, punching his arms gently, Tom bent over laughing.

"You looked so serious, I couldn't resist it," he explained. "If you help me collect up all of this mess, I'll give you a lift to mine?"

"Oh no, not after that little trick, I won't. I'll go and tend to my own carrots and beetroot thank you and then meet you back here for that lift!" She chuckled as she left him to finish his own job. Happy Tom was so much nicer than the old grumpy version. She wondered what happened to him.

The Theatre was the largest room on the ground floor, where Claremont & Butler hosted events, speeches and demonstrations, film viewings and like today, competitions. The entire back wall pulled forward and cinema style seats concertinaed out and the seats flopped down, nearly a hundred people already sat into the darkened space, no windows, dimmed lights with just a selection of kaleidoscope spotlights directed at the front of the room. There was no raised stage, various props were brought in depending on the event and set up on the floor at the front. Today a lectern stood to one side with a small light clipped over the edge to light up the scripts placed there. An enormous screen that would rival a West End cinema hung down from the ceiling, with the screensaver of the C&B logo bouncing around it, waiting for someone to spark it into life. Some teams had extra props that they would bring in when it was their turn to present.

On the front row sat some of C&B's top Directors and leadership teams. Katrina Everett, the Deputy CEO sat next to John Murray, Head of Procurement, who in turn sat next to Gregory Alford, Head of Human Resources. Various Heads of Departments had fingers poised on tablets ready to take notes and Petra, the P.A. ran around checking everyone was ready to start and giving out the order of presentations.

First up were four young men from the design department. The competition was open to all staff, not just those in the sales and marketing fields, so the ideas promised to be varied. They were all wearing green lycra suits with diodes attached to their joints and various parts of their clothing. Madeleine tried to keep her eyes on their faces as the costumes were revealing, to say the least. They introduced themselves as The Winning Team, a few polite laughs but a lot of groans told them they weren't off to the best start. The four disappeared behind a curtain and the screen woke into life. Images of the four were displayed on the screen but you couldn't see them fully, their bodies had been superimposed with robotic alien type characters, Madeleine recognised them as Anime style, the Japanese cartoons so popular all over the world. The four in the team proceeded to move around whilst a narrator boomed out through the sound system. Madeleine understood their concept, or rather what they were trying to portray but their haphazard dancing and prancing looked just like ridiculous schoolboys in a strobe-lit nightclub. They had gone for extreme digital imagery, but it was muddled and confusing. She saw the front row shaking the heads with the disappointing start.

Second to take the floor was a pair from the Marking Department, Hilary and Otis. As far as Madeleine knew, their day job was something to do with the radio advertising side of life, promos, jingles and adverts. She had seen them around the building of course but wasn't sure she had ever spoken to them. Understandably, they had developed a song with a catchy tagline that you could repeat after hearing it only once. It was the sort of tune she had heard people call an earworm. It worms its way into your ear drum, and you can't get it out. Madeleine thought their presentation was good, well-rehearsed and confident but it was only a song, nothing else to make a package or to tell you much about the Bittern Quays concept. The front row tapped their tablets, noting down their judgements.

Four or five other teams presented their pitches. Although a few had been very impressive, Madeleine was feeling confident. It was an odd feeling, she wanted to win, it's human nature in a competition, especially amongst your peers, to be seen to do well. Yes, now she was here in the Theatre, she really wanted to win. But she didn't want the prize. If the prize was a pat on the back and a 'well done' she would be happy. The idea of potential promotion filled her now with dread, she imagined a new pair of shackles that would see her into her forties at least. She would be tied to the company for many more years to come and all hope of changing direction, trying something new and exciting was disappearing.

She had laid awake early that morning imagining how she could sabotage their pitch, without anyone guessing it was her of course, just enough to throw them off the competition without losing face. Maybe a batch of homemade cookies with sick inducing qualities or she could file Roseanne's heels ever so slightly so that they snap just at the right moment, she falls headfirst into the front row and splits open the Deputy CEOs lip?

Last up was Insignia, the team name Dominic had labelled them. Madeleine felt it sounded more like a team from The Apprentice but without a better option herself, she accepted it gracefully. They had rehearsed, they were keeping it simple and letting the concept, the tagline and the themes speak for themselves. They would take turns with their introductions and explanations and finish with the TV advert that had been edited just two days before, with Tom's drawings layered against the images of shiny, happy people all at work in the new environment and Madeleine's soundtrack.

They came across as very professional and slick. Roseanne had used some of Tom's own words, from when he explained to them his ideas. She detailed how the green spaces supported health and well-being. Madeleine outlined the 'buy-in' that staff would be expected to have, how they would own their own space and nurture it. Dominic pulled it all together at the end, describing a possible future, the digital future weaved with nature, holistic and above all how Bittern Quays would set the standard and be a template for all future environmentally positive developments. The TV advert looked like the Aha video from the 1980's, line drawings and reality merged together, it was very effective. As the soundtrack faded out and the simple tagline loomed large on the screen 'Bittern Quays, for a Healthy Future' the presentation finished, the Theatre burst into applause.

Katrina Everett placed her tablet on her seat and moved to the lectern. After inviting the teams to take a seat she proceeded to thank them all for their time and efforts. She spoke of the company's reputation and what it would mean if it was one of C&B's teams who won the overall contract for the Bittern Quay's contract.

"Whilst I applaud the confidence some of the teams had in presenting today, we have agreed there are some of you who are not yet ready for the high stakes in pitching for this contract and need to get more experience first." Katrina called out half of the teams and thanked them and dismissed them from the auditorium. "From those of you left, we have selected three teams to go forward to the main competition with the Board at the Quays. The teams are, Collective Inc, Digi-blend and Insignia. Well done to you all and we will see you on the 18th at seven o'clock at the Quay's Showrooms. I expect you all do us proud. Good luck to you all and may the best team win…. as long as it's one of ours!" The room laughed and applauded as the lights went up.

Madeleine leant forward to look at Dominic and Roseanne sitting further along the row.

"Well done everyone, that went well didn't it? And even better, the main event is in the evening, so I'll be able to do my charity event and the competition too."

"Seriously Madeleine? Is that all you think about? We don't care what you are doing in the day as long as you're at the showrooms, on time and ready to win. After all of our work don't you let us down!" Roseanne stood up and pushed her way out of the row, the large tote handbag through the crook of her elbow narrowly missing Madeleine's face.

"Well what do you expect?" Dominic's sneer, as he followed Roseanne, was nasty and left Madeleine sitting alone as the Theatre emptied. There she stayed until a cleaner came in with a bin liner, collecting up bits of paper from the floor. Her only thoughts were replaying Filo's words, her past, her present and her future. What would the new Maddie look like, she thought, whatever it looked like, she hoped she wouldn't be sat feeling as miserable as the present version was today.

Madeleine heard James strumming on his guitar through his bedroom door. She knocked. They had always respected each other's space and even when they were young would wait to be invited in.

"Sis-ta," his exaggerated gangster style always made her laugh, "Yo!"

"Fool.... why are you cooped up in here on a Friday night? Surely you've got big plans?" Madeleine hadn't let on that she had seen her brother with Alice. Alice hadn't said a word to her either, so she assumed they had either broken up already or it was still a secret.

"I'm going out in a bit, don't worry little sis, I'm not going all old on you.... yet."

"Where is everyone? I've not seen mum and dad for days." Madeleine had been so busy she had hardly been home for tea all week.

"The sale of granddad's house completed today so dad's taken mum out for a meal, to make her feel a bit better."

Madeleine instantly felt bad, she had been so absorbed in work and the allotments that she hadn't realised the sale was nearly complete. She hadn't mentioned the sale to her parents, and she would have loved to have gone to the house for one last look around.

"That's a shame, I wanted to visit it before it sold. I bet mum's feeling weird, she lived there all her life. James, I wanted to run something by you and ask your opinion."

James sat up higher on his pillows and laid the guitar carefully on the floor by his bed. This was a very unusual request.

"You see, I've been thinking a lot lately about changing my job. I just don't feel the same about it anymore and I'm really not enjoying it. I have no idea what I will do instead but I need a change. I'm worried about what mum and dad will say. Will I really disappoint them, do you think?"

Madeleine had never consulted James on matters of her life before. They were on such different paths; she didn't think he would be able to empathise or understand enough to give a reliable response. But lately, she felt he was maturing a little and she found she was talking to him more as an equal. It was nice to have him to talk to as he is the only other person who understands their parents. James has found a way to live his own life without their scrutiny. She had always resented this but now she needed his insight and advice. She doesn't feel resentment now, he can't help the way he was brought up, to be left alone unchallenged, wrapped up in cotton wool. Now, she didn't blame him for taking advantage of it, she just wished they had treated her the same.

"Wow, I think they'll be shocked if you don't do something high-flying but at the end of the day, you have to do what's right for you. It's your life, not theirs' and no-one should be miserable at work. Is it that Dominic guy? Is he making it hard there for you?"

"No, no, he has nothing to do with it. It's me. I just don't recognise me there anymore, not just there at C&B but doing that type of work anywhere. I want a change. A big change. I want to feel I am in charge of what I do, I've always wanted my own business and if I don't try it soon, I'll be too old."

"Don't be daft, Madeleine, people start businesses at any age. But, yeah, I know what you mean. I couldn't stand working in an office every day, dancing to someone else's tune. I don't know how you've lasted so long to be honest."

"I feel I need a business-plan, a life-plan even, before broaching it with mum. She'll have every question for me and expect well thought out answers."

"Look, like I said, this is your life. You only have one of those. It's not mum's or dad's so you make yourself happy and sod everyone else."

"Ha ha, that's easy for you to say, I've got to explain how I'm going to pay the rent! And soon you'll be a homeowner when your trust fund pays out. I'll be left here alone and beaten on a daily basis." Madeleine was teasing and James knew it. "Thanks for the chat. I've got to be brave and speak out. I'll just wait until the right time, wait until she's had a glass of wine at least, then take the leap."

There was a nip in the air. The morning felt damp, although there had been no rain. Maddie felt the autumn in her bones. The leaves were turning to lime yellow and browning before their fall from this earth. Maddie's sandals and flip-flops were finally put away into boxes under her bed, now opting for leggings tucked into ankle boots with thick socks. The pick-up truck horn told her Tom was waiting, she grabbed her quilted jacket and ran downstairs.

"Are you out with him again?" Fiona called from the kitchen.

Madeleine sighed. This had been a running theme over the past week as each evening after work she had helped Tom gather equipment ready for the event. She had promised she would help all day today too, there was still so much to do.

"Mum, I've told you. Next Saturday is our charity event. That's only one week's time. It's going to be big and there's a lot to do and I've booked off Thursday and Friday from work. I've asked you to help and be part of it, if you'd like to, but I really need to go. Tom can't sit in the road for too long." She looked at her mother wiping up plates and wondered why she wasn't happy for her to be busy or more interested in what she was doing.

"I just can't see why it's taking up all of your time, that's all."

Madeleine's patience was rapidly wearing thin. "What else should I do with my time then, mum? Should I sit upstairs reading, go shopping, meet my friends at a golf club? Should I just do what you do, mum? Will that make you happy?" she sighed, she hated resorting to meanness, "I have to go..." Tom's car horn sounded impatiently. Madeleine never usually challenged and always opted for silence over confrontation but recently she felt more irked than usual. Was her mother's interference and disdain getting worse or was she just homing in on it more, each time it happened? She couldn't worry about it now, she had work to do.

As the front door shut, Henry stepped from the dining room where he had been standing listening to the two women in his life. He lent against the doorframe with his arms folded and looked sadly at his wife.

"You know, you are going to drive her away. You push, push, push and don't let her breathe. I've told you a thousand times Fiona, you must let her live her life."

"She's going to ruin all of the chances she has been given, Henry. I can't stand by and watch her do that."

"I don't see anyone ruining anything, do you? What I see is our daughter happier than she has been for a very long time. But what I also see, is my wife getting more and more unhappy. And why? Because our daughter is choosing her own path? That's how it should be Fiona. That's what children do, and we stand back and support them and pick them up if they fall. Look at James!"

"But Henry, you know as much as I do, James won't reach his potential, but Madeleine can, Madeleine can make something of her life."

"Fiona, I'm warning you. If you carry on with this, you'll lose her completely. James will move out soon enough and Madeleine will too and then what? She would have left because of you. How will you feel then?" Henry had said his piece, he wasn't prepared for an argument so quietly left Fiona to think about what he had said. He didn't see her wring the tea towel into the glass and break it in two.

"So, what's today's plan?" Maddie pulled herself up into the cab.

Tom passed her a cardboard cup of coffee from a takeaway machine and a warm croissant in a paper bag. His black wooden beanie hat suited him, his unshaven stubble was making him scratch his cheek and Maddie resisted the urge to pick the breakfast crumbs from his jumper.

"Today, you are my apprentice. We have got to build a stage! I've already picked up the materials," he motioned to the trailer attached to the back which was full of wooden panels strapped down with bungee ropes. "It's better to build it at the allotments as I can spread out and the Bowls Club are going to let me store it there for the week, which is really helpful. Here's the plans for it. Norris is going to help us too"

The plans were simply sketches of a series of boxes.

"We're going to build lots of boxes, they will be easier to carry and store and will be stronger than one large stage. We can fit them together into any shape. Pretty ingenious if I say so myself." Tom smirked. Maddie had to agree, it looked a good plan and would keep them busy all day.

Norris was waiting when they arrived. He guided Tom back into a space in the car park and helped undo the straps on the trailer. Norris had opened the front doors of the shed they called 'The Shop.' It stored secondhand gardening equipment that people could buy for a small price and large bags of soil conditioners, seed compost and various bottles of organic plant feed. It made a small profit which went back into the upkeep of the shared areas. There was an honesty box on an old desk and the last person out in the evening was responsible for locking it up.

"I've brought some of my tools down into the shop for you," Norris loved to help Tom, it made him feel useful and involved. He started setting up a range of rechargeable equipment and two portable workbenches.

"What can I do?" Maddie was wondering if she was really needed.

"Can you measure out these dimensions onto each panel for me and draw the lines where I need to cut them down?" Tom passed her the drawing again and explained what he needed from her.

The next few hours flew by. They became a production line, Maddie drawing and labelling the pieces, Tom cutting the shapes out, Norris lifting the pieces into place and holding them whilst Tom secured them with the drill. Norris had the foresight to bring extra power packs and by lunchtime they had a stack of cubes, solid and well built. They ferried them over to the storeroom in the Bowls Club and decided they were hungry.

The Breadmakers Arms was narrow, it was a former bakery shop, timber framed with an upstairs jetty jutting out over the pavement below. Inside was dark and dominated by the bar that ran down the left-hand side of the pub. Worn out wooden stools lined the front and music piped out of speakers hanging from brackets above. The bar top was stacked full of baskets of crisps, nuts and little chalkboards with descriptions of ciders and real ales. They chose their drinks and sat at a round table with a barrel as the base.

"Cheers," Tom raised his glass and touched theirs' gently, "Here's to teamwork."

"Cheers," they repeated and settled into the warmth of the welcoming room.

"You know, today reminded me of being with your grandfather, Maddie. It was just like the old days Tom, wasn't it? We would get together on a Saturday morning and potter about. He would have been proud of you today." Norris raised his glass towards Maddie to acknowledge her hard work.

The unexpected mention of her grandfather took her aback. She felt humbled to be accepted as his substitute and thanked Norris for his saying so.

"Of course, it's not been the same since the last time we were together," Norris continued. Tom glanced in his direction.

"What do you mean?" Maddie sipped her gin and tonic.

"Well the last time was the day we found him, your granddad. Collapsed in his caravan." Norris looked between Maddie and Tom and realised he was saying something that perhaps he shouldn't have.

"You found him? I thought he was ill?" Maddie didn't understand.

Norris looked at Tom with apologetic eyes. Tom picked up the story.

"I found him, Maddie. We'd been tinkering as we always did, on my plot. He said he was going to go and have a sit down for a while. I went to check on him a bit later and he was on the floor, he'd collapsed."

Maddie put her hand to her chest, she didn't know what to say.

"When I checked him, I couldn't see him breathing. Norris came in and I told him to call an ambulance." Tom spoke softly, she hadn't realised, but he had reached across and was holding her hand.

'What happened then?" Maddie didn't understand how she didn't know all of this.

"I gave him mouth-to-mouth and pumped his chest. I kept it going until the ambulance came." Tom's eyes reddened as he fought back the tears.

"Tom saved his life, Maddie. I'm so sorry, I thought you knew." Norris was distraught at bringing this up and upsetting everyone.

"Did you? I don't understand. He was ill in hospital."

Tom was squeezing her hand so hard, to take away the pain, "He had a heart attack and had stopped breathing. The paramedics stabilised him and took him to hospital. But, when he was due to come home, he had a massive stroke, they kept him in, and he never recovered. Maddie, I'm so sorry, I thought you knew."

"I went to see him in hospital, I knew he had the stroke, but I didn't know about him collapsing. No-one told me he had been found, or that you found him." Maddie was having trouble digesting the information and struggled to get the timeline straight in her memory. "So, you've already met my mother and father.... when it happened?"

"Yes, we saw them in the hospital. Your mum didn't really want to talk to us about it. She took charge, which was right of course, and we felt she didn't really want us there. I think she felt a bit guilty." Tom released his grip slightly.

"Guilty?"

"For not being there herself. I don't know, maybe I've got it all wrong, but she never saw him in the allotment and he used to say he hardly ever saw his daughter, so I'm just assuming, that's all. Sorry, I shouldn't say, it's not my business." Tom let go and sat back in his seat.

Maddie sat quietly. They all sipped their drinks in an awkward silence. How could she not know the details of her grandfather's illness and death. She had visited him but had been so wrapped up in her own world, she hadn't realised the enormity until the end. She had let him down, twice. She had stopped spending time with him as a young girl and again as an adult, when he really needed his family with him. The guilt consumed her. Here sat two people far more worthy of being his family than she. No-one had told her about his collapse, but then again, had she really been asking the questions? Had she taken enough time and effort herself? The day had darkened for her and she finished her drink.

"I think I'll walk home." She stood up and started to put her jacket on. Tom began to stand and picked up his keys, but she held out her hand. "No! Honestly, I'd rather walk if that's ok. Thank you, Tom. Thank you both for being there and for being my grandfather's friends. I'll see you on Thursday to help get everything sorted." She smiled weakly and left before the tears flowed.

"Why didn't you tell me Tom saved granddad's life?"

Madeleine had rehearsed a much softer opening line but when she saw her parents sitting in the conservatory, both reading quietly, classical music playing softly from the radio, the perfect scene, she couldn't think rationally. They both looked up in surprise. Henry removed his reading glasses and Fiona stared at her daughter over the top of hers'.

Fiona spoke first, calmly, "I thought you knew, it wasn't a secret."

Madeleine felt an angry pit of lava threatening to spill out; she kept it pushed down.

"So, you knew Tom the other day, when he was here, you knew what he had done and you never thought to mention it to me?"

"Madeleine, why would I? He helped your grandfather that day but then he got ill, he had a stroke. Really, we thought you knew all of this."

"No, I didn't. No one told me. Why were you so mean to Tom the other day then?"

"I wasn't mean."

"Alright then, dismissive."

"I wasn't aware I was dismissive. Does it matter how I was with him?" Fiona's voice was rising, she was becoming defensive with her daughter standing over her demanding answers.

Madeleine knew the conversation was fruitless. She felt angry, and when she was angry, she lost the ability to articulate.

"He was granddad's friend. He saved his life. He deserves more than you sneering at him.

"Madeleine, I'm not prepared to have this conversation," Fiona attempted to shut her down.

"No, we don't have any real conversations, do we? Why don't we have the conversation about why you stopped my grandfather seeing me?"

Madeleine shocked herself. She had had no intention of broaching that subject or discussing the letters that she had found in the caravan, but it burst out of her from somewhere hidden deep inside. Spontaneous and involuntary, it was out in the open, hanging in the air.

"What, what do you mean?" the surprise on Fiona's face was evident.

"I found the letters you wrote to him, saying he couldn't see me anymore. He kept them, he kept them in the caravan at the allotment. Along with all my things that he'd saved. He'd treasured them all over the years. How could you do that? Stop family seeing each other? It was cruel and I'll never forgive you."

At that moment she felt hate. Hate and rage. She had pushed her feelings down so far, deep inside, to keep the peace and to separate it from how she had been feeling lately. When the lid was opened, Pandora's Box spewed. Madeleine didn't want a scene; she had rehearsed a calm and adult discussion but the child once more crept out and defied her. She resorted to anger and tears. Henry stood and came towards her with his arms outstretched.

"Madeleine, it wasn't like that at all. You've got it all wrong."

"Have I? Not from where I'm standing!" Madeleine took a step back.

"Fiona, I told you this would happen. Your interference has gone too far." Henry made a stand against his wife. Fiona looked between the two of them in shock. Realising she was about to be corned by them both, overwhelmed Fiona rushed from the room. Madeleine couldn't remember the last time she saw her parents argue, they never did, their lives were stable and consistent.

"I have told her to talk to you about all of this, Madeline, honestly I have." Henry's voice quivered. Madeleine felt immediately guilty, she wouldn't have caused this upset intentionally. It had all gone wrong. It wasn't the way she wanted to deal with it.

"I'm sorry, dad. I really am. I'll go and see mum, shall I?"

"No love. Leave it for now. I'll talk to her first. She finds it very hard to express herself, you know that." Henry hugged his daughter, his loyalties cut in two. Why couldn't his wife connect with their daughter better? She only had to listen, really listen and for them to talk to each other. He would try again, be the voice of reason, he had to. His family were his world.

Filo placed the frog mug down on her kitchen table and opened the far end windows to let the fresh air gust in. Her house guest was unexpected but as Esther had already left, she was feeling lonely and the house felt empty. She welcomed Maddie into her home willingly, albeit a little worried about her.

"Sorry, Filo, I'd rather not talk about it. I appreciate you giving me the space I need. I must step back and look at my life and make some decisions. It's easier away from home at the minute if that's okay with you?"

"You stay as long as you need, m'love." The tea was sweet and the pastries warm and welcoming. Maddie felt instantly at home.

For two days, Maddie, Tom, Norris and Filo zigzagged between the allotments and Tom's garage to paint signs, test out electrics, gather chairs in the trailer, set up the gazeboes and fill canisters with fuel ready for the generators. They had begged and borrowed, Maddie using her brilliant persuasion skills with local companies in exchange for a few mentions on the loudspeaker system. She had spoken live on the local radio station to promote the event, the weather looked good, the dance and music acts had confirmed, and everything was coming together nicely. Maddie had drawn a plan sketch for the Bowls Club and the allotment areas and pinned it up in the shed shop. She had designed a route that she thought the families would walk around, moving from activities to food and refreshments. She didn't want anything missed out, there was nothing worse than being a stall holder, stuck in the corner with no foot traffic. She used all her knowledge and experience to think every aspect through carefully. The stalls, stage and areas for acts were labelled clearly and everyone could help out by easily referring to its notes. The others were in awe. Maddie directed and praised and ensured the troops were kept fed and watered. They were seeing her in full marketing manager mode and were seriously impressed. The phone calls from Dominic were an annoying distraction. He had seen she was on annual leave and was panicking she wouldn't show up on Saturday evening. She gave him constant reassurances that she would be there. He seemed to be part of another world already, she was so immersed in her new interests that he had faded away. In fact, that whole side of her life was disappearing fast. And she liked it.

By Friday afternoon, the others started filing into the allotments to help. Ranweer had finished work and collected his family to bring them along too. They offloaded his car of huge saucepans and woks, tabletop camping gas cookers and utensils. His wife, Janalee, took armfuls of tea towels and tablecloths into their caravan and instructed their sons to cut down long swathes of greenery to use as table decorations tomorrow.

Norris' wife, Jean, was filling large silver buckets full of water and setting them in a line, each containing different types of long -stemmed anemones, late flowering dahlias and autumn

French roses. She had also selected foliage for their interesting shapes and sizes, the green spindly fingers of the mock-orange bush, variegated euonymus, and traditional holly. She placed a bag of reels of silk ribbon, scissors, dried allium heads sprayed silver and gold and peacock feathers in the shed shop, tucked out of the way.

Maddie was busy hanging bunting across the front of the shop when she heard a car pull into the car park.

Jean called over. "Maddie! The police would like a word…."

Coming down from the stepladder, Maddie wiped her hands on her jeans. What is it about seeing the police that instantly makes you nervous?

"Hello again Maddie, I'm not sure if you remember me, I'm PC Bridgeman, I came here in May after you were burgled?"

Of course, Maddie remembered her now and the fact it wasn't bad news was a relief.

"I have some news for you, is Alice here too?"

"No, she hasn't come over yet, I'm not sure if she will be here before tomorrow?"

As if on cue, Alice strolled around the entrance gate hand-in-hand with James.

"Hello again Alice, I'm glad you're both here as I have an update for you. I'm sorry it's been so long but we haven't had any leads at all until last week. We were called to a house over on the Ashdown Pass Estate. We had reports of drug dealings and a team went over on a morning raid. We discovered quite a stash of random objects in a spare bedroom. One of the lads confessed straight away and told us he was part of a group who broke into the allotments that night. He gave us the name of another chap who liked to take anything and everything he found, regardless of worth. He sees it as a trophy apparently. Anyway, amongst the things were some boxes of games and in the lid was your name Maddie, Maddie Richards, written in a child's handwriting."

"Yes, yes, I used to write my name in everything!" Maddie was beyond excited.

"You are more than welcome to come to the police storage unit and identify anything that's yours. Alice, I know you didn't have anything stolen but I wanted to tell you we are sure we have the group who did the damage."

Alice hugged James around the waist and thanked the policewoman whole heartedly. PC Bridgeman left them her calling card and gave the times that the storage was open and left, but not after Maddie invited her to the open day tomorrow.

Maddie and Alice grabbed each other and jumped up and down.

"I can't believe it. I'd given up all hope. I know the things aren't worth a bean but it's the principle. And they are sentimental. I hope my little welly boots are there!" She paused for breath, "Anyhow, hello James.... nice to see you!" Maddie gave a sarcastic smile and teased him with a punch to the arm.

"We have something to tell you," He gave an embarrassed ruffle of his own hair. "We're seeing each other!"

"Old news!!" Maddie couldn't help it; she was in such a good mood that teasing him was a pleasure. "I saw you ages ago at the shops, it's about time you came clean, I'm so happy, Alice we're as good as sisters now! Sisters-in-law!"

"Steady on," James warned her laughing.

"I'm sorry, Maddie. I wanted to tell you, but James wanted to keep us in a little bubble for a while. Why didn't you tell me your brother is gorgeous?"

"Yuck! Really? I can't see it myself." she laughed at them both and hugged them before they skipped off to find Ranweer and get their instructions. Maddie went around the others sharing the police news.

"What did she want?" Tom had been tied up with electrical circuits and watched from afar. Maddie's joy was infectious, and he smiled at her childlike animation as she told him her belongings had been found. "I take it you're pleased then. I'm happy for you, I had a bike taken once and it was a terrible feeling."

"What a motorbike?"

"Did you get it back?"

"No silly, a pushbike, I was about seven and had left it out the front of the house. I never heard the end of it!"

Their easy warmth together was being watched, out of sight, by Filo and Esther who were filling up china cups, saucers and plates into boxes ready for the refreshment tent. They glanced at other with a knowing smile, wordless yet speaking volumes.

Maddie was wide awake at six o'clock. She crept down quietly to put Filo's kettle on, hoping for a chance to sit and enjoy some calm before the day ahead. She pulled up a chair to the large window in the kitchen, it was still dark outside, but the sun was breaking over the rooftops far away, enough to see the shapes of the small but neat garden. She hugged her mug of coffee to her chest, she wasn't cold, but she found the warmth comforting. She had enjoyed the last few days enormously; staying with Filo was easy, she was a laid-back and generous host. She had loved the planning and taking shape of the open day, it had elevated her inside, giving her the buzz of adrenaline, she has thrived on for so many years but coupled with the huge enjoyment of the people she was spending time with. She had spoken to her father briefly on the phone, just to say she was fine, busy and not staying away because of her mother but simply because of the logistics for the week. However deep down she knew she was staying away from home for a different reason. She was finding her lack of adult freedom stifling and knew it was time to leave. Maddie heard the creak of floorboards upstairs shortly followed by the toilet being flushed. At any moment the house would burst open into a bright new day. How the day would end was something Maddie couldn't think about yet, she had too much to do in between.

The ladies arrived in Filo's 2CV packed to the roof. Maddie sat in the seat whilst Filo bundled every piece of possible equipment on top of her. Lastly, she laid the dress and pair of shoes that Maddie would wear later in London. Already in the Bowls Club car park were Ranweer and Alice, setting up the trestle tables and cooking equipment. A menu board had been painted and stood propped up against a traffic cone; squash ravioli with a fresh tomato and herb sauce, served in a paper bowl or stir-fried vegetables, wrapped in a homemade tortilla with a choice of dressings, all homemade of course. Unbelievably at that time of the day, James was there, wrapping up wooden cutlery in paper napkins, grinning inanely whilst jigging to the music that Tom was setting up on the stage.

Tom nodded at her as she strolled over.

She called up, "Hi, is everything going okay?"

"Yes boss, I added some more bolts to keep these stage boxes together, they won't move an inch now. The mic's all set up and I've brought a playlist on an old iPod to play in-between the acts. We're all set for the musicians. How's everyone else doing?"

Maddie told him she was on her rounds, checking up, but so far everyone was calm and organised, just how she liked it. She found Craig setting up a tabletop with a few apple presses, tubes, demijohns and buckets. He had boxes of apples underneath, some from his plot (he was one of the lucky ones to have a tree already there) and others had donated more. His plan was to let children and adults have a go at pressing apples and they could take away the juice. He would charge for the lesson and the juice came free. That was a tip Maddie gave him, to avoid any complicated permissions.

The school brass band would be arriving soon, so she just had time to pop over the road to see how the allotment area was getting on. The demonstration marquee looked huge now it was up. Esther was walking around ordering the installers how much to tighten the straps and how to tie bright coloured flags to any ropes that could be a trip hazard. They smiled at her patiently. Maddie marvelled at how quickly Esther had started to get back to normal. She was extremely grateful to her for not wanting to pick up the reins again and to let her get on with the organisation. Esther had snapped at Norris who kept telling her to get off the ladder, stop picking up boxes, leave the tables where they were, so she decided to take her frustration out on the poor team who were only trying to put up a big tent.

The inside of the marquee was taking shape. Tom had placed a generator outside at the back, to run the lights and microphone. Norris was feeding the wires underneath to connect to the equipment inside. Ranweer's children were unfolding the chairs that the school had lent them and were setting them out neatly in rows facing the long tables at the front. Jean would decorate the table later, once everyone was out of her way.

Maddie wandered over to the shed shop which had been transformed into Filo's Tarot and Healing Emporium. Drapes had been hung over the panelled walls and thrown over the sacks of compost, Filo had hung small glass pots with tea light candles everywhere, crystals dangled in the doorway throwing multicoloured light dots inside which danced and pranced around Filo's head. She sat in the centre, laying out her cards and standing up leaflets advertising local alternative health and healing companies, a reiki centre, a homeopathy practitioner and a masseur amongst others.

"Welcome my dear, can I read your aura?" Filo waved her arms theatrically above her head.

"I don't have time, but maybe later. This is all looking really good, please just don't leave the candles alight, will you?"

"Stop worrying, you have done a great job instructing us all, now you can relax and let us get on with it!"

"I know, I know, I'm a control freak. When it comes to my work, I like to do a really good job. Sorry, I know you're all more than capable, I'll try and take a step back."

"Are you looking forward to tonight, your work's competition?" Filo didn't know how Maddie was managing to stay sane. Having two big events on the same day, one in Reigate and the other the centre of London, she didn't have a clue how she managed it. But that's Maddie's strength. She's capable and organised and has a good set of values, she wouldn't let anyone down.

"To be honest, I just want to get it over with now. As soon as we've finished this competition, I am going to look for another job. I've made up my mind and I feel better for making the decision."

"Good for you, Maddie. You'll be fine, honestly, I know it!"

A call from The Hedgehog Awareness group took Maddie away to help them find extra tables and sandbags to weigh down their notice and information boards.

By ten o'clock, crowds had already started to gather. Maddie felt someone take her hand and pull her gently backwards. Tom led her to the stage and ushered her up.

"You need to open the event, go on, it's your day Maddie, you can do this."

Maddie took a deep breath, tapped the microphone and glanced down to see Tom looking up with pride. She welcomed everyone warmly, explained the order of the day and where to find various activities, "Don't forget to have a go at CPR, you can learn how to save a life on our resuscitation dolls, also at one o'clock, we have the wonderful Jamie Snow, a local singer who got through to the next stages in X Factor two years ago, she'll be singing a wide range of songs for us all to enjoy but first, let's all welcome the children from our local school Brass Band who will be entertaining us with music from across the decades. And remember, every person on a stall today is an allotment owner and they are here to answer any gardening questions you may have and to sell their produce, so please ask them anything. Enjoy your day everyone and don't forget we are not only here to share our tips and help with all things gardening and horticulture but we are also raising money for the wonderful St Anne's Hospice, so please be generous and dig deep - pun intended! Enjoy and see you all later."

Tom held up his hand to help her off the stage and squeezed it tightly.

"You were brilliant," he whispered in her ear. The feel of his soft breath took her own away. Was she imagining it or was he finding reasons to touch her? Not that she minded, she found herself seeking him out, watching where he was and listening for his name. He had warmed himself to her, he no longer growled and snapped, he was tender and kind and there was no denying the feeling inside when he stood close. There was something he wanted to say, she sensed it, but the moment passed as he was called over to help carry a large tuba case.

Maddie spent the next few hours wandering between the stalls, checking and chatting, boldly encouraging the visitors to put their hands in their pockets, she rattled donation buckets, supervised the cadets with promises of food and found she didn't stop grinning from ear to ear. The cadets had agreed to sell raffle tickets, whilst they wandered around keeping everyone safe and informed. On the prize table sat an enormous basket filled with vegetables, except on closer inspection each carrot, onion, potato and broccoli were in fact a delicious sponge cake, in vanilla and chocolate flavours. Maddie and Filo had spent the last few evenings happily baking together and the result was spectacular.

The demonstrations were very popular, Norris and Jean had gone down a storm, they made simple and sparse materials into beautiful floral arrangements, showing everyone what they could easily achieve at home. They used dried oranges and lemons, pinecones, ribbons and even an old plastic milk bottle, with the top cut off and painted as a recycled vase. The Halloween themed arrangements went down so well they sold out of their pumpkins and squashes. Maddie couldn't have dreamt for a more perfect atmosphere, the crowds kept coming in waves, the whole place seemed full yet relaxed. She just had the final demonstration slot to join in with and then to help tidy up and then she had to step up another gear for the competition later. She hadn't had any time to think about that, this event was her full focus for now. She was going to sleep well tonight.

"Madeleine?"

She turned to be face-to-face with her parents.

Her mother looked around the allotment car park, she noted the crowds in the gazeboes, the beautifully decorated marquee and the buzz of the chatter and laughter and smiled weakly at her daughter.

"Madeleine, I was hoping to see you, can we talk do you think?" Fiona looked towards Henry who nodded in encouragement. Maddie led the way to her own allotment plot and opened the caravan door. Fiona looked around; little had changed in the many years since she was last stood inside. "There is a really good turnout, isn't there? You've done really well! I didn't realise it was going to be so big." Henry delicately excused himself to go and find tea for everyone.

"Thank you, yes, I'm really pleased. It's the first one and we weren't sure how popular it would be."

"Madeleine, I've come to say I'm sorry. I've been a stubborn fool lately, well all of my life really, but I didn't realise how bad I had become until you left the other day."

"Okay......" Maddie wasn't prepared to leave it at that and waited for more from her mother.

"Your father has had some stern words with me, he's right. I've been thinking so much about myself that I lost sight of what was important, you and James. It's no excuse but I have found it hard losing your grandfather and letting the house go has rather consumed me."

"But it's more than that though, isn't it mum? Things haven't been right for a lot longer than that." Maddie knew this was her chance to get the answers she wanted, the answers she needed, and she was determined to get them.

Fiona slumped in the bench chair, lent on the table and gazed at her hands. "When your brother was ill as a baby, it terrified me. I was young and didn't know what to do. I worried every minute that he would get ill again or worse and it changed me. I know now that I spoilt him, I didn't let him take any risks and as much as I love him, he is a lazy toad as a result." She gave a feeble laugh at her own joke to lighten the mood. "Then you came along so soon afterwards and I didn't have the strength to watch you in the same way, it was obvious you were different to him, you were tough right from the start, you walked early, refused to be fed by anyone, holding your own fork and doing everything yourself. I let you get on with things. You didn't seem to need me."

"But mum, you haven't let me get on with things. You're on my back with everything I do! I'm scrutinised all of the time."

"I know, I know, your father tells me to back away. It's just that you have every opportunity in life…and I don't. I lost that when I married and had children. I was going to be successful, I wanted to be, and the plan was after we married that I would have a career, but James needed me, you both needed me. It was a different world back then, harder to juggle both, there wasn't the child-care that there is today."

"But you've had all these years since we grew up to do whatever you want. That's no excuse, people do things at any age. Mum you can do anything for yourself, don't rely on me to live your life for you. It's too much pressure and it's not fair." Maddie felt strong, she felt brave and if ever there was a time to be honest it was now, whilst her mother was meeting her halfway. She then stepped into the arena that was the most painful.

"Mum, why did you tell my granddad he couldn't see me?"

"It wasn't like that, I promise. I could see how much you loved being here, with him. You only ever wanted to be here, and I was so worried you wouldn't do well and stretch yourself. I didn't have the career I wanted but you could. It was so important that you went to a good school and did well. It became such a battle getting you away from sitting here every evening and all weekend, I wanted you to widen yourself and try new things. I didn't want you to waste your life…. like me."

"But I saw the letters you sent him, you said I couldn't come anymore."

"I know, I'm so sorry Madeleine, honestly I am. He wouldn't meet me halfway and I felt I was losing you to him, you only wanted to be in his company. I was jealous, a stupid, jealous woman…. jealous of my own daughter and father having a good relationship. How awful does that make me? I'll never forgive myself Madeleine, I hope you know that! You still saw him when he came round to our house and when we went to his, it was only here at the allotment that I said no to. But he dug his heels in and hardly came round much after that. I know that was my fault and now he's gone I'd do anything to change it. I'll feel guilty forever. That's why I found it hard to talk to Tom and Norris, they were closer to him than me. I was embarrassed. I should have spent more time with him myself and I should have taken more care of him. They must think I'm an awful person."

"I don't know what they think, mum. They haven't spoken about you. I don't know what to say to you, this is all so sad. I've been feeling guilty too for not seeing him enough. Part of that is definitely your fault but I must be honest with myself, partly it was me too. When I was a teenager, I only ever wanted to see my friends. I let him down too."

"All I can say to you is I am so very sorry, and I'll do anything to try and make things better between us." Fiona was openly crying; Madeleine could see her mother was genuinely reaching out.

"Whilst we are talking, I need to tell you about work mum. I'm not happy and I don't want to do it. It's not me anymore, I'm not sure it really ever was. I want to have my own business, I always have. I don't want the corporate life; I want to be happy in my job. I'm not sure what to do yet but I'm going to leave after tonight's competition. I'll give my notice in and take a break until I figure things out."

Fiona inhaled, "But Madeleine, how can you just walk away from a career that you've worked so hard for?"

"Easily mum, it's not really my career, is it? I think it's more your career and you can't live your life through me, I must do what's right for me now."

They looked at each other intently, Fiona computing Madeleine's words with hurt and confusion.

"Is that really how you feel?" the truth had come as a shock to her mother.

"Yes, mum, I want to do the things that make *me* happy, not you. I want you to be proud of me whatever I do. I don't need to work in the City to be successful. I want a little of what you give James…. space. Back off me a bit and let me do things my way."

"I hadn't realised, there's so much I haven't seen or heard. Of course, I'm proud of you and I'll support you in whatever you choose to do. You're my Madeleine, I'll always be proud of you." She reached across and squeezed Madeleine's hands into her's tightly.

"Even enough to tell your golf club friends when I've failed miserably?" Madeleine tested the water whilst trying to break the somber mood.

Fiona actually laughed and joined in, "Yes, I'll even boast of my daughter's failings to them, if that'll make you happy?"

Henry beamed as he stepped back clutching cardboard cups between his fingers. "I see you ladies are talking again, thank goodness, I can come out of hiding now."

"You can both sit in here for a while if you like," Madeleine offered the caravan to them. "I need to go into the marquee for the question-and-answer session. They'll be waiting for me."

"Oh no, we'll come and watch that, it will be nice to see what you've been doing all these months over here." cautiously Fiona added, "and I'd like to meet your friends... properly."

Maddie gasped as she stepped into the marquee, it was packed. The chairs were full, people were standing around the edges to get a view. She pushed her way to the front where everyone was already sitting, the chair next to Tom was empty and he patted it for her to sit down. He had already started the session on her behalf, an opening question revolved around dealing with weeds. Tom had expertly explained their policy on organic and environmentally friendly measures but gave ways of finding out further information too. Hands were up for the next question. The next hour flew by, questions came thick and fast, which method is best for trimming rose bushes, how to grow cauliflower without them being eaten by bugs, what can children grow on a windowsill and Maddie surprised herself by answering one about starting out, she shared a potted version of her own experiences, warts and all and made the audience laugh. She was sorry when Tom nudged her and pointed to his watch, it was four o'clock, time to wrap everything up and get ready for tonight. She thanked the crowd and gave out a Facebook name of the new page she had started for them all. Any more questions could get posted on there.

As she stepped out of the tent, the light had already started to dim. It would be a race to get everything dismantled and stored away, ready for sorting out the next day. Everyone piled in to help. James had been amazing all day, he hadn't stopped going round to everyone, helping on their stalls so they could all take a break. He and Tom had spent a lot of time together, bonding over the cake stall and being at the beck and call of Esther and her demands for help. Ranweer and Alice had totally sold out of food and promised next year to make double. Filo had stuck to her word and only given out positive and encouraging messages to her visitors and was now pulling the bunting from the fence posts whilst the cadets were stacking tables and chairs into the trailer.

At five o'clock, Filo shooed Maddie into the toilets in the Bowls Club, clutching her dress and shoes and a small bag of toiletries. Only fifteen minutes later she emerged looking beautiful. Her old jeans, jumper and boots were stashed into a carrier bag. She stood in a floor length black cocktail dress fitted at the top and a slight fishtail flair at the bottom. A new, long silver necklace hung between her breasts with her locket attached securely. She had matching droplet earrings with thick crystal bracelets that jangled as she moved. She had scrubbed her hands clean and preempted the dirty fingernails with dark crimson nail varnish. Her stilettos were silver and she had to tiptoe across the dirty car park to find Filo for her lift to the station.

Without a chance to say goodbye to everyone, Filo sped Maddie off towards the station. "That was so much fun, wasn't it?" Filo was buzzing from the excitement, she had been received so well from the public, some had even asked for regular readings, she was overjoyed. "Maddie, you are brilliant! Well done, it was such a success. We were all like the celebrities on the TV gardening programmes today, being asked so many questions. People really want to know and learn, don't they? You know we could never had done this event without you. It would have been a tiny little affair; we wouldn't have known where to start. You are so good at planning; you should do it for a living!"

Maddie looked at Filo and smiled the broadest smile, "Do you know, you're right! I've enjoyed today so much, I haven't stopped smiling, I'm exhausted, but still smiling. Thank you, Filo, thank you for just being wonderful, I love you and I'm so happy we met. Friends forever!" They bumped fists and laughed. Filo wasn't sure what she'd said to deserve such an outburst but whatever it was, she liked it.

The train slowed before East Croydon station and just sat, waiting. Maddie kept checking her phone, the battery was low and at six thirty she knew she was going to be late. She ignored the thirteen voicemails and texts that Dominic had sent in the last hour, she didn't have the battery power to respond. She fired off one short message to say she was on her way but may be late and snapped the phone back off again.

A conductor eventually walked through the carriage, announcing a delay, there had been an incident further ahead. The train would get to the station shortly and buses would be there to take passengers any further. Maddie felt a burning acid rise to her throat, her heart was thudding, and she looked desperately out into the dark, seeing only her own reflection in the train window. Of all the nights to be stuck on a train! She pulled her jacket tighter around her to hide her glamorous outfit from the suits and families surrounding her. At six forty, she made a decision.

'Filo, I don't have much battery left. I am stuck at East Croydon station. I'll wait here. Can you come and collect me and bring me home? x "

By quarter past seven, the crowds had filtered out into buses, taxis and loved one's cars. Maddie sat alone at the front of the station, waiting for the 2CV to bounce into view. A car horn made her jump as a familiar black pick-up truck pulled up in front of her.

"Tom? What are you doing here?"

"Climb in, I'm your knight in shining armour, we're going to get you to this competition, you're not backing out now!" Without complaint, she climbed in. The truck cab was warm, and Maddie took off her jacket. As she did, Tom whistled. "Wow, you look amazing! Are you the same girl who's been running around an allotment all day?"

"The one and the same, thank you, I can't believe you're here. How come?"

"Filo told me about the train and there was no way we were going to let you just come home. You need to finish this, if you don't go tonight, you'll always wonder. Unfinished business is not healthy. And anyway, Filo's car would have got you there in time for breakfast!"

Maddie laughed gratefully and settled back into the leather seat, the red glow of the dashboard at night, the gentle rocking of the cab and Tom sitting next to her, she suddenly felt tired and laid her head back and closed her eyes.

"You did so well today, it's been a total success and you made that happen. You! My little Maddie. I didn't know you could do all of that. You should go into event planning or something, you're really good at it. You know, I was so proud of you...." But his words went unheard as she drifted off to sleep.

It took a moment to realise they were outside of the Bittern Quay showrooms. Tom gently shook Maddie's arm to wake her. "C'mon, you jump out and I'll park the truck."

At the entrance, the security men questioned her before agreeing to let her pass. She said she was with a colleague and waited for Tom who walked in looking totally out of place, his jeans and lumberjack coat were covered with the story of the day. Despite their mismatch, they were let through to follow the signs to the main presentation room. As they heard muffled voices through the vast wooden doors, Tom gently took her hand.

"Maddie, whatever happens in there tonight, I just want you to know I think you're wonderful. If you win or lose this thing, it doesn't matter. We're all the winners because we have you… I have you, or at least I hope I have, if you'll let me?" He searched her face for an answer, he didn't need to hear any words as she reached up and cupped his beautiful, rugged face and gently pressed her lips against his. The kiss consumed her, nothing else existed, his huge arms wrapped around her and she was home, safe and secure and blissfully happy.

The doors burst open and guests started to spill out into the main foyer. Maddie and Tom stepped out of the way to let the bubbling crowd through. She spotted Dominic and Roseanne at the back, deep in conversation and holding hands! She pushed her way towards them.

"I'm so sorry, the trains were cancelled, I've only just got here. What happened?"

"Well, we didn't win!" Roseanne sneered. "No thanks to you of course."

Dominic looked between the two women and mediated, "To be fair, we lost to a brilliant concept, a team from Manchester, who blew every one out of the water. Katrina is livid, you could see her seething that none of her teams even got a mention."

"I'm sorry to have missed it but look, it's only fair that you both know that I'm going to be leaving the company anyway. It nothing to do with tonight, I have other plans." Maddie glanced at Tom who was waiting patiently.

"So, I see," Dominic smiled. "Roseanne and I are going to make a go of things too; we're going to set up a company together." He took Roseanne's hand to show Madeleine that they were an item. She smiled a genuinely happy smile for them, they deserved each other, they were far more suited than she and Dominic ever were. She wished them a lovely evening and turned to join Tom.

"Excuse me, Miss Richards?" The top of a bowed head bent low in front of Maddie.

"Yes, I am Maddie Richards."

"Good evening, my name is Nobuaki Ito, I am one of the Directors here at the Quays." The old man held out his hand to shake Maddie's warmly. He turned to Tom. "And excuse me, are you the gentleman behind the garden designs?"

Tom nodded confused.

"I have been talking to your Deputy CEO who tells me you didn't present here this evening but spoke warmly of your work at Claremont and Butler. The Board have chosen our winner for the marketing of Bittern Quays, but I have been personally impressed with the concepts behind the Insignia presentation. Katrina tells me this part was both of you?"

Maddie was quick to correct Mr. Ito and lay the praise on Tom.

"I have a lot of interest in the well-being of my staff in the companies that I own across the world. I have been looking for ways to support them, especially in areas where morale is low, where there is deprivation and mental illness. I think your idea of giving them a piece of land, to grow and nurture, to make their work environment a happy and healthy place and provide them perhaps with food, herbs, flowers, space and calm and whatever it is they need or want is excellent. It matches my ethos entirely. I would be willing to give them the space and the time to do this within their working hours. I think the benefit would go both ways, I would have a happy and healthy staff and they will want to work for me in return."

"That's exactly how I envisaged it," Tom stepped forward, "I only take on design projects that benefit people's well-being in some way. I feel very strongly about that!"

"Then you and I have a lot to talk about then Mr.…...?"

"Mr. Squires, Tom Squires."

"Here is my card, Mr. Squires. Please call my secretary on Monday and we shall book a time to meet and make plans. I think we can help each other and do some very valuable work. Have a good evening, Miss Richards, Mr. Squires." Mr. Ito bent low to each of them and walked to join his colleagues at the bar.

Maddie pulled Tom behind a huge marble pillar, out of sight, and screamed silently into her hands.

"Oh my god, oh my god, you've done it! If you get a contract with him, you'll be famous, I'm so happy for you, I knew your designs were special. Oh Tom, it's amazing!"

Tom stood bewildered, not knowing what had just happened.

"Maddie, but what about you? This was your night? Not mine."

"Don't be so silly, this wasn't my night at all in the end, I don't belong here anymore. I'm over the moon for you, honestly. I'm so proud of you."

"What are you going to do though?"

"I am going to start my own business. Filo gave me the inspiration. I'm going to be an event planner. It's what I'm good at and love doing. I'm going to be my own boss and I'm going to move out and rent my own place too!"

"But you're still going to keep the allotment, aren't you?" Tom was worried where he figured into Maddie's new plans.

"You bet, you just try and keep me away! I'm going to need you more than ever now, to teach me how to grow enough to feed myself, after all I'm going to be poor for a while!" she laughed but felt freer than ever before.

"I'll always need you Maddie and I'll always be here for you. I think you and I are heading for amazing things.... together." His deep kiss took her breath away.

As they walked out into the city night, holding hands, Maddie knew her grandfather was smiling down at them, together at last, where she had always belonged. It took her a little while to figure it all out, but she got there in the end. She looked up at the stars and hoped he was proud.

Epilogue - JANUARY

"Seriously, will you two put that stuff down for a minute and come and have some breakfast! You've been working non-stop since early this morning."

Maddie and Fiona collapsed at one of the bare round tables, yet to be dressed in crisp white linen. Filo laid a plate piled high with croissants, a dish of homemade cherry jam and a pot of tea in front of them both.

Maddie looked around the community hall, filled with tasteful pink and white garlands strung across the ceiling, balloons and swags of foliage, weaved along the buffet table, intertwined with delicate pink French roses. She had created a soft and very beautiful welcome to the christening party due to arrive for lunchtime. The caterers, Filo and Esther, had baked huge, sumptuous cakes and filled wafer thin sandwiches. Norris had drilled tiny holes into antique china plates and threaded them onto metal stands, each table would have a cream tea selection loaded onto them to share.

Fiona had taught herself how to fold napkins into animal shapes, as a talking point for each guest. Jean, Norris's wife, had also taught her how to create small table centre arrangements from winter anemones, she told her the flower symbolised protection against evil, Fiona thought it sounded like a fairy tale christening. Maddie's mother had cautiously asked to help at one of the first events she was commissioned to do and since then had willingly helped at each one. She found she enjoyed learning new skills and having a real purpose. Maddie was surprised how much she enjoyed working with her mother and if the demand keeps growing, who knows, maybe her mother could go into the business with her, as a partner?

Esther was back on top form; Maddie could hear her bossing Filo around in the small kitchen, but she knew Filo wouldn't have it any other way.

As Tom sauntered into the back-kitchen door, he tried to swipe a homemade pork pie from under his mother's nose. She tapped his hand gently with the back of a wooden spoon and a smile. Maddie brought the plates back for washing up and lit up as she saw Tom standing there, scolded like a little boy. He grabbed her round the waist and stole a kiss.

"I'm too busy for you Tom Squires, I've got guests due in a couple of hours."

He grinned, enjoying having his favourite women in his life around him.

"Do you want me to read your tarot cards, I've got a pack in my bag?"

They both swung round to Filo, "NO!"

Laughing, Tom slung his arm around Filo's shoulders, "You know, I think I can take our fete from here thanks Filo, I've got our future all mapped out on a card that I like to call 'Forever.'

Printed in Great Britain
by Amazon

68402977R00317